THE HOUSE OF BAGHDAD

A Political Fantasy

By

Tony Sharp

Cover Designed By Ken Pyne

This book is a work of fiction. Places, events, and situations in this story are purely fictional. Any resemblance to actual persons, living or dead, is coincidental.

© 2003 by Tony Sharp. All rights reserved.

No part of this book may be reproduced, stored in a retrieval system, or transmitted by any means, electronic, mechanical, photocopying, recording, or otherwise, without written permission from the author.

ISBN: 1-4107-6365-X (e-book)
ISBN: 1-4107-6366-8 (Paperback)

This book is printed on acid-free paper.

To George V Scott without whose support and tenacity this book may never have been published.

1stBooks – rev. 08/23/03

THE HOUSE OF BAGHDAD

The characters and situations in this book are entirely imaginary and bear no relation to any real person or actual happening.

Best wishes to Samuel & Peter from

John Sharp

March 2004

Do you feel madness coming on?

JS

CHARACTERS

Colonel Doomsday, ('D-Day') ex-Dictator of Iraq
Mustafa, Colonel Doomsday's special bodyguard and friend
President Bazrani, constitutionally elected President of Iraq
Laura, wife of President Bazrani
Arid Aziz, Prime Minister of Iraq
Hattie, American-born wife of Arid Aziz
Faisal Hussein, Leader of the Opposition
The Caliph, brought in 'from the cold'
Manuel Gonzalez, President of Brazil
Maria, his wife and mistress
(Colonel Doomsday's mistress
and anybody else's mistress.)
Pepe Fernandez, Brazilian Foreign Minister, godfather to Maria
Fritz Krupp (alias Felix Esbano), German ex-pat, resident alien in Brazil
The 'Reverend' Biggs, British ex-pat, local character and entrepreneur
Franco Daconni, Brazilian Chief Detective Superintendent
Joshua Rainberg, member of MOSSAD
Dave Adams, Joshua's assistant
John Bullock, Prime Minister of Great Britain
David Shameer, Prime Minister of Israel
Dave Fletcher, BBC correspondent extraordinaire, Nobel Prize winner, etc.
Peter Watson, BBC, London
Tom Brown, BBC assistant, London
John Broadbridge, BBC man working in Iraq, good drinking partner of the Caliph
Kitty, John's long-suffering wife, kept at bay in Swindon, England
Dan Levy, American TV/film producer/entrepreneur in Iraq
Jim Rosenberg, Dan Levy's assistant, and director

PREFACE:

Baghdad, a likely story.

'It's *THE BIG CRUNCH*. And everybody knows it. This time the Colonel has gone too far - and even the patience of his own men has finally run dry. The tourists have long gone and what remains of a so-called economy is not worth saving. Food rations have been cut yet again and even the rats have taken on a decidedly worried look. But people are too tired and too angry to shudder when rodents and humans alike pop their heads up from under the rubble left behind in the streets from yesterday's riots. Indeed, compared with what is happening here, life in 'downtown' Ethiopia would seem like dignified High Tea.'

So reported the colourful BBC correspondent Dave Fletcher to a shock-proof world.

But something had to be done to rescue the country - and fast. The students, for their part, had wasted no time in organising themselves into a political force, left of centre - albeit with guns. Persuasion by words, naturally, had failed, and for them - as for almost everyone else - the sooner the Colonel was deposed the better.

Yet it was a surprise to the whole world how quickly the 'job' was done. For, ever since the United States' crude but effective exercise in clipping the wings of an elder, fellow dictator across the way in Libya, Colonel Doomsday - 'D Day' - as he came to be known even by his own countrymen - had built up within himself a seething well of resentment and hatred towards Uncle Sam. As expected, it appeared to be a shared and fairly popular sentiment among many Arabs. Moreover, when his own father - by mighty Allah's mercy or by the skin of his own teeth - had miraculously survived the indignity of defeat, not only at the hands of the Western Powers but by the unforgivable connivance of neighbouring Arab States, he had vowed that one day, he would throw down the gauntlet and, on his father's behalf, avenge what he perceived as a total outrage and betrayal.

He'd begin with America. He'd never been there. But he'd read about it. And he'd seen pictures. To his mind, at least, a nuclear bomb with a built-in sense of discretion - strategically dropped on New York - should be enough to get the ball rolling. And the descendants of the indigenous Indians who themselves had suffered humiliation at the hands of Uncle Sam in having their island wrested from them for a mere twenty-five dollars or so could, if only for a blinding second, afford that long awaited smile.

But, for 'D-Day', all this remained a pipe-dream, whilst through the years, he found himself being groomed for the role of his father's successor. He was soon promoted to Colonel-in-Chief, and, like his father before him, he quickly found his feet, indulging himself and enjoying every minute of his considerable power and predilection for mischief. 'Like father, like son', it is said. 'The sins of the father shall be visited upon the sons'. And in this case, 'two peas in a pod' could not have been more aptly applied. The young man, early on, came to learn of the many murders of supposed rivals to his father's throne, and he was urged by his advisers (with notable success) to continue the programme for his own benefit, of course, and until all signs of opposition were removed. Moreover, he saw no reason why his father's keen interest in new tortures, together with refinement of the old, should be discouraged.

But the people had had their fill. They had seen enough war to last them a thousand years. If the son of Sodom the Lesser continued in his father's footsteps there could be no hope. They weren't that stupid. Oh, how they yearned to be free, free like Westerners, to travel where and when they chose; to do all the things they had never been in a position to do; to be free from continually having a gun shoved in their hands - with a command to use it against others with whom they had no personal dispute.

How they yearned to speak their minds (and theirs were good minds), to oppose the antics of this new 'saviour' of their country - the favoured one - a chip off the old block. But the old block had scarcely crumbled before the might of the world. Must they wait to see the chip grow - only to be led by it into the fire once more? How long could they wait in the hope he would change? Must their lives be subjected to permanent fear that any moment there could be a knock on the door from army personnel or secret agents? How long could they endure hunger while their master strutted about in his Palaces as if the world revolved around him alone? Well, this time the people had risen and, suddenly, there was nowhere for him to go. Torture and hanging had been meted out to others - the same treatment would hardly be to his taste. If only he could leave the country as another man. But who could be trusted to do a plastic job on an ex-hero's face without letting the knife slip into a deeper and final cut?

Chapter I

It was gone 4.30 before Tom Brown received the call from Baghdad. His friend and BBC colleague had been shacked up for days in his hide-out. But, knowing Dave Fletcher as he did, it just had to be somewhere right near the action. Tom Brown, it seemed, would bloody well have to wait for the report which, no doubt, would be as poetically English as the last one. His friend's descriptions of 'natural disasters', wars, famines and other events of this crazy world had touched the hearts and minds of countless men and women everywhere - to the extent that his name had seriously been put forward for the Nobel Peace Prize.

The line crackled hopefully and Dave Fletcher's distinctive voice once more invaded the airwaves. 'It's bloody chaos here, dear boy… little to eat, panic, of course, looting, kids running about laying their hands on as many weapons as they can grab and then firing at anything that takes their fancy. And all the while, an old man still manages to sell a few tired-looking melons from his meagre stall - all, naturally, with the Colonel's face deftly charcoaled on one side. Nice touch, I think.'

Tom Brown laughed down the line, and, like the true Englishman he aspired to be, enquired after his friend's health.

'Tip top form, dear boy….. bit low on gin and tonic mind you. Otherwise, no complaints.'

The line had gone dead and Tom would have to sit it out again. Damn. He envied Dave's coolness and was jealous of his assignments. Increasingly, he'd become bored - kicking his heels in England, covering yet more puerile squabbles between MPs over issues which no party had ever got right despite what each continued to claim. All parties, it seemed, had conveniently short memories - and Joe Public had none at all. Oh, *when* would he be able to escape this mediocrity and embroil himself in something exciting?

'You should jolly well count yourself lucky,' advised Peter Watson, Tom's senior, crouching over his desk and eyeing his young charge with some suspicion. 'You have a cushy number, here, and.......'

'That's just it, Peter. It's too damned cushy. If only......'

'What's the matter with you for Heaven's sake? As a Jew, you ought to be glad of a bit of peace and quiet for a change. You *are* peace loving, I take it?'

Tom had ignored that last remark together with its implication. His mind was out on a day-trip of adventure. 'Perhaps I should go to Israel, and ......'

'What a good idea. I'm sure you could find a nice kind Arab nearby to blow your head off. And who knows? You might even get the opportunity to blow *his* off first. I wouldn't hesitate if I were you, old man. I really wouldn't.'

'Jesus, Peter. I think you've flipped. I only meant I could do with a bit of excitement, for a change. One doesn't have to be silly about these things.'

But Peter Watson had lost patience. Up to now he'd been a paragon of tolerance and understanding - a steady, long-suffering Englishman - slow to rise, but never unaware. He was not a racist by nature, yet he could see now how easily people can become one. In fact, if the truth were known, certain ethnic minorities - as they were still sparingly called - were beginning to irritate him. Moreover, racial tensions appeared increasingly to be the stuff of modern journalism. Quite frankly, he'd had enough and secretly pined for the good old days when an Englishman's home was his castle - and that included a bit of land and some white faces around the place. Peter's credentials as an open-minded journalist were already in the process of glorious, irreversible erosion. And he looked forward to his retirement and his books, in peaceful Devon.

But now, Dave Fletcher could be heard on the line again, anxious to reel off a report on the latest situation. This time he sounded breathless, in a hurry and even a little frightened.

'God, I hope he's all right.' Tom was doing his best to placate his boss.

'Shut up, and listen.'

'I think they've found our hide-away. They're coming for us, they're coming for us.' There was a crash of glass, some shots and then……

'Christ Almighty. He's been hit. The bastards, the…..'

'Steady, Peter. He may be OK. They've probably fired warning shots and taken him hostage.'

'Oh, I suppose that's all right, is it…..while *you* sit comfortably here in…?'

'I didn't mean it like….'

'Beginning to appreciate our cushy little number, after all, are we?' Tom tried to hide his face. But Peter's eyebrows had already risen a touch higher and despite a face flushed, it seemed, with a little more blood circulation than usual, his smirk would have stood an excellent chance of winning First Prize in the New Anglophile Award for Cynicism (belatedly set up in the UK in a desperate effort to preserve for all time the remains of a dying culture). After all, Peter Watson was, himself, an Englishman. The only trouble was - he wouldn't have been allowed into the club, being a real Englishman.

'OK, so, what d'we do now? You suggest something.' Tom decided to pursue the practical line.

'Call John Broadbridge on 9641 3899.'

'Typically bloody English. I suppose it's the bar of the Taunton Cricket Club?'

'No, silly. Prefix 00 - it's our back-up contact, outskirts of Baghdad. Don't argue. Get him on the line.'

This time Tom Brown knew for certain his boss wasn't fooling. Very English, damn him, the man most decidedly was. But Peter Watson, Esq., M.A. (Oxon), B.Sc. (London), still wielded considerable power in the corridors of the BBC - enough to sway things this way, or that. Tom had always been ambitious and a little too pushy for some people's tastes. However, there might, at some stage, be an opportunity to by-pass or even over-step Peter Watson in a perfectly legal or official manner. These things happened, just as they did - much to the chagrin of loyal, old-timers - in the teaching profession. He just knew he'd get there, one day, if only he could hang on a while longer to his over-stretched patience. And, working for the BBC, he'd had ample opportunity to test it.

Tom dialled the number, and waited ... Crackle, pop, crackle..

'Jesus. Some back-up contact. Whatever next?'

'Get off bloody line, English pig. You killed my mother; you killed my brother and my sisters. You think you can talk your way out of this.? Allah will....'

'Is John Broadbridge there, please?' Tom had suddenly become splendidly English. And Peter sat up with an appreciative smile on his face. After all, this was war. And all British subjects - whether they were of Scottish, Welsh or even Jewish extraction - were needed in times of war. If Tom maintained this refreshing stance, Peter would give him his full support.

'*No.* There is *no* Joan at the Broken Bridge. Fuck off to you, too.' And with that, the phone was firmly replaced on its Baghdadian hook.

Tom sat down and burst out laughing. And when he'd recovered sufficiently to relay the 'news', he was glad to see Peter relax with him. In fact, his boss went even farther. Without delay he proceeded to crack open a bottle of Scotch which he always kept for emergencies in his locker by the window.

'Here. Let's bury the hatchet, shall we, old man? At least, until after the war?'

'If you want to think of this thing as war, OK by me, Peter.'

And so, with a clink of glasses, they drank to a trial period of peaceful co-existence, at least within the walls of the office. There could always be a review of the situation - at a decent interval.

'By the way. What was the number you dialled?' Peter already suspected Tom to have got it wrong. Why he should have thought that, God alone knew.

'The one you gave me, of course. 964-1-3899.'

'That's right. Well, I wonder what young Broadbridge is up to? let me try.' Peter put down his glass and dialled the number, not forgetting, naturally, the prefix 00…

'You again? You English pigs. I told you to f….'

'Now, listen to me, my man,' began Peter in confident manner 'Let's drop the English pig bit, shall we? I happen to be of Irish descent and if you're thinking of….'

'I tell you there is no Broken Bridge, here.'

'Broadbridge, old man, Broadbridge.'

'Fuck off, Broadbridge.' Down went the phone once more and Peter wished he'd never mentioned the Irish bit in front of Tom. The point was bound to be taken up in no small measure.

'So, we're Irish now, are we? You sly old bugger. I just knew there had to be something in the old cupboard you didn't want me to know about.'

Peter grinned and clinked his glass again against Tom's.

'Sorry to disappoint you, old man. No Irish, I'm afraid. I just said that in the hope the bastard would change his tune....'

'If he believed you had certain sympathies?'

'Exactly. But I'm none too good at putting on the old brogue.' Tom smiled and felt himself warming to Peter.

'So, what d'we do now? Sweat it out, or try the Embassy again?'

Before Peter could answer his new drinking partner, the phone buzzed on his desk. 'Hello, Peter Watson here.'

'Peter. It's Broadbridge.'

'John.'

'I've been trying to get through to you all day. Bloody chaos here.'

'We've tried to contact you, too. But all we get is a tirade of abuse from a hot-head who insists upon calling you Broken Bridge.'

'Ah, that's a good one. Mind you, he's not far wrong, the way things are, at the moment. Do you have the right number?'

'964 -1-3899.'

'No, no. It's 964 -1- 38_5_9. Must have been a bad line.'

'OK. Got it.' Peter corrected the numbers on his pad.

'So, what's the latest? And what's happened to Dave Fletcher?'

'Don't panic, old chap. He's fine. A few of the old guard trying to hold on to things, you know. Tried to kidnap a few Westerners, cameramen and so on. Caught up with Dave. But they were overpowered by the students. Bloody determined, those youngsters,.....say what you like.'

'So, is it all under control now, John?'

'As under control as it will ever be in a place like this. Need I elaborate?'

'Just give us an update.'

'OK. The Colonel has gone into hiding. Most of the army has sided with the students and other opposing factions and together they occupy the TV/Radio station, Government buildings, Army headquarters - almost everything. They're a tough bunch, believe me. No, I think this one is for real, Peter; though, what sort of democracy it will turn out to be - if, indeed, democracy is what they really want - God only knows.'

'Right. We have it all recorded. Thanks John. Look after yourself. Regards to Dave, and keep the stuff rolling.'

'Call you within the hour. 'Bye.'

'Bye, John.'

Undetected, the helicopter rose up into the night sky above Baghdad. Its ascent was camouflaged by the trees surrounding the Colonel's hideout and by a ravine that had been secretly cut years before - for use, no doubt, in such an emergency as this. The machine soon turned and made for a private airstrip.

In no time at all the party transferred to a jet and were soon on their way to pretty Paris, ancient sanctuary to countless revolutionaries, maniacs and other deviant hopefuls, be they 'left' or 'right', a place where all kinds of unscrupulous deals were scrupulously dealt with in a setting of the best possible taste. The new President, a man of impeccable revolutionary lineage had guaranteed his 'prickly ally' a safe passage to his capital. Furthermore, another plane was already standing by to transfer the party and whisk them off to South America. The fewer stop-overs the better. And this plane was specially chartered. The President was sure of this much - the Colonel would need a safe haven for a long while to come; surely he would do nothing now to jeopardize the good life awaiting him in Brazil.

Moreover, the Colonel was certain to have a stack of money with him - to back up funds already accumulating interest in South America. It was not beyond the bounds of possibility that the President's good offices might, shall we say, be 'rewarded' in some way. No one's a saint. Besides, he was in a position to assure the Colonel (both through his high and low-profile contacts in Brazil) that he'd have quick access to money-laundering, especially, indeed, if he chose to reward the services of both Presidents. After all, everything has a price, and every man has his.

But the Colonel would have nothing to worry about. Brazil's world-wide reputation for hospitality to people on the run remained sacred, and undefiled.

Within a few hours the party had arrived in Paris. And with formalities waived, hands shaken, and a 'nod and a wink' in the right quarters, the party finally transferred to the big jet already warming up on the tarmac. There was no time to waste.

And so, as the special plane accelerated along the runway and rose up into the sky above the city, a new chapter in the Colonel's histrionic but ruthless life opened up before him. Back in his own country, the pace of change quickened further and foreign nations hovered to take their pickings - anxious as ever to show even-handedness and hide their cunning.

Chapter 2

'It's all over bar the shouting.' Dave Fletcher prepared to wrap up his latest revolution. He'd been covering bloody events for more than a decade and his soon-to-be released book on man's preoccupation with them together with his Nobel prize money (yes, it had happened, at last) would undoubtedly provide him with sufficient funds for a happy retirement in the country of his choice - supposing he'd ever lie down.

'But *this* revolution', he continued, 'will, in time, be seen to be different from the usual type in one very important aspect. Here, both the new régime and the people no longer care for retribution. They have not, after all, demanded their corrupt Colonel be tracked down, axed to death, cut to pieces, or brought back to the capital to face trial and then shot or hanged before a gawping public. Their only pleasure is that he is gone and that they are able at last to get on with rebuilding their lives. And to live them fully, to travel where they will, to worship whom they choose, vote for whom they prefer; say what they think. This is the real revolution. For the Middle East, it is unique. For anywhere, it is unique. Allah has either flown out with the Colonel, or he has had a change of heart, and stayed with the people. If God is not a reflection of man rather than the other way round, we may ask ourselves, how come he has so many different faces?'

The line went dead. Maybe Dave Fletcher's free and wicked throat, momentarily Americanised, had been cut by one of Allah's heavenly children - the revolution merely a dream. But he came back on the line as confident as ever.

'Now the people can begin to live as human beings and all of us in the civilized world wish them well.'

To everyone's amazement the streets were soon cleared and cleaned, and the rebuilding of the city began. Everybody got stuck in. Moreover, everyone seemed to have joy written across his or her face, though each child now had to learn to play with a toy gun rather than the real thing. Fortunately, most of the kids had seen enough bloodshed to last them a lifetime and were glad to help their parents clean up the mess. There was so much to do. On the political front a multi-party system, the first of its kind in the Arab world, was to be set up, elections held, new schools and hospitals built. Oh, the list was endless. But at least the Colonel had gone and some of the huge sums of money devoted to the armed forces could now be turned to constructive use. Yet the provisional Government was well aware that the country's new, fragile democracy would have to be protected from thieving, jealous, or merely opportunist hands. The question was - how the hell could all this be achieved, when so many other nations had clearly failed?

****

'But my dear Colonel. You look absolutely splendid. I would never have recognized you but for.......'

The Brazilian President's remarks were already beginning to irritate. The Colonel shot his bodyguard a sly look. Reluctantly, the bodyguard handed the President's aide a huge case of money 'for services rendered'. (The President could not be seen handling anything as vulgar as money. After all, Brazil, officially, was still a democracy). As the party bundled into the waiting cars, the pilot of the specially chartered plane, which had brought the ex-dictator to safety, was seen to give a curious little wave from the cockpit. He smiled and gently shook his head in barely disguised amusement. A British free-lance pilot, ex-B.A. who, over the years, had transported many a villain, many a tyrant across the continents of the world, he had seen it all.

And, for those services, he had been well paid. If only he were capable of writing a thriller, he'd make himself yet another fortune. Ah well. Mustn't be greedy, mustn't be greedy.

Through the streets of Brazilia the cavalcade wended its way. Yet, by Latin standards, it was a subtle cavalcade - three cars, top whack: no motorbike escorts with excited riders bedecked with immaculate uniforms, holsters and white gloves; no Rolls Royces piloted by Indian Chiefs-in-eternal-waiting, stabbing the clutch in blessed memory of ancient elephantine processions (London taxi-drivers will know what this means); no ostentatious flags on long bonnets, heralding a doomed, impoverished apology for a monarchy. This was modern Brazil - slick, dynamic, dangerous and complex. And corrupt - corrupt as no monarchy had ever been since the Middle Ages. Good men would come and go. Most, if they had ambition beyond their station, would either be eliminated or simply allowed to succumb to a smooth, easy sale of their souls. It was nothing to be ashamed of. Even England had caught up with the times and though the monarchy had survived, all the rest was for sale. Why the hell should Brazil, of all places, be any different?

At the Presidential Palace they soon got down to business. It was to be a pleasant meeting - polite but efficient. No one would be in any doubt as to his position. What more could one ask?

'Do take a seat, Colonel,' smiled the President, indicating a highly-decorated upright chair, while he himself sat in an even more ornate edifice of grand proportions.

After all, President Manuel Gonzalez was also of grand proportions with a head shaped like Marlon Brando. In fact, he was often mistaken for the great actor, and would always be given the benefit of the doubt. It seemed to please him and no one, for one moment, ever considered him a jumped-up villain of the first order.

Besides, his breezy Churchillian manner together with that huge cigar constantly hanging from his mouth gave him more than an air of authority. Moreover, he could charm the pants off most men and, when they weren't looking, the knickers off their ambitious wives. But opposite him, now, sat a man who not only had left his wives behind but who, also, was in need of protection despite Brazil's hospitable reputation. What possible reason had the President for using his famous charm? He had already taken possession of a substantial sum of money for services rendered. The deposed Colonel was on his country's soil. What more need he do for his guest?

But President Gonzalez was not a simple man. He thrived on intrigue; loved to live a little dangerously - near the edge. He liked to keep company not only with a number of stars of stage and screen but also a variety of high-powered villains and 'respectable businessmen'. After all, 'birds of a feather.....' Yet, apart from the usual crop of German ex-Nazis most of whom were too old to do anything out of order and in any case were fast dying off, there were few real monsters of international stature left to entertain him. Perhaps the Colonel, fresh from Iraq, might help to bridge that gap?

The President continued to smile and passed his cigar box across to the Colonel. 'No, thank you, Mr President. But I think Mustafa, here, would like one.'

'But, of course.'

The Colonel's bodyguard leant across the table and took hold of a handsome Havana. He put it in his mouth and, immediately, a hand came from nowhere to light it. 'UMP. p. p. Thanks.'

Mustafa had already decided he was going to love all this. If the Colonel played his cards right no one would have anything to fear.

'Now, my dear Colonel. We have arranged everything. There is a very spacious villa for you and your entourage, and…..'

'Forgive my interruption, Mr President. But it's hardly a large family. As you know, I had to leave my wife and children back home. I fear for their safety.'

'I quite understand your apprehension, Colonel. But from the latest reports that have come through to us, the provisional Government appears to consist of reasonable men. At least, so far. They don't seem to be interested in extracting any more blood from anyone at the moment except, of course, from bona fide donors.'

And with that, the President gave the Colonel a wry little smile, while the Colonel shifted uncomfortably in his chair, and bided his time.

****

Tony Sharp

Maria Gonzalez was a stunning beauty. For years she had modelled for the top Brazilian magazines. Tall, yet curvaceous and with the most wonderful eyes (not unlike those of the legendary Elizabeth Taylor), a small, gentle upturned nose and a bearing of graceful, easy elegance, she was, as they say, not to be sniffed at. Sniffed, yes - and was she sniffable - not with excessive perfume to cover a multitude of sanitary sins but with that aromatic, sweet-smelling natural odour one comes to expect of intelligent, moneyed Brazilian beauties. Her admirers were numerous, too numerous for her husband, the President, to take seriously. His was a mind given to life as it was - in practice, rather than in theory. Nevertheless, like any Latin worth his salt, he could, on occasions, be provoked into a burst of raging jealousy. But just as quickly as his feelings were aroused his wife, somehow, would be able to calm him with that seductive, never failing figure of hers - her soft, velvet voice caressing his big ears, ears that had too often and for too long been bombarded with ceaseless problems, gross statistics, sickening whingings and pressures from all sides. If he could trust no one, at least his wife would smooth troubled waters in a way no oil could ever quite do.

'But my dear,' he'd bleep in justifiable but useless protest, 'I have too much to do. The Finance Minister will be here at three, dear old Pepe Fernandez at 4, Chief of Police at 4.30. There's just no time to......'

Maria would have none of it. With a sensual caress of the back of his head with one hand and a slow brushing of his genitals with the other, her hand teasing his fly, unzipping it just enough to arouse his member from its slumber, they'd both sidle inevitably into the bedroom for an hour of passionate love-making that would, once more, make him forgive and forget. Besides, with a wife as insatiable as this, he was able to call on her at almost any time of the day or night and get his 'fix'. What need had he for anyone else? Who cared if she had a stableful of lovers? She was back with him. She always came back to him. What more evidence could he possibly seek of her need for him? Besides, the relief she afforded him was worth that of a thousand other women - he had tried them all - and found them wanting.

'Maria, Maria - I've just met a girl called.....' The famous song had stirred her time and time again and although she knew full well she could have almost any man in the Cabinet, for starters - and already had - even she could never resist her Manuel's singing. It may have been the association with an incident many years back when she'd first heard the 'wretched', magical song but she was powerless when Manuel began to get his tongue round........ 'Oh, Manuel, Manuel. Oh, God. You bastard, you bastard. I love it, I love it!'

A rude ring of the telephone disturbed their second course. Her Manuel would have to get out of bed and attend to matters of State. 'Matters of State'. How she hated that phrase. How she loathed the pretentiousness of the whole corrupt system. The money was a different matter. Money is money, anywhere. But 'Matters of State?' Huh. How she wished sometimes she could swap places with the Queen of England - to preside over a proper Royal Family. To be cosseted in real, lasting things of quality - surrounded by the ultimate in refinement, tradition, continuity; 'legitimacy'. How long, she wondered, could her kind of high living last? Just as long as Manuel remained President? Until he was removed from office? Until he was murdered? How many of her lovers could be relied upon to treat her as well as her Manuel had always done? How many could make her feel like a woman rather than a common whore? Would they all fade into the woodwork when the chips were down? People were weak - bumped up, pumped up machos or mercenary witches. She had been around and was hardly blind. Moreover, she possessed an intelligence which unnerved her rivals, unnerved more than a few Government Ministers, unnerved anyone who was shallow, transparent, obsequious - or just a plain, common creep. She could suss them all and longed for the day when she would meet another man like Manuel - a real man, someone of substance, a tyrant even, just so long as he was 'his own man'. She had tired of little crooks, 'yes men' who crept round her husband, currying his favour, each constantly smiling the smile of treachery, the smile of the traitor. She loved her Manuel - *in a way* - and could always get the best out of him - *when* he was available. But that was the trouble - he was always so busy. She needed a man and was honest enough to admit it.

'But, my dear Maria,' gasped Pepe Fernandez, the Foreign Minister, a gentleman of the old school, a man of impeccable manners and with a virtuous family life, to boot - how *he* ever got into the cabinet God alone knew. 'You can't tell Manuel. It would hurt him too much. It's enough for him to accept a thousand or so rivals... the idea, in reality, as we all know, is quite preposterous. But..'

'Preposterous? What a thing to say to a lady.'

You're no lady, thought the Minister. But he controlled his tongue.

'Well, you know what I mean, my dear. He knows you love him still, and that is enough. But to actually tell him you *need* another would....'

'Nonsense, Pepe. I'll pick my moment to tell him. Don't worry so. He'll see sense in the end. Besides, he's so busy with Matters of S..... .'

She stopped herself completing the dreaded, preposterous phrase. Yes, if anything was preposterous, it was her Country's 'Matters of State'.

Chapter 3

Within a week the whole of the free world had celebrated a rare event - the declaration of a democratic Arab State.

'Though, what sort of a democracy it will turn out to be, God alone knows.' John Broadbridge, quite naturally, had his doubts. He'd been studying Middle East affairs for many years and had grown quite fond of the Arabs, though no one could ever accuse him of aspiring to the 'heights' of Lawrence of Arabia. That would have been taking things a little too far. Nice man though he undoubtedly was, the extent of his romanticism was somewhat limited - stretching as it did to a rose-covered cottage in Dorset. Like Peter Watson, tucked up in his BBC office in London and whose own heart was set on Devon, John Broadbridge aspired to the quiet life. He had done his stint, to the best of his ability. He was no Tom Brown who yearned for a posting right near the action - no Dave Fletcher, long embroiled in the thick of it, spewing out his despatches with the glee of a young Churchill. 'Joan at the Broken Bridge' was a family man - with a wife, two kids and a dog - solid, down to earth; reliable. His assignments had always been taken up on the strict understanding they would be of a limited period. He would adhere to the contract and expected others to do the same. So, what the hell was he doing in the Middle East, you may ask? Well, his knowledge and command of Arabic was second to none - his ability to get the best out of people; his very physique - 6' 4" - and a girth and muscles to match; a strong jaw (yet bearded in deference to local customs) with bright blue eyes all played their part in impressing the natives. He towered over most of the Sheiks with whom he came in contact. But he would never threaten, never patronize. He was, as they say, a gentle giant. And they loved him for it. And just as Iraq, against all odds, was about to become free - though no one in his right mind could predict for how long it would stay that way - John Broadbridge approached the T-junction of his own life. Cross-roads were for others, braver or more foolhardy, the type never to blame themselves for taking the wrong turning since, to begin with, there were more than two choices over which to puzzle. But, for John, one choice out of two was sufficient. "One challenge at a time", he was fond of saying. "I am a simple man. Mazes are not for me. Life is difficult enough for there to be room for complications". He was not a man endowed with great imagination. And so, for him, even a T-junction posed a difficult question. For days, he agonized. And the question was - should he agree to a straight-forward extension of his contract already offered him on even better terms than before, or should he pack up and go back home to a simple, family life - in Swindon?

For Iraq, the choice posed no such problem. The Colonel had gone and for most people, now that they were allowed free rein to an honest tongue - or any other sort, if they so desired - it was 'good riddance'. Within two weeks, detailed plans were drawn up for free elections and a multi-party system on British lines. And since, for years, that system merely boiled down to a matter of two main parties - albeit with hopeless attempts to jig things up via splinter groups or the eternal flogging of that loveable old Liberal horse - it did not appear to anyone to be such a daunting task, after all. Even Arabs can 'see their way clear', sometimes. And in

The House of Baghdad

England, much to the chagrin of poorer, indigenous locals, they have frequently proved the point.

So there it was - for all the world to see, while astronomical bets were placed even by wealthy Arabs as to the time it would take for the system to break down and for a popular demand, if not for the return of the Colonel, at least for a decent '80s style dictator - perhaps, on British lines?

Yet within nine months, most of the world's bookmakers were sporting decidedly long faces. Few Westerners felt the new enlightened régime would last more than two months. But last it did - and longer. Moreover, the eyes of the locals were beginning to take on an international, almost humorous gaze. It was a rare phenomenon and purists began to be concerned for the future of Islam. If people were learning to laugh at themselves, how in hell was the world to be saved? It was no laughing matter.

But the provisional Government was determined to pursue its chosen path. It was, after all, made up not only of students, some of whom had been lucky enough to escape and study abroad and had now returned to the Country of their birth but also of disgruntled army personnel who'd suffered heavy family losses at the hand of the Colonel's ruthless 'cleansing programme'. Most surprising of all, however, was the fact there was such a substantial core of underground intelligentsia remaining who had, over the years, avidly listened to the BBC and rather liked what they'd heard. Like their 'cousins' in the Himalayas who insisted upon keeping their Gilbert and Sullivan up to scratch, they were somewhat dangerously close to becoming irreversible anglophiles. They even held secret meetings in the course of which they entertained each other in BBC accents. Had their hard-line fellow countrymen known of these meetings, the whole network would have been hunted down and all members exterminated without mercy. In fact, as was only to be expected, a number of the old guard remained in the Country, making plans and biding their time. Some even took advantage of the general lifting of travel restrictions and flew out, disguised as happy members of the public to join their 'brothers in the cause'. Like cynical Westerners, they too did not hold out much hope for the new liberal régime.

The difference was - they were determined to overthrow and stamp out what they saw as a Western plot, albeit of an enlightened kind. And since they knew not the meaning of enlightenment...... It was all very distressing.

Another two weeks passed and at last the provisional Government announced the date of the elections. To experienced Western eyes it was a rushed job. But at least *they were trying*. Many parties sprang up and they all squabbled with each other - so much so, that a couple of well-respected British ex-pats who, over the years, had managed to entertain some of the 'leading lights-in-waiting', even suggested a competition with a prize of £10,000 for the party who could out-squabble all others. Since all political coffers were desperately low, the suggestion was eagerly taken up. Moreover, a representative of an American TV network offered the parties an open forum to be shot for screening back in the States as an alternative to 'The British House of Commons'. Why the man should have believed the alternative would be so very different no one could make out. But there it was. At least the people were beginning to have fun. And the blood of fundamentalists boiled yet again.

'Well, Mr Broadbridge? Have you made a decision?' Safe in the interior the Caliph sat in his chair and eyed his foreign friend with some amusement.

'Yes, sir. I have. But it was a difficult choice.'

'Difficult choice? Even I have heard of Swindon. You are well treated here, are you not?' The Caliph looked deep into the eyes of John Broadbridge and tried to fathom the depths of an Englishman's soul. Despite the continual ravages, rape and pillage exercised during the forging of the great British Empire, out of it all - even the Caliph would have admitted - came a few nice people. And though he'd had nothing to do with it, personally, John Broadbridge, by the look of him, was certainly a product of that unspeakable tribe. So, what happened?

The Caliph spoke again. 'How in Allah's name, sir… oh, well, in God's name, if you must, can you even think about going back?'

'I'm not going back, sir.'

'Not going back?' The Caliph's mouth stood open in mock surprise. He'd been educated at Cambridge and, despite the bleak flatness of the Fens, the wind and the cold and the damp, he'd survived it all with a remarkable lack of resentment and more than a wry sense of humour. He was unique among his fellow Caliphs.

'Well, sir,' plodded John Broadbridge, 'I've turned it over in my mind very carefully, again and again and though I love my wife and family, I must say - the thought of….'

'Don't tell me you've got used to our funny little ways, my friend?'

'It is rather colourful, here, sir.' John Broadbridge was beginning to brighten up but had decided to keep it short and uncomplicated. The Caliph smiled and ordered his house boy to bring some tea.

'Well, allow me to be the first to congratulate you and wish you a further happy stay with us.'

'Thank you, sir.'

'After all, there is so much to be done, now that the tiresome Colonel is out of the way. You could be of invaluable service to us. And since the indefatigable Dave Fletcher has won his Nobel Prize and will doubtless be off again somewhere to report on yet another upheaval,' (here, the Caliph looked for signs of pleasure or otherwise from his guest but found not a flicker) 'there will be no one but yourself on whom we can rely.'

'I could hardly count myself in his league, sir. He's....'

'Nonsense. He's colourful, I grant you - to match our little Country eh?'

The Caliph gave his guest a wee wink which instantly reminded John Broadbridge of the sheep's eye blinking at Charlie Drake in 'Sands of the Desert'. He was but a lad of 10 when he'd seen that film in the local cinema with his mother and had never forgotten the funny yet rather nauseating frame. He was a grown man now but associations can play havoc on one's body functions. His stomach began to turn but the Caliph had not finished....

'But you, my dear friend, are - shall we say, a little more solid, and dependable?' John Broadbridge was feeling anything but solid, at that moment. He hung on like grim death to his 'dependability'.

'Dull, you mean, sir?'

'Don't demean yourself, my friend. You English are always doing that. I hate it.'

'But that's what makes us English.'

'I cannot agree. The English, I have observed, have too many fine qualities to warrant self deprecation.'

'Would you rather have a German?'

'Don't be vulgar.' And with that the Caliph proceeded to sign his guest's new contract, while the houseboy poured the tea.

He could have been deluding himself but John Broadbridge was feeling better already.

Chapter 4

The Colonel put his feet up on the bed and opened his magazine.

'Maria, Maria. I've just met......' Where had he heard those mawkish words before? Wasn't it from a tape one of his men had confiscated from that spotted-dick, loud-mouthed American agent last summer? But the Colonel hadn't seen this magazine before - not in Iraq, nor had he seen such a luscious beauty filling any pages - with 'Eyes like precious jewels, breasts like prick-teasing mountain tops, legs like never ending silken....'

'Did you call, sir?' Mustafa popped his head round the door to make sure his master and employer was all right. He always addressed him as 'sir', for unlike most of his fellow Arab heavies, he had served many masters of different nationalities and cultures including a particularly pernickety 'Englishman' for whom, nevertheless, he had built up considerable respect. It was difficult to get out of the habit.

'No, Mustafa, thank you. I was just taking a peep at this magazine and thinking..'.

Mustafa grinned and walked across to the bed to take a look. 'Well, what do *you* think?'

Mustafa looked at the pictures and gulped. 'Beautiful, sir. But that's the President's wife. I should forget about that one.'

'What did you say? The President's wife? Forget about her? Could *you?*'

'If it's the President's wife.' Mustafa had always been succinct and to the point. Moreover, unlike the Colonel, he had travelled the world. Up to now, the Colonel had tended to stick with local bodyguards who, like him, had never wandered much beyond their 'safe' Bedouin tents. But Mustafa had been thoroughly de-coded, de-briefed, de-contaminated - and Allah knows what else - before he was given the job of protecting the Colonel.

And now that 'the master' had found himself so far away from home, ("What have I done, O Allah, to deserve this?") an intelligent, well-travelled, well-read, and, it seemed, well informed heavy, would be invaluable.

'If this is the President's wife,' postulated the Colonel, pointing a lustful finger at a particularly provocative pose in the now well-thumbed magazine, 'I'll eat my hat.'

'Start eating, sir.'

The Colonel laughed at Mustafa's easy impertinence. Already he'd learned to appreciate his man's little quips, despite the fact they were decidedly too American, for his taste. Not that his own language was so pure, with all this 'literature' around the place. Perhaps the President had set a trap for him. Who could tell?

'Nevertheless, I want to meet her. I'm sure we can find a way.'

Well, if you're adamant about it, sir, it shouldn't be too difficult. She's bound to turn up at one of the President's little 'do's' to which, no doubt, you will be invited. But I strongly urge you to be careful. By all accounts Manuel Gonzalez can, on occasion, throw an almighty fit of rage.'

'My word, Mustafa. What a speech you've just made. You're getting to be quite English, these days. Are you feeling well?'

'Perfectly, thank you, sir.'

'You only have to say - if it's getting to be too much for you. Or perhaps you're still pining over that English tycoon? What did you say his name was?'

'Robert Maxwell.'

'Robert Maxwell? He's no Englishman, I fear. Tried hard to be, though, I must say.'

Mustafa began to laugh. 'In Allah's name, what were you doing with him? The mind, er ....'

'Boggles, sir?'

'Something like that.'

'Well, I don't really want to go into it, tonight, if you don't mind, sir. Just let's say... I was keeping an eye on him.' Mustafa's facial expression assured the Colonel that whatever it was that had contributed to Maxwell's final demise had, at least, brought a certain amount of poetic justice to bear upon 'The Struggle'. As to his own position, the Colonel, for all his quirks, would have nothing to worry about - if Mustafa had anything to do with it.

'All right, my friend. You go and rest - while I pour over this magazine a little longer.'

'You'll go blind.'

'I'll go blind if I don't have her. Out, Mustafa.'

****

It was a very grand affair. Ministers of State and their mistresses, bishops and their boyfriends, international entrepreneurs, well established gangsters - including one ex-Nazi, looking very healthy and distinguished in his chic 'off the peg' mohair suit, fully complementing his upright bearing (it was as if he'd refused to have the peg removed) and three famous actresses, one of whom had, that year, won the annual award for best Porno Movie - Expo Brazil. There was the French President who, no doubt, had turned up to cast a beady eye over his 'prickly ally', the latter, despite his other reputation for the quiet, secret life was bound to attend such a gathering as this, if he knew the Colonel and, last but not least, a drag queen of the most gigantic proportions - a creature some said had years ago outstripped Linda Lovelace's epiglottal acrobatics by more than a hair's breadth, but who now had settled down to become one of the most 'suckcessful' and entertaining TV evangelists of all time.

Maybe grand is too stiff and formal a word with which to describe that affair. Colourful, perhaps, would be more appropriate. The gathering, certainly, reflected all possible tastes. Manuel Perez Gonzalez, President of all Brazil, could always be relied upon to whisk up a motley crew (not a momentous task in Brazil, after all); besides, he'd always been a very human man - tough when necessary, yet tolerant and yielding when appropriate. In fact, on this particular occasion he seemed so yielding that his Maria decided it was the night for her to 'look over' the guests more carefully and to seek out that new lover of hers. Who could tell? It could be her night. Again!

The table was laden with mountains of rich food - all sorts of dead meat spluttered and groaned under the weight of yet another slice of its own kind. After all, the President had his quirks - he would never allow a whole pig or ox to be displayed within his sight. Strangely, it wasn't the blood or other natural juices dripping down that turned his stomach, it was the fatuous idea that somehow the carcass would suddenly revolt and get up and walk away. He had never entirely got over one particular childhood nightmare

The House of Baghdad

in the course of which all kinds of bodies rose from their graves and terrorised the whole neighbourhood in which he was still spending his impressionable years. That damned silly priest of forty odd years ago would have much to answer for -whether they met each other in Heaven or the other place. Trouble was - they'd be eternally missing each other 'between shows'.

The President stood up and banged on the table. All chatter and giggling subsided and all eyes were turned and concentrated upon him - this magnificent Brando look-alike. Even the stance was the same as the original model's - the angle and turn of that noble, intelligent head, the quiet, powerful confidence – an alchemy superbly honed to create a presence no one could ignore and to which all were inevitably drawn.

'Your Graces, Ladies and Gentlemen. My friends.' With this last acknowledgement, the President glanced across to the Colonel who appeared somewhat sheepish and out of place in his getup of mohair suit and silk tie.

Though the tie was of a different pattern, the suit was exactly the same type, cut and colour as the ex-Nazi's. In fact, from the very start of the proceedings the German gentleman had been practising some of his blackest looks in the direction of the newcomer. For the time being, however, those looks were lost on the Colonel. His mind was bent on a more interesting pursuit. Indeed, the rather obvious machinations now being set in motion had not gone un-noticed by the President. For, as he continued his address, out of the corner of his eye he caught sight not only of the Colonel's 'indiscretions' but also those of his wife. She'd been making passes at the Colonel ever since she'd clapped eyes on him. 'Clapped' on him, indeed, were her eyes - he was just the sort of man she'd been looking for over the past year and a half and, though the face was perhaps a wee bit too spotty for her individual taste, nevertheless it exuded a certain attractive arrogance - the sort of pose people round the world seemed to go in for in a big way during those hard '80s but which now, alas for Maria, was fast being replaced with a gentle, friendly smile. Yes, people wore silly, human faces, faces that permitted every nuance of feeling, every compassionate thought, every weakness, every kindness. Or so it seemed, to her. She was old enough to remember the '80s faces. They were the kind that turned her on - hard, determined, taut, mean faces that disparaged human tenderness but aped the '20s, faces whose owners could know little of the real sophistication, wherewithal or humour of that era. The get-rich-quick philosophy and brutality of the '80s was all-pervading and affected everyone - whether they were 'making it' or not. But, for Maria, it was the decade. With so many friendly faces around these days, it was refreshing to see such a puffed-up, arrogant countenance as the Colonel's. Judging by the bulge in his trousers, he also appeared to possess (for Maria) the most important wherewithal of all - it would keep her happy for a long time to come, she decided.

Manuel's 'thing' was such a circumspect attachment that she had often found it difficult to concentrate. Mind you, he knew just what to do with it - she'd give him that. And his imagination never seemed to run out of steam. Moreover, his tongue would not be idle for a second. Nevertheless, she could hardly deny she preferred the big ones - if only the dummies knew how to use them. Yet, from what she had already deduced, the Colonel seemed to possess a power and an intelligence to make all his equipment function beautifully - not only for his own gratification but also for hers.

Yes, the more Maria studied the man, the more she knew she had to have him. He was so darned sexy - in an Arab sort of way; in command of himself, laid-back. She had no prejudices, no hang-ups or mental constrictions of the kind that seemed to inhibit other people's natural enjoyment. If she liked someone, she'd always go for it. Oh yes, the Colonel would have to watch out. Maria would be there.

But so would the Colonel, it appeared. As the two of them continued to exchange glances the President made a mental note - first to tackle Maria after dinner; then he'd have a little chat with his guest, the Colonel. It shouldn't take long to sort out. Or so he believed.

'Ladies and Gentlemen,' he continued. 'you can see what a colourful bunch of people I have gathered under this roof, tonight.' Nudges, winks and laughter ensued all around the vast dining room. It could almost have been the occasion of a very informal and friendly lodge meeting except for the fact that none of the guests had the slightest interest in either puerile ritual or suppressed, yet thinly disguised, incest. Here, certainly, was a motley crowd of individuals but with cutting edges and the widest experience of life in all its anger, all its terror and with softer edges too - volumes of experience in all its gentler moods, all its colours, all its delicate and not so delicate intricacies.

No one here had need of the insincere pat on the back, a crocodile tear, or a worthless silver-plated candlestick won in a childish raffle. These people possessed imagination beyond the norm. Who cared if they'd 'blown it' in the eyes of the world? To their mind the world itself was stupid - an incestuous, self-perpetuating, boring old blancmange. They were in it; they were not of it.

The voice of the President raised itself a touch higher as he lifted his arms to embrace, as it were, the whole room. 'My dear friends. Most of you have known each other for many years. But I would like us to extend a particular welcome to a man newly arrived from another rather colourful spot in the world - namely, Iraq.' Renewed laughter and cynical giggles broke out and all eyes turned to the new man in the mohair. Only now did the ex-Nazi (he'd been a real officer in Rommel's crack Afrika Corps before falling out with the great man) allow himself a proper smile. He'd been thinking. Could the reason the 'upstart' was wearing the same suit be an omen, a sign the two of them should get together and work out a strategy? Something, surely, could be worked out? For too long the German had languished in Brazil, kicking his heels - not in command or honour of his country, but, for him at any rate, in frustration, ignominy, anonymity.

But the only sign acknowledged by the majority of the guests was one from the President to the musicians. He had lashed out and booked the best Brazil could offer. As far as he was concerned it was going to be a great night. And, as he turned to face the band - with a wink and a nod - the room lit up with the strains of the latest Latin American number which, like its predecessor, had, not surprisingly (considering its pedigree and determined sponsorship) shot straight to Number One in those pop charts. 'Ladies and Gentlemen,' beamed the President. 'Take your partners, please, for the Ronnie Biggs Rumba.'

Chapter 5

It was fast becoming a night to remember. The 'Reverend' Biggs himself had indicated a wish to attend but had not yet arrived. 'A spot of business' would have been the only genuine reason for his failure to appear. However, there were a couple of long-standing associates of his who, it seemed, had shown willing - to make up the numbers, so to speak. Like others from the great era of British 'comedians', they had tired of Marbella and its narrow clique and had taken the plunge and moved to Brazil.

On cracked the band. The sound was superb - dynamic, stimulating - inspiring; one bishop even neglected his young friend in order to entangle himself with the outrageous drag queen. Perhaps he was hoping for a favour from the lips of a legend. Much as the bishop undoubtedly loved his pretty friend, for some time now he'd increasingly felt there had been something missing. To his mind the young man had never quite mastered the art of fellatio and the bishop had always been very demanding. After all - 'When in Rome'. The Colonel, on the other hand, would, it seemed, want for nothing. The mere outline of his equipment through the cloth of his trousers had aroused Maria to such an extent that, as soon as the band had struck up with Ronnie's Rumba, she had made straight for him.

The Colonel could hardly believe his luck. It was all happening so quickly. It seemed only five minutes ago that he was ogling those pictures of her in his magazine and trusty Mustafa had warned him not to get involved. Not get involved? What a ridiculous, old-fashioned, English idea.

The very thought of ignoring a creature like Maria. She had got him to his feet and they were already on the dance-floor.

He had made a half-hearted plea to be excused from the dance but she would have none of it. She'd be teacher tonight, she joked and, with no further ado, she had him locked in a hopeless embrace. Already, her leg had slid near to his leg. Her shapely body closed on his rather less shapely - yet no longer - hesitant body. She could feel him getting hard as they moved tightly together. 'The Bulge' was certainly going to live up to expectations, as far as she was concerned. It would only be a matter of time before he'd be in full flow. Perhaps he'd whisk her off suddenly in the middle of the dance when Manuel wasn't looking. Perhaps…..

The Colonel felt a tap on his shoulder. It was an interruption he could well do without but the German gentleman was insistent. 'My dear Colonel,' he coughed, trying to ignore his dancing partner busying herself nibbling his ear, 'we've heard so much about you. I'd like very much to have a chat with you after this dance.'

Maria raised her eyes to the ceiling in exasperation. Just as she was beginning to enjoy herself. Damn the man. 'Not tonight, Felix. I think the Colonel will be occupied for a little while.'

And with that, both Maria and the Colonel began to laugh.

But, then, quite suddenly, they found themselves locked in a lingering French kiss. 'Disgraceful woman,' whispered the German's partner under her hypocritical breath as she extricated herself from her partner's ear. 'Oh, well,' soothed the German gentleman, 'we all know Maria, my dear. Maria is Maria. Manuel never seems to complain. Why should we worry?'

'I think we could all consider the Colonel to be something of a different kettle of fish to her other admirers?'

'It may seem that way, my dear. But remember, he is here with the help of our President. If he has any intelligence, he'd do well to watch his..... what do you English say - P's and....?'

'P's and Q's, my foot. It's much too late for that sort of nicety, sweetie. Look, they've gone.'

A solid, reliable German head turned to find not another mohair to be seen for dust. The couple had escaped - skilfully, smoothly - the whole operation as smooth as …….. and talking of bottoms…..

'Oh, Colonel, you naughty boy. You… ouch. That hurts. Ou…..oo….. Oh. My God. Oh My God. Oh, that's nice… that's nice! Keep going, keep….. Go on, harder, harder, harder. Oh, that's wonderful. I can feel your balls right up against my……'

'Maria, Maria… I want you….Ah … all day….every day……. every which way….'

The Colonel had learned a great many Western phrases and, besides, he was hardly in need of tuition from any jumped-up sex guru. He was an Arab, through and through. And here, snug in his bedroom, so thoughtfully loaned to him by the Brazilian Government, he was at last enjoying himself with the woman in the magazine. OK……she happened to be the President's wife….. but, right now, he couldn't be bothered about trifling details of ownership or etiquette. His mind and body were on an exciting course of exploration.

'OK. Now the other way.'

'The normal way, you mean?'

'Right way, normal way, who cares, Maria? Do *you*?'

'Not any more, my beautiful monster. You can have me any way you like.'

She turned on her back and prepared to lie there, supine - at least until she got her breath back. She reckoned she'd worked almost as hard as he during Phase 1 of this little session. But he'd tolerate no respite, no slacking, no sleeping on the job; he'd known too many of those women back home. With an expert flick of his hands and wrists, Maria's legs were thrown over his shoulders and, instantly, he found her warm natural opening, a welcoming natural orifice and one which could only be matched by another kind which now pouted and opened in harmony yet barely in patient expectation. If only he had three cocks she'd have nothing to complain about, but there it was... Mustn't be greedy, mustn't be greedy. There was only one of him - and his weapon, so far, was working beautifully. If he had enough seed inside his balls after this lot, she'd certainly help herself to it. After all, he'd only have to kneel over her. This time she would be doing most of the work.

Forward, back, forward, back, forward... The lovemaking continued apace. And now she found herself really getting into it. Her legs quivered and moved in lustful harmony and she began to moan for more. On and on it went and at last he let out a great groan and shuddered his sperm into her.

'God..... that was wonderful, wonderful!' His eyes looked down at her with joyous pride and satisfaction. She smiled at him and parted her lips, the only ones that so far had not tasted the fruits of his member. She was sure it would not be long before Phase 3 of their love session would begin and she would at last come 'face to face' with his huge organ. She'd been buggered, she'd been fucked and had not been too disappointed. But she never wanted to give up sucking. She loved to see a man straddle his legs over her while she drew his penis into her mouth. She loved to see him slide it backwards and forwards while she adjusted her own rhythm. Then she'd suck harder and stare straight at his beautiful pulsating pelvis. God, the thought of his huge cock fucking her mouth was making her come again, it was.......

The Colonel had returned from the bathroom and was here - just as she had dreamed and hoped for, he was here, right up and into her mouth, stretching it, filling it, invading it. 'Oh God, Oh..... arrh, arrrh.'

He came into her mouth - she came, too, and......

Of course, he'd been a little crude. And for Maria, it was all over a touch too quickly. But what the hell? There was always next time. Next time? Supposing Manuel put a stop to it? Supposing he set to work on the Colonel, or had one of his men 'do the job'? Easy-going though he undoubtedly was on certain matters, there were limits to his patience. And he owed the Colonel nothing. It was surely the other way round. But the excitement, the danger... Oh, how it all appealed to Maria. And, judging by the nonchalance of his present demeanour, it appealed to her new lover, too.

'Has anyone seen Maria?' This could well have been the question on the lips of the average, concerned male on finding his wife so conspicuously absent. But President Gonzalez was anything but average; nor would he dream of making such a parochial enquiry. Despite the occasional bout of jealousy in matters of personal relationships, he would always do his best to rationalise any problem with which he was faced. And in spite of his intention to confront Maria over her obvious attraction to the Colonel, the fact they had both slipped away like naughty schoolchildren had given him an idea. He was always full of ideas - possessing, as he did, a quick mind and a judicious cunning to go with it. Moreover, he had the enviable ability to turn what at first seemed a tragedy, outrage, or mere disappointment into a distinct advantage to himself. If the Colonel was stupid enough to get involved with Maria in such an obvious, unsubtle way, ignoring normal protocol and good manners towards his host in the process, then he'd make sure of using him for as long as he stayed in Brazil. And that could easily become rather a long stay. If he had a mind to do it, not only could Manuel seize all the Colonel's assets but could also allow himself the pleasure of watching the little bastard work for a living. The powers of the President were considerable, to say the least.

The more Manuel Gonzalez thought on these matters the more he liked the idea. Besides, Maria only respected strong men. With the Colonel put in his place, Manuel would, in her eyes, remain the clear favourite - despite her one-off, indiscreet romp with the Colonel. Moreover, her own indiscretion would further strengthen Manuel's hand. At any rate, this was his thinking.

****

'Good morning, Maria. How are you, today?' Breakfast, it seemed, had at least got off to a civilized start.

'I'm fine, Manuel, thank you.' She returned his smile and sat down to open her fan mail, a selection of which her personal secretary had laid out on the table a half hour earlier.

'Seems as if you have quite a bundle, today, my dear.'

'Yes. But then I've had more than the usual number of sessions to get through.' Manuel looked up from his paper to smile his special smile, the one that suggested Maria's photo sessions (she'd never been able to give them all up) would invariably be spiced with another sort of activity for which she was undoubtedly well equipped. She caught his expression and wondered who'd be the first to broach the subject of last night's little episode with the Colonel. But Manuel said nothing and she began to worry. If he maintained this commendable but irritating constraint, he just had to have something up his sleeve. She had never underestimated the old bugger's intelligence and ingenuity when it came to the crunch. But was this the crunch? Perhaps he didn't care any more? Perhaps he was losing his touch and turning himself into an Englishman? God forbid. As she ploughed through the mound of mail cluttering the breakfast table, she felt her face flush. He was so quiet, so at ease with himself. She felt uncomfortable, hemmed in, trapped. His silence at the other end of the table would drive her mad - if she allowed it. But she was determined to stick it out. That was her intention.

He'd finished reading the papers and had started on his fruit. He always ate fruit after his cereal. But this morning, he appeared to be in less of a hurry. Normally he ate a few grapes or an apple with his orange juice and coffee before shooting off to deal with those 'Matters of State'. Today he seemed bent on tackling a banana, carefully and deliberately peeling it back so that the fruit stood tall, proud and naked - exposed for all the world to see ..... and the world was Maria - beautiful Maria. The huge fruit was poised in front of his mouth. He angled it towards him, taking the tip in his mouth and then more of it - closing his mouth firmly over the shaft. He looked up to Maria and closed his eyes mockingly in the belief one at least of last night's activities would be rekindled in her mind. Maybe she would crack and then tell him everything he wanted to know. He opened his eyes again and caught her smile. But it merely suggested she knew he knew, but that she didn't care, anyway. Let him make the first move, if he wanted. She wouldn't be rushed. It was a game of cat and mouse and they were both more than capable of playing it... He had already consumed the top of the banana. But now he put more of the fruit into his mouth, sliding his mouth over it - up and down, up and down......

He was no homosexual. But he could be a damned tiresome child, at times. What did he care - as long as it got to the truth? He was sure Maria would explode any second and bring the whole subject of the Colonel out into the open - and to a head.

'All right, you silly sod,' she began predictably, 'I just couldn't resist him. I'm back with you, am I not? I always come back to you.'

It was his turn to smile and, as he did so, he rose from the table and walked over to her to touch her hand that still clasped one of those fan letters.

'I want you to be happy, my dear. You know that.'

He gave her hand a squeeze, and calmly walked out of the room.

Damn him. Damn his coolness, his understanding, his control. For, underneath that calm exterior, she knew throbbed a calculating brain which, together with his powerful position and a sadistic streak to match it, could spell the end of her beautiful new affair.

Chapter 6

In Swindon, life posed somewhat tamer problems. Kitty Broadbridge turned the key of her front door and only just managed to avoid treading straight onto a matful of letters. She had been away for a fortnight's holiday with the children, Polly and Davy, and was glad to get home. Even the kids had had enough Devon cream to last them a lifetime: they had stuffed their faces with it until they were sick. And the real country air - to their seasoned minds - was hardly a match for Swindon. Say what you like, people were very accommodating in Swindon and no-one shot anyone funny looks…… stares, yes. But then at least they were Swindonian - blank, complete, reliable.

Polly put the kettle on and young Davy - no, he didn't take it off again but simply scooped out the remnants of Mum's flan, left in the fridge, "just in case", while Mum herself made a start on the letters. My word, what a lot she'd received; a postcard from Auntie Ivy from her holiday hole in Jersey (she'd always been in the money, blast her); then there was a letter from her brother Jack, pleading poverty again and promising to be helpful if only Kitty would let him stay for a couple of months - maybe six or nine, 'top whack', then there was the bloody phone bill - how much? Oh, God - it can't be. The usual commercial bumph fell through her hands - straight into the bin and then - the one with the foreign postmark, which she'd saved till last. Of course, must be from her John. About time he came home. And now that the situation in Iraq, by all reports, looked settled and…… What, What? The bugger. Oh, no - he can't. Must be a mistake. Must be a joke. Damn silly one, stupid man. In their fifteen years together, he'd never played a trick on her. What a time to start. Must be a joke. Don't like it though. Better ring the BBC. They would know what he's up to, *surely*?

On Peter Watson's desk, a labyrinth of phones had been buzzing all day. Conflicting stories were still pouring out of Baghdad over who really was in charge and also the possible direction of the new régime, regardless of the supposed good intentions of the victorious. There was no question the Colonel had gone but all other questions - as was only to be expected - were 'up for grabs'.

At last Kitty succeeded in making her connection.

'Oh, Peter. Thank God I've reached you. I'm so upset by this letter from John. What's going on? What's he…?'

'Kitty, don't panic, my dear. He's OK. Quite OK. I've only just heard the news myself. Seems as if he wanted to break it to you first.'

'I've just come back from the country, Peter.'

'Oh, yes. Had a good time?'

'Hardly. I've been so worried. And now he's gone and signed another contract. Has he gone mad? What did he say to you?'

'Well, he sounded in great spirits. Just said he'd explain it all to you by letter and that you'd understand.'

'Understand? He knows where home is. He……' (Here, Peter stifled a wee giggle as best he could. Kitty, bless her, had never possessed what one might call a wild imagination but John Broadbridge, up to now her reliable, loving spouse, was, it seemed, already preparing to broaden his horizons. Indeed, if wonders never ceased, he might even stretch out his contract for ever - just so long as he didn't have to see Swindon again. But Peter was never a man to spend time fathoming the whys and wherefores of other people's domestic arrangements - however unfortunate they might turn out to be.)

'Well, Kitty. As far as I can tell, John is in good shape and of sound mind. Is there anything you wish me to convey to him? I'm sure he'll be in touch again, soon.'

'Yes, Peter. Give him my love, of course... and from the children and tell him I'm none too happy about him staying out there. And not to worry so much about the money. We can manage - as long as he's home.'

'I'll do my best, Kitty, don't worry. Call us again in a couple of days... if you don't hear from him yourself.'

'May I?'

'Of course. Must go. God bless.'

'You too. 'Bye, Peter.'

Peter replaced the receiver with a smile. He'd been a bachelor for many years now. However, he'd recently decided to take the plunge with a young lady at the Beeb on the strict understanding that, once hitched, neither would get in the other's way. "Absence makes the heart grow fonder" had long been his catch-phrase and, judging by this little phone call from Kitty over John's 'surprise' decision to stay on in the Middle East, he was provided with yet another ready-made example to prove his point. Not that he'd ever consider making his bed in.......

No sooner had he made a move to leave the office for his lunch-break than the phone rang again. Christ, the phones had not stopped ringing all morning. And today he was short-staffed. Tom Brown had been called out to cover the Chancellor's Budget proposals and the remaining typist was new and inexperienced. Damn. It might even be Dave Fletcher. The man moved so fast these days - not even

Peter, with all his fine intellect and imagination, could ever hazard a guess as to where the man would turn up next.

'Hello, Peter. It's John.'

'Oh, John. I thought it might have been Dave Fletcher, but……

'Sorry to disappoint you.'

'Now, whatever gave you that idea?'

Peter detected a little giggle coming down the line together with a slight slur in John's speech pattern. Maybe the desert, even for a Broadbridge, had never been entirely dry?

'How's life, anyway?'

'Bloody marvellous. I'm beginning to enjoy myself. Gettin' on fine with the Caliph. Good sport. I think he's pleased to have one of us here to hang out with. Get my drift? Hic.'

It was the first time Peter had known John to get this far in the liquid stakes. Presumably the Caliph knew what he was doing. Whatever it took to keep Mr Broadbridge in his employ, it seemed, was worth the risk. John's reliability, even Peter would have admitted, had never been in doubt. So, what was a wee drink or two between friends in the comparative privacy, presumably, of the Caliph's 'little palace'?

But John Broadbridge had not finished. 'By the way, hic. The Caliph would like a word. Hic.' The phone was plonked down on to a table or something very hard before Peter had time to pass on any message from Kitty. Not that it would have been received with much sympathy, today.

'Hello, Mr Watson.' The Caliph's voice was clear and well modulated,

'Good morning to you, sir. How is everything?'

The House of Baghdad

'Everything is, how do you say - hunky dory?'

'An American expression, sir. But we'll let it pass.'

'I am speaking to a real Englishman, then?'

'Indeed, sir.'

'Very good. Well now, Mr Watson. What Mr Broadbridge and I are proposing is this...... With the help of the BBC, we would like to set up a new regular radio programme entitled, say 'The Baghdad Line' which should give the British public a better understanding of what is happening here. May I continue?'

'Please do.' Peter Watson was hooked. The Caliph sounded such a reasonable man, and well educated into the bargain.

'Well, considering our recent bloody history in the eyes of the world and, indeed, in the eyes of the more civilized of us Iraqis, the programme should help, you might say, to 'put the record straight.' Or is this phrase also to be excluded from the English language?'

Peter laughed down the line and found himself warming to this Caliph. Besides, the voice was so like that of Sir Alec Guinness that he was beginning to hope the two men were one and the same. After all, who could fail to be impressed by the great actor's portrayal of the Emir Faisal in 'Lawrence of Arabia'?

'I think it's a sound idea, sir. Moreover, if we obtain the full approval of the British Ambassador in Baghdad, I believe it could serve nothing but good.'

'I agree, Mr Watson. In fact, I have already held a meeting with Sir Thomas this very morning. He is all for the idea.'

'Splendid. Of course, if it could be arranged to have an occasional television programme to bring it further to the public's attention, so much the better.'

'I agree. But we would be unwise, would we not, to over-expose the matter? I myself know how sensitive you are in the West over this particular danger.'

'You took the words right out of my mouth, sir. Thank you for being so understanding.'

'Aware, perhaps, would be the correct analysis?'

Peter laughed in appreciation of the Caliph's grasp of British sensibilities. 'I shall do my best, sir.'

'I'm sure you will. And I wish you to know you can count on my full co-operation in this project.'

'Thank you, sir.'

'But now Mr Broadbridge would like to speak with you, again. Goodbye from me, Mr Watson.'

'Goodbye, sir.'

And so, after what sounded like a difficult tussle with the phone cord, John Broadbridge once more came on the line - excited, and very happy. In fact, his happiness seemed so complete, so delightfully genuine that Peter could hardly bring himself to mention Kitty's call. He decided he would wait for his colleague to make his own enquiry after his family's welfare (despite what he'd promised Kitty), for the man appeared so bent on describing how happy he'd become since signing his new contract, that it seemed a pity to bring him down with talk of Swindon - or such places.

Chapter 7

John Broadbridge leant across to his bedside table, and grabbed his watch. 10.15 a.m. Damn. He'd overslept. First time in years. It was certainly not his style. But he had to admit, he'd had a peaceful and undisturbed night's sleep and was feeling quite refreshed. Moreover, he had no hangover to worry about. He knew that sort of experience came only from drinking too much cheap booze. Good Islay malt could never be relegated to that category. Nevertheless, it had relaxed him sufficiently to forget to put on the alarm.

'Ah, well, I'm sure the Caliph will forgive me this once. After all, it was he who was the host and he who introduced me to that wondrous brand of whisky. Oh, the ironies of life.'

He remembered the 'obligatory' orange juice being replaced very rapidly by the powerful, aromatic yet smooth malt. The Caliph's hand had remained steady and firm and his little grunts of pleasure and sighs of appreciation after each sip, could hardly be eradicated from John's memory. In fact, as time went by, the two men had successfully subjugated their cultural differences to a pleasant and misty celebration of well being and brotherly love. There was no suggestion of standing on ceremony, no suggestion of manning medieval fortresses of religious fervour, or chasing hopeless long-lost dreams. This was life - as it really was. And if drowning in a vat of Lagavulin sixteen-year-old malt was the penalty, so be it.

It was on this note of wistful light-heartedness, that John decided to put in a call to Kitty. He was sure he'd be able to handle any situation arising from his wife's misgivings about his new contract. He'd already prepared himself for that probability. Besides, he'd be making damned good money and when the time came for him to return to England he would surely have had enough of the desert, of the souks, of the latest Arab pop record blaring out of every other shop front and especially enough of 'Allahu Akhbar' wailing from every mosque, every hour of the day, invading his English ears and providing a particularly unnerving background to his Mozart records which he'd managed to buy cheaply from a friend who'd already given up the struggle. But even if he did make enough money to move the whole family to Dorset, had his time to retire really arrived? He thought not. Or was it merely a case of holding at bay the very idea of retirement? Retirement? A disturbing concept to an active man. How it conjured up visions of dreams unfulfilled, broken promises - promises solemnly given to good people already dead and to whom those promises could and should have been kept if only one had had the time. Now that there was plenty of time, the need was gone - gone forever. The good people were dead. Oh, if only, if only.....

Harbouring regrets had never been a pastime of John Broadbridge. Yet here and now he was beginning to think in the vein of a true romantic, a poet even, a .... no. He would not blame it on the whisky. After all, he had not drunk it in order to get through a sticky patch - he'd heard that excuse from too many friends back home. He'd not even drunk it just to make himself happy. But, by golly, it had made him happy. Moreover, it had had no unwelcome after-effects - apart, perhaps, from making him forget to put the alarm on. No, the more he pondered on his little drinking session with the Caliph, the more he approved. He could well understand how the man (unbeknown to the outside world, of course) had become hooked on the stuff.

'What?' exploded Kitty, readily clipping young Davy round the ear as he ran past her down the hallway pulling a particularly unattractive face. 'What are you doing, John? Why have you signed another contract, for God's sake? You know we can manage if we put our heads together....'

John detected the start of a snivel at the end of the line, an anxiousness, a hurt and a tone bordering on the aggressive - a tone he always knew to be a cover for a string of other grievances - some legitimate, some, well... right down to the real core of her discontent. Did he really love her? Did he? She had previously accepted his postings to various parts of the world with reasonable equanimity. He'd always come home, not only with loads of money but with a willingness to attend to her physical and emotional needs; to her fears of insecurity. So, why should a simple, straightforward extension of this contract (and with more money) upset her so?

'But Kitty, dear. What could be more secure than *Swindon*?'

She did not laugh. It was no laughing matter, apparently. The fact was, he was the one always "gallivanting about", as she liked to put it. He was the one who seemed to be having all the fun, though he'd never show it when he was in England. Not really. Not properly. How could she feel secure? He had signed that damned contract that would keep him even longer in the Middle East. If that wasn't evidence enough that he'd gone mad, then it amounted to a personal insult to her - which was worse.

'So why did you do it?' she kept saying. 'Why did you do it?'

'Well. Look at it this way, Kitty. The money I shall make this time out here will help us to invest in that cottage we keep promising ourselves. And....'

'You keep promising yourself, John. You're the one who always wants to get away. What's wrong with our home, here?'

An awkward silence permeated the line, while Kitty began to wonder why John was so reticent. He'd never been a great talker at the best of times. But this was beginning to get on her nerves. What was he up to? Had he, perhaps, procured himself a lover on the side - a wide-hipped Arab woman, or even a young, dark-eyed sexy-looking girl whom one of his wealthy Arab friends had thrown him as a sop, or worse (to Kitty's mind) - as a genuine reward for his 'reliable' services to the man's Country? Yes. What was John really up to? Most of his friends in England had considered him a bit of a dark horse - bit of an unknown quantity. They were always somewhat wary of him - his imposing figure unwittingly subduing them, his clear blue eyes penetrating their every little thought. Swindon had that effect. No wonder he was quiet.

While John Broadbridge busied himself explaining his way out of his 'little local difficulty' both to his wife and then to the Caliph, events in downtown Baghdad were moving apace. Soon, it was hoped, there would be a properly elected Government and soon, some said, 'we will have real Houses of Parliament to boast of, designed and constructed on British lines.' Oh, it was all very silly. But most entertaining. And enthusiasm for the idea was spreading. Several prospective and hopeful Members of the new Parliament had often seen videos and even the occasional broadcast of the English system on their televisions via satellite. Yes, they'd seen the two main British parties slogging it out with each other with apparent venom (though hardly to be compared with their own) - only to disappoint their unsuspecting audience by suddenly breaking out into ridiculous laughter which, surely, negated the whole argument? How strange were the British. Could anyone take them seriously? Yet, somehow, they got by, muddling through, pottering about. And most of those MPs eventually arrived safely at their homes (or wherever they went.) only to return the next day to do the same thing all over again. Incomprehensible. Nevertheless, it occurred to some of the local 'leading lights', that the same thing might well be right for Iraq. And who could tell? Maybe if the seats were designed correctly, they could all get down to some good hubble- bubble? Now, that was one occupation the West had never appreciated. Not properly.

The argument over the design of the new debating Chamber raged on. No-one really cared if the Country would have to make do with one. After all, how many Countries could afford two? (The American system hardly counted - to sophisticated minds. It could hardly compare with the fine, subtle balance of the British class system, forged over centuries. And no Prime Minister, however well meaning, could change that). One alternative scheme, however, suggested by a cynical English architect was of a rather attractive debating Chamber on the lines of the Spanish Parliament. Maybe the Englishman judged the idea of MPs cowering for their lives in the midst of an attempted coup in full view of the TV cameras, could not fail to appeal to the Iraqi mind, despite everything that had happened to the Country. But four pairs of irate Iraqi eyes bore through him and the idea was quickly dropped.

Meanwhile, the competition for the best squabbling Party was fast approaching and the two English ex-pats who had put up the money were due to have themselves a whale of a time judging the event. Not that it would be a particularly easy task. The parties who'd entered, were known to be so vociferous, so experienced in squabbling to the point of exclusion of all other activities, that even the judges felt that some sort of discipline might have to be injected into the proceedings - a decision which, naturally, they were loath to make. Indeed, on second thoughts, they decided it would be fun just to play the game. A completely free rein to tongues was to be the order of the day and all parties looked forward to that £10,000 prize money which by now (by an unprecedented act of generosity on the part of one of the judges) had been increased to £20,000. It would, it was thought, pay someone's gas bill. Besides, the two Englishmen were having the time of their lives. They were, after all, surviving Members of that dying breed. The British Government of the '8Os had done a pretty good job knocking any sort of nonsense out of the English psyche.

The American film crew were making the final adjustments to their equipment. The producer, the director, the warm-up man, the usual crop of freelance commentators and hangers-on, all contributed to giving the impression that the squabbling competition would at least look professional - on American lines, naturally. A few remnants of the demoted and disgraced Ba'ath Party, re-grouped into a suitably ragged shadow of their former selves, were among the first to have a go. After all, it was supposed to be a squabbling-match and the newly-found enlightened Parties of the Left were already determined to test their own patience and recently acquired tolerance. If the Ba'ath Party

The House of Baghdad

won fairly it would be accepted, for at least it was no longer propped up by force, repression and murder.

But traditions die hard and few people really believed 'the old dog' could learn new tricks. Some people will believe anything. Nevertheless, there were so many challenges to the old Party, that nobody really worried and the American producer continued to wear that never-ending grin - the coffers would soon be flowing as a result of the constant stream of applicants for his TV programme. If he could manage to organize the damned thing without its developing into uncontrollable violence, he'd be guaranteed instant success. The programme would be a smash hit - back in the States, for ever since Mrs Thatcher departed the fray, 'Live at Westminster' had never been the same: the edge had gone - perhaps for ever; no more could we watch that beacon of contentious light, ruffling the feathers of the male Members of the House, causing dismay or striking terror in their wet, whimpering hearts. She was gone. The dust had settled and it was back to a cosy men's club. But Dan Levy's TV programme would top even Maggie - not so much in terms of good old-fashioned cut-and-thrust within the law but of hot-blooded barely-disguised threats of murder, rape and pillage - underpinned, naturally, with the garlic of Arab revenge. All this, conducted within the confines of a regular meeting-place, had the makings - to Mr Levy's mind - of huge viewing ratings and a large bank balance to accompany it. He was on a winner. And woe betide anyone who tried to plagiarize the idea. Dan Levy saw no reason why the programme should not have a run at least as long as 'Desert Island Discs.'

Until the new debating-Chamber could be completed, however, the old assembly hall would have to be used, though it was some time before the benches were ripped away and rearranged to resemble a façade of democratic government. So the squabbling continued unabated in the streets and, for a while, both the English ex-pats and Dan Levy wondered what the hell they'd let themselves in for. But the newly injected humour (the Country had been starved of that essential ingredient for years) helped to save the day.

At last the Chamber was ready, though neither the English nor the Spanish architect could bring himself to give it his blessing. There had, after all, been a few Iraqi enthusiasts who disagreed with their colleagues and had taken up the Englishman's wicked suggestion but had 'gone native' and summoned a Spanish architect – "just in case". In the end, an Iraqi architect clinched the contract and, well, ... that was that. The only trouble was, he was given a free hand and he'd constructed the Opposition benches so that they faced the wrong way. The backs were firmly positioned opposite the 'Government' benches. At least the English architect could treat himself to another good laugh. He could never forget the arrangement at Gatwick North where the departure monitor screens could only be seen if passengers had eyes at the back of their heads. Once he pointed out this little English discrepancy, the Iraqi architect seemed to cheer up and no longer resented having to make good his charming faux pas.

By a supreme effort of self-sacrifice, a system of squabbling by rota was devised - to allow everyone to have a fair crack of the whip whilst giving the cameramen free rein to their instincts, not only of self-preservation but for sensation, free shots and creative improvisation.

The House of Baghdad

Oh, the scoops they'd soon be able to boast of back home would add more than a few points to some of their otherwise prosaic and ineffectual C.V.s.

Chapter 8

'Pilot programme for the Opening Session of Iraqi Parliament. Take 1.' The voice of the man with the clapper-board reverberated through the packed Chamber. Excitement filled the air. *Clap* went the board and, with a smirk that spoke volumes, the man turned to face the director. Everyone waited with bated breath. They were partaking in a unique and historic event and they wouldn't have missed it for the world.

'Action', boomed the director and waited for the clatter of over-excited sounds he'd heard these men make so often in the streets during the past few weeks.

'Action', he repeated, somewhat anxiously a few seconds later. Still nothing happened. No one spoke and no one moved. Dan Levy's smile vanished. It was as if God had handed him yet another huge white elephant on a flimsy plate. And for a while the two English ex-pats sitting up in the gallery, eagerly waiting for the show to begin, could hardly believe their eyes and ears. Lord knows the times they had both dozed off in front of their television sets back home while watching the House of Lords 'in action', to be happily woken by their wives for an appropriate and welcome gin and tonic refresher. 'What was it Lord Young said?'

But *this* was ridiculous. What had got into these buggers? Only yesterday, yet another pretender to the throne of P.M. had biffed a harmless-looking Liberal on the nose while the watching crowd respectfully hushed for a second before reverting to the unruly rabble it really was. What was going on? Had the occasion - in the splendour of their new Chamber - frozen their balls? Who could possibly be frightened of that swaggering Jim Rosenberg, bawling out a director's vitriolic commands with the self-conscious imitation of a Hollywood great? Who could be unnerved by the sight of the camera crew, shuffling and squeaking around the marble floor, trying to find a sure footing before zooming into a particularly interesting head? Who could possibly freeze in front of Dan Levy, stock still in his Producer's chair, his never-ending grin at last ended?

Something had gone wrong, *very* wrong - and no one knew who was to blame. Dan Levy had an idea. Maybe the participants could only be fired up when out on the streets: the people, the noise, the bustle, the confusion - all helped to stir the blood. Yes, that was it. If he could film the first part of the programme in the street outside the Parliament building and then persuade the politicians to continue the proceedings inside, bringing with them a scaled-down crowd - perhaps the more articulate rather than merely vociferous among them - maybe that would do the trick.

'OK., Dan. Anything. Anythin' to get this thing rolling. You're paying the bill, for Chrissake.' Dan smiled at Jim Rosenberg's simple statement. Thank God the Englishmen were sharing the cost via the competition. But the way things were going, it looked as if there'd be no goddam competition, let alone a professional Parliament.

'OK.,, fellas. Let's put some beef into it.' The director's voice boomed out once more with Dan Levy's idea that had suddenly become his own. 'I have an idea.'

'Gosh. The man has an idea,' came from the gallery. The politicians began to smile. Could this be the start of something new? Could humour really be here to stay?

'We're going out into the street. And we'll film this thing there. Any objections?'

'Yes. I object.'

'So do I.'

'Me, too.' And so it continued. Politicians of all shapes and sizes (except they were mainly well set and all moustached) began to murmur, then shout, and then..... by golly - a leader had emerged. And all the while the cameras had never stopped rolling. Who could tell what priceless scenes of black humour would be found there, in embryo - all ready to be tarted up and cut into money- making spin-offs?

Arid Aziz stood in a quiet corner of the Chamber with Dan Levy and Jim Rosenberg and spelt out his terms. A flashback of the situation before the Gulf War, flooded the Americans' minds, a situation wherein Tariq Aziz (Arid was no relation of the famous diplomat) did much the same thing with apparent, terrifying skill. But this was different. The dictators, father and son had gone - gone forever, it was hoped - and the country was set on a course of democratization. There had not been a costly war and a bloody revolution for nothing. Yet, like his namesake, Arid Aziz exuded a quiet strength that not only impressed people but unnerved them. His very presence, his steady gaze, his grasp of the facts, an insight into people's intentions and motives within the context of historical patterns, could not be lightly dismissed and never ignored without a price. But unlike his namesake, Arid Aziz was a free man. And the irony was, unlike the famous Foreign Minister who was a Christian, Arid was a Muslim. But his tolerance of other faiths and political views was legendary. If he was not entirely unique among his fellow politicians, at least he was the best man Iraq could now have to become her leader.

Yes, Arid did remind Dan and Jim of old Tariq. But whereas the Christian was determined not to permit the anomaly of being one to stand in the way of politics, Arid was equally determined not to allow the late Ayatollah All-Meanie's vision of Islam to stifle his natural sense of humour. It had, he said, been a gift from God. So, why should he throttle it out of existence just to satisfy the edicts of a man who, like Sodom the Lesser, had brought death and untold suffering to his own and to his neighbours Country - and more than a little pain and inconvenience to the rest of the world? It didn't make sense. And Arid was a sensible man.

The more Dan Levy and Jim Rosenberg bent their ears to Arid's good sense, the more they found themselves getting to like the man. Maybe the whole idea of a squabbling match - to be filmed and paraded in front of a gawping, gloating TV audience back home - was all wrong, anyway. It was, after all, the bloody Englishmen's dream. Trust English alcoholics to come up with something as crazy as this. Nevertheless, they both had to admit they'd been attracted to the idea at first and had cottoned on to its potential like bees round a honey pot.

After further discussion and argument, it was decided the 'session' be called off (much to the disappointment of the less mature Members of the assembly), or postponed until something better organized and more 'constructive' could be filmed for world viewing. The various parties would just have to forego the pleasure of uncontrolled, riotous contest together with the chance of that elusive £20,000. On the other hand, if the Englishmen could be persuaded to part with a cancellation fee of £10,000, or even the revised figure of £20,000, towards the upkeep of the new Parliament building, the money would, in Iraqi eyes, not be wasted. All contributions, however small, were always welcome.

'You clever old dog, Aziz. I knew you weren't just a pretty face.' The politician smiled at the director's quaint remark while homing in to Dan Levy whom he considered might be looking for far more substantial compensation, if not an alternative to the aborted contest.

He was not wrong. 'Well, sir. Why don't we discuss all this with these crazy Englishmen who seem to have money to burn? And in the meantime…'

'In the meantime, Mr Levy, we draw up plans for televising the Real Thing.'

It was Dan's turn to smile and his mind was quickly set alight. Yes, of course. It was foolish to play around with 'pilots' and childish mud slinging when there was the opportunity to film the "Real Thing". Besides, perversely, some darned serious black humour could come out of it if things unwittingly or inadvertently went wrong during transmission of the 'Real Thing'. Dan Levy had long been jealous of the success and money that had accrued from the straight screening of the British House of Commons. 'Prime Minister's Question Time' had really taken off in the States. Moreover, his own network had never been averse to creating a bit of rude, gutsy competition, to say the least. 'House of Baghdad' couldn't fail to stir the old blood for one reason or another and millions would be glued to their TV sets - if only to watch the impossible - an Arab nation, not only with an elected Parliament but with real live Members, some Government, some Opposition - standing up and sitting down, delivering little speeches, caustic, clever quips, arguing with reason, challenging, inspiring.

'Possible?' Of course it's possible,' insisted Arid Aziz. In my country, all things are possible.' His eyes twinkled wickedly. And Dan Levy had gained a new friend.

Much to the surprise of everyone concerned, the two Englishmen conceded that the squabbling competition had proved an unmitigated disaster. But no harm had been done. They'd both had a bit of a laugh and, besides, they'd jolly-well saved some money.

'But, what we were thinking,' prodded Dan Levy.

'Ah yes,' spewed one of the ex-pats. 'I'll tell you what. I'd hate to be accused of total meanness. Mr Poulton and I have talked the whole thing over and we've come up with a scheme that could be of interest and benefit to us all. Want to hear about it?'

'Fire away.'

Everyone crowded round the small conference table and listened to what the crazy Englishmen had to say. There was Arid, wearing the bemused smile that most foreigners had, in time, come to appreciate and there was Abbi, his right-hand man, who sat looking into space but whom everyone knew to be a wily intellectual, one of yet another breed most people thought extinct. Ah, but for those BBC broadcasts….. Then there was the Caliph - always a man of colourful dignity, draping his dish-dash around him with regal elegance and, on his left, was John Broadbridge, looking remarkably fit and at ease in his new, 'extended' capacity. There were a couple of the many hopefuls for the post of Leader of the Opposition - though, with so many over-excited politicians around these days, it was a wonder anyone could be patient or tenacious enough to hold down a job as dishonourable as Leader of the Opposition. 'But that's all part of true democracy', they were constantly told. It was something most of the politicians did not wish to hear, despite the years of brutal dictatorship thrust upon their country. And finally, there were Dan Levy and Jim Rosenberg, each leaning forward, eager to hear what the Englishmen had to say. In spite of a British tendency to make for the bottle a little too often (few people seemed to know of the Caliph's 'indiscretions') together with an irritating habit of playing down everything while making jokes in all the wrong places, they knew they were dealing with solid, reliable people. Never would a war go by, it seemed, without the British rushing to the side of Uncle Sam. It was as if they couldn't get enough of the stuff. If whisky was the food of their quirky inspiration, war came a close second. Anyway, these two had some money……..

'Ian and I are willing to put up £75,000 as a kick-off in a new company for this project. Not much, we know, but hear us out.'

'You have the floor, gentlemen.' Arid smiled. Dan Levy smiled. Jim Rosenberg, the two 'Opposition' leaders, John Broadbridge, the Caliph….. they all smiled. Wouldn't it be nice if all Parliaments could be like this - small, cosy, experimental, a womb of original ideas, potential business, fun and with tea and biscuits brought in by…….?

'Who was that?' Dan Levy followed the line of a silky female body who had slipped silently into the room with the tea things and out again, leaving a trail of sweet-smelling perfume behind her. It was more than a welcome relief to John Broadbridge's disgustingly pungent pipe smoke, to Dan's mind.

'That's Meridia.'

'Sounds a little fancy, to me. But I like her.'

'She's like a star at its highest point - wouldn't you agree, Mr Levy? We have merely cut off the last letter to give the name..... er, shall we. say, a more Continental flavour?'

The Caliph shot Dan Levy a look that suggested there might be others in his stable of stars. But what was the Caliph doing with them if not......? Dan checked himself. There was work to be done. And maybe these two Englishmen had their heads screwed on, after all.

'Now, I suggest we keep this syndicate small, nice 'n tidy, and clean,' said one of them.

Where had Dan Levy heard this sort of talk before? He'd been brought up in the Bronx; he'd been around - enough to know people all right, to know where things led, to know the pit falls, blind alleys, end of the line. But hang on, hang on. This wasn't the Bronx. This was...

'The Middle East, Mr Levy, has its compensations, wouldn't you agree?' The Caliph smiled at the producer - already beginning to appreciate the Arab way of doing things. It was such a civilized cunning, no wonder the English liked it here.

The Caliph spoke again. 'Gentlemen. Mr Broadbridge, as you know, has excellent contacts with the BBC. But he also has friends in most of the independent companies. Is that not so, John?'

John took the pipe from his mouth and grinned. 'A few.'

'OK. Where's all this leading?' Dan had become impatient and began to think about that girl Meridian, Mer....... whatever her name was. She was nice.

The Caliph had been studying Dan for some time and could read his thoughts - one by one. As he watched him splaying his hairy arms across the table, his podgy legs never still, underneath, he wondered what the English had in common with their cousins across the pond. It couldn't be the same tongue, nor the fact that George III could hardly hold on to his own sanity - let alone a continent as determinedly insane as America. What could it be? Maybe it all boiled down to the fact that the Atlantic had shrunk to a 'back-to-the-future' trip on Concorde, resulting in two breakfasts, two lunches, at least four large Scotches, good business, a show, a girl - and all was forgiven? The Caliph might never understand. But with a Cambridge education under his belt, he was entitled to try.

'In answer to your question,' he continued undeterred, 'Mr Broadbridge and I have discussed this idea with all our friends here and with the British Ambassador. We believe it will interest you.'

'Well, let's have it.' Dan's patience was in the process of being stretched to the glorious limit. He kept thinking about that girl. Maybe it was the best way to help him keep calm. He stopped tapping his fingers on the table and looked up into the faces of the men gathered together for this strange meeting. They all wore smiles. Smiles - smiles! What the hell did it mean? Was it good, bad, or just plain crazy?

'Here, Mr Levy.' Arid Aziz slid the envelope across to Dan and looked him in the eye with a 'I think you will like it.'

Dan took the envelope and opened it. He pulled out the fancy contract and scanned its contents. It was looking good, for Chrissake. He was relaxing by the second and then a tinge of genuine excitement ran through his weather beaten body. He could feel his pulse quicken as he read on...... hereby gives exclusive rights to Dan Levy & Co for the broadcasting of 'The House Of Baghdad', coast to coast and in the U.K. for a period of three years - with options on both sides for a further three. Furthermore,........ .

At last Dan broke into a smile and looked up to his hosts. 'You like it, Mr Levy?'

'I sure do.'

'Then welcome to the club.'

Chapter 9

'Maria, my dear. I beg you. Please be careful of this man.'

'What man?'

'What man? You know who I mean. Now, come on. You can't fool me.'

'I'm a big girl, now, Pepe. Even you can see that.'

'I can, indeed, my dear. And a very lovely one. And that is why I'm concerned.'

'Concerned?'

Old Pepe Fernandez sighed again. He knew he'd have his work cut out making her see sense. His only real motive, he'd convinced himself, was to protect Maria from what he knew to be a nasty piece of work..

Yet he did not want to be accused of merely interfering. He'd known and loved Maria's parents for many years and felt responsible for their lovely daughter.

'And as your god father,' he went on, 'I consider it my duty to warn and protect you. I owe that much to your dear mother and father - God rest their souls.'

'Warn and protect……? Oh, Pepe. You are sweet.' She tried to soften him with those big eyes of hers. But he stood his ground.

'I can look after myself, now. I'm a big girl, remember?'

'I know, dear. But this man is dangerous.'

'Dangerous? But I like dangerous men. They excite me.'

'Even murderers?'

'Even…… What did you say?'

'He's a murderer, my dear. Make no mistake. And what is more, he's a murderer of a particularly sadistic kind.'

'I don't believe it.'

'He enjoys torturing people, personally, and has done so for many years. He's not his father's son for nothing.'

'Stop it, stop it, Pepe. I can't bear it when you go on like this.'

'It's hardly a case of 'going on', as you so innocently put it. These are stark, cruel facts I am giving you for your own protection. You must be careful.'

She did not want to believe these awful stories any more than she'd give up lightly the excitement of being with the Colonel.

'They're just stories Manuel has made up to frighten me. Yes, he's told you to give me a pack of lies to frighten me, *hasn't he*, hasn't he, Pepe?'

She would not cry in front of Pepe Fernandez. Not any more. She wasn't a child now. She was......

'Have I ever lied to you, Maria?' He looked deep into her eyes.

As a child she had often suspected him of lying - as part of 'his duty', part of doing Daddy's dirty work - he would never be around when she needed him. But 'Uncle' Pepe' would always be there, always there to back up Mummy, always there to guide her, correct her, love her, cuddle her.

'Pepe. You're jealous. My God. That's what it is. I'm a damned fool. I should have known all along. I......'

'I am not jealous, my dear, in spite of what you may think of me. I have my faults. But as far as you are concerned, I am not jealous.'

He began to blush a little as he spoke - enough to give Maria a prop for a while. But it was only to be for a while.

'There. I have proved it. You're blushing, Pepe.' She moved close to him and threw her arms around him - just as she had done so often as a little child. Oh, she had been so happy then - before Daddy went away. He went away and there was only one man left in the house.

'Uncle' Pepe had taken on a new role in her life. He had become her father. But he wasn't her father, he wasn't. 'Oh, Mummy. When is Daddy coming home?' And Mummy would answer: 'When he has finished his business, dear.'

Business - everything was business. And then came the war, the one everybody had said would happen one day as sure as eggs are eggs. It would start in the Middle East and spread, and then... But where was Daddy? What was he doing in......? The telegram had arrived. 'Let me see it, Mummy'. 'No, dear. No.' And Mummy had burst into tears, great floods of tears running down her cheeks. And then she clung to her child. She clung to her child tighter than she'd ever done before. But it was a terrible embrace. Mummy was crying and oh, oh God.......

'Oh, Pepe.' He held her in his arms while she cried her heart out.

****

In the Colonel's villa, old Felix Esbano (real name Fritz Krupp) - distant member of the all powerful industrial family whose factories forged the military might of the Third Reich - sat in a high, upright wicker chair. He always preferred this kind of chair - they kept his back straight. And at the age of 98, he could at least get out of them with a degree of dignity and the minimum of fuss. At his side, on a table set at the perfect height and angle, stood a glass of fine whisky. Up until his 70s, he'd been a regular imbiber not only of ideas both emotional and intellectual but also of the best Napoleon brandy to accompany them. Yet, since reading an article in an English newspaper, describing the habits of the late Lord Shinwell, who, after years of consuming good whisky, called for a dram of his favourite malt, drank it, put his hands in the air and with a contented "I've had enough" gladly gave up the ghost at the age of 101, he considered that what had been good enough for a damned lucky old Jew-boy, might well be good enough for him.

Ever since the night of the President's elaborate party, from whence the Colonel had successfully 'eloped' with the beautiful Maria, Felix had been eager to have a proper chat. There was a certain aura about the man which, as a fellow 'heavy-weight' (though now long retired), Fritz Krupp could hardly fail to recognize: the set of the jowl, the thick neck, the eyes.......

'Another whisky, Mr Esbano?'

'Ah, thank you. Call me Felix, Colonel. I think, at my time of life, formalities can safely be dispensed with.'

Colonel D-Day smiled and suggested he too, might similarly be honoured.

'Call me Yudie. They all do - all except Mustafa who insists upon 'sir'. Maybe a spell in this country will knock that silly nonsense out of him?'

Felix laughed and downed another measure of whisky.

Time passed. But still they played cat and mouse with each other. What did the Colonel want? What did Felix Esbano want? They were drawn to each other but demarcation lines were hazy, fluid, moveable. Neither man was in a hurry. They had both seen action - lots of it. Maybe too much. But it had been tremendous fun. Too much fun to forget about. And now, they were both 'on vacation', émigrés from their respective countries. The age difference between them hardly mattered. What mattered was: how were they to get back into the swim of things? At least, this was the Colonel's thinking. For him, it would be a matter of biding his time until the new Iraqi political system disintegrated - until they called for his glorious return. And like the Ayatollah Khomeini, who flew from Paris to Tehran, descending the steps from his aircraft in awesome triumph, Colonel D-Day would return from Brazilia - perhaps via Paris, for appearances sake - to Baghdad, to be finally greeted with cat-calls, machine-gun fire, or, at best, shouts of 'Fuck off, Yudie. Can't ya take a hint?' He pulled himself together. He'd been watching too many black comedy videos. But seriously, he might have to resort to plastic surgery, after all, as an aid in penetrating the old country. There had to be some way, for God's sake, of getting back into the right circles before seizing power once more? Much as Yudie had enjoyed his little session with the lovely Maria and hoped for more of the same (these things were such stimulating excursions), he remained a fish out of water, despite anything he said to the contrary.

As for old Felix Esbano, it was, naturally, a more delicate matter. He had no intention of leaving Brazil. He'd seen it all - done it all. He was comfortable. But 98 years notwithstanding, the man was in fantastic shape. He had his wits about him, and his knowledge and experience would be invaluable to any fascist worth his salt. It was always nice to feel wanted - and doubly so, at the age of 98! But the fact Felix no longer supported the more manic aspects of 'the cause', hardly bothered the Colonel. He knew his guest had 'been there' - his credentials were impeccable. For his part, Felix had long enjoyed watching the antics of his host's father, whose pathetic attempts to emulate Adolf Hitler the whole world had been watching every night on television. The plain fact was: the man just hadn't quite got it. He seemed to forget his hero possessed a monumental power base. As Chancellor of all Germany, Adolf Hitler had built up overwhelming support from powerful, self-sufficient German businessmen whose money, armaments and drive were unstoppable. And unlike Sodom the Lesser, Adolf Hitler did not 'neglect' the people but worked ceaselessly to arouse and inspire them to rise up with him in a supreme, awesome effort. For a few gloriously vibrant years, a great nation was swept along on the crest of a wave. Sodom the Lesser's lethargic little walk-abouts and edited trips to remote villages were hardly a match for the Fuehrer's grand, heady stuff. Far from taking to his bunker at the first sign of enemy aircraft in the skies, Hitler would at least bide his time before shooting another batch of experienced officers. No, Sodom had been doing it all wrong. The desire was there but,....... well, if D-Day had thoughts of following in every one of his father's cumbersome footsteps, as far as Felix could sense (and he'd seen it all), he'd better think again - if he knew what was good for him.

'So, what can I do for you, Colonel D-Day? Sorry. Yudie?' The Colonel put down his glass, and looked old Felix in the eye.

'It is, perhaps, more a matter of what we can do for each other.'

'Oh?' Felix continued to play it cool. He'd been doing it for most of his life. Why should he change now? Besides, how could he possibly come clean with the Colonel over the real reason for his visit? He had made it look like a normal social call - a welcome to Brazil, while honouring his host with an appeal to his pride. If D-Day was anything like his father, then, apart from an inordinate interest in war, murder and torture, a visit from another V.I.P. would always be preferable to being seen running around with 'cap in hand'. If Felix played his cards right, the Colonel would probably never suspect his guest to be in any way working for the President. Felix would use the smoke screen of his advanced years to put the Colonel off the scent, whilst making no attempt to deny his personal friendship with Manuel Gonzalez. Indeed, to Felix's thinking, it would appear very odd to someone like the Colonel if he had not been a friend of the President. All in all, Señor Esbano's skills in deception remained considerable and no amount of liquor plied seemed to blunt his senses or grip on things. He'd been hardened. And in such a pleasant manner.

'Another Scotch, Felix?' The Colonel allowed himself a smile as he poured an even larger measure into the old man's glass.

'Whoa.' Felix gave the Colonel the satisfaction of having his hand steadied over the pouring.

'Well, how is everything going for you, here, Yudie?'

'Very well, so far, Felix. Yes, I believe I could get to like it here?'

Both men grinned. There was no need to comment further upon the source of the Colonel's 'lucky strike'.

'Good. I wish you every success and happiness in our adopted country.'

Felix searched for a sign his host would soon talk about Brazil in general - en route, as it were, back to his own country, with just a dash of Germany to keep the guest happy. But D-Day was no fool. He was in no hurry to divulge his real aim of returning to Iraq to become its Dictator once more. Not yet, at any rate. Not directly.

Into the night they talked, 'circling' and 'sniffing' like two ancient dogs too old to make rash decisions. Though not yet of Felix's advanced years, Yudie was learning fast. Besides, 'like father like son', he had inherited his father's cunning and ability to size up his man. That much could be said for him. And so they drank and they laughed (in this respect Yudie was 'far from home'). Yes, they drank and laughed; and laughed again, touching on this and that but only touching - until at last.......

'When do you hope to return to Baghdad?'

'When do you hope to return to Germany?' Yudie's cruelty had never confined itself to the torture chamber. For an hour, they had skimmed the surface of philosophy, religion, world politics, world power, and then came the subject of personal power - the kind that stemmed from frustrated ambition, hopes, desires and more than a few lost dreams.

'At my age, Yudie, one has learnt to be practical. But you are a young man. I'm sure you'll find a way to get back into the big league.'

At that remark, the Colonel had suddenly become silent, almost maudlin. And for a while, old Felix Esbano wondered whether he'd said the wrong thing. But his host held his arm and looked him in the eye with measured words - 'I would like you to be my mentor.'

Felix took another sip of his whisky and prepared to take up this new and unexpected challenge. 'Why, my dear fellow, I am honoured. When do we start?' he joked.

'Why not now?'

Could the Colonel be serious? True, old Felix Esbano was famed throughout Brazil for his seminars on philosophy, as well as his clear and articulate views on world politics, propounded under yet another pen name in a regular column of the Brazilia_Times. But despite his connections with the German hierarchy during World War 2, he had grown accustomed to living in peace without too much challenge to his equilibrium. Yet, before him now, sat a man he could hardly ignore. He'd expected to glean all kinds of interesting information about him during the course of the evening. He never expected this. But Fritz Krupp, alias Felix Esbano, had never been a man to be caught with his trousers down. The Colonel appeared to have taken the bait of the old man's clever but charming cunning. Yet no one - not even a hand as experienced as Señor Esbano, could have foreseen this. Could it be a trap? The old man had to find out. But, for the moment he was content to play the game. He put down his glass and prepared his new pupil for a few hard facts.

'I hope you can take it.'

'I am here to learn. You are the teacher.'

'Right. Here goes. Lesson Number One: Strategy. You must have strategy. But it will not be effective without a proper power base. Too much for one night?'

Felix was never a man to waste words on hard lessons. And there was something in his eye that suggested he knew more about Sodom the Lesser's weaknesses than the Colonel cared to be reminded of.

Chapter 10

'You're doing a great job,' enthused the President. 'Find out what you can of his real intentions.'

'I shall do my best, sir. You know me.'

The President beamed and poured his friend Felix a large whisky.

'I know no one more fitted to the task in the whole of Brazil.'

'You're too kind.'

'Much as I am proud of our reputation for hospitality to the 'waifs and strays' of other countries, though most tend to be of the richer breed, I must admit, there is a line over which even I will not step.'

'Quite.'

'And though I have no intention of introducing extradition laws,' ('God forbid' thought Felix Esbano), 'I would hate to think we are harbouring people who one day intend to blow up our touchy neighbours in the North.'

'He appears to be a chip off the old block, sir. And we all know how much trouble he gave the Americans.'

'My point, exactly.'

'Leave the Colonel to me. I'm sure I can handle him.'

'My dear friend, of that I have no doubt. If Kennedy's assassination had coincided with the placing of Kruschev's missiles in Cuba, I am certain you would have dropped everything and stepped into the breach.'

'You flatter me, sir. I have never been able to save anyone's face.'

'Don't underestimate yourself, my friend. Your diplomatic skills are legendary.'

It was music to Felix's ears. But a phone buzzed on the President's desk, interrupting the flow of this most pleasing eulogy.

'Yes, Janet?'

'A call, sir, from the Iraqi Ambassador.'

'Thank you, Janet. I'll take it......... Hello, Mr Bazrani. What can I do for you?' Felix rose to leave.

'Er, stay, Felix. Stay if you can,' whispered the President. Felix nodded and sat down again.

'Mr President. I have just received a communication from Baghdad indicating my Government's wish to apply for the extradition of Colonel D-Day. Please don't jump down my throat. I know how you feel about introducing such a measure as.......'

'It's not only me, Mr Bazrani. Our tradition of 'Open House' goes back a long way. You don't need me to tell you that.'

'I know, I know, sir. I keep telling them but they don't seem to understand.'

'Perhaps the idea of democracy is already going to their heads, Mr Bazrani?'

Cynical laughter came from the other end of the line. The Iraqi Ambassador was one of the growing number of Iraqis who could not (with any degree of honesty) put much on the new system lasting beyond the year.

'So, what can I tell our new Prime Minister?'

'Tell him what all other Governments know perfectly well: Brazil's is a special system. And considering the civilized life-styles enjoyed by most of our well-heeled fugitives over many years, it would hardly behove us as a Government to disturb an alternative economy that has served us so well. No need to elaborate, is there, Ambassador?'

Bazrani smiled to himself in sympathy with life as it was - rather than as it might be. After all, he had not become an Ambassador for nothing - democratic Government or no. He could always 'see his way clear' by saying the right things in the right places while turning a temporarily blind eye to apparent impasses.

'I shall do my best, sir,' he insisted with renewed confidence.

'Or your worst?' Bazrani laughed openly. He'd always held a particular affection for Manuel Gonzalez ever since they'd met at an exhibition of Brazilian art in London, back in the '80s. Señor Gonzalez had immediately struck Bazrani as the ideal man to lead a country as vibrant and diverse as Brazil. What he did not expect - now that Manuel had finally 'made it', as it were, was the President to invite him to phone direct if matters ever became a little sticky. And now that Bazrani himself had risen in the world, almost the first assignment thrown in his lap was beginning to look particularly sticky.

But President Gonzalez did not see things the same way. He liked what others saw as sticky problems. The stickier the better. Besides, there was nothing like a bit of danger to stir the blood. 'Know thine enemy' it is often said. It was not the President's style to miss out on anything. And so, with Colonel D-Day now ensconced in his country and already taking chances with his wife, it was not difficult to arrange 'a little accident' or a warning, or even a deal, if he felt like it. Nothing was impossible. This was Brazil. And with Felix Esbano 'indebted' to him, and the Iraqi Ambassador 'in his pocket', the President saw little chance of Colonel D-Day being allowed (like some people he knew in Rio) to scream for even bigger boots.

The telephone conversation was dragging on. But the President didn't care. He liked talking to Bazrani. Besides, if the Ambassador could be persuaded to see things his way, so much the better.

'Mind you,' he continued, 'with your country's economy due to pick up at last - now that your military expenditure has been so drastically reduced, if our Colonel does become unmanageable......'

'I think I get your drift, Mr President.......'

'He doesn't seem to be complaining at the moment, although I dare say a friend of mine could tell me about a few skeletons in the cupboard?'

'Don't remind me.'

'But I thought your people no longer cared about bringing him to justice?'

'It started off like that, sir. But you know how these things are. Liberal ideas are all very fine for a while......'

'And then when things get tough.'

'Exactly. As expected, the economy has not picked up as quickly as we'd all like and so a scapegoat has to be found.'

'Or diversion?'

'If you insist upon a euphemism.'

'I'm not sure Colonel D-Day would like to be called a euphemism. Doesn't seem his style.'

Bazrani laughed. So did Felix whom, his patience notwithstanding, wished he could be in on this conversation. Within the time they had spent on the phone, the Ambassador could have popped across to this damned office, imbibed, had the conversation, and gone home.

The House of Baghdad

But the President had his reasons. He wanted to keep Felix's efforts and Bazrani's possible machinations separated. Only when he was ready would he get the two men together in the office. He would add the persons of the Foreign Minister and the Chief of Police only if things got out of hand. He was confident, nevertheless, that Colonel D-Day could be contained without too much bother. He might even allow sessions with Maria to continue unabated. At least he'd know where she was. And when they weren't 'at it', Felix Esbano could continue exercising his role of mentor, whilst obtaining valuable information and insight into the bastard's mind. The President would have the Colonel just where he wanted him.

'OK., Mr Bazrani. Do what you can to put your people off the idea of extradition. Much as many other countries would like us to oblige, I can't see our people going for it. That's the official line. Now, if enough money can somehow find its way in the direction of the Brazilian economy, I'm sure we can………'

'See our way clear?' The Ambassador had never forgotten one of the President's favourite phrases. Not only did it seem to cover a multitude of sins, but it had that certain, hopeful, ring to it - as if just by saying it, all those sins would be absolved. If 'Matters of State' was anathema to Maria, 'Seeing Our Way Clear' had become a panacea for all problems to Manuel.

'You're a clever man, Mr President.'

'I didn't get where I am without some grey matter, Mr Bazrani.'

The Ambassador would probably have substituted 'guile' for 'grey matter' in this case. But, for the moment, he was happy to leave things as they were. Over all the years he'd known the President, he would always recognize the line over which it would not be in his interest to cross.

'Allow me to work something out, Mr President. Our people have always been capable of pragmatism - despite the West's predilection for viewing us differently.'

'I'm glad to hear it, Ambassador. And now, I must........'

'I understand.'

'Ring me when your people have decided. The ball's in their court.'

'I will, sir. Thank you, and goodbye.'

The President put his phone-piece down and turned his attention once more to Felix Esbano, so patiently sitting there, wondering how big or how small a part his particular talents would play in the saga currently absorbing Brazilian society.

'My dear Felix. You must forgive me. Bazrani does go on so, but then, so do I, eh?'

'I quite understand, sir. You have your job - and you have your reasons.'

Old Felix looked up to the President for a little more information than he had been able to pick up from one side of the telephone. Yet he instinctively felt his boss would not be forthcoming. At any rate not today.

'Hey. Let me top you up.'

'Just a small one, sir.'

'Just a small one? It's not like you, Felix.'

The President poured out a large one for his friend - and a large one for himself. He'd deserved it, he told himself. And then he sat down, next to the old man.

'Cheers, Felix.'

'Cheers, sir.'

The House of Baghdad

They lifted their glasses and drank to happiness and friendship.

'And talking of friendship... How long have I known you, Felix?'

The old man shifted a little in his chair and a suggestion of a frown crossed his experienced, craggy face. Could it be he was about to be pensioned off, just as he was getting into an exciting new assignment?

'No, my dear fellow. I am not going to pension you off - even after your assignment.' God, the President was psychic, or at least a mind reader. 'I just want you to call me Manuel.'

Chapter 11

'Oh, you bastard, you bastard! I love it, I love it! Oh, God……..'

They were at it again! And though Maria's vocabulary, quite understandably, tended to be somewhat limited on these occasions, she had no intention of limiting her appetite for such occasions to one man.

Manuel was always busy. And now that the Colonel had made himself both known and available to her, what could she do other than give full vent to her frustrations?……

'Oh, God, that's nice... Keep going, keep going, you bastard. *Oh*!…….'

Colonel D-Day was not used to being called a bastard - no matter what people thought of him - even by his women back home - *especially* his women back home. But this woman, this beauty of Brazil, the President's wife……. somehow, it no longer mattered. It no longer seemed an offensive word. The way she uttered it, well…….

He raised his head to look at her. It was the first time he'd gone down on her. Not the last, he hoped. But today, he would not hurry. Somehow, neither of them felt the pressure to show their faces again before the evening was over…….

'Oh, hello. The Colonel and I have been having a most interesting conversation. Haven't we, Colonel?'

'Most interesting.' The guests would raise their eyebrows or look the other way or they would be so busy with each other, that they would have forgotten Maria and the Colonel had even left the room.

Besides, Manuel would be engrossed with politicians, businessmen and the like. Even the wildest party provided him opportunities to do business. Not that he was a stuffed shirt. Anything but. He was hardly a man to miss an opportunity if one presented itself. The trouble was - there were so many. Nowadays, his reactions to such approaches tended to be more measured, more thoughtful, wiser. He would enjoy himself and join in many of the dances. But when it 'came to it', he'd be much more selective than even five years ago. It wasn't so much a question of diminishing sexual appetite - rather, it was a question of quality.

"Every way, which way". On it went. To Maria, the Colonel seemed tireless. And when he had whispered to her that he could come at least ten times in a night, she did not disbelieve him. Now that Manuel knew what was going on and so far had not really scolded her (not directly), there seemed little point in hurrying - especially an activity as pleasurable as..........'Oh, oh......oh, my God, that's wonderful'.

But when everything in the garden looks lovely.......

There was a rude knock on the main door of the villa.

'If it's that Felix Esbano, he will have to understand I do not need a mentor for everything.'

'Felix Esbano?' Maria took a short break and lowered her legs from her lover's shoulders. 'What's he want, Yudie?' She looked worried - almost as if the gentle straight-backed old 'ex-pat' could pose a far greater threat to her happiness than even Manuel. All her antennae had started to bristle and she began to put more than two and two together.

'Don't worry so, Maria. Mustafa will see to him. He'll settle him in his chair and with a large whisky to keep him company, he'll be as happy as....... what is it the English say..?'

'Umm. Don't kid yourself Felix is as innocent as a sand boy. He's just got to be up to something. I don't like it, Yudie, I.......'

'Calm down, Maria. And keep your voice down. I don't want him to know everything.'

'Oh, come on, Yudie. He's not stupid. He can guess what we've been up to ever since the night of Manuel's party. He knows 'everything' - as you like to put it.'

They had both sat up and begun to get dressed. Their concentration had been broken anyway, and.........

'No, no. What I mean is, I don't want him to feel ostracized in any way just because he was a member of the Nazi party Allah knows how many years ago.'

'What are you talking about, Yudie?' Maria looked into her lover's eyes and marvelled at the extent of feeling between some villains and tyrants, particularly when they had fallen from grace. "Honour among thieves" was one thing: love between serious heavies was another. 'I think you're really getting to like him, aren't you, Yudie?'

'Yes, I am. There's a certain poise and elegance about the man that I find very impressive.'

Maria began to recall some of the pictures Yudie had shown her of his father - just after their first love session - Sodom the Lesser in his most famous pose of calm omnipotence, or could it merely have been the pose of a dangerous and wicked slob? Calm he may have been, but elegant? Against such a background, she conceded almost anything would seem elegant, though she could not quite see Felix Esbano in Anthony Eden's league. Now, there was an elegant man, if ever there was one. Maria had been shown pictures of him many years ago by her grandmother who, despite her Latin blood could never resist a real English gentleman. Churchill's bulldog features she could do without - but Anthony Eden - oh boy. But for Maria, elegance in a man held little personal attraction, though she could recognize it for what it was. If Felix possessed any of it, as far as she could see it would only be used as a camouflage for his guile.

In this respect he was little different from Manuel. In fact, for some time now, Maria had had the distinct feeling that the reason Felix maintained that old-fashioned principle of addressing his President as 'Sir' or 'Mr President', was to provide himself a measure of distance with which to feel superior. She would not put such perversity past him despite his 98 years. And with the cloak of those years he had wormed his way into the Colonel's life. Just *what was* he up to?

A respectful knock on the bedroom door had the effect of hurrying their dressing.

'Yes, Mustafa?' The bodyguard had put an ear to the door, and waited.

'Mr Esbano is here, Sir. I have shown him into the drawing room and given him a large Scotch.'

'Well done, Mustafa. I'll be there in five minutes.'

'Very good, Sir.'

Mustafa's politeness was legendary. But this was becoming ridiculous. He had become so polite since arriving in Brazil that the Colonel wondered whether his trusty bodyguard could really have been reared by his mother. Or perhaps, like Moses, he had been found abandoned by the riverbank - but with a dog collar on him with the words: 'This baby is English. Please handle with care'. But he stifled the idea. After all, the 'disease' was even beginning to rub off on him.

'Felix. How nice to see you.' The Colonel was the first of the lovers to enter the drawing room to greet the old man. 'Is Mustafa attending to your needs?'

'He is, indeed.' Felix Esbano began to rise from his chair before the Colonel could stop him. 'Please, Felix.' But the old man was on is feet with outstretched hand. 'I trust I am not interrupting anything?'

The two men shook hands and grinned at each other.

'She'll be joining us in a moment.'

'Splendid.' And, with the tiniest suspicion of a blush, Felix Esbano returned to his chair to rescue his whisky.

'Ah, Mustafa. Thank you.' The Colonel sat in a chair opposite his new friend and mentor with a gin and tonic poured out by his bodyguard - the man who had travelled far and wide, who'd educated himself in the intricacies of the world, its languages, its people, its ugliness and its compensations. If General Norman Schwartzkopf had ever needed someone close to him when walking down the Edgware Road in London at the end of the Gulf War, Mustafa would have been his man.

Not only did he have a high I.Q. to match the General's, but he also possessed a physique even more unnerving to anyone foolish enough to try his hand. Certainly, Colonel Doomsday had been impressed when making his first acquaintance with Mustafa. He had quite literally bumped into him in a Baghdad boutique where the owner of the shop had told the Colonel that Mustafa was looking for a job. Since leaving Mr. Maxwell's employ back in England, he had wandered the earth like a lost but uncharacteristically intelligent sheep. The Colonel had tried to figure out the moral of the story, without success. But after even more thorough checkouts than usual, he decided to take a chance on Mustafa and had never looked back. The revolution was quite another matter.

'Maria, my dear. Will you join us?'

'Good evening Maria. You look lovely.' Maria had thought about slipping quietly out of the house and leaving the men to it. But she had thought better of it. That sort of thing might be all right for the menial millions. She had more confidence.

'Good evening Felix. And thank you for your kind compliment.' She turned to face the Colonel with a smile. 'I think not, thank you, Yudie. I'd rather leave you two er.....uninhibited by my presence.' She shot Felix an especially wry smile - not enough to be unnerving but bright and steady enough to make him think twice about ever betraying her. It was one thing to know about her indiscretions: another thing to use them against her. Yet, despite her earlier misgivings over what he might be up to, she somehow knew he'd got the message and that all would be well. Besides, Yudie seemed so relaxed in the old man's company, that she decided if Manuel really wanted to put a stop to her little affair, it would not be too long before either she, or her lover, was duly informed. In the meantime, she'd have herself a damned good time. It would always be better to love and to lose than never to love at all. That was her theory, and she was sticking to it.

'Mustafa will run you back, my dear.' The Colonel turned to call his man. But trusty Mustafa was already in the room. As he stood there, a few paces behind the Colonel's chair, Maria began to think of him as a man rather than a hired hand. What did he look like in bed? What would he

The House of Baghdad

look like in hers? Would his muscles bulge even more under the strain of his weight above her? Would he be even more dominant than Yudie had shown himself to be? Or would he be like a bloody heavy sheep, shooting his load, in a final fling before the slaughter? The idea nauseated her and she contented herself with the manservant image - and a damned impressive image - at that. The way things were going, she might even need him for herself.

As the Colonel's car left with Maria and Mustafa at the wheel, Felix Esbano and his host got down to some serious drinking. It would not be a long lesson tonight but, if Felix were to impart a few vital home truths during the course of the evening, he wanted to test the Colonel on his memory for detail the very next day. It was agreed by both men that this would be - at least for Yudie (who up to now had never been a heavy drinker) - a damned useful test for the future. It was at this point that a loud bang was heard coming from the direction of the departing car. The blast rocked the drinks table and a million possibilities raced through the minds of the two men. Yudie's first thought was: 'had his car been hit by a mercenary expecting him to be inside it?' Two opposing thoughts battled for supremacy in Felix's mind: one, a consideration that after all these years of such pleasant sanctuary in Brazil, building up an enviable reputation in the social graces - he was a good dancer (despite his age); something of a diplomat; and no mean raconteur - they had 'come for him' at last. (Their thinking would be simple: if they couldn't have Hitler, then at least they'd nab all the other bastards who were still around.) The other thought? Well, would the President be so stupid as to make an assassination attempt on the Colonel without first making full use of him? Then Felix suddenly remembered.

Of course, it was the night of a special fireworks display in honour of Saint……. Who the hell was it, this time? People kept telling him he should jolly well be used to bangs and crashes after what he'd been through in his long, active life. They seemed to forget that all those years - even when attached to a Prussian of such intelligence and magnificent stature as Fritz Krupp, sorry - Felix Esbano - must eventually take their toll. But then, how could they know that, just by looking at him?

The men breathed a sigh of relief as the first of the sprinkler rockets shot up in the sky right outside the window. Maybe the President was trying to tell Yudie something? After all, Manuel had always loved fireworks - ever since the day when he tried to get his own back on that damned silly priest whose stories so disturbed his sleep as a boy. No one in the village had forgotten the young Manuel's attempts give the priest a nasty shock with a rocket strategically placed under the man's cassock when he wasn't looking. The experiment was not a complete success but a bit of a mess was made of the priest's under-garments - and there was hell to pay.

'Damn fiestas. Any excuse to make a racket.'

'The penalty of living among the Latins, Felix?'

'I dare say you had your fair share of irritations in Baghdad, Yudie?' smiled Felix, stretching to pick out a large havana from the box handed him by the Colonel who merely grinned, while concentrating on lighting his own cigar. Felix remained convinced the regular wailings of 'Allahu Akhbar' had unnerved more than a few petulant Englishmen though no Arab, even a military man, could be expected to admit as much.

'So, what shall we discuss tonight, Felix?' The Colonel took a pull on his cigar and eyed his guest with bemused expectancy. He was determined to keep his guard on a tight rein - and bide his time. He knew Felix Esbano was no fool: one only had to look in his eyes to see that. They were the mirror of the soul and though Sodom the Lesser's own soul had need of urgent repairs, to say the least, his son had inherited his gift of sixth sense in making an accurate assessment of anyone set before him. Pity the father heeded no one who possessed a similar gift.

'Let's talk about ambition. It's always been an absorbing subject, to my mind.'

The Colonel studied his guest even more closely. But he said nothing and allowed him to continue.

'Seems to me, most people either deny it entirely, or define it as something very simple and straightforward. Maybe that's healthy. Personally, I think it goes far deeper.'

'You are a disciple of Freud, then?'

'Good Lord. Are you trying to make the argument singular?'

Felix took a sip of his whisky and looked into the Colonel's eyes - testing, probing for a level. Maybe his host was not so bright, after all. But Felix's objective was merely to draw his man out into the open and encourage him to declare his avowed intentions. Even if he had read Freud, Jung and all other known gurus of psychology, it remained doubtful Colonel D-Day would ever have the slightest interest in their findings, especially if those findings found him wanting. His was a mind given to stubbornness, aggression, cruelty; to uncontrolled, unreasoned passions of vengeance. What need had he to question such passions?

"Vengeance is Mine" might be acceptable to some people but his passions were given him by Allah. And who was Colonel Doomsday to argue with Allah?

'I have never had a problem with sex, Herr Esbano. Why should I have a problem with anything else?'

As Felix had feared, the Colonel had suddenly become very singular in his argument. But just as Felix began to wonder how the devil he could best expand his host's horizons, the Colonel spoke again. 'You want to know my ambition?' Ah, this was it. As long as Felix took care not to assume Yudie had limitations (even if he had) then he could probe as much as he liked. He might even get an answer: whether it turned out to be the answer he required could be another matter. As the old man sat there, gently puffing away on his cigar, whisky in hand, his eyes set on this fascinating newcomer to Brazilian society, he could sense growing in him the beginnings, if nothing more, of an appreciation of the Arab mind. The central and all-pervading theme of that mind, after all was said and done, might still remain that of justice. Judging by the response of his own people back in Iraq, there was little evidence the Colonel had measured up to this high ideal. But if the West refused even to consider the nature and sensitivities of the Arab psyche - let alone understand it - then they would remain fools forever.

Chapter 12

The Colonel lent back in his chair and took another pull on his cigar. 'Tell me more about the super-gun your people were developing back in the '40s'.'

They were still at it - talking, drinking - (the Colonel had stuck to gin and tonic. Yet, on Scotch, Felix Esbano had remained compos mentis).

The smoke from their cigars pervaded the room, reaching the nostrils of one of the Colonel's Dobermanns lying on a rug by his feet. The dog lifted his head and gave his master a brief look of disdain and went back to sleep. The time had reached 1.30 am. but the night was young: Felix Esbano was determined once and for all to pin down the Colonel on the delicate matter of the bombing of New York. His own bombing days were clearly over and the one assassination plot he had been invited to join, which stood any chance of dislodging Herr Hitler, somehow seemed inappropriate and, to Felix's mind, too childish to talk about. The fact that had it succeeded, millions of lives would have been saved, never entered Fritz Krupp's idealistic mind - so caught up was he in the heady euphoria and passions of the hour.

'Ah, the super-gun. Yes, that Canadian lad Gerry Bull knew all about our designs, of course. I'm damned sure he'd have had a field day, working for the Fuehrer.'

Yudie laughed. But Felix had not finished.

'No need to tell *you,* is there? - Had Gerry lived, your father would have taken delivery of the biggest and the best in time for his own little war.'

At this remark, the Colonel's face momentarily dropped (perhaps in memory of his 'unlucky' father). But suddenly it lit up again. Felix could hardly believe his eyes. As he watched his host's face grow in animation, he recalled the occasions on which he'd been summoned to meet his Fuehrer. My God. The Colonel's face had taken on an uncanny likeness. Felix felt hot, locked in a time capsule, while he watched every muscular movement of the Colonel's cruel mouth, every twitch of his obligatory moustache. The eyes began to sparkle and shine in the way Hitler's did. Could Felix ever forget the magnetism of his Fuehrer - his manic, terrifying, but inspiring eyes? If Sodom the Lesser was merely a lethargic shadow of the German Chancellor after a particularly tedious meeting of foreign Heads of State, then Yudie was an Arab equivalent of a jubilant Fuehrer after the successful bombing of Poland. Felix pondered the question further. No sooner had the world put down one Middle-East monster with designs beyond his station, than it was faced with another who, by the will of his own people, had mercifully been denied the fulfilment of his true, but perhaps even grosser, potential. Would fate take a hand? Would Felix reach the age of 100 only to find himself the catalyst or even the accomplice in the bombing of New York?

The Colonel's eyes continued to blaze in ecstasy. Felix Esbano was clearly the man to bring him out of his shell. No other man he'd so far met in Brazil, had got what it takes to inspire him like this old warrior. 98 he may be but naughty old Fritz Krupp was dynamite. Yudie felt perfectly at ease in his company. He felt he could tell him anything - even his secrets: his hidden agenda. Little did he realise the old man had a shrewd idea of what that hidden agenda amounted to and that he was merely seeking confirmation of his well-founded suspicions.

Yudie rose from his chair and walked across the room - so finely furnished with subtle-dye Persian carpets, tapestries, Monets and selected pieces of Brazilian sculpture to add an indigenous air and respect for the host country. A magnificent walnut writing desk completed the picture: if this was to be the seat of the true Iraqi Government in exile, at least it could not be accused of lacking elegance. Yudie stood behind the desk with his back to Felix and pulled aside one of the lighter tapestries. Built into the wall was a modest-looking safe (so kindly loaned by the Brazilian Government for personal effects and the like.) Yudie selected the combination, turned the handle and opened the safe door. He drew out a folder and closed the safe door, turning the handle and securing the combination. He carefully covered the safe with the tapestry and walked over to his guest, patiently waiting in eager anticipation. Whatever was in that folder would be worth millions, maybe billions to anyone determined enough to cause mayhem. Of this Felix had no doubt. And no TV game of 'Open the Box' could ever be farther from this moment of tension, excitement and sheer fearfulness.

'Tell me what you think of this.' The Colonel plonked down the folder in Felix's lap and returned to his chair to await the reaction. Felix put down his whisky, pulled out his reading glasses from his jacket, put them on and took his first look at the title on the folder. In neat, almost ashamedly modest lettering, stood the title: 'Project Jerusalem.' It could have been the title of a novel: the folder itself hardly seemed different from yet another hopeful author's. But Felix knew better. He turned the page to reveal the sub-title: 'Super Gun - Top Secret.' He turned again and what he saw there left him in no doubt as to its real meaning. If people shrunk in fear of Project Babylon, they had seen nothing like this. In graphic detail, the working plans described a gun that could deliver a rocket into space (complete with nuclear war-head) which could then travel 6,000 miles in orbit, re-enter the atmosphere and, with pin-point accuracy, deposit itself on top of the Empire State Building. As the old man read on, his very being seemed to change from a benign ex-Nazi who'd seen it all, done it all, and whose eyes at last looked out on to the world with some degree of compassion, to a re-created Member of the Third Reich, a highly-motivated disciple of the great Lucifer. Every little detail of 'Project Jerusalem' - the immaculate description of the bore, the thrust, the range, the sheer fire-power of those huge, high quality guns and their deadly rockets, increased his excitement by the second. As he pored over the awesome plans, his 98 years began to shrink into insignificance; the cloak of civility, his knowledge and appreciation of fine literature, the weekly classes of philosophy he'd held to an ever increasing and spell-bound body of students, even his consumption of fine food and fine liquor seemed to recede into the background - all memories erased to make room for this new and terrifying obsession. How much longer should he hide his true nature from the world? If he hung on until he was 100, he had paid his dues to society, given back more than he'd taken, disciplined himself to 'do as the Romans do'. Would they now condemn him for having a final fling before his inevitable demise? Would his old masters allow themselves a fleeting chuckle in hell when Fritz Krupp, alias Felix Esbano, finally made it to the gates? His whole life flashed

The House of Baghdad

before him. Yet he was not dying - not yet. He was fitter than most men half his age. If he had had his own rocket, he would have been up there. Ah. Maybe this was the answer: he should co-operate with Yudie on 'Project Jerusalem' and volunteer to sit in the nose of the rocket and sacrifice himself on the altar of the Empire State Building? He pulled himself together. Maybe the whisky was getting to him, after all; maybe all the years he'd spent in Brazil as an ex-Pat, ex-Nazi, ex-everything else had finally unhinged him - civility merely a myth.

He raised his eyes from the folder and its contents. 'Yes, Yudie. I think you have something, here.'

'I thought you'd be interested. Will you help me?'

It seemed an eternity before Felix answered. But Yudie was in no particular hurry. He knew he 'had something' - something that would make the nations sit up and take notice; something they would never forget. Felix closed the folder and stretched himself in his chair. Could he now betray his President, the man who'd protected him, affording him the freedom to live all these years in comfort; the man whose own wife was having it off with the Colonel, whose own safety depended upon the generosity or whim of Manuel Gonzalez? Corrupt he might be but President Gonzalez had done more than anyone he knew to bring succour to the 'lost sheep' of this world. How could Felix allow himself a final aberration of the mind and let down a man to whom he owed so much?

It was decision time. While Yudie's face moved in ugly contortions, his eyes blazed with excitement, like those of a torturer who'd been given a free hand to do his worst (O, if only the world knew), Felix began to harbour serious doubts about supporting his host in his devilish plan. If Sodom the

Lesser's modest aim of bombing Israel via the super-gun had, at the time, seemed despicable enough, his son's monstrous scheme of attacking America from space was not only horrifying but certain to bring retribution the like of which Baghdad could never imagine. 'Any other madcap ideas, Yudie?' This would have been a question any normal, level-headed intelligent man might well have posed the Colonel at this juncture. But Felix Esbano was anything but the world's average, prosaic, level-headed citizen. He instinctively knew his host was ready, and more than willing, to share his secrets with him in a display of terrifying, manic gestures that would jog his own memory of those 'halcyon days' of German supremacy and military force. All he had to do would be to keep his host talking by supplying him the occasional feed-line and continue drinking his whisky without falling asleep.

'But my dear friend. Have you forgotten what the West did to your father's own rather less ambitious plans for the super-gun?'

'No, I have not. But, don't you see, Felix? When I return to power in Iraq.......' (here Felix managed to stifle any expression of doubt over his host's dream. He simply wished to remind the Colonel that Russia and America were still co-operating with each other and were ready and waiting for any rogue attack from space) .. 'I shall simply take advantage,' droned Yudie, 'of the new political climate.'

'What are you driving at, my friend?' Felix was not without imagination but he could hardly have been prepared for what was to come......

'I have an idea which should guarantee a swift subjugation of America,' continued Yudie with prophetic smugness. 'It shouldn't be too difficult to execute. Moreover, it would be entirely unexpected.'

'Fire away,' encouraged Felix, beginning to sense his host's enthusiasm for overkill might just be the trigger for his inevitable downfall. The question was: would the world be spared the inconveniences of yet another madman's will?

'Now that my country is a so-called democratic State I could, as I say, take advantage of this otherwise unfortunate condition and drop my nuclear bomb via an ordinary innocent-looking jet airliner.'

Felix swallowed another measure of whisky and looked up into Yudie's face with a gasp. He wanted to say something important, something of substance, something... But nothing would come out and Yudie continued to describe in graphic, horrifying detail, the first ever bombing of New York City by a chartered airliner which came from.......... Yes, where the hell did that damned thing come from? It had suddenly flown off course like a mute, deaf Korean Airliner and had deposited its lethal load, banked and flown away 'off screen', back to........? Panic had broken out; the military and air command were confused, caught napping and all that could be detected flying back across the Atlantic at the time were a British Airways Concorde, a TWA Jumbo jet and the President's own Airforce 1 on a relaxed trip to a European summit. The bastards had struck and not a little pandemonium and sickening death and destruction had ensued.

Yudie's flow of monstrous thoughts seemed unstoppable. His eyes burned bright, boring through the soul of Felix Esbano. A thousand scenarios flashed through the old man's mind - all of which bore huge penalty tags. In his long active life he had never liked being boxed in. But, on each of these occasions (and, mercifully, they had been few), he had managed by a supreme effort of self-control coupled with innate wisdom and guile to remain calm, whilst giving away little. Moreover, he had lived to tell the tale. But now that he'd reached the twilight of his life, living out his days in the comforts of Brazilian society, who should confront him with a potentially earth-shattering decision but an Arab exile with an impeccable pedigree of infamy? Could this be yet another variation of Sod's Law so beautifully timed to see him off the face of the earth?

God knows how, but suddenly, everything appeared to click into place. In Felix's mind, the die had been cast. He would not let his President down. The heinous crimes of the Third Reich, with which he'd had such illustrious connections so long ago, screamed out in his mind and soul; the spirits of the victims summoned him to do everything in his power to stop this man before him treading the same fatal path as the Fuehrer. And if a little deception was needed in order to achieve the desired result, then so be it. No, he would not let his President down. Even a man as devious as Manuel Gonzalez, had his good points. Moreover, the man had friends in high places; and some of them resided in the United States. Any alteration to the map of America, however timely or desirable to some comedians he knew, would have serious repercussions upon his own back yard. And since Felix Esbano also had the good fortune to live in it.......

'Yes, I think you have something, here,' repeated Felix, wistfully. But his cool, almost throwaway intonation was lost on the Colonel. The old man looked up again into his host's eyes and detected the pleasure he continued to show in believing he had found an accomplice to his monumental crime, a crime which if executed, would guarantee the perpetrator a huge black mark in 'The Guinness Book Of Records'. It might at least make up for the indignity of being kicked out of his own Country. As far as Felix was concerned, such a record (and at the age of 100 it would amount to the jackpot) no longer represented the accolade it might once have been.

And now he needed another drink. 'Allow me.' Yudie rose from his chair, lifted the decanter and poured his friend - looking stunned and uncharacteristically 'at sea' - another large drink. This time Felix did not attempt 'Whoa', 'Steady', or any other feigned admonishment. He drank deep and allowed his fine mind a well-earned rest - to linger a while before succumbing to a welcome and much-needed anaesthetization.

Chapter 13

In Baghdad, things were really moving apace. Dan Levy's 'House of Baghdad' and John Broadbridge's 'Baghdad Line' were going great guns.

Judging by the sheer noise engendered during the broadcasts, it was felt the Iraqis would have little to complain about. It was not long, however, before Westerners began to appreciate the strength of the Iraqi character. Now that the dictators had gone, the people could, at last speak their minds and what those minds were saying was this: 'Give us the tools and we will finish the job'. For once, they were not speaking of war and though the phrase smacked too much of an imperialist Churchill for some memories, it was a phrase that somehow stuck. Money simply poured into the country from all over the world as, indeed, did those foreign helpers - whether they were needed or not.

Officially, the West had declared itself 'neutral' in terms of interference in the internal affairs of the fledgling democracy, though, naturally, it could not resist taking advantage of business opportunities presented by the rebuilding programme worked out by the new Government.

And talking of Government - the Iraqis were not slow in realising the weakness of proportional representation. For, very soon after the aborted Squabbling Competition - and more likely as a direct result of the same - they had put their heads together and decided by a huge majority to reject it as a system for their country. 'It may be fine for the Germans,' one politician was heard to shout 'but for us Arabs, I ask you.' A great laugh went up in the Chamber and the man was inundated with inquiries about the source of his humour. There seemed no need to mention France or Italy - ever again. Nevertheless, the French President was only too keen to prevent potential breaches, not so much in security as in good relations. His 'two-handed' approach over the safe conduct of Colonel Doomsday could not be entirely over-looked, even by the pragmatic Iraqis. Historical links with France was one thing, a lifeline to a brutal dictator - who had brought ruin to his own country - quite another. What guarantee had they that the bastard would not return to Baghdad with the connivance of the French President and seize power yet again?

The German Ambassador, for his part, remained keen to arrange a meeting between his country's Finance Minister and Iraq's opposite number to be held either in Berlin or Baghdad. Iraq's rejection of the German PR system notwithstanding, a substantial aid-package was still on the table - provided Iraq not only developed and upheld its new democratic system but also gave up that silly nonsense of pursuing the extradition of their 'beloved' Colonel. Maybe the Ambassador knew too much about President Gonzalez's 'guests'. It would be foolish to stir up a hornets' nest, particularly when the nest still contained a number of high ranking German ex-pats.

As for Arid Aziz - he was enjoying himself more than he'd ever thought possible. His party - the Sensible Arab Conservative Party - had clinched a 130-seat majority over the rival Social Liberals (an optimistic euphemism, in this case, for the Communist Party) or, as some cynics had dubbed it, 'the only Loony Left'. Nevertheless, Iraq - maybe for too long - had been ruled by strong men and, despite Arid Aziz's disturbing sense of humour and diplomatic skills, no one considered him a fool. He had not promised the earth; he had not promised another bloody holy war; but he had promised strong Government - together with open, honest trading with the rest of the world. Besides, with the prospect of so much money being saved as a result of drastic reductions in military spending, the people could at last look forward to a better standard of living. And, by Allah - they deserved it.

Yes, there was little doubt. Arid Aziz had the gift of the gab - not only in Parliament but on the 'hustings'. And on his little walkabouts, not only did he stay to argue his case but his case appeared to be understood and accepted as very sensible indeed.

It had been agreed by general consensus that Arid Aziz would make the best Foreign Minister Iraq had ever had since his famous ill-fated namesake. Flattered though he undoubtedly was by the weight of such praises, Arid insisted there was far too much to do at home which would need his personal attention and that, unlike one famous British Prime Minister of the '80s, he would find no difficulty in relinquishing any desire to break other people's cricket bats. No, he would be content to be Prime Minister and delegate the jobs of Foreign Minister, Finance Minister, Health Minister, Education Minister - you name it - to other people. If folks wished to accuse him of having no balls, that was up to them. His balls were reserved for his wife and occasional 'secretary'. His head would be used to conduct the nation's business.

As for the idea of extraditing Colonel Doomsday from Brazil, Arid himself did not share the enthusiasm of some of his colleagues. He would have some sharp words for a rather vociferous and over-eager young member of the new

Foreign Office spouting his head off on the phone to his country's Ambassador in Brazil. Maybe that famous British Prime Minister's distrust of her own Foreign Office was justified after all?

****

Bazrani's plane touched down at Baghdad and, within the hour, he was shown into Arid's new office, specially built to withstand terrorist attacks. In fact, the whole building had been thoughtfully constructed so as to house the whole cabinet - should Arid decide to implement some necessary but 'unpopular' measures. It was hoped Draconian methods could be avoided. But no one could be certain how many 'old guard' cells remained in the country or if they would suddenly take it into their heads to strike at the very seat of democratic Government. The new Chamber - for all its Arabic splendour - still remained too reminiscent of the Spanish model for Arid's taste. Maybe he'd seen the video of that attempted coup in Madrid too many times but he was not without imagination.

'My dear Bazrani. Welcome. Judging by your complexion I think Brazil is beginning to agree with you.'

Arid Aziz extended his hand to his guest and indicated a chair opposite his desk.

'Thank you, sir. Indeed, I think Brazil has a lot going for it. A very stimulating society.'

'Unlike ours, eh?'

'Oh, I wouldn't go so far as to say that, sir. It's just that........'

'No need to elaborate, Mr Bazrani. Even I have a pretty good idea of the life-style on offer to the likes of us.'

The House of Baghdad

Arid Aziz raised his eyebrows and winked. It was the first time Bazrani had ever seen his P.M. raise his eyebrows. It was the first time he'd ever seen him wink. To be able to perform both feats at the same time was truly remarkable.

The Ambassador sat down and waited upon Arid to open the conversation proper.

He had a shrewd idea of the PM's personal view of the possible extradition of Colonel D-Day but he'd been led to believe by several high-ranking officials that the Government wished to track down the Colonel. Moreover, that telephone call from the Foreign Office seemed so genuine, so........

'Now, I will make the position absolutely clear, Mr Bazrani.' This was it. No argy-bargy. This new P.M., Iraq's first real P.M., would be as decisive as any dictator. 'I have been approached by MOSSAD with a plan to track down the Colonel for us in return for a guarantee of peace and trade. And I have been approached by the German Government with an offer of cash as long as we not only maintain our new democratic system but also drop the idea of extradition. What should I do, Mr Bazrani?' Again the P.M. raised his eyebrows but this time he did not wink. Could this be genuine indecision on his part? Could this be weakness, after all? Or could he be on the point of offering him, Mr Bazrani, a new assignment - one that involved his making decisions? Oh God, no. He was used to carrying out orders. He would never be able to take responsibility for making a decision. Oh God - please take this cup from me. Anything, anything - just so long as it doesn't involve making a decision. Thank God for Prime Ministers. They were welcome to the top job. There were reasons for everything. There were reasons why they called him 'Baby Bazrani' - for that was the name to which he answered when pressed by…….

'Ambassador. Are you listening to what I'm saying?'

'Who? Oh, yes, yes, of course, Prime Minister. You were saying something about MOSSAD. It was quite a shock.'

'A shock? You are a man of the world, are you not? In politics, anything and everything is possible. I would have thought you'd be the first to know that?'

'But Israel, sir………'

'You have heard of it, I presume?' This time the P.M. did not bother to raise his eyebrows. Nor even his voice - which drifted across his desk, past Bazrani's big ears and as far as the walls, where it was quickly absorbed by heavy curtains and reinforced concrete.

'Now, listen to me, Mr Bazrani. By Allah's good grace, we now have a democratically elected Government, of which I am the head.' Bazrani allowed himself a tiny smirk behind the official alignment of his features. 'At last we are at peace with our neighbours,' continued the P.M.

'Praise be to God,' interjected the Ambassador.

But the P.M. had not finished. 'We have offers of financial and technical assistance from everywhere we care to look. If we play our cards right, as they say, we can be a great country again. *But, Mr Bazrani* - we have to live in the real world. You have heard of Egypt, I trust?'

The Ambassador looked sheepish. 'Dare I say it, Bazrani, we could be more successful than your beautiful…….'

'Launderette?' Arid Aziz did not have much opportunity to go to the cinema these days, and whatever Bazrani was thinking about was no concern of his.

'Oh, I'm sorry, sir. Brazil does have its effect on one. 'Blame it on Rio' as they say.'

These constant references to films - past, present or future - were beginning to irritate and Arid would soon have to leave for 'Prime Minister's Question Time'. Despite all the risks, it was a TV transmission he wouldn't miss for the world. After all, it was he - more than anyone - who was the instigator of the idea, in spite of what some people continued to claim.

'So, what do I advise Manuel Gonzalez, Sir?'

'You simply tell him a very junior member of the Foreign Office had misinformed you. Needless to say, the culprit will lose his job.'

'I have it on your authority, then, Sir, that we will not be pursuing the matter?'

'You have. After all, we must respect the Brazilian way of doing things, mustn't we, Mr Ambassador?'

Once again the P.M. treated his guest to another of those strange winks.

'Oh, quite.' Bazrani's thoughts were rather less concentrated upon respect than on personal gain. Bang had gone his chance of creaming off a little of that money that would undoubtedly change hands in return, as it were, for the Colonel. It was not unknown for President Gonzalez to reward, quite generously, people who had scratched his demanding back. But now Arid Aziz was looking his guest in the eye. The Ambassador had better pay attention if he valued his job.

'On the other hand,' continued the P.M., 'if MOSSAD take the trouble to track down the Colonel whilst searching for a few of those German gentlemen they seem unable to forget about, who are we to stop them?'

Arid Aziz rewarded his guest with yet another of those disconcerting winks. And Baby Bazrani was glad to be out of that office and on the plane again, heading for Rio.

Chapter 14

'Hey, Martha... Come take a look at this.' On the huge TV screen dominating the Johnsons' sitting room in Atlanta, loomed the imposing face of Arid Ariz. For years he'd secretly fancied himself as a film star - this, he believed, was his chance. Perhaps, his only chance. And now that the bloody dictators had gone he could afford to put himself about a bit. If he, too, grew to be a dictator - in the normal course of political intrigue - at least he would not be a bloody one. The country had seen enough of that stuff and there were other pursuits to occupy the people's time. Iraq had at last been received into the United Nations as a worthy partner in peace. How reliable it would be, remained a matter of conjecture. 'Time will tell', they all said. 'Time will tell'.

But Arid Aziz was determined to prove himself a great Prime Minister of the new Iraqi Government. And what better way to do this than to be seen on television, arguing and bawling with the best of 'em? To be fair, these sudden and disconcerting outbursts were kept to a minimum - not so much through Arid's own self-control (commendable though it was), as by reason of the fact that a young and particularly poncey-looking cameraman, too frequently employed by Jim Rosenberg (for Arid's taste), seemed to have a bit of a yen for the more handsome Leader of the Opposition. Too often the camera would zoom onto the charismatic figure of Faisal Hussein, eager to steal Arid's thunder. "The Only Loony Left" this young man may well have been but no one could accuse him of lacking guts, or a healthy determination to win the battle of the TV stakes. If not every day, certainly every other day, people were glued to their TV sets in Baghdad to watch the on-going saga of their very own Parliament. Indeed, all over the world, people sat, mesmerized, for within the space of two months Dan Levy's 'House of Baghdad' had topped the charts for 'The Soap of the World'. And Iraq was proud. Worried looks furrowed the brows of the presenters of Britain's 'Prime Minister's Question Time'. Heart-attacks, suicides and sackings were primed for activation in the decision-making offices of New York and L.A.. Dan Levy's programme was the tops and his havanas got bigger by the day.

John Broadbridge's 'Baghdad Line', on the other hand, though successful, could not quite match up to its American rival. After all, no one could deny the power of television. And with Dan Levy firmly in charge of that particular avenue - as far as his contract would allow - John Broadbridge's nose, if not exactly put out of joint, had to be satisfied with a BBC radio programme and generous helpings of fine whisky from the ever-smiling Caliph. There was no question 'The House of Baghdad' had scooped the market. The very sight of Arid Aziz throwing back his newly-grown locks with the panache of a 'Tarzan' and tapping the despatch box with the authority of a Perry Mason, contributed to the fascination of a world audience. His eyes would sparkle at the right time, his head would turn to the camera at the exact moment of his punch-line. He would even take on the guise of a Jewish trader - raising his shoulders and hands to signal the problem he'd struggled with in getting the price just right - for the customer, of course. Even Adolf Hitler, in his early attempts at mimicry, was hardly a match for Arid. It was all very confusing. For fellow Arabs would try to take him on and question his motives. 'Show business', he'd say. 'It's show business', and carry on as if he'd been used to it all his life.

One thing was certain: the coffers of the Treasury were beginning to fill up very nicely. For in exchange for the excellent returns from world-wide transmissions of his programme, Dan Levy was committed to parting with substantial fees to the Baghdad Government. After all, business is business. And a deal is a deal. But Dan Levy continued to wear that famous grin: the spin-offs from his programme seemed to provide a never-ending source of income for both sides. There were commercials, feature films and even a curious little pop record of Arid Aziz himself - overdubbing his party's new policy document against the hubbub of a crowded and over-excited House.

Even the Caliph began attending the House to see what tips he could pick up for a book he was considering writing about his unusual life. 'Well, my dear Broadbridge', he was heard to grunt one afternoon in the House after a particularly energetic speech from a member of the Opposition, 'Dan Levy seems - as you might say - to have cracked it?'

John Broadbridge happened to be in the House on a rare day off and had decided to pop in - in order to give Levy's damned programme the 'once-over'. He was not by nature a jealous person but the speed with which this money-spinner had taken off had done little to discourage an outbreak of the dreaded disease. For years he'd been suggesting a regular radio programme from Baghdad, and now that the revolution had swept aside the fearful dictators, even a television series was possible. But as soon as he makes an attempt at this, along comes a damned American loudmouth, and takes the cherry. It was bloody typical. And what could one say about the BBC? Well, much as he'd always held a particular affection for 'Auntie', his ideas had all too often been dismissed as too expensive, too impractical, or (in their words) just 'too tiresome to entertain'. (He'd overheard them say it - more than once) Someone even had the cheek to suggest that the cause of his failure to convince the corporation, might lie in his postal address - somewhere between Paddington and Reading. But this rather unkind analysis of the problem was swiftly waived by his immediate boss as bearing no proven correlation with the facts. No, despite an unfortunate meeting of bodies (so early in his life), which subsequently produced an honest woman, two kids and a dog to look after, John Broadbridge had continued to exercise what he saw as his right of free movement. His physical attributes, temperament and language qualifications, all guaranteed a certain amount of success in the Middle East. And just as he was really beginning to loosen up and enjoy himself, along comes Dan Levy and his bloody 'flying circus'.

'Now, now, Mr Broadbridge. Jealousy will get you nowhere. After all, it is an emotion with which we Arabs have had to struggle. The radio programme is going well, so why should you worry?'

'Doesn't quite have the same impact, sir, does it?'

'But, my dear fellow. Radio is so civilized. You are an Englishman, are you not?' The Caliph smiled sweetly at John Broadbridge who finally relented with a healthy grin stretching his earthy face.

'You say the nicest things.'

'OK. *Cut*. Camera 3. Take it. The man in the gallery is going to........ Oh, Jesus.' Yet another broadcast had captured the attention of a huge world audience. A man sitting up in the gallery had fallen back on the bench after uttering a great cry to Allah. He had been incensed by what he considered the talk of infidels, a betrayal of Islam, a loathsome disgrace and had thrown his hands up in the air in a final act of defiance. But the politicians had carried on and the TV cameras had never stopped rolling until the man plonked down and promptly collapsed over the lap of a highly emotional young student who'd quietly slipped in to gather research for his week's essay.

'Oh my *God*,' he screamed. 'This man is dead. Oh my *God*!'

A commotion broke out in the House and another man in the gallery stood up and began to harangue the Prime Minister, accusing him of insensitivity, of lying to the nation, of taking on the garb, methods and aims of Westerners. 'You will be punished.' he screamed. 'Allah will pun.......'

'Now, sir. You come along with me.' A hefty security guard, looking and speaking remarkably like a British bobby had taken control and calmly - but firmly - dragged the screaming man out of the gallery and into custody.

'Well, for all of you watching at home,' interjected the TV announcer, 'perhaps this would be a good moment to take a break for a commercial or two. We will do our best to resume this programme as soon as it is technically possible.' And on that optimistic note, Arid Aziz could be seen to make one of his last minute and specially wry glances at a stray camera.

'Did you see that, Martha? Marth...... What the hell ya up ta in that kitchen? Ya like some goddam English housewife fussing over this, broodin' ov.....'

'Pack it in, Jack.'

'Come 'n sit down, will ya? This crazy programme'll be back in a jiffy. Christ, have I gotta have some of this. I'll put in a call to Roy Abrahams when this is over. Those shares are gonna move like crazy.'

Martha Johnson finally returned to the sitting room and sat down on the sofa next to her Jack.

'Here. *That's* what I've been up ta.' She passed a mountainous plate of freshly cut sandwiches to Jack who grunted his grudging appreciation. At least the beef looked bloody and generous enough. He'd be content to overlook dinner tonight, in the circumstances.

'Here it comes. Take a look at this.'

'OK. Shoosh.'

'Mr Speaker, I believe the whole house will want to join me in expressing sorrow for the death of the unfortunate gentleman in the gallery who was so tragically overcome by the occasion. We offer our condolences, of course, to his widow and children and trust all future business in this House may be free of......'

'Such inconveniences?' The Leader of the Opposition could always be relied upon to supply any of Arid Aziz's missing lines.

'Did you get that, Martha? The guy is dead. Little guy in the gallery jest keeled over. Guess this democracy game is a bit too much for the Iraqis.'

'Shoosh.' Martha passed the plate back to her husband who took another sandwich and fell silent, absorbed in the 'House of Baghdad'.

'And now, gentlemen, I would urge you to consider carefully not only the motives, but the consequences of voting for this bill. The extradition of Colonel Doomsday,

The House of Baghdad

in my opinion, would serve only to revive and inflame all the unwelcome and dangerous emotions that surrounded and accompanied his ruthless reign - here in Baghdad. Let us be thankful and satisfied he is gone. Why should we go to the trouble *and* expense of bringing him back from Brazil - assuming that's where he is' (derisive laughs accompanied this remark) 'and assuming the feasibility of such an operation, putting him on trial, a trial that would incur further considerable expense to the taxpayer?'

'Because the people demand it.' shouted an Opposition MP.

'How do we know the people demand it?'

'Why don't you ask them?' shouted another Opposition Member.

'Because I believe our people are not as stupid as to waste time and money on someone who has already been driven from his homeland.'

'If he believes that he'll believe anything.'

'Shoosh, Jack.'

The Leader of the Opposition stood up and the P.M. gave way.

Faisal Hussein acknowledged the P.M. and smiled at the camera trained on him by his young admirer. 'It seems to me, Mr Speaker,' he began confidently, 'we have a unique opportunity to show the world how much we have matured as a nation.'

'Chrissake. Who's he kiddin'?'

'Shoosh. Have another sandwich.'

Several looks of disdain were caught by the cameras. And some MPs considered themselves so mature that they sat back on their benches and simply closed their eyes.

'I would like to say something that may well surprise the members opposite.'

Looks of horror - as well as derision - flicked across the faces of many MPs. Could Faisal Hussein - this good-looking young politician, eager to make his début in the full glare of a world audience - be suicidal? Or was he merely making a bid for the leadership of the nation in a manner so subtle as to wash over their confused heads?

He bided his time, waiting for the right moment when all murmuring would cease and all eyes would be fixed on him - this upstart, this inexperienced youngster with film-star looks who, in the run-up to the elections, revelled in the cut and thrust of argument and opposition to anything and everything, almost on principle.

'I shall be voting against the bill, honourable Members.'

This did the trick. The MPs fell silent and all eyes were, indeed, firmly fixed on him.

'I would rather leave it to the Israelis to continue this immature pursuit of tired old men who are past posing a threat to any country. I would rather forgive and forget.'

And with that, the young man sat down to a stunned and angry House. Scuffling broke out and the Chamber had to be cleared. If this sort of freethinking was allowed airtime, there could be no hope for the country. If Western perversions were allowed a free rein in Iraq, it would be the end of civilization.

'Get that, Marth.'

'What does it mean, Jack?'

'What does it mean? It means revolution, you stupid woman. It means.......'

'After what those poor people have been through?'

'Those poor people - as you choose to call 'em - are maniacs, They're never happy till they're either driving a tank or got their Goddam butts in the air. They're......'

'Stop it, Jack. Don't be so crude. Give 'em a chance, will ya? They're trying to put their country straight, aren't they? After that Sodom guy and then wha's 'is name.....?'

'Doomsday.'

'Yeah. Doomsday. They've had enough, can't ya see?'

'All I see is a load of Goddam Arabs trying ta beat us at our own game.'

'Oh, that's it, is it? I see. You're just mad they've gotta darned good TV programme going. What happened to the shares?'

Jack looked sheepish and buried himself in another sandwich.

'What happened, Jack?'

'Dunno. Gone off the idea.'

'Hell. That's quick. Where's ya staying power, Jack?'

Jack shot his wife a sly look. He knew his staying power in the bedroom was second to none. So he believed. But this conversation, he decided, was beginning to irritate.

'OK. Have it your way. Those creeps are nice. They're just having teething troubles. Is that it?'

'Jack......'

'OK., OK. Let's calm down. Fancy an early night?'

Chapter 15

Arid Aziz was pleased with himself. He had resisted the temptation to feign over-enthusiastic anger following Faisal Hussein's apparent conversion to Christianity. He put the sudden and un-Arab outburst down to his rival's youth and lack of experience rather than to the young man's avid reading of Tariq Aziz's Memoirs. Nevertheless, he was glad his opponent had decided to 'come out'. It would allow Arid to somewhat distance himself from such dangerous sentiments whilst proceeding in secret to meet MOSSAD half way in their own pursuit of Colonel D-Day. He knew MOSSAD would appreciate his difficulty in openly pursuing the man (the Iraqi Parliament had, after all, defeated the motion on a free vote. Wonders will never cease.) At the same time, he was conscious of the fact Colonel D-Day still posed a threat to Iraq if, God forbid, he should ever manage to return to the Middle East. Despite repeated assurances from both the French and the Brazilian Presidents that the ex-dictator would never again cause trouble, what water-tight guarantees could there ever be that he would not, one day, slip through that fragile net? 'Where there's a will……' had never been far from the lips and soul of Colonel Doomsday. And since neither Iraq nor Israel could afford a repeat of Sodom the Lesser's escapades - still less the fulfilment and consequences of his son's avowed intentions of horrific revenge - a 'Get the Colonel' campaign was soon agreed upon. It would simply be called 'Operation Moonlight'.

So, this part of Arid's plan would remain a covert arrangement. But the PM was quick to capitalize on Faisal

Hussein's sudden 'conversion'. He had no intention of being caught napping and planned to remove the ground from under his rival's feet as adeptly as possible. Within a week he had worked out a deal with the Israelis for peace, security and trade. If Egypt could do such a thing with the aid of an American President, surely Iraq could do better? If agreement could not be reached without Uncle Sam poking his big nose in Arab affairs or posturing as the 'honest broker', something was clearly amiss. After all, when all the gloss and sophistication was stripped away Arid Aziz remained an Arab. Besides, he could never quite forget what happened to Sadat.

A deal was struck. And what a deal. But first MOSSAD would pay a little visit to the Colonel in Brazil - whilst tracking down a few of those stray German dogs. The secret service had already gathered enough intelligence to enable them to locate one Fritz Krupp currently enjoying the hospitality, under an assumed name, of the Gonzalez Government. The fact the man was fast approaching his centenary failed to make the slightest difference in the Israelis' attitude. If they could have 'hit' the Fuehrer himself, they would have gladly done so. In fact, even in the face of historical records and all probabilities, a number of Israelis still clung to the belief that Adolf Hitler was still alive (and maybe even kicking) - somewhere. If that were the case, he would be a similar age to Fritz Krupp. One member of MOSSAD even proffered the suggestion that Fritz and Adolf were one and the same man. But judging by recent photographs of the former brought back by some Israelis who at a garden party given by Manuel Gonzalez were convinced they had found the Fuehrer, it was quite obvious - even to the keener members of MOSSAD - that their friends could not have been more mistaken in their 'find'. The figure in the photographs presented an old yet tall, upright man of magnificent, chiselled features with bright blue eyes, a full head of thick white hair and the easy, confident bearing of a Prussian aristocrat - still in possession of his money. Apart from the bright blue eyes, these photographs could not have been farther from the image of the wretched, decidedly 'un-Aryan' and paranoiac image of the Fuehrer that the world had come to fear.

'Still, it's the thought that counts,' insisted the disappointed and somewhat disillusioned student.

'Yes.' The secret-serviceman was glad no one, at least in his organisation, would be stupid enough to entertain this young man's application to join.

****

A call was put through to Arid Aziz's private line. It was the call the PM had been eagerly awaiting for several days. If he could pull off this diplomatic and economic coup he'd be hailed as the saviour of Iraq not only by more than a few Iraqis who had finally comprehended where their dictators' monstrous ambitions had led but by the rest of the 'civilized' world - whether believers or non-believers. Yes, the Israeli Government had discussed Arid's proposals in detail and saw no reason why - in return for a favourable deal on oil and a mutual non-aggression pact - it should not go so far as to protect Iraq from all predators, be they Arab or non-Arab. Besides, Israel would thereby be doing itself a favour - it would be importing oil at a competitive price whilst safeguarding its own security as well as that of Iraq. Iraq in turn could relax in the knowledge it could safely keep its armed forces down to a minimum, while devoting its cash to re-building the country into a truly modern and prosperous state.

'Mr Shameer, this is very good news. If we can get it through Parliament here, I will be the happiest man in Iraq.'

'We wish you well.'

'Thank you. But as you know, despite my large majority, I still have a few... er - what can one say - hard nuts to crack?'

Mr Shameer sympathized but remained silent.

'However, with a little bit of persuasion, arm-twisting and whatever else I can think of',' (Mr Shameer allowed himself a more than sympathetic laugh) 'I am confident we will be in business. After all, Mr Shameer, it is time, is it not, to bury the hatchet?'

'If you say so, Mr Aziz.' Arid didn't quite know what to make of this but he pressed on. 'I do say so, Mr Shameer. I shall do my best to convince, not only my own colleagues, but also as many members of the so-called Opposition of the wisdom of the deal.'

'I'm sure you will, Mr Aziz. And, seriously, I wish you every success in your task.'

'You don't sound too sure of my ability to persuade, Mr Shameer?'

The line suddenly seemed to have gone dead and Arid Aziz wondered whether his brilliant and innovative idea had run into the sand before it had even been aired in the Baghdad Chamber. Or maybe he had got the Israeli Prime Minister's name wrong. But a man could be heard to cough on the other end of the phone and Mr Shameer had returned with renewed confidence. 'I'm sorry about that, Mr Aziz but

I get taken short every now and then. That was one of those moments. Hope you understand.'

'Oh, I do, my friend. I used to have the same trouble during my military service. To make matters worse, one never knew whether someone had been planted in the toilet, ready to chop you down to size.'

Mr Shameer laughed out loud and began to believe that, after all, he really could do business with this entertaining and very human Arab gentleman. Nevertheless, he did not envy the man's task of persuading the Iraqi Parliament - a task that even God would find daunting.

Much to the surprise and delight of Arid Aziz a large number of MPs thought the idea brilliant - a major breakthrough at last in Arab-Israeli relations. But then the expected voices of doubt and dissent began to echo round the Chamber and Arid wondered whether his sense of relief and barely controlled excitement had been too good to be true. Suddenly, an enterprising Opposition member suggested: 'Mr Speaker, could not Israel find a space in her heart for a Palestinian or two?'

'Only in Cloud Cuckoo Land.' Derisive laughter greeted this last remark from all sides of the House but the brave, perhaps foolhardy MP - though embarrassed and angered by the remark from a member of his own party - persevered with, 'Could she not give up, if not the West Bank or Gaza Strip, then a small portion of her land, maybe near the border between herself and Jordan - then Jordan could do the same on her side, and......?'

'No!' came from a large body of MPs on both sides of the House. 'Go back to school,' came from his colleague who'd embarrassed him earlier. And Arid Aziz could see his brain child of a deal with Israel withering away before his

eyes, a deal he'd believed could put him, Arid Aziz - the first freely and properly elected Prime Minister of an unoccupied Iraq - squarely and firmly in that Guinness Book of Records as a very good guy indeed.

But then came his time to speak. He rose from his seat, his face showing the first signs of anxiety, seeds of doubt and insecurity. Visible on his forehead were a few beads of discernible sweat - hallmarks of a man treading a tight-rope that was new, untried, unknown. But this was a tight-rope of his own making. He knew that if Iraq wished to 'get somewhere' in the world - as opposed to lurching from one disaster to another - it would have to put its own house in order. But more than this. Now that the Country was a democracy - albeit a fragile fledgling - it must take the courageous step of using the opportunity to examine all avenues of procedure, all reasonable diplomatic channels, all alternatives to the methods previously used- methods that only served to wreak havoc upon itself. It must reach out and lift its spirit beyond those narrow confines of God versus the Devil. Even Arid could see there was good in everyone - if only one took the time to find it. Why, then, shouldn't the nation co-operate - even with its supposed arch enemy, Israel? If this could be achieved, the sky would be the limit.

'Mr Speaker.' Arid's voice cracked a little and he looked into the Speaker's face - pleading almost, appealing to the man's innate sense of justice, fairness and good sense. 'Mr Speaker,' he repeated, at last finding his voice and straightening up into a figure more like a Prime Minister. 'I feel this is going to be the most difficult speech of my life.....'

'Well, don't make it,' came from the front bench of the Opposition. The cruel jibe, flung at him with the reckless abandon of a British MP, stung the sensitive breast of Arid Aziz, but his strength of character and amazing power of self-control, rushed to his aid...... 'I shall make it,' he said, quickly recovering himself, 'because it is essential that we re-examine our attitude to the outside world.'

'What outside world? There is no outside world. Only Satan.' Arid appeared not to hear this interruption but continued like the seasoned, skilful politician that he was. 'If we continue to ignore the rest of the world - like the honourable gentleman opposite - then we do so at our peril.'

'Israel is our enemy and will always be so.' shouted a member of his own party. Arid made a mental note to have a quiet word with the gentleman in the committee room after he'd finished speaking. 'Israel, sir, is only our enemy if we allow her to be so,' Arid hit back.

'What's that supposed to mean?' came from across the floor.

'Israel will remain our enemy, as you choose to call her, as long as we neither recognize her *nor* have the good sense to reach agreement on security and trade.'

'Rubbish!'

'Now, I am pleased to inform you,' continued the PM undeterred, 'that Mr Shameer and I have produced a plan whereby Israel guarantees our security in return for oil.' Shouts of abuse and derision filled the air but Arid bravely continued. 'In this way - I believe it will be obvious even to our more backward honourable members,' (with a smile, Arid gained a few friendly laughs and he carried on somewhat heartened) 'our nation will be able to use its money to build roads, schools, hospitals and all the other facilities of a modern, sophisticated State. We will be able to raise our standard of living, repay some of our debts,' (looks of horror and surprise greeted the PM that any country should ever want to do such a thing) 'we will be able to take part in the decisions of the nations of the world, instead of burying our heads in our convenient and plentiful sand. We will......'

'Hey. What's going on?' Suddenly all the lights had gone out. The TV cameras had stopped whirling. Confusion and uproar, fear and anger gripped the Chamber. Could this be the price to pay for so-called democracy? Could it be a hoax, or harmless prank? Or could it be, as Arid now feared, a serious attempt to disrupt the business of an elected Government by a few of those hard-liners whom he was never quite convinced had entirely been put to sleep?

Chapter 16

In the UK, the papers took a bold yet essentially jaundiced view of the situation in the Middle East. Having had some experience of propping up an unpopular puppet Government of its own creation after the First World War, the UK quite naturally felt (bombing of Kurdish villages notwithstanding) that at least it had an inkling of the aspirations of ordinary people. Strange how history repeats itself. But here was a new situation - a democratically-elected Iraqi Government agreeing by means of a simple majority on a free vote to sign a peace and trade agreement with Israel. The mind boggled. How long would it last? Who would be the first politician to get shot?

'AZIZ ACHIEVES THE IMPOSSIBLE' proclaimed the Daily Telegraph.

'SUN GOES DOWN ON IRAQI PARLIAMENT' gloated a facetious planetary paper.

'FIGHT THE IMPERIALISTS' insisted the Daily Star, whilst Private Eye, running a new political cartoon series for young cynics, suggested God was having a field-day watching the world destroy itself.

'GOD GIVES UP' was the title of the week's contribution. And a picture of the Almighty in whose hands the globe had so lovingly been held for the last three weeks had suddenly turned itself into a disappointed creator with angry blood-red hands through whose fingers a broken world had just been allowed to slip.

The 'Sundays', in turn, provided their readers a magnificent spread and expanded upon the latest analysis of the Iraqi phenomenon. Prime Minister Bullock professed himself quite happy with the efforts of Arid Aziz and continued to insist we must all "wait and see". Cautious yet articulate as ever, his interview with Mr Bumblebee on BBC1, served to emphasize his personal view of the situation and, once again, proved a testimony of his ability to fill up a half-hour without giving away a single piece of news on which he could be challenged. Ending the interview with a friendly smile across his pug face and indubitable humanity penetrating his new bullet-proof glasses, he expressed the hope that, after so many years of blood and suffering, Iraq would finally emerge as a prosperous democratic State.

'Isn't that really asking too much?' Mr Bumblebee had retained his sting to the last, determined that Mr John Bullock would not get away with mere platitudes or idle dreams. But he had.

'If you were an Iraqi, Mr Bumblebee, would it be asking too much?'

'That's not quite what I meant, Mr Bullock. But I get the point.'

And with that Mr Bumblebee thanked his guest for the interview and rounded off the programme with a wicked full frontal at the camera. 'We must all "wait and see".'

****

'I don't know how Aziz does it,' grunted Lord Brocklehurst as he downed another brandy brought over to him by the barman. The 'Smoking Room' of the House of Lords had filled up with an unusually depressed bunch of long-suffering veterans. They were badly in need of a drink. Their Lordships had been debating yet another reading of the Bill on euthanasia tabled in the Commons by an enthusiastic campaigner who saw no reason why she should have to go to Holland every time she felt the desire for a dignified end coming on. 'Damned civilized, the Dutch', she'd say and plonk down on the bench to wait for the next debate on her Bill. She had been waiting for fifteen years. The prospect that one day it would be on the statute-book was the only thing that kept her alive.

'Arid Aziz? I'm afraid he stands a damned good chance of being bumped off, old man,' responded Lord Partridge, taking another pull on his cigar. Brave fella, though. And a nice man, so I'm told.'

'Yes, I believe Shameer has taken to 'im. Turn up for the books, eh?'

Lord Brocklehurst shifted in his armchair and then sat back to enjoy his brandy.

'We can't count the old chickens - just yet, Charles. Wish I could share your optimism, old man. But experience shows......'

'You're a damned cynic, Henry. Remind me not to invite you to Celia's dinner party.'

'Oh yes. When is it? Promise I'll be jolly and all that.'

'25th of this month. Put it in the diary. Expect you'll be bringing one of your dolly birds?'

'Why not? You know me, Charles. Can't change at my age.'

'At the age of 83, I rather feel it's time you thought of settling down, old man. Now, what d'you say?'

'Can I think it over?'

'Drink ya brandy before it gets cold.'

The friendly banter was interrupted by a sprightly middle-aged Member charging into the room with a red face. 'Bloody fools, bloody fools.' he kept saying. 'When will they ever learn?'

It was hardly unexpected. News had just come in that Arid Aziz had indeed been shot, not, as was first thought, in the Iraqi Chamber when the lights went out but just as he'd turned the key to the front door of his house. For nearly two weeks, he'd hardly had time to hold a civilized conversation with his wife and just as he'd arrived at his home to enjoy a well-earned quiet weekend - they had struck.

'Bastards.' spat Lord Brocklehurst.

'Oh, my God.' echoed Henry Partridge. 'Hate it when my damned hunches come true. Have the bastards killed him, Peter?' Having already buried his angry face on the mantelpiece, the bringer of bad tidings slowly turned to face his companions. 'Let's pray not. They've rushed him to hospital... Just a chance it's a bungled hit and run and that he may pull through. Oh, God. *why*, whenever we get a good man in the world, who tries his damnedest to mend fences, does some maniac have to come along and put the clock back a thousand years?'

'... sympathize, old chap, but it seems as if those old fences were never meant to be mended. Get my drift?'

'I do, Henry. And it hurts. Why the hell do we go on with this? Is it worth it? Is anything worth it?'

'Got to keep trying, Peter. Everything takes time.'

Lord Brocklehurst had taken up the mantle of hope. 'Even at my age I can see it will be worth it if we never give up.'

'If you say so, Charles.' And with steady hands, another measure of fine brandy slid down the throats of at least two wise old men. The world always looked better through large bulb glasses.

The House of Baghdad

****

In Baghdad, the streets were alive with anxious and angry people. Could it be that the years of repression and torture were not just a long nightmare but part and parcel of Iraqi life - its very nature - its soul? But why? Why should they submit to dictator after dictator? Why must they stand and watch helplessly as their sons are dragged off to yet another war-front or torture chamber? Whose country was it, anyway? Why should one man be allowed to wreck the lives of good, honest working people? Why shouldn't they take to the streets and demand their rights - as they do in Russia?

'You think they'll give us our rights if we do what you're suggesting?' asked one old man who'd seen it all before and even knew what had happened in Russia.

'If they don't, we will fight.' insisted a young man, punching the air with his fist.

'What with?' asked the old man, looking the young man in the face with compassion whilst curling his bitter lip. His facial contortions were amazingly skilful. But then, he'd seen it all.

But the young man had not finished. 'Leave it to us younger ones, my friend. With respect, we must not allow these brutal, bitter old men to infiltrate the country again.'

'But they're here, son. How could this have happened without them?'

The young man was in a hurry. With a friendly squeeze of the old man's arm he rushed off down the street to gather some of his friends for 'the fight'.

Tony Sharp

****

By nightfall the news was better. Arid Aziz appeared to be pulling through. Both bullets had been removed 'just in time'. The doctors, it appeared, had done a remarkable job. With their skills, and Arid's strong constitution and will to live, the Sensible Arab Conservative Party, it was thought, would pick up even more popular support; the terrorists would be found and put on trial and everyone would rally round the brave PM.

In London, Prime Minister Bullock awoke to the news on radio. He picked up the phone and dialled Baghdad. There was always someone in Arid Aziz's office - day and night, and with the warm, personal relationship he'd already built up with his Iraqi counterpart, Mr Bullock knew he would not be denied a speedy answer to his genuinely anxious enquiry.

'Ah, thank you, Mr Bullock. It is most kind of you to telephone. Yes, I am pleased to inform you that Mr Aziz has not only survived but has been sitting up in bed, drinking coffee.' An astonished Mr Bullock responded to the Iraqi secretary with a sigh of relief and admiration for the patient. But he added a word of caution. 'This is very good news, Mr Hashif. Please convey my good wishes to Prime Minister Aziz and urge him to take things easy for a while.'

'But I can do better than that, Mr Bullock. I will transfer you direct to the hospital.'

'That's marvellous. Thank you.'

'Hold the line, please……'

'Hello, hello. John. How are you?'

'How are *you* would be more to the point, Arid?'

'I am fine, thank you, my friend. Just a little achy but that will soon pass - with a bit of luck.'

'You are amazing, Arid. Thank God you are in good hands.'

'The doctors were wonderful. If everyone in Iraq could get the same attention in an emergency I would be happy, indeed.'

'With you at the helm, Arid, at least they'll have a chance.'

'Thank you, my friend.'

'But get yourself well, first. Is there anyone to hold the fort while you're recovering? You know.......?'

Anyone I can trust, you mean? Ah,... trust. What an elusive concept, eh John?'

'Indeed.'

'But in answer to your question - yes, I think my deputy will do a fine job 'holding the fort', as you put it.'

'Good. Now, if there is anything I can do, please don't hesitate to ask.'

'John, my friend. *You* I trust - like this nurse, here.'

At the other end of the line Mr Bullock smiled. He knew of Arid's penchant for pretty young things and took it as yet another good sign that his friend was on the mend.

'I'll leave it to you, then. Phone me when you're back in action.'

'UMM. Won't be very long, now, John, if she keeps doing that.'

Mr Bullock laughed down the line and bade 'au revoir' to his courageous new partner in democracy. He hoped to God the terrorists would not try again. But, considering a former Prime Minister's miraculous escape from the supposed sanctity of 10, Downing Street, he began to wonder.

England was one matter; Iraq, another. And with Arid's determination to launch his country - even drag it - screaming into the twenty-first century (it might not necessarily be a step in the right direction), things could get very sticky indeed. Even if Colonel D-Day never returned, there would always be other wicked men to take his place.

Chapter 17

A great cheer went up in the Iraqi Chamber. Arid Aziz had appeared with a broad grin and a magnanimous wave to Members on both sides of the House. He prepared to take his seat with the minimum of delay but they would not let him. The cheering continued and he was forced to remain standing, acknowledging the admiration and good wishes of the whole House. Indeed, when at last the cheering subsided and he sat down on the Government front bench, the Leader of the Opposition - the ever effervescent Faisal Hussein - took up the initiative and delivered his own tribute to the PM's courage and tenacity and went on to say... 'And so, Honourable Members, I'm sure we would all agree that this despicable outrage upon our new democracy will serve only to strengthen our resolve. ('Hear, hear,' clucked MPs on both sides). And the perpetrators of such foul acts will see that nothing they do will alter the course of this democracy.' ('Hear hear, hear hear.')

Faisal Hussein sat down to the admiration of his own side and an acknowledgement of his act of decency from the Government benches. In fact, Arid rose again to thank the honourable gentleman personally for the sentiments and convictions expressed and added, 'And now, Honourable Members, I should like to take this opportunity to say I will not personally be pressing for the rescinding of the vote democratically reached against the extradition of Colonel Doomsday. To quote the words of the honourable gentleman opposite, "I would rather leave it to the Israelis to continue this immature pursuit".' Laughter broke out in the Chamber but Faisal Hussein, though pleased and touched by the PM's gracious acknowledgement of his philosophy, remained determined the PM should not overlook the important last part of his now famous quote. 'And 'I would rather forgive and forget'?'

'Forgive, I can, sir. Forget,... never.' ('Hear hear,' came from all sides of the House, and Faisal Hussein had been adroitly checked.)

But the PM had not finished. 'And while I am on my feet, gentlemen, or should I say - before I feel the need to sit out this afternoon's session - ('Don't tire yourself, Prime Minister. Sit down . It's all right by us,' came from several Members). 'No, no. I'm all right....I wish to urge upon you all the wisdom of pursuing our adopted line of pragmatism. Now, I know it is not the done thing in the West to advertise the fact one is pragmatic. To hell with all that. This is Iraq. We do things our way.'

At that remark, spontaneous cheering broke out in the Chamber and Arid's standing in the admiration stakes had risen at least another five points.

'I will go even further...' Several people in the public gallery - including the two English ex-pats who had vested interests in all this - bit their lips and wondered how far this incredible and already world-famous Prime Minister would, in fact, go. Would he throw over all traces of common sense, reason and expediency - as the UK had done - and allow any old Tom, Dick or Harry to enter the country? Or would he go completely mad and sign every contract that was offered from whatever quarter and leave them all to sue him or each other or everyone if things went wrong? But the PM remained calm, precise; unequivocal. 'It is clear, gentlemen, that we can have our cake and eat it.' Beyond that statement, he would not go. And the Englishmen in the gallery could relax again. It was one thing for Arid to admit to being pragmatic; another to actually broadcast every damned detail. Arid Aziz had sat down to a suddenly hushed and curious Chamber. To 'have our cake and eat it.' What did it mean? Increasingly, the PM had come out with confusing foreign expressions - complicating matters, talking in riddles. For some tastes, his gestures too often were those of a man in search of a part in an American 'soap'. It never seemed to dawn on many MPs that they were actually part of a 'soap'. The fact Dan Levy and Jim Rosenberg would be milling about - or the occasional cameraman could be seen lingering in the Members' toilets after a broadcast - never really impinged upon their political minds. Much as most Members respected both the PM and Faisal Hussein they believed both men tended to overdo things a bit, playing up to the camera...... Too many words, too many gestures - raising of the arms, turns of the head. Even Sodom the Lesser knew how to calm and control an audience before attending to his next murder. Nevertheless, when all was said and done, things were better now. At least Arid Aziz was approachable; one could even get near enough to shoot him. But his sense of humour worried some people. What was its meaning? Was he allowing the British and Americans to influence him - for the worse?

Arid was on his feet again. 'Honourable Members. Before I go and take a little rest, I would like to inform you of two very important engagements in my diary for next week. On Monday I fly to Tel Aviv for talks with Mr Shameer. It is our intention to work out that treaty on security and trade. And on Wednesday, I fly to Berlin for talks with Finance Minister Herr Fockel. Many of you already know that Germany will be offering Iraq a substantial aid-package in return for oil, and on the understanding that it remains our intention to maintain and develop our new democratic system. As long as that doesn't involve proportional representation, gentlemen, I will continue to be a happy man.'

At last the whole Chamber burst out laughing. On many issues, Members would continue to disagree with the PM. On this one, however, all were united. 'Could it be, gentlemen, you are beginning to appreciate my brand of pragmatism?'

On that happy note, Arid Aziz left the Chamber to huge applause from both sides. And most MPs waved their order papers with such a genuine feeling of admiration for their country's leader that many a British Prime Minister watching would have turned green with envy.

'Democracy we all welcome,' said one of the English ex-pats up in the gallery. 'But this is ridiculous.'

'Who cares?' responded his partner-in-crime. 'We have a hit on our hands.'

****

At home, Arid was made to put his feet up by Hattie, his American-born wife. She had come to Iraq before the war. Despite Sodom the Lesser - or Sodom the Greater - she would still have stuck it out just to be with her Arid. He was a lovely man: cuddly, funny, but sensible and strong. If he needed mothering, she'd be there. Besides, in bed - no mother ever had such luck. No, she had no complaints - she simply adored him. And he adored her. If he survived all they could throw at him in Iraq (barring further shootings, naturally) and could have the satisfaction that he had led his country irreversibly on the path of good democratic Government, he would consider retiring somewhere with his Hattie - maybe France, or Spain. Hattie herself had no particular desire to return to the States and live the life of a celebrity - partying and socializing all over the place and fussing over her coiffure. Chic she could be - when the occasion demanded. But she was much more comfortable in old jeans and pullovers - feeding the chickens or planting a fruit tree. She was no dummy, no intellectual sluggard. Her taste in books was catholic, comprehensive, sometimes deep. But she was no intellectual's intellectual; who the hell wanted to be one of those? She was merely intelligent, imaginative, fun - and very human. That was enough for her. It was enough for Arid and he counted himself the luckiest man alive. The occasional nurse apart, there was no substitute for Hattie.

With a smile she handed him his tea and sat down on the pouffe to be by his feet. He took a couple of sips and put the cup down on the sidetable. He began to stroke her hair and she leant back towards him. Without a sound she lay there, her head cupped in his hands, tender hands - stroking, loving; calming. He was supposed to be the patient but he did not want to be pampered - not tonight. He was content to be master - a gentle master in no hurry. In perfect peace, they stayed there - maybe for several minutes. Then Hattie sat up, turned and smiled. They kissed, and made for bed.

****

The plane touched down at Tel Aviv. The time: exactly 9 a.m. David Shameer held out a large hand to welcome his guest on the tarmac. It was unusual for a top Arab politician to come to Israel with such a positive and constructive attitude. It was their first meeting and, immediately, the Israeli Prime Minister could sense the warmth of human feeling emanating from the person of Arid Aziz with whom he'd held such pleasant telephone conversations. The feeling was mutual, despite Mr Shameer's reputation for maintaining the hard line and stubborn image. It was to be a meeting the world would not forget, for out of it would be born a new spirit of co-operation between Iraq and Israel, a spirit that - for as long as Arid stayed in power - would be difficult to break.

They soon arrived at Mr Shameer's official residence and began their discussions without delay. There were so many items they could have dealt with - if only there were sufficient time. But time - *time* - the enslaver of man, just ticked away. And Arid would soon have to go to Berlin, to Paris, to London, to... 'You must be careful of your health, Arid. After your frightful experience, I mean.'

'Thank you for your kind concern. But I feel fine. My lovely wife keeps me young.'

'Ah, give her my kindest regards, won't you?'

'I will, indeed.'

'Well, how are things going for you in that new Parliament of yours?. You're quite a star, these days. I'm rather envious.'

Arid laughed and looked kindly on his host. 'It's tough at times, of course. But I'm enjoying it. And so, it seems, are Mr Dan Levy and Jim Rosenberg.'

'They must be raking it in - with those TV ratings.'

'*We* get *our* share as well, you know.'

'Hope you do. Well now, what are the chances of getting any deal you and I work out ratified in your Chamber?'

'Well, despite the expected protestations - from all sides of the House, I might say - towards *any* deal with your country, I am convinced they are coming round to the realisation that our two States are on the same planet.'

Mr Shameer laughed heartily and leant across to his guest. 'I think,' he said deliberately, 'this is going to be a good meeting.'

In fact, the meeting was to become one of many. And even at this one, it was not long before protocol had been broken with brotherly pats on each other's backs together with a natural and irrevocable drift to 'Christian-name' terms. Reagan and Gorbachev may have started it but the David & Goliath meetings, as they came to be unkindly dubbed in the Middle East - 'the Dave & 'Arry' in the West - were destined to become a yardstick for how sticky problems should be tackled.

After lunch they would be joined by members of the inner Cabinet. But this first get-together was to be a one-to-one meeting, for there were delicate matters to be discussed which were not on the official agenda - and none more delicate than the question of Colonel Doomsday. 'As you probably read, the Leader of the Opposition - Faisal Hussein - made a very interesting statement that I managed to turn to my advantage.'

'I should imagine it wasn't the first of its kind, Arid?' The two men grinned at each other, while Arid continued: 'After saying he'd be voting against the Bill for the Colonel's extradition he went on to say, and I quote: "I would rather leave it to the Israelis to continue this immature pursuit of tired old men who are past posing a threat to any country. I would rather forgive and forget".'

'Huh. I can imagine the reaction in the Chamber.'

'Yes, it caused quite a stir. Anyway, the point I'm making, David, is that most of our people expect MOSSAD to make a move to track down the Colonel - if only for your own country's security. You and I both know, he should at least be 'monitored' if not, er, exactly.......'

'Hit?' David Shameer preferred to be succinct when he could. Besides, it was quite evident he was dealing with a man of the world.

'Let's put it like this, David. If Iraq resists the temptation (understandable though it is in the eyes of the world) to spend time and resources on dragging the Colonel back to the Middle East she stands to gain a great deal.'

'From Germany, you mean?'

'Not only from Germany but from Brazil and France - in terms, of course, of goodwill.' Arid tried one of his special winks on his host. Unlike the earlier uneasy response of Ambassador Bazrani who had quickly slipped back to Brazil, David Shameer's reaction to Arid's little foible was one of pure pleasure. He leant back and laughed out loud and made a mental note that should his host ever be in need of a job, he, Prime Minister Shameer, would not be ashamed to personally hire him for a cabaret spot on the Tel Aviv hotel circuit. Arid would be a smash hit - if he knew his own people.

'So you want us to 'get the Colonel' - while you look the other way?'

'I couldn't have put it better myself.'

'I'll speak to MOSSAD in the morning.'

'Good. Now we can get down to our little deal, eh?'

It was Mr Shameer's turn to wink. And the two men settled down to a cosy, private chat on 'equal' and very friendly terms.

Chapter 18

It was party-time again in Brazil. For this occasion, President Gonzalez had really lashed out on the music - courtesy of Herb Alpert himself with his Tijuana Brass. Yet another version of the Ronnie Biggs Rumba had topped the charts: the 'Reverend' Biggs, after all, could still cut a dash with the best of 'em. He still had plenty of muscle and people loved him. 'Let me tell ya, son. If people like ya, yoo can 'ave anything!'

'Thanks, Dad. You've given me plenty.' And with that, family smiles and love would break out like a rash on the backside. Biggs junior had topped the charts before - with a little help… But now it was Dad's turn - with the assistance of Tijuana Brass. Herb Alpert and his band had long been one of Dad's favourite sounds and, by means of singin' on the tape while sittin' on the loo, Ronnie had come up with a great new number. Besides, why should Lionel Bart have all the best tunes?

There was no sign of that monstrous drag queen who had entertained the licentious bishop at Manuel's last 'do'. Her evangelical work had been occupying so much of her time that it seemed her energy had been drained to the limit. But who could tell what she still got up to behind closed doors? Better than anyone, she knew there was more than one way to cure a sagging faith.

Nor, too, was there any sign of the Colonel. He had tendered his regrets to Manuel by phone, giving the excuse that he wished to catch up on all the news back home and make, as he put it, some delicate phone calls. The 'House of Baghdad' was due to be transmitted that night and Yudie needed to be alone - ready to telephone 'friends of the Cause' immediately after the broadcast. He had been informed that despite the vote against his extradition from Brazil the argument 'for' simply would not go away and enough Government backbenchers as well as Opposition Members had forced a re-opening of the debate. Rather like the eternal argument for the reintroduction of hanging in the UK, the 'extradition of Colonel Doomsday', it seemed, would continue to rear its head if only to satisfy MP's sensibilities towards a supposedly affronted or insecure public, hungry for justice. Yudie had no doubts that should his job as Prime Minister be put at risk, that damned Arid Aziz would find a way to change sides with the ease of an experienced and wily old python.

'Good to see you, Felix.' Manuel Gonzalez extended his arms to greet a man who had done so much in bringing a little order and dignity to Court life. Yet, from his old friend's response and demeanour the President detected there was something not quite right. Elizabeth, Felix's old English dancing partner, had died just two weeks ago and the old man had lost a proven confidante. His own 'mentor' sessions with the Colonel, too, seemed to have taken their toll. Despite his initial excitement over Yudie's Project Jerusalem, he had clearly become bored with the idea - rather like a small boy losing interest in a cheap toy; except the super-gun was anything but a cheap toy. No, now that he'd thought about it, the idea had become increasingly ominous - a nightmare in embryo and already he'd begun to have a few very peculiar dreams. God knows the horrifying experiences of the Second World War were enough to send more than a few shivers down anyone's back who'd been through it - the slaughter of innocent people, the treachery, betrayals and lies, the fear of being shot by one's own people, the sheer destruction and waste. But Project Jerusalem? If Yudie got his way (and who could be sure that eventually he would not?) no one could lie safe in his bed. Just one little nuclear bomb neatly dropped on New York during the Easter Parade and all hell would be let loose. Much as Felix had always held reservations about the New Yorkers, he instinctively felt Yudie's plan was no way to conduct foreign affairs. Colonel Doomsday would have to be stopped.

'How are things going in the mentor department?' Manuel Gonzalez was determined to drop a quiet word in Felix's ear before anyone else claimed the old man's attention.

'Very well indeed, Manuel. Too well, in fact.'

'Oh? Fancy a chat in my office in the morning - say, eleven o'clock?'

'I'll be there.'

'Why, - you old dog.' The rather shrill voice came from the other side of the room. And Manuel left Felix to it. A large German lady who had known 'the old dog' for years - back in the Fatherland - had only recently emigrated to Brazil but she had been invited, via Pepe Fernandez, to the President's party. She bounded over to where Felix stood and put out her arms. 'Goodness gracious me. It's Anna Schönberg, unless my eyes deceive me?'

'No, they do not deceive you. Anna Schönberg - at your service.' And without further ado she hugged him tight and plonked a huge kiss fully on his lips.

'Anna, my dear girl.' A noticeable blush coloured his fine old face and she sensed he still reserved an undoubtable affection for her. They had never consummated their love but, years before Felix's wife died, they had met at a small café near party headquarters in Bonn. Felix, or Fritz as he was known then, would often pop into the café after another hair-raising meeting - if only to calm himself down over a good cup of coffee and a good book. God knows how, willy-nilly, he'd been inextricably caught up with the propaganda and euphoria of it all, allowing himself to be swept along the crest of an unstoppable wave. For unstoppable it was: anyone declaring himself against the Fuehrer was considered a bad egg - or a traitor, in plain German. Tolerance was relegated to the mists of time. Yet through it all Fritz Krupp managed to retain his sanity. Perhaps it was the exalted position of the Krupp name, in the hierarchy of favoured families, which somehow afforded him the luxury of remaining a little less demonstrative than most of his contemporaries. Besides, it would have been a very odd Krupp indeed who made a point of sticking out like a sore thumb against a régime the head of the family so patently supported. And so it was that Anna Schönberg had never thought of challenging Fritz on his own views of the policies and events fast overtaking a worried world. His physical presence alone was enough to remove all doubt about his credentials and she had found herself increasingly drawn to him.

So now she had caught up with him - after all these years. Her husband had died five years ago, her family were all grown up with families of their own and she was still healthy and fancy free.

'Damn it. I'd almost forgotten what a good-looking woman you were, Anna.'

'Were?'

'Are.'

'Thank you, my dear sir. I would like to return the compliment and say, in all sincerity, that in all my years in the old country, I have never met a finer looking gentleman than your good self. And here you are in Brazil. My Rupert was a dear, make no mistake. But *you*, my dear Fritz, I have......'

'Shoosh, Anna. Felix is the name. You do understand?'

The old man looked kindly upon a suddenly hushed lady. 'Oh, of course. How silly of me. I.......'

'Esbano is the surname.'

'I see. You must tell me more when we have a chance.'

'I will, my dear... but I can see Manuel beckoning me. Must be important, my dear. One should never keep one's President waiting, eh?'

'Indeed not. You do what you have to do, while I mingle. I'll see you a little later?' She smiled the promise of good things to come. And notwithstanding his advanced years, he was still a man.

'It will be a pleasure.' With an old-fashioned kiss of her hand, Felix Esbano took his leave and joined the President, already heavily engaged in conversation with Pepe Fernandez. Both men wore worried looks and, as Felix drew near, a tinge of anxiety pierced his worldly breast.

'Ah, Felix,' intimated the President, 'we have just heard through Ambassador Bazrani that MOSSAD have planned a little operation in these parts which could - shall we say - upset the apple-cart? Need I elaborate?'

'Oh dear,' swallowed Felix. 'that would implicate both the Colonel and me, I presume?'

'I'm afraid so, Felix,' confirmed Pepe Fernandez, 'we were all hoping Iraq would put that final nail in the extradition coffin and bury the damned thing for good. But even if their Parliament throws out the revised Bill, we have reason to believe Arid Aziz has given a nod and a wink to the Israelis to, er…..do their worst?'

'Oh, my God.' Ninety-eight years was a damned good innings by anyone's standards. But Felix Esbano was still enjoying life. And with Anna Schönberg newly-arrived - ready and willing - he judged there was more to come. Why should he - now, of all times - have his past dragged up by people who could have little conception of the intricacies and reasons for non-resistance during the years of the Third Reich? How could they possibly believe all Germans were bad because they fought for their country? Wouldn't each one of them have done the same if he had been a German Gentile?

'But isn't there anything you can do to stop these people entering the country?' A momentary shiver passed along Felix's spine with the thought of remaining a sitting duck while professional killers freely entered Brazil and, unhindered, made determined tracks for him.

'We will do our best, Felix. But you know how difficult it is to scan everyone.' The President shot Felix a wry smile as if to suggest he should count himself lucky to have escaped the clutches of 'authority' for so long. But he had not finished. 'The Israelis are clever little devils, are they not? And it's almost impossible to watch the whole coastline - just supposing they attempt to enter the country in that rather wet and uncomfortable way. Bit old hat, wouldn't you say?' The President seemed to be enjoying himself and his remarks offered precious little comfort to an old ex-pat warrior, already in the throes of a dwindling confidence in the Brazilian system. But the President had more to say. 'And who knows? They might merely activate sleeping cells - already here in Brazil?'

My God. Had Manuel Gonzalez turned out to be a slimy, treacherous bastard, after all? Was he prepared to sacrifice a dear old man who had more than paid his dues to society - just for the sake of good relations with Israel, Iraq, Saudi Arabia, Syria, Egypt,...... the whole damned caboodle? Was he.......?

'Don't worry, my dear friend. I will make a personal plea for you to be spared. Let's face it, Felix, they are really more interested in getting the Colonel. Now, here is where *you* come in.......'

This was it, thought Felix. In return for his life, he would be required to divulge all he knew about the Colonel, all he knew of his plans for the super-gun, his ultimate ambitions, his thinking,......everything. If he finally betrayed the Colonel, his own life......what could it amount to...... one, two, three more years at the most, would be spared? He'd even be able to make up for lost time with the magnificent Anna Schönberg, and, like more than one of his old comrades, go out with a bang.

'Tomorrow at eleven, then, Felix?' The President remained nonchalant.

'Um?..... Oh, yes. Yes.' Felix's mind had wandered free, free as a bird - soaring over the plain - up, up and swooping down; up again, over the countryside and down onto the first available fruit tree, shaking it with his unusually heavy landing, shaking it to see who would pick up the fruit that had fallen to the ground. The 'humans' would pick up the fruit and laugh and giggle and look up and call him funny names. He had shaken the tree of life and spilled the fruit on to the ground and they had stooped to pick it all up. And he would just have to fly away again and seek new pastures. His life was nearly over and no one would be there to comfort him. He had reached the end of the line - caught between the Devil and the deep blue sea.

'My dear Felix. *There* you are!' Anna had finished circulating and had homed back to the old warrior. 'But my dear man. You look as if you've just seen a ghost. What happened?' Manuel Gonzalez and Pepe Fernandez had together left Felix with his thoughts and to the attentions of his new dancing partner. 'Now, come on. Cheer up, and let's boogey.' But Felix was in no mood for such trifles. His mind and soul remained heavy with concern, heavy with the decision he would soon have to make. His life was on the line - together with the Colonel's. But Felix was the man upon whose strong but old shoulders - once more burdened with conscience - Manuel Gonzalez had laid such awesome responsibility.

Chapter 19

With apologies made, and a hurried peck on the cheeks, Felix Esbano finally extricated himself from the bosom of Anna Schönberg. She had kicked up a bit of a fuss about his leaving. But it couldn't be helped. He had to be alone. And with a sinking heart he was driven back to his flat to chew over what the President and Foreign Minister had said to him.

What the hell should he do? If he betrayed the Colonel - but that, after all, was what he was really doing all the time - he should, at least, do it properly. If he could surreptitiously take some pictures with his micro-camera while Yudie was in the loo, he would be betraying the man for a good reason - saving the world from the ultimate showdown. It would be so easy to do - in fact, it would be his duty to do it. And with clear, unequivocal evidence of Yudie's plans firmly in the President's hands, Felix would be let off the hook. Even the Israelis might view the old German warrior in a different light and allow him to live out the rest of his twilight years in peace.

Felix paid the taxi-man and entered the lobby of the building. He took the lift to his apartment and stepped across to his door to put the key in the latch. Already he could hear the phone buzzing on his writing desk. He turned the key and stepped inside. He closed his door and hurried to the phone as fast as his legs would carry him. 'Hello?'

'Felix? It's Yudie here. Can you come over tonight? I know it's late and I'm sorry if I disturbed your evening, but.......'

'My dear fellow. Of course you haven't.' Felix was determined to use the occasion as a test of his famous self-control. 'In fact, I've only just returned from Manuel's party,' he added as nonchalantly as possible.

'Oh, how was it? I'm afraid I had too much to do.'

'Well, you know about these things, don't you? I met up with a long-lost lady friend of mine I haven't seen in years. But enough's enough,' he lied.

'I know what you mean. Well, if you feel too tired, let's leave it till tomorrow morning, then?'

'I think it would be better, if you don't mind. A good night's sleep might even make a new man of me.'

'But I like you as you are, Felix.' They both laughed and agreed upon 11 a.m. for a good chat, lunch and a car (Yudie insisted) to pick Felix up and bring him back for his siesta. After what Yudie had lined up for him, he would need it.

Felix replaced the phone on the hook and sat down to think.

Damn it. In his anxiousness to appease the Colonel, he'd omitted to say he already had an appointment at 11 with the President. By golly, things were hotting up. Yudie had, no doubt, been informed from some little dicky bird that MOSSAD were out for him. Why was Yudie seeking Felix's advice? He'd already told him enough, perhaps too much about his insane plans to bomb America when he'd re-establish himself in power in his beloved Baghdad. Huh. What a laugh. How the hell did he think he could swing that one? Even Adolf Hitler knew his limitations (though he would never admit it to the world). He knew he'd have problems if America entered the war. Blast those Japs. Why should Colonel Doomsday be any luckier? But that was the trouble. The man knew no limits. And to his mind his banishment from Iraq was but temporary. His very being, his bullish arrogance, his tunnel vision, his faith in God, all drove him on - on and on and on. He would not have had to look as far as America to see a perfect example of this type - forced from power, tearful in disbelief that such a thing could ever happen - wondering what had hit her. But he had chosen not to look. He was destined to lead, to lead his people from disaster to disaster. If *they* wanted to kick and scream in the process, all well and good. For himself, he would just lead. After all, he could always witness plenty of kicking and screaming in the properly appointed torture chambers. Oh, how he missed them. How he missed watching his men gouging out the eyes of political 'misfits' or lopping off the fingers of someone who dared to spit in his monstrous, greedy face. Despite its obvious corruption, life in Brazil, for him, was becoming too predictable, too comfortable, too easy. Even his affair with Maria, steamy as it continued to be, presented too few problems, too few edges. He liked to fight for something. If he didn't have to fight, he'd begin to lose interest. Oh yes - the edge was beginning to go, the fear, the danger, the adrenaline - the raison d'être. Perhaps his new role as a fugitive from MOSSAD would provide all the adrenaline any man could wish for.

Felix got up from his chair and walked into the bathroom to make ready for bed. After his ablutions, he walked into the bedroom and sat down on the bed. He picked up the phone and dialled the President's number.

'Ah, Felix. I'm glad you've phoned. Pepe and I have been worried about you. I hope you've not taken my warnings too much to heart?'

'How would *you* react to such news if you were me?' In all the long years of their association and friendship, it was the first time Felix had shown hurt towards his President. The point was taken and Manuel decided to come clean. 'Listen, Felix. It *is* a very serious situation - all joking aside. But, at the risk of sounding arrogant, there is nothing much which I cannot fix in this country. If you play ball with me, MOSSAD will not touch you. I think you get my drift?'

'I know what I have to do.'

'Good. And since you have taken the trouble to phone me, Felix, I think we can postpone our 11 o'clock meeting until after you've seen Yudie. Do you agree?'

'My thinking entirely, Manuel.' Felix had never been one for tittle-tattle and there seemed no need to mention Yudie's phone call. Besides, despite the man's monstrous reputation, he had found himself warming to the comparative newcomer to the ranks of Brazilian heavies. 'I'll report back to you as soon as I have the material.'

'Good man, Felix. Get some rest now, and call me soon. 'Bye for now.'

'Bye, Manuel.'

With the phone replaced on the hook, Felix slipped back the sheets and eased himself into bed. Ah, nice. He set the alarm for 8 a.m. Normally he would lie awake in bed for an hour before dropping off, or he'd read some of his own philosophy papers in order to make himself sleepy, yet tonight, despite his anxiousness over his 'part in the plot', he was going to be lucky. Within five minutes he was out cold. He slept like a log. And when his alarm bell buzzed dead on 8 a.m. he was already awake - refreshed and confident.

Yes, he'd always believed in fate. After all, what could one really do about it? But supposing someone knew what decisions you would make - in advance? Supposing someone in the next world could foresee every move you make and could see every pitfall, every danger, every......? Why can't one appeal to that person or spirit for guidance - to prevent that awful thing happening? Why can't we do deals with the spirits?

Even while he shaved, his whole life seemed to flash before him. He'd had this feeling before, not so long ago. Perhaps, deep down, he damned well knew his time was running out. But he was still fit - and looking forward to his centenary. What a party he'd throw. But this business over the Colonel - and more ominously, an intimation from the President, that the Israelis might also come for him, unless... Ah, yes, a nice bit of blackmail had not come amiss. The bastard. After all these years of 'serving' him - in return for which, admittedly, he'd enjoyed a very comfortable existence - could he look forward only to an ignominious end to their friendship?

By 9 a.m., he had finally made up his mind. With his micro-camera neatly concealed in his jacket pocket, he sat down to read a few chapters of Graham Green's Monsignor Quixote, a delightful little novel that somehow had never failed to calm him and put him in a more than otherwise mellow mood in situations like this. Come to think of it, the friendship and personal rapport he'd built up with the Colonel since the man arrived in the 'parish', was not too dissimilar to that of the Spanish priest and Communist mayor in Greene's story. True, the characters in the book could hardly be described as murderers or mere heavies by any stretch of the imagination. Yet, there was something charmingly attractive in the conspiratorial friendship of Felix and Yudie - like two naughty schoolboys - that could appeal, perhaps, to the Israeli's sense of humour? No? No, 'spose that would be asking a little too much of them.

At 10.30 the car arrived. The chauffeur rang Felix's bell and waited.

'Mr Felix Esbano?'

'Yes, thank you. I'll be down in a jiffy.'

'All right sir. I'll wait.'

As they prepared to set off in the direction of Yudie's villa, all kinds of thoughts fought for possession of Felix's mind. But as he fastened his seat-belt and looked across with a smile at the driver, smartly attired in his blue suit and peak cap, he decided to let things take their own course. The only thing he'd attempt to engineer would be to get another look at those super-gun plans and snap pictures of them while Yudie was taking a leak. He could hardly imagine the man letting him take them home with 'Here, would you like to borrow these, old man? Let me have them back when you can'. No, he'd have to find a way to snap them when Yudie wasn't looking.

The car pulled up outside the villa and Felix could see Yudie anxiously looking out of one of the larger windows. The chauffeur opened the car door for Felix who stepped out, thanked the man with a comment on his very circumspect attire and attitude, and made for Yudie's front door. With a rather strained smile across his face, Yudie opened the door for his friend and mentor. With little delay, he showed him into the study and the two men sat down to……..

'Felix, I'm worried.'

'I can see that. Get it off your chest, my friend. That's why I'm here.'

'You are the only one I can tell, apart, of course, from Mustafa.'

'Go on.'

The Colonel got straight to the point. 'It's MOSSAD They're after me, and, I'm told, they are very interested in your whereabouts. My dear Felix.......'

Felix knew there'd be no point in feigning surprise or shock. No, it would be much better calmly to suggest a positive plan to deal with this new situation. 'Well,' he began, as if he were delivering one of his famous lectures, 'after spending many delightful years here in Brazil, Yudie, I suppose I cannot expect to get off entirely, er...... scot-free, as they say?'

'But you are.....'

'An old man?' Felix smiled and continued with the balming process. 'For myself, I am hardly concerned. But for you,... Where, may I ask, or should I say from whom, did you glean this information, if information it is - rather than tittle-tattle?'

'I'm afraid it's serious and I'm sorry, Felix: I'm not at liberty to disclose the source, even to you. I trust you understand?' Felix's mind was working up to full throttle. Now he'd have no conscience about filming the documents on the super-gun and handing them to the President as soon as...... 'But I want you to keep these'. Could Felix be dreaming? What the hell was Yudie doing opening his safe and getting out those lethal documents? If they ever got into the wrong hands... Wrong hands?... 'Into thine hands I commend my project... Oh Lord Esbano, can you refuse Project Jerusalem?'.... Felix's mind came down to earth. 'But you said they'd be coming for me, too?'

Yudie smiled at the old man. 'I don't believe they will touch you.'

'If they know I have these, they most certainly will. What *can* you be thinking?'

'Trust me, Felix.' How often in his long, turbulent life had Felix been subject to that notoriously earnest yet loaded appeal? And now, at the age of 98, he is hearing the same plea. "Trust me". Was this extraordinary newcomer to Brazil, this ex-Colonel, ex-dictator, this murderer (if those stories were to be believed) planning to fly off again somewhere - leaving Felix Esbano holding the baby? If Felix declined to accept the super-gun plans, Yudie would surely suspect him - not only of weakness or sheer timidity but of the treachery which so often accompanies such negativity. After all they had discussed - all they had shared in calm, intelligent conversation over fine liquor and cigars - it would not do for Felix to let down his new friend and refuse to hold the plans in safe keeping until......

'So, where are you thinking of flying? Back to Baghdad?' Felix had found it hard to resist a little tease but there was nothing in his voice or face to suggest he was anything other than concerned for his friend.

'Eventually, of course. All I ask of you is that you 'bury' these plans somewhere until the heat is off. Will you do that for me?'

'My dear fellow... . Felix's thoughts raced on. Once in his care, these plans, whether they were the originals or duplicates would implicate him, willy-nilly. Yet, if by passing them on to the 'authorities', he could save the world from the final catastrophe, he could at least salvage a vestige of his fast-dwindling honour.

'Where will you put them? In the President's safe?' The Colonel allowed himself a half-hearted chuckle and Felix felt obliged to join him.

'Very funny. Do you take me for a fool?' The words were out of his mouth. Before he could retract them, he knew he'd committed himself in the eyes of his friend to safeguarding the plans from the eyes of all officialdom.

So the die was cast. There was no going back. If the Colonel came out of this thing alive, Felix would be considered an accomplice to the crime if the plans got into the wrong hands - and his life would not be worth living.

Oh, God. What had he done? For too long, he had lived the life of peace; he had prided himself on his civility, courtesy and wise counselling. Would his last pupil be the trigger to his own demise? Were the fates about to conspire in his long-delayed, cruel comeuppance or shameful downfall?

Chapter 20

Back in his flat, Felix plonked down the file of Project Jerusalem on his desk in the study. Oh, the ironies of life. What was the betrayal of one man compared with saving the world from ultimate disaster? For in this ex-Nazi's hands, lay the key to Mother Earth's salvation. Would Hell ever understand? Would it forgive? The earth could hardly be expected to show gratitude.

He made himself a cup of coffee and sat down to take his final look before photographing each sheet with his trusty micro-camera. With the original file in his possession (unless Yudie had palmed him off with duds), there was really no need to do this. But habits die hard and Felix's memory was still in perfect order. My God, there could be little doubt Manuel Gonzalez would show considerable interest in this file and would doubtless congratulate his old friend on a job well done.

In a few minutes the task was complete. Felix deposited the file and film in his safe and returned to his desk to ring the President.

'My God,' gasped Manuel Gonzalez. - 'To think I have been wining and dining this monster, harbouring him from every conceivable retribution, allowing gratification with my wife and all the while he'd been planning a little bombing campaign that would involve us all.'

'Well, Manuel, at least you have your worst fears confirmed.'

'Yes, indeed. And I have you to thank for bringing this episode to a head, if not to an end.'

Ah, the President was getting to it. Felix's reward would be spelt out loud and clear - unequivocally; irreversibly: MOSSAD could have the Colonel on condition Felix was spared. No matter what ghastly operations Fritz Krupp had been involved in, no matter what directives he had issued that had brought about swift elimination of innocent lives, so long ago, the life of Felix Esbano - honoured citizen of the Republic of Brazil - would remain sacrosanct.

But the President, if nothing else, remained a politician.

'I have to be seen to be doing something about Nazi runaways, Felix,' he continued, 'even if nothing happens, in practice. Do you get my point?'

"Seen to be doing something". Perhaps this was another of those little epigrams that somehow stuck unhealthily to the person of Manuel Gonzalez and continued to be the source of either irritation or amusement to onlookers, intermediaries, or family.

Like 'Matters of State' and 'Seeing our way clear', 'seen to be doing something' was beginning to take on the ghostly guise of an English Civil Service Department. In all his long, languishing years in Brazil - eating, drinking and living it up in return for a few odd seminars on philosophy - Felix Esbano would never in his wildest dreams have imagined a Brazilian President to admit to being 'seen to be doing something'. Though officially Protestant himself, Felix at least possessed an imagination. It was inconceivable a true Brazilian would ever have to fall back on Protestant practices of deception (he had plenty of his own) in the face of a Public, hungry for information. In Brazil, everything was expected to be corrupt - it was accepted; and no excuse was expected from a public who couldn't care less about information. Accountability had never featured in a truly Brazilian dictionary. So why should it suddenly appear from nowhere?

'But my dear Felix. You have nothing to worry about. Have I ever let you down? All things are possible in Brazil. *You* should know that.'

'Yes,' replied Felix wistfully.

'Now, come on, old friend. Cheer up. I'm busy again with our Finance Minister today. But tomorrow morning I could see you earlyish, say 10?'

'All......'

'I'll send a car for you. Mustn't let that file fall into the wrong hands, eh?' The wrong hands. Which were the right ones?

'Do you expect me to be mugged as soon as I step outside this flat?'

'Can't be too careful, Felix. I advise you to stay in tonight.'

'Oh?'

'Just in case Yudie decides to, ...'

'Grouse on me, as the English would put it?'

'Can't put anything past him. We must be careful.'

'All right, all right.'

'If you like, I'll send a security man along to keep you company. Or perhaps you have much better plans?' The President ventured a chuckle. He knew Felix's penchant for buxom women.

And Anna Schönberg's statistics, from what he had gleaned at the party, appeared more than able to fit the bill. Felix smiled to himself. 'No, no, thank you, Manuel. No security man necessary. As for Anna Schönberg, much as I adore her I think a nice quiet night on my own will be best.'

'Best for what? Sorry Felix. Just teasing. Must go. See you in the morning. 'Bye, my friend. And thanks for your good work.'

The phone was firmly replaced on the President's hook. But Felix put his phone down with a heavy heart. The deed had been done. He had betrayed his new friend, Yudie, who had opened his soul to him. Felix Esbano had accepted the Project Jerusalem file for safe keeping, a file that could only be entrusted to a madman or.......what? Responsible person? What responsible person could ever view it with anything other than utter contempt or horror? What responsible person could dismiss it with a nonchalant wave of the hand, or simply lock it away in the safe for a rainy day? God knows the number of occasions back in Germany in the '40s when matters had begun to get out of hand, when the tide had finally turned in favour of the Allies, when tempers began to fray, dreams faded and hopes were dashed; when the Fuehrer would bang his fist down on the table and splutter obscenities in outrageous tantrums, when officers squirmed and flushed or stood their ground with shaking knees and wet pants. And Felix had been there. How could he forget that one occasion when the tension generated in the room was such that he couldn't decide whether to pee or shit himself? The fact he wanted to indulge in both pleasures at the same time was really neither here nor there. If circumstances had been different, he would have laughed the whole thing off as a one-off abandonment of self-control.

But now - it was as if he himself had become the Fuehrer incarnate, strutting alone in his room - with a secret weapon in the safe, a weapon that, with its modern and devastating technical accuracy, could launch a war to end all wars. For this reason alone, some would welcome such a weapon. But the nations of the world had grown up - even Iraq. The antics of Sodom the Lesser had been truncated only just in time. And if Felix played his part right, the chip off the old block would never be allowed to succeed in his avowed ambition. Shame the sacrificial lamb had seemed so colourful.

Felix's hour of temptation had come and gone. His flush of personal power had defused itself as quickly as it had risen into being. He was an old man - and an old man should do the decent thing. The decent thing? Perhaps Yudie was already on his way over to the flat? Perhaps he'd send his chauffeur along again - this time with a feeble excuse that he'd left something in Felix's flat, or he'd come to deliver a message, a message or a......*bang*!. And Felix would be dead, dead as a....... He switched on the television set to relieve his growing anxiety. Maybe........ Oh, *no*. It was that damned 'House of Baghdad' soap opera again. But this time it was different - the camera zoomed in to a close-up of a dead man slumped over the lap of a delirious student. The camera switched to a crowded Chamber of MPs, shouting and screaming and then to a whimsical Prime Minister trying to appear as cool and collected as an Englishman - then to an American in a chair who smiled and simply shrugged his shoulders like a Frenchman. The programme presenter came on the air and peered full face to announce that that was 'Yesterday in Parliament'. 'Today', he went on, with the most cynical smile Felix had seen in a long while, 'we hope to bring all of you watching at home another gem - yes, another debate on an issue that never quite goes away - the extradition of Colonel Doomsday. And so, without further ado, we are taking you over to the Chamber, live in 'The House of Baghdad' ".

Felix poured himself a large scotch and soda and slumped into his leather sofa which he kept mainly for visitors and for the rare occasions when he was feeling particularly tired or lazy. Today, however, he was feeling neither tired nor lazy -merely anxious. His agitation was compounded by the day's events which had witnessed a worried Colonel who had deposited Project Jerusalem in his lap as if it were a brand-new novel, hot off the press (or was it a red-hot potato?); and there had been the President, who, so far, had done little to alleviate either his worst fears or his shame. And now this TV broadcast, with a picture of a dead man as an hors d'ouevre, followed by……..

Jesus. Even Felix remembered watching a clip of the attempted hijacking of the Spanish Parliament. That was frightening enough. But now, someone had suddenly produced a gun at the back of the Prime Minister's head. A member of his own Party, it seemed, had decided this was the time, in the full glare of publicity, to put an end to the career of a man whose only crime was to attempt to drag Iraq into the twenty-first century. The twenty-second would just have to wait. With one shot, the assailant could pull the country back to where it belonged……. The Middle Ages had never properly been appreciated. Here was another chance for Iraq……. Felix's eyes were glued to the television screen but mercifully, in an instant, another member of Arid Aziz's team, sitting behind the would-be assassin, spotted the man's ungainly action in taking out the pistol from under his jacket and smartly leant over and knocked the gun from his hand. There was instant uproar and, amid an unceremonious bundling of the terrorist out of the Chamber by beefy-looking stewards, a gawping public were treated to yet another dish of the Baghdadian day. The presenter even had time to discuss the producer, Dan Levy, while a wayward camera zoomed into his burly figure sitting up in the gods with a contented smile stretching his cigar-filled mouth.

'Ladies and Gentlemen. We offer our apologies to you at home for this truncated transmission of 'The House of Baghdad' but we hope you will join us again next week at the same time.'

Truncated transmission or no, Dan Levy still had a hit on his hands. And whether each programme lasted thirty or five minutes it mattered not - just so long as these Arabic histrionics kept rolling. And so long as his bank balance continued to expand, he'd allow not a word said against his playful hosts.

But Felix Esbano saw nothing to laugh about. This day was fast becoming the watershed of his long and eventful life. Everything seemed to converge upon this hour, an hour during which the only missing piece was for a couple of MOSSAD members to burst into the flat and shoot him point blank. Even the whisky was beginning to affect him in a strange way. His normal capacity had never been in doubt - for he could drink a professional lush under the table with no trouble at all and still 'come out fighting'. Yet now it seemed a case of his pickled innards at last breaking out in revolt. No, he would not go out this way. He got up from the sofa and walked over to the bookcase from which he withdrew his treasured copy of Monsignor Quixote. If he was to die, he would die reading Graham Greene. Yudie could sit on top of his own super-gun if he wished. Felix Esbano would take his communion with Father Quixote and end his days in the tranquillity of his own monastic flat - far from the madding crowd.

He walked into the bedroom and placed the book on the bed. Then he went back into the study and sat down at his desk to write his note. He had always been methodical - retaining, as if by Divine Providence, the German characteristic of order. But for a personal touch of capriciousness, the note would be precise and clear. No one reading it would have any doubt as to what he or she should do.

'Dear World,' it began, 'I go now to meet my Maker upon whose mercy I rely. For all the unspeakable horrors brought to bear upon you by the German Nation in the two World Wars, I beg your forgiveness. And I would be failing in my duty if I did not take up the mantle of peace as expressed in the constitution of the present German Republic. The other nations of the world should be glad the new Germany embraces such an ethos. They should, therefore, refrain from encouraging us to take up arms every time someone gets up to a little mischief outside the boundaries of NATO. I pray that MOSSAD does not think even less of me for taking this way out. But it is my choice. And at least they will have satisfaction in the sure knowledge their organisation can never be taken lightly. The plans of Colonel Doomsday are here for all the world to see. I will have done my duty to humanity. I have saved you the trouble of photographing the file. Please open the top right-hand drawer of this desk for the combination of the safe in which will be found Project Jerusalem together with the film.
    Fritz Krupp
    pp. Felix Esbano

NB. As a rider to this file, I think you should know that the Colonel has something else up his sleeve. During one of our frequent meetings, he intimated an outrageous alternative method in the destruction of New York - yes, an almost casual blitz one might say - a totally unexpected dropping of a nuclear bomb by a harmless-looking jet airliner. I think you will agree this man, with whom I had struck up a remarkable friendship and had grown to like, should be stopped in his tracks. A joke's a joke; but you ignore this one at your peril.

I have had a long life and I now have few regrets. Happy hunting.

FK'

It was a peaceful night. And the pills worked beautifully.

Chapter 21

The news broke in all the papers around the world……..
'NAZI COMMITS SUICIDE IN BRAZILIAN FLAT', stated most of the European rags with clinical inaccuracy.

'HE WAS A LOVELY OLD MAN, SAYS LANDLADY', blazoned itself across Brazilian papers and magazines together with articles of remembrance and respect from the President downwards.

'MOSSAD ON THE WAR-PATH', warned British journalist Dave Fletcher, having set himself up as an untouchable, non-aligned and rich ex-BBC correspondent tapping away on his word processor in his clean, 'non-aligned' flat overlooking Lake Geneva.

Not a word was seen to come from the pen of John Broadbridge who, it was thought, had succumbed more to the balming influence of the Caliph and his splendid liquor than to a self-destructive jealousy of Dan Levy and his TV success.

On Brazilian television, it was as if a world leader the calibre of Winston Churchill had just passed away and nothing short of a state funeral would suffice in his honour. And Mustafa, glued to the TV set and in an attempt to comfort a very anxious boss, could not recall seeing so many Moira Stewart look-a-likes bearing down on him from the screen. But suddenly, the face of the President appeared - seated at his desk in the Presidential Palace. Colonel Doomsday leaned forward in anticipation.

'Fellow citizens,' began Manuel Gonzalez gloomily, 'today I bring you sad news indeed, for, from our midst, a man of outstanding dignity and courage has been taken. Some people would say he had been too lucky and deserved to reap some sort of comeuppance for past sins or omissions. But Jesus is reported to have said: "He who is without sin among you, let him cast the first stone". And who are we, dear friends, to argue with that? For my part, I would like to assure you that whatever sins - whether of commission or omission - attending our dear brother departed, Brazil, this day, has lost a good citizen and advocate of peace. I refer, of course, to the late Felix Esbano. Some people say he was a racist,' (at this, Mustafa laughed over the President's euphemism, whilst Yudie simply shrugged his shoulders), 'others, that he was simply a victim of circumstances, hemmed in by the pressures of a great nation rising from the ashes of an ignoble defeat at the hands of greedy, vengeful victors of World War 1. Whatever may be the truth of the man's past, we know, to our constant delight and gratitude, that Felix Esbano never failed to do his best in enriching our society by his ever-popular seminars, his availability to all in need of counsel, his charity work and his humour in dealing with the most tricky and delicate of problems. And it is about this last aspect of his character that I should like to speak to you tonight......'

What the hell was Manuel Gonzalez up to? His speech so far was sickly enough. Surely he was not about to spill the beans about the Colonel and Project Jerusalem? But the flow of the President's soliloquy seemed unstoppable. As he rabbited on, Yudie's face took on the guise of a man not only doomed to the gallows, but one who'd been fattened up for the kill. His present life-style could hardly be described as that of a common thief - it was the envy of most of

Manuel's Ministers, many of whom, having sampled the joys of Maria's talents, had been smartly dropped by her after only one session. What was the special secret of this outsider, this ex-dictator, this alleged mass-murderer? He had not only dined on the best food and wine available in Brazil but he could still command the attention of the President that few of them really enjoyed. What had this man got - besides money and a big cock?

'I want to talk about a so-called Project Jerusalem.'

What? Had the President gone mad? No statesman, Western, Eastern or even Middle Eastern worth his salt, would dream of divulging such information. The fool. Fancy blowing the chance of trapping the Colonel in quiet secrecy once and for all. What the hell was he playing at, if not a clever and final turn of the screw?

'Well, at least we know now what sort of person we're dealing with.' Mustafa had never had any illusions about Manuel Gonzalez's motives. The bastard had extracted stacks of money from his boss - one way or another - and, the fact he allowed Yudie's affair with Maria to continue, only suggested he was dangling him on a string until a convenient time - either to demand even more or to cut him loose. The wolves would do the rest. If MOSSAD had a free run on the Colonel, Manuel would be in line for yet another tasty back-hander. Either way, he couldn't lose. The whole thing stank to high Heaven.

'What are you thinking?' Yudie looked across to his faithful bodyguard. But Mustafa had become more than that. He had blossomed into a true friend and would go through hell to protect his boss. Moreover, he was intelligent and imaginative - yet he saw no reason to leave the Colonel. Any decent psychiatrist would have given up on him in a week or taken the money and run.

'I have an idea, sir.'

'As they say - shoot.'

'It may sound a little far-fetched, but I think it will work.'

'All right. Let's have it.'

'Well, first I think we should contact the President and commiserate over Felix's death. Then we should ask to attend the funeral. That way, supposing he agrees - and I'm sure he will - he'll inform the Israelis who will doubtless be there to pick us up. Only, we won't be there.'

'Fine, so far. Where's the far-fetched bit?'

'Promise not to laugh?'

'Promise.'

'OK. I will go to the local mortuary and pick out a couple of stiffs.' (Yudie stifled a guffaw. After all, a promise is a promise).... 'You know, those with no dependants and all that. I'll drop the man a good tip to keep his mouth shut and bring them back here.......'

'Then we make our escape?'

'Not without a fire, sir. I'll pick out two guys as near as damn it to our type, cover them in petrol, light 'em up, and away we go.'

'On the day of Felix's funeral?'

'You've got it. Of course, it has to be well timed. But I'll do it - for you, sir.'

Mustafa smiled at Yudie who returned the gesture with a slow shake of his head. 'What a find I have in you, Mustafa. I suppose you got up to these sort of tricks when you were with that Maxwell man?'

Mustafa laughed and waited upon his boss for an analysis of his wild plan.

'Let's go for it.' shouted the Colonel with abandon. 'Let's live a little dangerously, my friend.'

'I thought that's what we'd been doing ever since we arrived here?' The two men chuckled together and decided to put Phase One into operation.

'All right Mustafa. I'll ring him myself.'

'Right, sir.' Mustafa handed the phone to his boss, while the Dobermann growled gently in the background. Perhaps he had some inkling of his and his owner's fate.

'Is that the President?'

'President Gonzalez here. Oh, it's you, Yudie. Have you heard the news?'

'Of course. I'm very upset. We had become such good friends.'

'So had he and I. He was a grand old fella, wasn't he? Are you attending the funeral?'

'Well, of course - if I'm invited.'

'You are invited, my friend - you and Mustafa.'

'Thank you. Then we will be there.'

'I will let you know the date and time as soon as I have them. By the way, I hope my TV broadcast didn't upset you?'

'Whatever gave you that idea?' Yudie remained determined to keep calm and show no fear. Every remark the President made seemed loaded. 'At least you eventually pooh-poohed the idea of Project Jerusalem.'

'Wherever did you learn that hyphened expression, Yudie?'

'From Mustafa. He's been to some very strange places in his time.'

The President burst out laughing. It had the effect of releasing the tension and gave Yudie time to take the initiative. 'Nor did you mention my name. I think you did a good job in quashing one of my best efforts.' The President laughed again and assured the Colonel that in spite of Felix's revelation of his plans to blow up New York, he was determined to assuage the fears of the public that the author of such a potentially monstrous crime would never be allowed a free hand - even in Brazil - and that, in any case, the whole idea was too ridiculous for words. It could never be taken seriously.

'But it *is* serious, Mr President.' If only the Colonel had been an Englishman he could have swallowed his pride and laughed the whole thing off as just one of his own little pranks. But the Colonel wasn't an Englishman. Mustafa intervened to save his master's face. Surprisingly, Yudie conceded and handed him back the phone.

'The Colonel's a little upset at the moment sir - as you can imagine.'

'Oh, I quite understand, Mustafa. Please assure him from me that he has nothing to fear. My only purpose in mentioning Project Jerusalem was to bury it, along with poor old Felix, once and for all. You get my point?'

'Oh, yes.' Mustafa's mind was ticking like mad. If people thought his master had a gift for cunning, they had never heard of Manuel Gonzalez. This President really took the biscuit.

'The public have to be reassured,' he droned on, 'I think it was best for me to take the initiative and quell all silly rumours that would have undoubtedly ensued from Felix's death. I still have some very strange Ministers, you understand?'

'I can imagine.'

'What I did, in fact, should only serve to protect Yudie. I trust you will make him see that?'

'I shall do my best, sir.'

'I know you will, Mustafa. He has a good friend in you. I hope he's paying you well?'

'Very well, sir, thank you. We shall both be at the funeral.'

'Very good. We can have a good talk afterwards, back here. By that time, I will know whether there are any special precautions I think both of you should take - to, er… shall we say - keep out of harm's way?' Mustafa grinned to himself. Crafty old bugger, Manuel Gonzalez. What a slippery customer. Who was he trying to fool? 'We'll see you at the funeral, sir.'

'Yes, indeed, Mustafa. 'Bye for now.'

'Bye, sir.'

Mustafa replaced the receiver and turned to his boss. But Yudie was sitting in his chair with a glum face. He had taken on the expression of a young schoolboy who had just had his toffee apple taken away from him. Perhaps he had. Project Jerusalem, it seemed, had finally proved too sticky an idea ever to get off the ground. And just as soon as he'd decided to share it with a friend, the friend has to go and die, leaving a trail of unequivocal evidence behind him. 'Oh, Allah. What have I done? What's it all about? And what should I do now?'

'Come on, sir. Cheer up. Here's a little refresher.' Mustafa handed Yudie a large gin and tonic and waited for the follow-up.

'Thank you, Mustafa. Help yourself to one too, and let's work this thing out between us.' Ah, at last the Colonel was getting rid of negative thoughts and beginning to look to the future. Mustafa returned to the drinks cabinet and poured himself a good measure of gin, topping it up with tonic. Umm. Lovely. He turned and walked back to his chair. 'OK, sir,' he began, splaying his legs out on the great Persian carpet already disfigured by the Dobermann's dribblings. It wasn't the dog's fault he had a lousy master.

Yudie sank into his chair and switched off the television set with the remote control. He drank deep into his G & T and, gradually, the idea of pinching a couple of stiffs from the mortuary began to have its appeal to his macabre sense of humour. Somehow, the thought of running away again with his trusty body-guard (with all the inherent dangers of pursuit) began to seem attractive. He still had a considerable amount of money stashed away in the safe. It was nice to look at it occasionally, to touch it, then lock it away again with the satisfaction 'the bastards' had been paid off and that what he could see in front of him was his to use as he pleased. Even if he never managed to return to Iraq, he and Mustafa could live very comfortably for the rest of their lives on the interest alone. Women could always be bought - love had never really been in the picture, anyway. Why should he seek it now?

'Just run over the plan again, Mustafa, will you?'

'With pleasure, sir…'

Into the night they talked. By 2 a.m., the whole schedule had been worked out and agreed upon. All eventualities were covered. It was even agreed both men should volunteer as pallbearers in order to further reassure the President of their intentions and trust in him. They must both act as normally as possible whilst making the plan watertight. Neither man had any intention of remaining in

Brazil to be a sitting duck for MOSSAD. "A man's gotta do what a man's gotta do". And that goes for an Arab, too.

Chapter 22

Maria continued to be upset by Felix's death. She had become very fond of the old soldier despite the niggling feeling he'd been spying on the Colonel all along. Notwithstanding her most enjoyable sessions with Yudie, to whom she had awarded more than a hundred per cent for performance (there was no style) she would still have liked to have had the opportunity to 'try' Felix Esbano, at least once, before he departed this mortal life. Maria had never had qualms over what people thought of her. And if so-called perversity had featured somewhere in the epithets bandied about by lesser, jealous little scandal - mongers, so be it.

But now he was gone and the world suddenly seemed emptier, sadder and less civilized. It was as if a whole era had finally come to an end, and a generation who had seen two World Wars, who had lived through hell yet come out of it to tell the tale and live a better day, had passed for ever through the 'best forgotten' annals of time. Some, like Felix, had much to teach the world - if only the world had listened. But it would not listen, preferring to make its own mistakes. Too bad if they turned out to be the same ones.

'Is Yudie attending the funeral, Manuel?'

'Yes, he is, my dear. I shall phone him after lunch to give him all the details. Unless, of course, you would like to tell him yourself?' Manuel looked across to his wife with those silly, accusing eyes of his that never seemed to have any effect upon their subject. If only the man could see that he might save himself so much unnecessary anxiety. Maria always came back to him, so why couldn't he take a leaf out of the book of those wise, ancient but civilized Greeks? Why couldn't he live and let live? Why did he continue to fight Nature? The fact Manuel had never fought Nature, had never really occurred to Maria.

'You'll be happy to know I shan't be seeing Yudie until after the funeral. Despite what you think of me, Manuel, there are some things that take preference over sex.'

'Really?'

'Yes. really.'

Manuel had begun to soften those eyes of his and, had she not been so concerned to avoid blowing her case, Maria would have taken him by the hand and dragged him into the bedroom - there and then. But a girl has her pride. She must always give a little plausibility to her most recent words.

'All right,' countered Manuel, 'I'll phone him and tell him I shall be expecting him.'

'Expecting him? What the hell are you up to, Manuel? After your boob on television last night, you can hardly expect him to trust you.' Maria shot her husband a wicked side-long glance, just to rub things in. But Manuel remained unperturbed.

'I am expecting him to attend the funeral, Maria. And in spite of what I said last night on the box, I have no reason to believe he mistrusts me. After all, I neither gave credence to Project Jerusalem, nor did I mention his name.'

'Oh, so you think people will be gullible enough to swallow what you say - just because you're the President? There is no smoke without fire, Manuel. *You* should know that. The mere mention of Project Jerusalem has set them thinking. The fact you denied its validity or its feasibility only makes matters worse. Why did you do it?'

'I have my reasons, my dear.'

"Matters of State", 'I presume?'

'Quite so.'

'My God, Manuel. Why do I put up with you?'

Manuel gave Maria such a look of nonchalant disdain that she wished she'd kept her mouth shut.

'You run along, my dear, while I get on with those "Matters of State".' If looks could kill, then Maria displayed the whole caboodle.

'Yudie? It's Manuel here.'

'Oh, hello, Mr President. What can I do for you?'

'No, it's just to tell you the funeral is next Friday, 21st, at 12 noon. Felix did not want a fuss, so we are holding it at the crematorium.'

'I will be there, with Mustafa. Thank you for informing me, sir.'

'Not at all. I look forward to seeing you both despite the unhappy circumstances. We'll have a good chat after the service. You are both invited back here and when the others have gone, we'll discuss any little worries you might have over security etc. No need to elaborate now, is there?'

'None whatsoever, sir. I'm sure we can work something out.'

'Well, we haven't done so badly up to now, have we, Yudie?'

'No complaints, sir, no complaints.'

'And you can drop this 'sir' bit. 'Manuel' will do nicely.'

'Thank you, s... er, Manuel.' What the hell was the President up to now? Was he merely buttering up Yudie for the kill? Let him think so. Yudie was no fool. And with a man like Mustafa as his friend, he would soon have the pleasure of seeing Manuel Gonzalez stuffing his little games right up his own orifice! Not a pretty sight, perhaps. But fun.

'So, until the 21st, then?'

'We look forward to seeing you then, despite the unhappy circumstances - as you so rightly put it. 'Bye for now, Manuel.'

"Bye, Yudie.'

There was no time to lose. From his tone, demeanour and invitation back to the Presidential Palace, Yudie figured the last thing Manuel would expect would be for his guests to arrive limping from the exertion of carrying the coffin. Nevertheless, if he heard from the lips of the undertaker that both Yudie and Mustafa had volunteered their services, he'd be in no doubt as to their intention to attend. Moreover, the gesture would be a clear sign that they harboured little fear of being tracked down and that they had trust in the President's assurances..........

'Why, Mr Yudie. This is very gracious of you. But we have a sufficient number of pallbearers, thank you. I'm quite certain your attendance alone will be sufficient and much appreciated.'

The undertaker was doing his best not to offend the deceased's grieving friend. But Yudie was much relieved that neither his nor Mustafa's services were, after all, required. Oddly, a vision of the late Ayatollah Khomeini's macabre and obscene final journey through the streets of Tehran flashed through his mind. How could he forget those delirious, grasping hands threatening to spill the body from its open casket? But mercifully, the memory disappeared as quickly as it had manifested itself. Felix's body, too, would doubtless be heavy and a sudden removal of support from both Yudie and Mustafa while they made a dash for freedom from the Israelis' hot pursuit of them over the gravestones, would inevitably result in considerable embarrassment, if nothing else.

'I will no doubt see you at the service,' said Yudie.

'No doubt, sir. Thank you so much for your call.'

"Bye.' Yudie put the phone down and turned to Mustafa. 'Well, that's one hurdle out of the way. We'll let that 'feed through the system' and await Manuel's next call.'

'Exactly.'

'In the meantime?'

'Phase 2. Right. I'll drive over to the mortuary. The guy in charge, would you believe, is a Mr O'Death? I met him at that strange night club we visited a few weeks ago. Remember?'

'The Peabody Club?'

'That's the one. Turned out to be a really nice man. With a job like his, he has need of a sense of humour.'

'And with a name like that. Nevertheless, he seems to have chosen an appropriate profession?'

'Quite. Anyway, I'm sure he'd be open to a bribe or two.'

'Make it one, if you can.'

'I'll try, sir. Must be off.'

'Be careful, Mustafa.'

'I will.'

Mustafa opened the front door of the villa, got into the car and drove away. Yudie walked back into the lounge and awaited the President's next call. He did not have to wait long.

'Hello?'

'Yudie. It's Manuel again. Just to say how much I appreciate your offer to help as pallbearer.'

'Not at all.'

'But my dear fellow, despite your obvious feeling for our dear departed friend, it's enough you are attending. But I am touched by your gesture. Thank you.'

'My pleasure, Manuel. See you on Friday.'

'Yes, indeed.'

Good. The President, it seemed, swallowed it - hook, line and sinker. Yudie and Mustafa would be there and so would MOSSAD. There would be no party afterwards - just an unceremonious bundling into the car, or a muffled shooting behind one of the more substantial gravestones. Perhaps, there would even be a newly dug grave, conveniently to hand, in which to dump the bodies whilst the service for Felix was being taken by a well-paid and well-silenced priest.

Umm. Colonel Doomsday would be no son of Sodom the Lesser if he were to allow such transparent trickery to have its day. No, sir.

Within the hour, Mustafa had returned from his visit to the mortuary. He flopped down into an armchair as soon as he'd followed Yudie into the lounge.

'Mustafa, you need a drink. I'll fix you one myself.'

'Thank you, sir.'

'Well, tell me all.' Yudie poured out two large measures of gin and tonic and brought them over to the table between the two armchairs. He handed his brave bodyguard his drink and waited with bated breath to hear the story. 'How was Mr O'Death, today?', Yudie wanted to say. But he held his anxious and excited tongue.

Mustafa drank practically half a glassful of G & T and gasped, 'no ghost could ever come near some of those apparitions, sir. Of all the bodies you and I have seen back home,' (Yudie chose not to remember) 'none come up to any of this lot.'

'Spare me the details, Mustafa. Did you find two of our type?'

'Now, *there* I had better luck. Indeed, I found two that, well, …… er..'

'Go on.'

'Well,' (Mustafa drank another measure of his fast-vanishing drink) 'they might as well have been…….'

'Go on.'

'*You* and I. That was the real shock. Damned unreal, sir. Most disconcerting.'

'But most convenient, is it not?'

'Well, yes. I have to agree. By the time they check dental records and all that, we'll be miles away. Most convenient, as you say, sir. It's all going a bit too well for……'

'Now, come on, Mustafa. You've been reading too many thrillers. Nothing's going to go wrong. Let's turn everything to our advantage. It looks as if Allah is working…..'

'Overtime?'

'He is always on our side, Mustafa. Never forget that.'

'I don't, sir.' Mustafa drained his glass and wondered what religion he'd embrace in his next life. But then, if Heaven is paved with gold for the likes of him, why should he worry?

'So, what is all this going to cost?'

'$20,000, sir. That's the lowest he'd go. I'm sure the guy's done this sort of thing before.'

'No doubt. All right, when do we pick them up? And can this man be trusted?' Mustafa shot Yudie a wry look. 'I think he gets the message that if he squeals, he's a…….'

'Oh Death, where is thy sting?' Mustafa laughed and assured his boss that despite possessing such an evocative name, Mr O'Death would be a 'doddle' to handle.

'We pick them up on Friday, at 10a.m.'

'The day of the funeral?'

'Yes. They'll still be reasonably fresh, as it were.'

'Don't be disgusting, Mustafa.'

Both men laughed, agreed to have another gin and tonic and go out to dinner. Mustafa often cooked the meals himself. He was a damned good cook and Yudie never had tummy trouble as a result of his endeavours. If all else failed, Yudie was certain his bodyguard could always find a job as top chef - almost anywhere. But this evening they decided a trip to their favourite little French restaurant, barely a mile away, would be a good ploy, if only to gather any gossip or test the temperature of the locals who'd become accustomed to the presence of an ex-dictator and his man in their midst. Yudie and Mustafa had always behaved discreetly and in any case the other diners were invariably having too good a time themselves to worry about two heavy-looking Arabs tucking into their coq au vin. Now that Felix Esbano was dead, however, things might be different. Everyone seemed to know the old man had been "one of them Nazis" in his younger days and that he had friends "in high places". Moreover, he had himself occasionally dined in this restaurant and his gracious manners and imposing bearing would hardly go unnoticed, if only for a moment, before everyone would revert to their own devices - gabbling and gorging to their hearts' content. Yudie and Mustafa had never been seen there in the company of Felix, yet it might be interesting and instructive if they went along tonight - to test the water, so to speak.

And for this purpose, they would tune their antennae to maximum sensitivity.

Chapter 23

'Good evening, sir. May I take your jacket?'

'No, you may not,' teased Mustafa with a wink at the head waiter. There was a buzz in the air, and the entrance of Yudie and his bodyguard turned heads that normally would not have turned. Yes, the antennae of both men were bristling like mad; they even considered leaving on the spot and making the excuse that it was a little too crowded tonight. But they thought better of it. Instantly, they realized they could not withdraw without arousing further suspicion. And if all eyes were firmly on them, so be it. Those people would soon get tired of it and revert to their own company.

But as Yudie and Mustafa sat down and took hold of the short and excellent menu handed to them by their favourite little waiter called Pierre, they knew that tonight would be the night they would have to watch their words lest one or two stray ears might misinterpret what was said and their owners got up and phoned the President. But the world wasn't really like that, was it?

'Good to see you, Colonel. And you, too, sir.' Pierre smiled sweetly at his 'guests' and apologized for the people being somewhat over-excited tonight - on account of Felix Esbano's sudden death. 'But I will tip you off if any spy of 'you know who' comes in while you're eating. Don't worry.'

'Thank you, Pierre. But why should we worry?' Yudie looked up into the young man's face for the slightest give away. The waiter loved talking so much that any customer of intelligence could glean a ream of juicy facts and figures, and more than a few naughty goings-on in the town, just by keeping his own mouth firmly shut. All one had to do to encourage Pierre was to look him in the eyes with an adoring smile. The waiter was never fussy about the face to which the smile was attached.

'Rumour has it,' he intimated, bending down with lowered voice and even wider eyes, 'that the President has invited MOSSAD to investigate a few people here in Brazil. He's done it before, I hear, when he's been unable to resolve the matter himself.'

'How interesting.' Mustafa remained non-committal about the whole thing whilst shielding Yudie from any obligation to respond to this flood of tittle-tattle.

'Oh, but I'm keeping you from ordering. I'm so sorry.'

'Not at all, Pierre. Feel free. I must say, that lamb looks inviting.' Mustafa had swung his head in the direction of the table opposite on which stood a succulent leg of lamb and a fine bottle of claret. An elderly couple were tucking into their meal with obvious relish.

Mustafa turned back to Yudie.

'You fancy the lamb, Mustafa?'

'That's for me, sir. How about you?'

'Umm.' Yudie looked up into the waiter's face. 'Is the fish any good tonight, young man?'

'No, sir.'

'Right. Well, I think I'll join my friend, here.'

'Leg of lamb for two, then?'

'Yes. And a good bottle of burgundy?'

'I recommend the claret, sir. The '82 is superb.'

'All right Mustafa?'

'Let's go for it. How about croquettes, cauliflower and garlic bread?'

'Fine.'

The House of Baghdad

The waiter smiled, picked up the menus and turned to go into the kitchen. It was at this point that the man on the opposite table, a well-dressed old gentleman of around.......well - it was hard to tell - anything from seventy to, say, eighty something, leant across to Mustafa and commended him on his choice. It was an opening remark which led to a commiseration over the death of Felix Esbano.

'Did you know him, then?'

'Yes, we did,' interjected Yudie smartly.

'A fine old man,' continued the stranger, 'any country would have been proud to have him as a senior citizen.'

'Do I take it he would not have been so welcome as a young man?' Mustafa had stuck his neck out and Yudie wondered whether his bodyguard was already becoming a little too adventurous. The stranger shot a curious look in the direction of... well, at whom was the look aimed? Mustafa well remembered those hilarious films of Marty Feldman which he'd brought out from England on video in order to provide himself with light relief after witnessing one of Yudie's torture sessions. Yet somehow, this man 'eyeing' him, did not possess quite such an endearing appeal as that much loved and much missed comedian of the early '70s.

The stranger chose not to answer Mustafa's loaded question, whilst his lady companion (presumed his wife), attempted to rescue the situation with: 'I suppose you'll be attending the funeral? He was such a dear man.'

'Of course we will,' Yudie hastened to assure her, 'will you be there?'

'Oh yes, Bernard and I practically lived with him back in the old country when we were toddlers.' She touched the arm of her husband whose eyes somehow seemed to encompass an amazingly wide arc. Yudie and Mustafa began to feel somewhat uncomfortable. 'How times have changed,' continued the lady, 'every-thing's changed, hasn't it? And the prices. Well, I said to Bernard only the other day - 'If we hadn't been so frugal in the early years we would never have managed over here.' How the government can just ignore inflation and laugh it off with all the other bad debts I just do not know. And as for the drug problem.....' The lady rabbited on at ten to the dozen, whilst Yudie and Mustafa wondered whether the man was a plant and his wife, with her incessant gabbling, a decoy to put them off the scent. But just as Mustafa began to light up a cigar in an attempt to break the monotony, a nervous little man in an ill-fitting suit entered the restaurant and drew close to the lady's table.

'Good evening, madam.'

'Good evening.' She shut up like a clam, clearly annoyed. The man turned to her spouse and whispered something in his ear.

'For God's sake, man, stop whispering. And sit down. I want you to meet Colonel Doomsday and his man, Mustafa.'

The mouths of Yudie and Mustafa would have dropped wide open if they had been amateurs. But they were not. Nevertheless, the fact that the stranger called Bernard had known who they were was most interesting.

'Pleased to meet you.'

'Touché,' said the nervous little man.

'And who are *you,* sir?' enquired Yudie, working on the nearest eye of 'Marty Feldman'. The nervous little man sat down diffidently next to his boss's wife. Her Bernard's other eye seemed to be clouding over - in sympathy with the over-worked one upon which Yudie was now concentrating. He was giving it all he had and was doing a remarkable job of demolition.

'I am Felix's half-brother,' croaked the slightly unnerved diner. Mustafa decided it was his cue to back up his boss's effort in counter-attack. 'Don't worry,' he assured the man, 'the Colonel and I will be at the funeral.'

And with a firm handshake from his massive hand, he left Bernard in no doubt that far from cowering from any possible threat to their persons, he and his boss would not hesitate to initiate a little 'cleansing programme' of their own, should circumstances dictate.

The strangers were on the point of leaving. Yudie himself rose from the table and stretched out his own impressive hand. It was uncharacteristic of this Arab that he should squeeze the hand of Felix's half-brother with the firmness of a Rugger Blue. But squeeze it he did.

'See you at the funeral, Bernard. My sincerest condolences to you. In the short time I knew him, I got to love him very much.'

'Thank you. And au revoir, gentlemen.'

'Goodbye, Mr,….. hic….Bernard. What have you put in this wine?'

'Come along, my dear.' The couple left the table with the nervous little man trailing behind. A waiter opened the door for them and they disappeared into the night.

'Well, Mustafa,' sighed Yudie, settling once more in his seat, 'what do you make of that?'

'Glad to hear he's only a half-brother. With eyes like those, who needs a whole one?'

They laughed freely, while Mustafa poured the rest of the wine into their glasses.

'Cheers, sir.'

'Cheers, Mustafa. We make a good team, don't we?'

'You bet. Ah, here comes Pierre with the food. Umm. Glad we didn't bother with a starter. That smells good. Can't wait.'

Pierre drew near and, with the help of an assistant, he served his illustrious guests a wonderful meal. Even Mustafa could hardly have done better.

'I thought you were going to warn us about spies, Pierre?'

'Ah, but Mr Bernard. He's not a spy. What could he possibly spy with...... er,.....?'

'Yes, quite.' Mustafa grinned and passed his boss the condiments.

'Thanks. Let's have another bottle of claret, shall we?'

'Another '82, sir?'

'Thank you, Pierre. We'll drink to the Marty Feldman Road Show.'

'You're a cruel man, Mustafa.' Yudie's bodyguard looked across to his boss and conjured up a few of the more horrific events of the Colonel's reign back home. Look who's talking, he mused. But he kept those thoughts to himself.

****

The day of the funeral had arrived. And despite the fact Felix had expressed, many years before to his lawyer, that his funeral should be a quiet affair (not all funerals are, after all) it seemed the whole of Brazil had turned out to pay its respects. Yet no official announcement had been made and, notwithstanding the President's eulogy, nothing on television had subsequently suggested there would be a motorcade. Maybe the people were really expected to forget the whole thing and go out and have themselves a good time, instead. But, just as Maria had indicated, Manuel's TV appearance had stirred people's curiosity. How important had this ex-Nazi really been? Would there be a German salute ready to greet the cortège as it arrived at the chapel?

Yudie and Mustafa had risen early and had done most of their packing by 9 a.m. Mustafa was not particularly looking forward to picking up those stiffs. But the job had to be done. He picked up the telephone and dialled the number of the mortuary.

'O'Death, here.' The voice, mournful and whining at the same time, invaded the line.

'It's Mr Malcolm, here,' responded Mustafa cautiously.

'Ah, yes, Mr Malcolm. I have them ready for you. No questions asked. Just $20,000 and all will be well. No one will know.'

'Fine. I shall be there at 10, as arranged.'

'Very good. I look forward to seeing you.'

'Till 10, then.' Mustafa quickly replaced the receiver. If anyone had ever told him that one day, a Mr O'Death would look forward to seeing him, he would have... Yes, quite. A shiver passed along his spine with the thought. But he pulled himself together.

'I'm off now, sir. Hope O'Death doesn't throw a fit when he sees me dressing up the bodies with some of our clothes.'

'I'm sure he's seen more peculiar things in his time. Besides, with $20, 000 in his pocket, why should he care if you're just another weirdo?' Mustafa laughed at the thought, appreciating his boss's sense of humour during this tense period of their lives. South America had somehow relaxed his master in a way Iraq never quite did. Shame they had to leave so soon.

'But do be careful, Mustafa.'

'Don't worry about me, sir. I'll be back before eleven.'

'All right. I'll just tidy up a few things.'

'Tidy up? When we're going to have a fire?'

'Well, I'll just wash the glasses.' It was the first time Yudie had winked at Mustafa but the gesture, together with his light hearted remarks, had the effect of making him as relaxed as his boss appeared to be. He suddenly felt as if he was on his way to pick up a pair of highly recommended whores rather than a couple of gruesome stiffs.

While Mustafa was away, Yudie picked up the phone for the final details of their flight to Dublin. He got through immediately.

'O'Casey, here.'

'Ah, Shaun. It's Yudie, here.'

'Yudie. Good to hear yer little ol' voice. I've fixed everytin'. Don't ye worry yer little ol' self, now. The chopper will be at the villa at 11.30. We leave straight away after you start the fire, fly to our little ol' airstrip and then off we go in the jet to Dublin, care of dear ol' British Airways.'

Yudie laughed. He'd known Shaun O'Casey for years. Not only had the man become a master of international intrigue, to put it mildly, but he could show a sense of humour in the tightest of corners. 'Anyt'in' else worryin' ye?'

'No, Shaun, thank you. You've been...... what do the English say, a brick?'

'Don't mention the English to me, me friend.'

The House of Baghdad

'I thought that was ………?'
'Water under the bridge?'
'Something like that.'
'Don't ye believe it. I'll see ye at 11.30 - sharp?'
'Yes, Shaun. And thanks again.'
'Don't mention it.'

There was only one other thing to do before Mustafa's return. The money in the safe had already been checked before breakfast. It now had to be removed and packed into the strongboxes. Yudie was half way through this procedure when the phone rang. Damn.

Should he answer it? Well,…

'Manuel here, Yudie.'

A slight shiver passed down Yudie's back. 'Do you want to be picked up? Save you the tedious drive?'

'No, thank you, Manuel. It's kind of you. But Mustafa is more than happy. He likes to keep busy, as you know.'

'OK., my friend. Just a thought.'

'And I appreciate it. But we'll be fine. See you around, oh…… I'd say 11.30 to quarter to 12?'

That's perfect. Look forward to our little chat afterwards.'

'So do I.'

Jesus. What a fright. The final check out on him, eh? But lying and deception were nothing new to Yudie. As Colonel Doomsday, he'd had ample opportunity to refine and test the art until it had become second nature. And who better than his own father, Sodom the Lesser, to teach him?

He returned to the job of packing the money. And sooner than expected the work was done. Perhaps there was some missing, after all? Ah well, there was enough here with which to live out his days in comfort. And now there was the matter of the dog. Where was he? Perhaps the great Dobermann sensed the two men were about to leave, and had decided to run away before anything really nasty occurred. But just as Yudie began to rack his brains over the whereabouts of the animal, a car drew up outside.

Good. It was Mustafa. And in good time. The dog jumped out of the car and made for Yudie. 'Down, Brutus. Down.'

'I think he senses we're leaving, sir.' Mustafa drew near and led the dog into his bedroom and locked the door.

'Right. I'll help you with the bodies.'

'Thanks, sir. They're pretty heavy.'

Mustafa was right. It took them nearly twenty minutes to get them into the villa, out of the caskets and splayed out to look 'natural'.

At last they got the fire going but only when they'd made sure the helicopter just coming in was friendly. To be sure, to be sure, it was O'Casey himself - on time. He entered the villa, his bright eyes burning with excitement. The luggage was quickly loaded up, including the caskets which had contained the bodies. The dog was let out and he immediately ran towards the helicopter. He'd be left behind, of course, but Yudie and Mustafa had no time to spare on sentiment. The fire soon began to blaze around the bodies and then the carpets, curtains and chairs joined in the chorus of angry flames. O'Casey, Yudie and Mustafa boarded the helicopter, finally shutting the door on the Dobermann, anxious to join them. As the machine rose into the bright blue sky, the dog looked up with sad, pleading eyes, his heart pounding in fear and desperation. Only then did Yudie and Mustafa look down with human regret and human pity.

Chapter 24

The cortège moved along the aisle of the chapel at a slow, mournful pace. The coffin was placed on the trestle and the men stepped back and moved out of sight. The priest raised his eyes to 'Heaven' as if to grasp the remaining straws of wisdom that for years had eluded him. How often he had presided over farewells to cruel men and women; how often he'd been offered money to oil his tongue in the paths of blessed hypocrisy. In the confessional, at least, he could trot out the usual, invariably unheeded advice, without the embarrassment of having to look at the culprit. But here, in the middle of the chapel, the shiny splendour of the expensive polished oak cask somehow demanded more of him. Starkly, perversely (for the sun shines on the wicked and the just alike) he was reminded of the lives of ruthless men. And many of them were so charming. Felix had been a charming man. And now, a little late in the day, he had been dragged to his confessional - helpless, still, demanding the blessing of forgiveness. The blessing was his right. Dead or alive.

All around the chapel sat the faces, the faces of the Establishment - the Government who'd given refuge to this old warrior and others like him. They had given succour to those unwilling to pay the unthinkable price in their own countries, to those who had robbed and cheated, to those who had merely murdered. For what were a few more murderers when the country housed so many of its own? Besides, foreign murderers had money. And the country could never be accused of refusing to open its doors to those with spunk enough to go through them.

The service began with an introductory prayer for the deceased and an opening hymn - 'For all the Saints - who from their labours rest' - a wry choice considering Herr Krupp's track record. But the President had insisted: Felix Esbano was a saint, and if a man could not forgive someone who had done so much to atone for his sins, what the hell was he doing in this chapel?

Even now, the absence of Colonel Doomsday, though disappointing, had so far, failed to arouse suspicion in the President's mind. He was convinced Yudie would turn up halfway through the service and sit at the back with Mustafa until it was over. Even now, there were no telltale signs of MOSSAD having infiltrated the congregation. When the pallbearers had first entered the chapel with their charge, Manuel had made a discreet survey of the gathering and had detected no one who could fit the bill of a secret agent. But then, times change, don't they? And not all covert operators insist upon dark glasses and heavy vibes. Like the new generation of American Mafia college boys, who had already learned to relax and smile whilst 'doing their worst', MOSSAD had come of age and trained at least a proportion of their team in the ways of civilized cunning.

'For all the Saints' at last was laid to rest. And the congregation sat down to hear the priest's address. Manuel, for one, was thankful for the respite, for, during the singing, as verse followed verse, Maria had begun to let herself go. She had long fancied herself as a Maria Callas rather than Maria Gonzalez, for at least the former had possessed more than one talent. Unfortunately, the wild imaginings and energy put into each successive verse by the President's beautiful wife, matched neither the idol's immortal sound nor her own magnificent image. Indeed, the result would have made the efforts of Edith in BBC TV's 'Allo,' 'Allo' series seem almost blissful by comparison.

The priest began quietly, for he remained conscious of the fact his congregation knew far more about the ins and outs of villainy, skulduggery and political manoeuvring than ever he would be allowed to know. He knew something of what was going on, of course. He wasn't unobservant by nature, but he always knew when to turn that blind eye and keep his sermon as short and sweet as possible.

'My dear friends,' he began innocuously, 'we come here today to honour our dear departed brother, a man of immense charm and stature, a man who has seen life in all its different colours, all its trials and tribulations, its.......'

'Huh.' The sudden, almost violent interruption momentarily fazed the priest whose beady eyes searched the congregation for the culprit who, he hoped, would somehow acknowledge his guilt and apologize. The priest could never quite forget the occasion when, in São Paulo Cathedral ten years before, a man had shouted out during an elaborate wedding. 'Huh,' he shouted during the traditional space allotted to public objections to the marriage, 'I've been fucking that little girl since she was fourteen.'

'Well, *I'm* fucking her, now,' came the equally spicy reply from an unhesitating bridegroom. Laughter, tears and deep embarrassment ensued, to say nothing of an almighty brawl which guaranteed yet another postponement of the tearful bride's beautiful day. But that was somehow fun. This funeral service could hardly be put in the same category. A man had chosen to interrupt the flow of the priest's difficult oration - a delicate balancing act which, if he didn't get right, would fester in the minds of this heavy, powerful entourage and might even put his own life in some difficulty.

'Huh,' repeated the man at the back. But as the congregation turned like distraught, disgusted sheep to the source of the commotion, all they could see was a wizened little old man on a bench at the back who, subsequently, it was found, took delight in doing the rounds of baptisms, weddings and funerals. The man was not a wino; nor was he a mischievous trouble-maker - merely a disgruntled, cynical old man who thought the whole business was a farce and wished to say so.

The congregation relaxed once more and the priest was allowed to continue……

'And so, brothers and sisters, we commend the soul of our dear brother to the Lord God in whom we all trust. And may the Lord keep you and…….' And, with the parting of the curtains, the coffin which had been moved in silence from the trestle slowly slid into its compartment and thence into the consuming fire like a doomed ship sinking inexorably into its watery grave.

Manuel was spared a final hymn and, springing to his feet, walked out of the chapel with Maria by his side. As he neared the door, he spotted a couple of well-dressed, well-built men in their late 30's moving into the aisle towards him. Manuel's detective quickly stepped in front of his boss to protect him and deal with any potential trouble. But the two men flashed their cards to the detective who acknowledged them as bona-fide members of MOSSAD.

'The Colonel is not here,' intervened the President.

'We know that, sir. Any ideas?'

'Try his villa……..Then phone me before you do anything silly.'

'Call us anything you like, sir. But not silly. Thanks for the tip.'

And with that the two beefy men left the chapel, ran to their car and accelerated away to track down their quarry.

As they drove along the dusty roads at breakneck speed, the men scanned the scenery for anything resembling either an official car or a fast getaway job. But the traffic was unusually light for a Friday and nothing was seen bar a battered old Hillman Imp with Mum and Dad in the front seats and two dirty-looking kids in the back, followed by a bus, full of old folks on an outing. And within a mile of the address given to them by the President, they sensed something else was wrong - fundamentally wrong - not only was the sky exceptionally overcast for the time of year but, as they drove on, they could see bright flickering lights penetrating the trees on one side of the road. The burning Manderley in the classic film 'Rebecca' could not have looked as foreboding as the sight coming into view just as the men rounded the bend leading to the Colonel's villa. Gigantic flames leapt on all sides of the building as if the Colonel's father had taken a personal interest in the affair and ignited it himself in a fit of destructive jealousy - as part of his scorched-earth policy. If anything had survived in that inferno, thought the men, it would have their admiration, if not their sympathy.

They stopped the car a distance away and got out to survey the situation. No one, it seemed, had bothered to contact the fire service or any other help. The villa was isolated but not *that* isolated. Maybe the fact it was the day of Felix Esbano's funeral had somehow numbed the reflexes of anyone with sight, sense of smell or just plain common sense. The place was deserted save for a lone, sad-looking

Dobermann, whom the men found whimpering and wandering around the place and looking up to the sky with an excruciating bark.

'Hey, fella. What you looking up there for, eh? Is your master in the sky?' The dog barked again but was soon licking the hand of one of the nice men. He was a very silly dog. But the nice men had no intention of doing anything silly (as the President liked to put it).

'So, the bird has flown, Josh. Next move?'

'We contact the President. After all, he must know about this. He seemed too off-hand at the crematorium to be genuine. Know what I mean, Dave?'

'I do. Maybe he's protecting the Colonel.'

'We'll find out and then inform our People.'

The men walked back to the car and got in. 'Hello, hello? Is that the President?' The car-phone crackled and spat in sympathetic frustration.

'It's his secretary, here. Who is this?'

'It's Joshua Rainberg from MOSSAD. It's very urgent, sir. The President knows we are here and asked us to contact him.'

'Very good, sir. Hold the line, would you please?' The secretary happened to be a few feet away from the President at the time. He cupped the phone in his hand and relayed the message to his boss.

'All right. I'll take it. Thanks.... Hello?'

'It's Joshua Rainberg from MOSSAD here, sir. My colleague and I met you a little while ago at the crematorium.'

'Oh, yes. What's news?'

'The news is, the bird has flown.'

'The bird has flown, eh? Well, well, well. Now we know.'

The President's secretary had been listening intently and had pretended to be busy with official papers. He had never before heard his boss repeat himself three times. It must be something very important. And he wondered what the President did know.

'What are you planning on doing, now?' continued Manuel with a rather off-hand intonation.

'Well, sir. We thought you may be able to help us. You know, spurious airfields, underground escape routes. Stuff like that?' What would the president know about "stuff like that?" Brazil was a free society. Very free.

'Stuff like that? What do you take us for, Mr Rainberg?'

Joshua Rainberg knew exactly what to take the President for but he kept his counsel. 'Have you checked the villa?'

'Impossible at the moment, sir. The flames are too fierce.'

'Flames?'

'Yes. He's burned the place down. Seems like he's done a pretty good job of it.'

'Oh, has he? But who knows?' suggested the President quickly. 'It may be a genuine fire. And there might be genuine bodies in there, my friend. Have you considered that?'

'Of course we have, sir. But it seems more likely he's escaped by chopper.'

The President had always disliked these North American expressions for mechanical objects. Helicopter was a perfectly good name for the machine in question and for him - helicopter it would remain.

'I think you have helicopters on the brain, Mr Rainberg.'

'It appears the dog also has one particular chopper on the brain.' All sorts of obscene thoughts ran through Manuel's mind at that remark but he ruthlessly banished them.

'Now, what do you mean by that?'

'Well, sir, the Dobermann - the Colonel's dog, we presume - keeps looking up at the sky and whimpering. Sure sign, sir, 'the bird has flown', wouldn't you say?'

'Not before the remains of that villa are examined, no.'

While the President and Joshua Rainberg continued to discuss the situation, quite suddenly - almost as if by Royal Command - the heavens opened and a timely monsoon descended upon the whole area, stifling the flames that had so magnificently lit up the sky barely a few minutes ago.

'Jesus, we're getting wet, here. It's teeming down, sir.'

'How fortunate for you. You'll soon be able to take a look, won't you?'

The President sounded callous, as if he didn't care how difficult or uncomfortable MOSSAD's work became. Maybe he'd set the whole thing up and was hiding the Colonel himself - somewhere in this vast, sprawling country called Brazil. Maybe Joshua's bosses at home had underestimated this President's guile. They should have known there would be frustrations and obstructions put in the way of extradition from a country of Brazil's reputation. Prime Minister Shameer was an intelligent man. Yet maybe even he could not foresee the suicide of Fritz Krupp, or a sudden Brazilian downpour - timed to delay the pursuit of a colonel not only with time, but money, a corrupt President and, doubtless, God on his side?

'OK., sir,' sighed Joshua Rainberg, 'we'll try taking a look inside, now, and report back to you.'

'You do that. I shall be here for the next hour.'

The House of Baghdad

'Very good, Mr President. We'll be back to you in a jiffy.'

The men drove the car within a few yards of the villa and got out to take a closer look. The rain was doing a good job of subduing the flames which now spluttered and hissed in protest, whilst the Dobermann drew near to inspect, as it were, the remains of his once comfortable home, now almost unrecognisable from its former glory. Maybe his interest in the sky was merely a temporary aberration of his feeble mind, his real interest lying in a desire to get back inside to sniff at his unfortunate master?

'My God, Dave. Take a look at this.' Joshua had turned over the remains of the bodies lying there, charred, scarred and mangled in the fire. With the rain which had poured through the disintegrating roof, they had taken on a gruesome life of their own, parts glistening in the wet, one face looking up to Joshua with the sure curse of hell, fire and brimstone. It was not a pretty sight. Of all the pictures of the Colonel and his bodyguard that Joshua had studied back in Israel, none were as terrifying as the images staring back at him, now. But the bodies - or what remained of them - certainly appeared to be of the same build. Who knows? Maybe they were the remains of his quarry, after all?

Dave led the Dobermann to the bodies. But the dog appeared strangely disinterested in their welfare - fear had become his dominant emotion. With a particularly nasty snarl he backed away from them and turned to run out of the house.

'Let him go, Dave. He's told us something, at least.'
'You don't think these bodies are genuine?'

'They're genuine, all right. But I doubt they belonged to the Colonel and his man. No, I don't like it, Dave. President Gonzalez is a cunning, slippery man. He's just *got* to be hiding that bastard.'

'Well, what can we do if he won't co-operate?'

'First, I'm getting cleaned up at the hotel. I'll put in a call to our people. Then I'll phone Gonzalez again and give him hell.'

'Like ya style, Josh. But we're in his damned country, remember.'

'Leave it to me.'

'What d'we do about the stiffs? Want me to stay till you get back?'

'You'd better, Dave, in case some little bastard decides to whisk even these away.'

'Now, who'd wanna do that?'

Joshua laughed. But he was in a hurry. 'Don't worry. I'll phone through to the hotel. Our Pete will send a car for you with dry clothing and something to eat. He'd better get on to the airports, too. We can't let this little bastard go, Dave. Our jobs are on the line.'

'What jobs', thought Dave. The rain had stopped but, at that moment, he looked anything but a happy worker.

Chapter 25

By the time Joshua had been put through once more to the President, the plane with the Colonel, Mustafa and O'Casey on board, was already on its way to Dublin's fair city. At the hotel, Pete, Joshua's other colleague and co-ordinator of operations for this case, had worked his arse off to find the whereabouts of the fugitives. Joshua had felt no hesitation in giving his friend a blunt character analysis of the President. Of all the operators in MOSSAD over the past twenty years, the name of Joshua Rainberg had been cited most often in the top league of bright lads. He could smell a rat a thousand miles off and, as far as he was concerned, the President stank. Despite what he may have agreed with Tel Aviv, this cunning smoothy liked to play as many hands as possible. From now on, whatever the man said to Joshua would be vetted, scrutinized, turned over and still taken with a pinch of salt. If the Israeli Government had authorized money to be telexed to Brazil in return for a 'free hand' over the Colonel they must be mad, thought Joshua. He'd always held his country's politicians in great respect. But…… In disbelief, he shrugged his shoulders, and continued the conversation as best he could…….. 'But Mr President, it's in the interest of both our countries that we find him.'

'Of course it is, my friend. But I have told you all I know. God knows I telephoned him enough times to make sure he would be at Felix Esbano's funeral. It is a disappointment to me, too, that he failed to appear. And so, I repeat,' (the President sounded annoyed and somewhat impatient with his inquisitor) 'check those bodies and the remains of the villa; then report back to me. I myself will make sure all airports, etc. are checked for suspicious passengers. Does *that* satisfy you, Mr Rainberg?'

'Thank you for your help, sir. But we must stop this man.'

'Someone else may have done it for you, my friend. Check out those bodies - but don't move them. My people are on their way.'

Oh, Jesus. That's all Joshua needed - a bunch of chattering South American bunglers who were, no doubt, in the President's personal employ. They'd take one look at the bodies and pronounce them to be those of the Colonel and his bodyguard. The case would be wrapped up there and then and life in Brazil would go on as before.

Driving back to the 'scene of the crime', Joshua felt his blood pressure rising in frustration. Sod it. He'd do a little 'autopsy' of his own - he wasn't a bright member of MOSSAD for nothing. Besides, the President himself had encouraged him to go ahead. But one thing could be said of Joshua - he knew his limitations. As he began to study the bone structure of the men's remains, comparing them with the pictures and physical details on his file, he knew he'd need the assistance of an expert. A quick call to the nearest hospital or morgue would not come amiss. He would dearly loved to have bundled the bodies in the boot of the car and driven off with Dave back to the hotel, to re-contact his people. At least they could not accuse him of neglecting his duty - habeas corpus should always be taken seriously. And since these two bodies were the only ones lying around the Colonel's villa at the time, there was a slight possibility they could be the 'right' ones.

But Joshua's instincts had always been acute. Something told him these 'effigies' of the Colonel and his bodyguard were mere decoys. Two unsuspecting stiffs had been 'spirited' away from the morgue and placed in the lounge of the villa. A fire had been started and the bastards had made their escape. But where, for Chrissake?

'Hey, hey, hey. What's going on?' Detective Daconni and his men found Joshua and Dave standing over the bodies as if they had partaken in a macabre and ritualistic picnic. The place was a mess. What had once been a well-constructed and elegant villa - the envy of the local people - now stood wretched, broken, charred and wet - all at the same time - just like the bodies of its occupants. To Daconni's mind it was quite obvious - MOSSAD new the whereabouts of the Colonel's villa and had invaded the man's privacy either during the night or on this very morning of Felix Esbano's funeral; they had shot dead the Colonel and his bodyguard, started a fire, left the villa to burn itself down and had calmly driven to Felix's funeral service in time to foist themselves onto the President. It was bloody outrageous. The Colonel may well have been a villain, a murderer and many of the other things that tend to accompany dictatorship but, whilst he was here in Brazil, he had certainly done as the Romans do - Maria, for one, could testify as much. For MOSSAD to come over here and casually knock off a couple of ex-pats, drive to the funeral of another and then hustle the President whilst pleading ignorance was beyond the pale.

'OK, you two. I think we'd better have a little chat.'

'Joshua Rainberg is the name.' Joshua took the initiative and held out his huge hand to the 'leader of the pack', Franco Daconni, who reeled as much from the Israeli's nerve as from the power of his grip. 'The President knows we're here. Even suggested we take a look at the bodies.'

'Did he, now? Well, let *me* take a look. Shouldn't be too difficult to determine their identity.' Daconni glanced at Joshua Rainberg with a look of disdain. How dare MOSSAD come barging their way in here, taking over the reins of power from Brazil's lawful detectives. This pushy upstart may well have spoken to the President but, when Franco Daconni had been assigned by him to a case, then no one, but no one, would be allowed to come between Chief Detective Daconni and the solution to the crime..........

He looked down at the wretched corpses with a triumphant, self-satisfied smile. Yes, at last Colonel D-Day, whom Chief Daconni had never really liked, had come to a sticky end. The fates had joined forces to give him his just deserts, and Maria would be back 'on the market' again. Oh, the possibilities opening up for him now seemed limitless. Before this upstart from Iraq had come along, things were beginning to go his way in the love stakes. He had met Maria at one of Manuel's 'little do's' and was utterly convinced Maria fancied him.

'Oh, the delusions of the Latins.', sighed Felix Esbano's English dancing partner at the time. And to that remark Daconni had simply responded, 'I don't think so, madam. Besides, it's better than remaining a cold fish.'

The woman had slapped his face and dragged Felix off the dance floor to abandon herself to Felix's inevitable soothing sympathies.

'Well, my friend,' sneered Daconni, raising his voice to Joshua Rainberg busying himself examining the remaining contents of the lounge, 'I think your little chase is over. No question this is Colonel D-Day, and *that,*' (he pointed a stubby finger at the bedraggled corpse beside him) 'is his loyal bodyguard. His loyalty didn't do him much good, did it?'

Joshua kept his mouth shut. He was beginning to take a certain amount of delight in Daconni's glib self-satisfied analysis.

'But just to make sure and also, to satisfy your overstretched imagination, we'll take the bodies down to the morgue,' suggested the 'official' detective. 'There's a man there I'd like you two to meet - Mr O'Death.'

Dave's mouth fell open wide and he treated himself to a sudden nervous little giggle. 'No joke, I'm afraid,' pressed Daconni, 'you see, we like to have things in their proper places, here in Brazil. Would you care to join us?'

Joshua nudged his companion's arm. 'Why not have ourselves a bit of fun while we're here, Dave? Can't do any harm.' Dave pulled himself together and returned Joshua's wicked grin. They followed Daconni out to the cars, while the great detective's men wrapped the bodies in blankets and carried them out and into the back of the shooting brake. 'Thanks, fellas. If you two ride with Mr Rainberg and his friend here, you can direct them to the morgue if we get separated.'

'Separated?'

'You never know.' Franco Daconni, apparently, was not prepared to take any chances with these two unwelcome Israelis.

'OK, boss.'

****

Carl Rufus O'Death had never been a man to hurry. Ever since his school days when he had early discovered there was pleasure to be had in chasing other children who tended to keep their distance, so to speak, he was determined to turn his otherwise unfortunate name to his advantage. And when in adulthood, he rose within a few years to the position not only of Head of the Forensic Department but also of 'Curator' as it were of his local mortuary, he knew he had found his rightful niche. Moreover, he seemed to take a fiendish delight in the knowledge of his clients' discomfort. His name alone appeared to set the 'mood' of his dealings with all his customers. And though he remained polite while interviewing people, whether distraught relatives, helpers, hinderers, busy bodies or 'moneyed dealers', he always managed to extract the right amount of respect from each one of them. And they always paid up. It was as if they couldn't wait to get away. "There's nowt so queer as folk", he was fond of quoting as he slid open another drawer, full of frozen meat. "Nowt so queer as folk". He seemed happy in his work.

The 'cavalcade' had arrived. Daconni was the first to jump out and enter the mortuary. Joshua and Dave followed close behind.

'We have to watch this customer, Dave,' whispered Joshua in his companion's ear. Dave nodded in agreement, while Daconni's men lifted the corpses from the back of the shooting brake and carried them into the place from whence they had so recently been taken.

Now, whilst Mr O'Death may well have had his little quirks - and to some people he remained decidedly odd - never in any way could he have been considered a fool. And though he still had a clear recollection of receiving $20,000 from someone eager to purchase two of his heaviest-looking stiffs, he had no intention of admitting to such a transaction to anyone. Besides giving his word to keep his mouth shut (Mr O'Death always kept his word), he jolly well knew it would behove him to do just that if he wanted to hold on to that money. Moreover, neither of the dead men appeared to have relatives or any other inconvenient incumbents. All O'Death had to do was to keep his mouth shut.

'Can I help you, gentlemen?' O'Death looked up from his latest post-mortem examination and displayed a toothy grin that would have made Dracula seem like a kindly old clergyman. A shudder passed along Dave's spine. But Joshua remained calm and expressionless, his mind concentrated upon solving the mystery of the bodies. Daconni's men appeared in the doorway with their charge and Mr O'Death gave them a brief glance before fixing his eyes on Daconni.

'O'Death. This is Joshua Rainberg of the Israeli Secret Service. You have heard of MOSSAD, I presume?'

'Oh, yes. But what has it got to do with me?'

'With your assistance, old chap, we will be able to clear up any misunderstanding between Mr Rainberg and me. Let's leave it at that.'

'So, what d'you want me to do?'

'Identify these two guys - cause, and time, of death.'

The men slapped the bodies heavily on two tables cleared by O'Death, and everyone waited for the verdict.

'Cause of death - broken backs, I shouldn't wonder,' jested O'Death.

'Oh, very funny, old man.' Daconni was determined the verdict should be one of murder and that the victims' identities should be Colonel D-Day and Mustafa, his bodyguard. If he could pin the murders on MOSSAD, so much the better. It would be yet another feather in his inflated cap. His fame would spread throughout the land, he'd be honoured by the President, the Colonel would be laid to rest and Maria would be his - at last.

O'Death began his examination of the bodies. 'Difficult to say, Mr Daconni. The fire has done a pretty good job of mutilation.'

'Fire? Who said anything about a fire?'

'These bodies have been in an almighty fire.'

'And you remember seeing them in good condition *before* the fire?' Joshua held O'Death with a searching, determined look. No little mortuary man, even with a name as definitive as O'Death, would frighten him.

'What the hell ya getting at, Rainberg?'

'What I'm getting at, Daconni, is that I believe these bodies were used as decoys - the Colonel and his man have escaped. Well, Mr O'Death?'

'Oh, come on, Rainberg.' Daconni was not having it. 'Why would they go to all that trouble? They'd just get the hell out of it.'

'Not if they intended us to waste time examining these two stiffs. They've certainly achieved that objective. Well, Mr O'Death?'

'No, I have not seen these two before, sir.'

'Not seen these two before? Take a look here.' Daconni reached in his jacket pocket and pulled out a number of photographs. Some were shots of the Colonel in the company of the President at one of his extravagant parties; others, of the Colonel with his bodyguard beside him, walking in the grounds of the villa - taken by an inquisitive snooper. Daconni would never turn down the offer of such photos, from whatever source. If nothing else, they served further to stoke up his loathing and envy of the man and give him something to live for.

O'Death remained expressionless. He glanced at the photos of the Colonel and his man. 'If you're trying to get me to say these bodies once belonged to the two men in the photos..... ' (Ah, he was getting to it. Daconni's theory would be proven right......) 'it's impossible to say, at the moment. Could anyone identify these faces? Look at them - burnt beyond recognition. Have you the dental records?'

'Of course not,' snapped Daconni.

'Ah well,...I don't think I will be able to help even you, Mr Daconni. Time of death is easy - between one to two hours ago, I'd say. Cause of death - asphyxiation and burns. And what burns.'

'I want these bodies examined for bullet wounds, too.'

Daconni shot Joshua a sly glance.

'Bullet wounds?' O'Death remained sceptical. 'What a job you've given me, Mr Daconni. It may take me some time to ascertain what you require of me. The fire has made such a pretty mess of the flesh that.......'

Oh, Jesus. Mr O'Death was becoming rather tiresome. Time was slipping by and the Colonel, Joshua believed, was getting farther and farther away. His frustration in letting him slip through his fingers was bad enough. Daconni's frustration in being unable to pin anything on MOSSAD was clearly unbearable. He banged his fist on one of O'Death's lockers and out slid a particularly gruesome body of a woman who'd been strangled a couple of days before. Her eyes were still open and they stared up at Daconni with a look of wild agony. 'Jesus Christ!' Daconni quickly backed away and wiped his sweating forehead with his handkerchief.

'What the hell are ya trying to do to me, O'Death?' The proud curator of the mortuary looked up at the distressed detective and giggled. 'Don't worry about nosy old Bertha. She often pops out for a look around.' He calmly slid Bertha back into her quiet resting-place. Joshua nudged Dave and grinned. He was beginning to warm to Mr O'Death. As far as he was concerned, this one had a nice sting and seemed to know just how to use it on irate and boring nonentities.

'OK. How long d'ya need to give us a verdict either of murder or misadventure?" O'Death smiled to himself. If only he could afford to tell the truth about the two unfortunate clients on the slabs. He knew Rainberg already suspected what had really happened but, thanks to Daconni's constant interruptions, there had been no pressure on him, properly, to answer his inquiry. Besides, he'd given his word to the kind gentleman who had parted with $20,000 to keep quiet about the transaction. And Mr O'Death always kept his word.

'You will have to be patient, Mr Daconni.'

'OK., OK.. May I use your phone?'

'Go right ahead.' Daconni picked up the phone on the desk in the corner of the room. He dialled the number and got straight through to the President. 'Mr President?'

'Franco. How's it going?'

'Not too well, I'm afraid, sir. The fire in the villa has burned the bodies pretty badly. O'Death is checking for bullet wounds now, and........'

'Is Rainberg of MOSSAD with you?'

'Er,.. yes, sir, he is. Why?'

'Well, let me speak with him, man.'

'Right, sir. Just a moment.' Daconni grudgingly held the phone out to Joshua who smiled and calmly 'took up the reins' from his sulky rival.

'Hello, sir.'

'Mr Rainberg. I may have seemed a little sharp with you earlier but I have never had anything less than the greatest respect for your people's talents.'

'Thank you, sir.'

'So, what's your theory?'

'Well, sir, I believe these bodies to be decoys and that the Colonel and his man have escaped.'

'Do you, now? What does O'Death say?'

'He says he's never seen these bodies before and that the men died around two hours ago.'

'OK. Let me speak to him. And come and see me at my office at 5 p.m. - without Daconni, got it?'

'I'll be there, sir.'

O'Death stopped what he was doing and took the phone back from Joshua. 'Yes, Mr President?'

'O'Death? You up to your old tricks again?'

'What could they be, sir?'

'Making people jump with bodies shooting out of drawers, for instance?'

O'Death breathed a sigh of relief. As far as he knew, the President had no knowledge of his little deals with customers for the purchase of a body or two. If he had, he'd never let it be known to him. But the disappearance of the Colonel and his bodyguard could hardly be expected to go unnoticed. If these two bodies were not those of the President's 'guests', where then, did they come from, so conveniently?

But O'Death had never been afraid of anyone, and even the President, it seemed, would just have to accept his diagnosis of the situation. 'So far, Mr President, I can find no trace of bullets or bullet wounds. Both men appear to have suffered blows on the head - either from a fall or fight and one has a nasty cut on the right cheek which seems to have healed up in the fire.'

'Spare me the jokes, O'Death.'

'But Mr President. It's almost impossible to say whether it's the Colonel and his bodyguard. There are no dental records, I understand?'

'Huh. Highly unlikely. All right, O'Death. Thanks for your help. Keep working on it and let me have a full report. Drop everything for this.'

'I will, sir. Goodbye.'

'Oh, before you go. Tell Rainberg there is so far no trace of our fugitives from airport sources or coast guards. It's damned frustrating for us all.'

'I'll tell him, sir.'

Chapter 26

While O'Death continued to waste time and drag out the verdict on the men lying on his slabs - the cause of whose deaths he knew so well - Colonel D-Day, Mustafa and O'Casey were busy enjoying champagne on board the jet making good time for Dublin. Within a few hours, they would be guests of Shaun O'Casey's friends and sympathizers. After a night's rest, there would be meetings the next day and a dinner party with a few folks in high places. Then, it was planned, the guests would be accompanied to Cork and thence to Clonakilty on the West Coast where they'd rest and hide out before the next move. A seventeenth-century farmhouse had been chosen for this purpose - nothing flashy but, with around four acres stretching down to the Atlantic Ocean, it was considered ideal for people on the run. Moreover, it was assumed the Colonel was a romantic. But if he wasn't, at least he could have a bracing swim when he felt like being foolish. O'Casey would also stay at the farmhouse, ready to ferry the Colonel and his man away in the helicopter should time be of the essence.

'I t'ink it's going well, me friends,' suggested O'Casey upon hearing the news from the captain that Dublin was but one hour away. 'A toast, gentlemen.'

'A toast to Ireland,' was graciously proposed by Mustafa and seconded by the Colonel.

'To Ireland.' They all drank.

'And a toast to a restored Iraq,' suggested the Colonel, dreaming of his own restoration to power.

'To President Yudie Doomsday,' toasted Mustafa and O'Casey, winking at each other. Why they should ever have thought such an idea unlikely, God alone knew. But the Colonel had always been a man of conviction and if his bodyguard occasionally suffered periodic lapses of faith in his ideas at least his loyalty could never be in doubt.

'Life will always be stranger than fiction, my brothers,' Yudie prophesied. 'You mark my words. Before the year is out, I shall once more be master of Iraq.'

O'Casey and Mustafa glanced across to each other again but dared not risk another wink. They raised their glasses and toasted the Colonel a second time. 'To Colonel D-Day.'

"President D-Day', my brothers.'

'President D-Day.'

Yudie smiled and thanked both men for their good wishes. He was beginning to feel a little tired and would take a catnap before touchdown. Mustafa watched over his master with affection. He tried to think of his charge as a kind of Messiah. Indeed, his very words had had a certain ring to them – "Before the year is out, I shall once more be master of Iraq". The Colonel had raised his eyes as he spoke. It might have been Christ himself saying, "Today, thou shalt be with me in paradise". Yet, even Mustafa would have admitted such a comparison with his own country - if not with Christ - to be stretching one's imagination a little too far.

****

O'Death, bless him, had at long last finished his work. He was ready to pronounce the verdict - 'death by concussion, asphyxiation and burns.'

'Well? Who did it, O'Death?'

'Who did it?' O'Death stood back and looked Daconni firmly in the eye. If looks could kill, O'Death took the biscuit. He had them all. He'd always had them. Even as a small boy, when he indulged himself in staring matches with other children, he would sometimes be challenged with - 'What's yer name, weirdo?' 'O'DEATH', he'd pronounce dryly. It was enough to do the trick. And the unlucky taunter would run off screaming, ice-cream dripping and unwilling to wait for an explanation why the boy had chosen to linger over the charming and rather Irish inflexion in front of his name.

'Who did it?' mocked O'Death again. I'm not a detective, Mr Daconni. You are the one who is supposed to be clever enough to find that one out.'

'OK., OK.' Daconni gritted his teeth and began to pace the room towards the lockers, remembering what happened last time he knocked into one of them. 'Rainberg. We'd better take a little trip over to the President. You and I together. What d'ya say?'

'But Mr Daconni......'

'Yes?' Daconni hardened his expression.

'The President asked me to see him at 5.'

'Since when did he ask you this?'

'Just a while ago, on that phone.'

Blast. This damned Israeli guy is here just five minutes in Brazil and he's wangled a private meeting with the President as if they'd been buddies for years.

'Is that so?' Daconni was running out of inane responses. And he knew it. 'Christ Almighty, Rainberg. OK, you do your thing and I'll do mine and then we'll see who wins.'

'Fine.' Joshua could not have been happier. He had finally got the man off his back. For he'd no intention of divulging his every move to the President's man.

'Come on, fellas. Let's go.' Daconni and his crew left the premises, got into the shooting brake and drove away, leaving Joshua and Dave to their little chat with nice Mr O'Death. "Where there's a will there's a way" had always been Joshua's maxim. Before the day was out, he was sure to have a lead on the Colonel's whereabouts. If not, then he'd know the Colonel and the President had colluded, and his report to his bosses in Tel Aviv would reflect as much. It would be no less juicy for that.

'President Gonzalez and his men have not been slow in alerting the airport authorities of the world'. That was the impression Manuel Gonzalez wished to give his MOSSAD friend. Of course, the President had made no such moves. The file of Project Jerusalem was firmly in his control (thanks to the late Felix Esbano and the supposed ineptitude of the Colonel). But MOSSAD would go on searching not only for the Colonel but also for those plans for the 'nuclear-headed super-gun'. They were not without experience, and what happened to Gerry Bull could happen to Colonel D-Day. He would be pursued with cool efficiency and shot. In the meantime, the President would have himself a little game with MOSSAD - it would be dangerous. But then, President Manuel Gonzalez liked to live a little dangerously, didn't he? He liked to live near the edge. And if, one day, he fell, or was even pushed over it, well,....... what the hell? Anything to save himself from boredom.

At 5 p.m. exactly, Joshua, and his colleague Dave Adams, were shown into the President's office.

'Mr Rainberg. You are very punctual.' The President held out his hand to the secret agent.

'I try to be, sir. This is my colleague, Dave Adams.'

'Pleased to meet you, sir.'

The men settled themselves into comfortable chairs whilst the clock on the mantelpiece finished striking the hour. It's tones reminded Joshua of Big Ben in London but he could not be quite sure. ' 'Little Ben', I call it, Mr Rainberg. One can't have everything.' Joshua smiled and waited for his host to get down to business.

'Well now. Your theory, Mr Rainberg. You seem convinced the Colonel and his bodyguard have - how would the English so charmingly put it - scarpered? But I prefer your style. 'The bird has flown?''

'Yes, sir. We have reason to believe the Colonel had struck up a friendship with Fritz Krupp, who, as you know, had been living under the name of Felix Esbano.'

'God rest his soul.'

'Yes, well, most of us in Israel, Mr President, would not be inclined to share your sentiments or generosity concerning this man.'

'We all have our faults, Mr Rainberg, and we all have souls - if my memories of simple theology are to be believed.'

'That may be so, Mr President. But my job is to hunt down the men who have shared not only in the responsibility for the Holocaust but who may even be instrumental in bringing about another.'

'I can understand your feelings, my friend.'

Joshua wondered but allowed the President to continue.

'But you see, ours is a society where people are free to come and go. It would be difficult to reverse a policy that has served us so well for so long. That's official. *Now*', whispered the President, 'what we could do - off the record, of course - is to co-operate with you over certain individuals who could pose a danger to our common security and stability.'

The President gave Joshua a wee wink which might (if it had been up to the standard of one from the eye of Arid Aziz), have stood a good chance of upsetting the guest. But Joshua Rainberg was no Bazrani. He was tough, his own man, and very determined. After leaving O'Death's place, he had returned to his hotel and contacted Tel Aviv. Having given his people his report and diagnosis of the situation they had voiced their agreement with him and instructed him, moreover, to remain canny over the President and his tricks. As yet, no money had been telexed to Brazil; nor would it be - so long as President Gonzalez remained difficult.

'What have you in mind, sir?' Joshua put the ball back in his host's court.

'Well, since you seem convinced "the bird has flown", I suggest we use our respective contacts to track his whereabouts and then liaise when either of us has found him.'

'Agreed.'

'And in the meantime our Mr Daconni will, no doubt, continue his own line?' The President softened his words and gave Joshua a human glance of understanding. He clearly had little time for his home-grown detective and, were Joshua not paid so well by his own people, it was conceivable the President would have made his guest an offer he could not refuse.

'I am happy with that, Mr President. Now, these plans the Colonel has for the super-gun......'

'Ah, yes.'

'We are very anxious to get hold of them since, as you probably know, they are detailed plans of a gun with a range capable of reaching New York. We're talking here of a nuclear head launched into space.'

'You mean to tell me the man would not be satisfied with Tel Aviv?'

Joshua could not be certain whether the President was seriously concerned or indulging in an unkind dig against Middle-East politics. But he let it go.

'You have the picture, Mr President.'

'Good heavens.' Manuel Gonzalez continued to act the innocent. 'I don't suppose our North American friends would find the prospect very funny?'

'Exactly. If only you'd known what sort of man you've been harbouring, sir.'

The President knew exactly the sort of man to whom he'd given refuge. But he held his tongue. He had no intention of calmly handing over the file of Project Jerusalem to Joshua Rainberg, much as he respected the man. If the Colonel was not caught he could barter the file for considerable favours, elsewhere.

'Well, I must say, Mr Rainberg - you have not been idle, have you?'

'No, sir. It's imperative we find that file.'

'Not much chance in that fire, I suppose?'

'We started searching the place, sir. Even the remnants of papers of all kinds scattered about. But then Daconni insisted we cool it.'

'Ah, Franco Daconni doesn't like anyone else on his patch, Mr Rainberg. He's very touchy about that.'

'Don't remind me, sir.'

The President gave a sigh, stood up in front of his desk and stretched out his hand to Joshua once more. 'Well, my friend. Keep in touch. I wish you well in your pursuit. We'll get in touch as soon as we have anything. And you do the same, eh?'

'Sure thing, sir. And thank you.'

'Thank you for coming, Mr Rainberg. You, too, Mr Adams. Happy hunting.'

Joshua and Dave smiled to themselves and left the President's office dissatisfied. It had been too short a meeting and Joshua damn well knew Manuel Gonzalez was hiding something. Maybe he'd set the whole thing up. But despite Brazil's reputation for corruption, what hard evidence had he to support his suspicions?

Chapter 27

As time ticked by, the distance put between the Colonel and the 'authorities' had widened further. After a splendid reception given by 'friends' in Dublin and a feast fit for……. well, yes,…… the party left by helicopter for Clonakilty. The farm house where they would stay had been renovated by a work-force brought in from Cork. O'Casey had purchased the property some years back for his clandestine operations. His dealings with various organisations had always been conducted in a civilized manner. And though the world might never understand or sympathize with his approach to political issues, it would, if it had known about it, surely have approved of his life-style.

The house was ready. The guests would be comfortable for as long as it was necessary to stay. There was even a boardroom, superbly decorated with oak panelling, oak table and Regency chairs. The bar in the lounge would have graced the finest club in the land. In fact, if only they knew it, it was the finest club in the land. O'Casey had done his homework. Neither the Colonel nor Mustafa had pleaded tee-total and O'Casey was determined that, even if Yudie never managed to pull off an outrageous coup back in Iraq, he would neither forget the hospitality of the people of Ireland nor the man who had made his escape possible.

There was even a cinema with films to satisfy all tastes - and O'Casey had a shrewd idea of the main thrust of the Colonel's tastes. The television set could pick up all stations via satellite and the bedrooms and bathrooms were straight out of dreamland. Seventeenth-century farmhouse it may once have been but O'Casey had spared nothing to guarantee comfort and peace of mind for his honoured guests. W.R.Hearst's 'San Simeon', in Los Angeles, may well have attracted the great and the famous in the '30s but O'Casey's 'Little Caprice' had already outstripped the newspaper magnate's offerings by more than a Guinness or two. Moreover, if people wished to fornicate after dinner, they were free to do so.

But fornication could not have been farther from the Colonel's mind at this moment. Much as he'd begun to miss his wild sessions with the lovely Maria, matters of anonymity had taken prime consideration in his active brain. Here, in the south of Ireland, he would not only have to reorientate himself (already he'd tried a couple of pints of Guinness followed by some old Jameson - and had, as a result, been inclined to put off doing things) but he would have to devise a foolproof plan not only to retain that anonymity but to enable him to infiltrate his own homeland at the right time. God, how he missed it. How he missed watching his father stirring the pots of meagre soup as a gesture to his men before sending them off to die. How he missed looking in on the torture of the day, or spitting in the face of a foreign agent, or even a brave countryman who had found himself out of line. How he missed his own programme of torture, designed to carry on and develop what his father had shown him. How he missed hearing the screams of the Kurds on film at private showings of Iraqi bombing raids. After all, why should the British have all the best tunes? He missed his wife and children, of course, but they could hardly match up to the pleasures of war.

They settled down to relax in the lounge after a superb meal prepared by O'Casey's cook. She had been in his employ for over fifteen years and had always kept her mouth shut about people she met there - and what they discussed. As far as Mary O'Reilly was concerned, she would rather die than speak about Shaun O'Casey's business associates. If, on occasions, the delivery service failed to deliver, necessitating a personal trip into town, she would be doubly careful of her tongue. And if anyone mentioned 'Little Caprice' in her company, she would shut up like a clam. Everyone respected her.

'Thank you, Mary, for that wonderful meal. The lamb was delicious.'

'Yes, thank you, Mrs O'Reilly', concurred Mustafa with his customary politeness.

'Call me Mary, sir. They all do.' She turned to face the Colonel, already settling himself in a capacious armchair by the fireside. He looked up into her wonderful eyes, huge liquid green eyes, eyes that had seen everything, eyes that could never be fooled. 'Very good meal, Mary. Thank you.' He patted his stomach to indicate satisfaction and wondered what those eyes really wanted to say.

The wind began to howl outside the house, for it was already mid-October. The Atlantic Ocean at the bottom of the garden swelled and hurled itself against the rocks below and opened its freezing arms to anyone crazy enough to have a dip. The house lights brought a glow to the faces of the people inside, relaxing in comfortable easy chairs round the inglenook alive with the fire-crackle of logs. It was a million miles from Brazil with its brash, don't-care attitudes, its sticky heat, its pressures, even its sordid, glutinous politics. This was Ireland - seat of Guinness and poetry; wit and hospitality. Outside strolled a couple of guards, hardened to the life and to the weather, permanently on O'Casey's pay-roll. Whatever their private thoughts and ambitions they had learned, like Mary the cook, to hold their tongues over the comings and goings of their boss's guests. Theirs was not to reason why the helicopter, parked to one side of the house, was necessary or even desirable in a place like Clonakilty. The boss paid them well, treated them right and they thanked their lucky stars they were no longer in that eternal dole queue with the rest of their mates.

'Well now, me old friends,' began Shaun, sinking back into his chair with a large Jameson by his side, 'I t'ink we should finalize the plan we discussed on the plane and tie up any loose ends. What d'ya say Colonel?'

'What happened to Yudie?'

'I was trying to be polite - just like Mustafa, here,' teased Shaun O'Casey.

'Oh, come on now. God knows the number of times I've tried to get Mustafa to call me Yudie, but to no avail.'

'I feel comfortable with 'sir', sir.' Mustafa winked at his boss. It was one of life's little anomalies.

They all had a good laugh to clear the air, if not matters of address. 'All right Shaun. What is the latest inside information you have?'

'Well, much to everyone's surprise, not least to Arid Aziz himself, the Government has held up pretty well. Unlike the Russian experiment, at least people can get food. Even the Kurds are integrating themselves into the mainstream and the whole place is in danger of becoming a tolerant melting pot.'

'God forbid' - if things continued in the way O'Casey had described them, on what possible hook could Yudie hang his ambitions?

'I have an idea, sir.' Mustafa put down his whiskey, and lit up a Havana.

'Let's have it, Mustafa.'

'Ump.....p....p.... Well, if you have no fundamental objection, nor have I.'

'What fundamental objection?' Had Mustafa pushed his luck with the Colonel's innermost sensibilities? Shaun O'Casey, for one, had never gone in for fundamental objections of any kind, though he perceived other people could become very heated over such 'technicalities'.

'Now, don't laugh if I say it. It's only a suggestion, sir.'

'Don't tease the Colonel, Mustafa.'

'Well?' Even Yudie primed himself for the ridiculous.

'Why don't we both have plastic surgery? New faces?'

'New faces. Don't be vulgar, Mustafa,' O'Casey stifled a guffaw.

'Michael Jackson hasn't done so bad, sir.'

'Who's Michael Jackson?'

'He's an American pop star, sir.'

'Oh.' The Colonel did not appear keen to continue the line of Mustafa's argument, though the idea of a slight alteration to his image, merely for the purpose of getting back into Iraq, had already begun to filter through his Jameson-inspired brain cells. To his mind, dark glasses and beards had not outlived their day.

'If Shaun's analysis is correct, sir, there seems little chance of stepping off the plane at Baghdad airport a free man, looking as you do.' The Colonel shot his bodyguard a particularly sly glance. He'd always rated his looks fairly highly. And it was still painful to him to accept the idea that those looks might be advantageously altered. But he was not entirely stupid and he could see that all avenues of procedure had to be examined if he ever stood that chance of returning to Iraq and gaining power once more.

O'Casey had been biding his time. He knew damned well the Colonel hadn't a hope in hell of realizing his ambition through the normal means of a military coup. Not unless or until the present system failed beyond redemption. The people had begun to enjoy their new freedoms and, if life was still a bit tough in economic terms, at least they could voice their dissatisfaction without being tortured or merely shot for their efforts. No, the more O'Casey thought about it, the more he considered the benefits of plastic surgery for both the Colonel and his bodyguard. Besides, Mustafa was someone Yudie could trust. And if he was willing to take a chance, why shouldn't the Colonel? They could both hang around 'Little Caprice' until they got used to their new faces. And after trying them out in the local boozer, they'd have even more confidence to take a trip to Cork, or Dublin, or even London. Maybe, within the year, the Colonel's dream would come true, or perhaps, part of it?

He suggested, 'if you cannot gain control of Iraq in one fell swoop, you might at least be able to live there as a resident alien.'

'Resident alien? Why do you insult me, O'Casey?'

'No insult, sir. I assure you.'

Mustafa breathed a sigh of relief. The conversation could easily become somewhat touchy and he wondered whether O'Casey was up to handling the delicacies of the Colonel's 'face-saving' yet ruthless background. He decided to step in and calm the ruffled feathers.

'Resident Alien is merely a technical term, sir. They even used it in Spain. None of the ex-pats I knew who lived there seemed to be troubled. Besides, I believe any sacrifice is worth making in order to return to the homeland.'

The House of Baghdad

This did the trick. The Colonel looked at his bodyguard with growing pride. Who else in the history of great men could have boasted of a friend like Mustafa? He was much more than a bodyguard. He was a companion, an intelligent man, a loyal subject and a believer.

'Mustafa, I love you. If you are willing to go through hell with me, who am I to forsake you?' A tear dripped down the left cheek of the Colonel as he spoke. If only a woman could be like a man. He had never seen My Fair Lady but his thoughts would surely have found echo in more than a few men's breasts?

'But, sir, plastic surgery is not hell - necessarily.'

'Not all surgeons allow their hands to slip, Yudie.' O'Casey was doing his best to keep up the spirits of his guests. But Mustafa doubted he'd yet learned the trick - where his master was concerned. Luckily for both men, the Colonel suddenly let out a robust guffaw. It may have been the Jameson - it may have been the sound of the howling wind outside. But the image of himself stepping off the plane at Baghdad, looking like Michael Jackson, had tickled his fancy. 'Michael Jackson, eh?'

Mustafa and O'Casey looked at each other in astonishment and then to the Colonel - who proceeded to giggle with delight and foolish imaginings. 'But, bu.... I thought you'd never heard of him, sir?'

'Course I have, Mustafa. I was just trying to be,.... er, cool, man, *cool*.'

Casey and Mustafa rocked with laughter. If only 'they' could see him now. If only... The people of Iraq would drop - if not their knickers - then their new democratic Government, squabbling on TV in ridiculous parody of the British House of Commons. They'd drop it and welcome the

Colonel back with open arms. Mustafa, for his part, was determined to pursue the argument, now that the ice had been broken - now that his boss had begun to loosen up and enjoy himself. 'Well, sir, if not Michael Jackson - how about Anthony Eden?'

'What?' The Colonel dropped his glass on to the carpet. But it was not so much out of anger or disgust as...... well, the Jameson was indeed very, very good.

'A brilliant idea, Mustafa, if I may say so.' O'Casey's eyes had lit up. Although the man never exactly endeared himself to the Irish heart, by golly, he was handsome. 'Oh yes, Mustafa, I t'ink you've hit it.'

O'Casey and Mustafa proceeded to study more closely the features of the Colonel, now sitting there in bemused, soused repose.

'Oh yes, sir. There's no doubt. With a little trimming here, a little something there and the job's done.'

'What about the eyes, Mustafa?'

'The,....... ah, yes, now we may have a slight problem there, I must admit.

'I'd really rather be Nasser,' pronounced the Colonel unequivocally.

'Well, at least his moustache was decently trimmed, like Eden's,' offered O'Casey.

'But the build, and the head is all wrong,' added Mustafa. O'Casey giggled.

'Hey, hey, you two monkeys. And who, may I ask, have you in mind to carry out this risky operation, my dear Shaun?'

'Well, now, it just so happens....... I have the perfect man for such a venture, here in County Cork. His name is Dr Kochs.'

The House of Baghdad

The Colonel's mouth and that of Mustafa fell wide open. The Colonel almost choked on his whiskey, so quickly replaced by O'Casey after seeing his guest's glass go down on the floor.

'Ah yes, me old friends,' continued O'Casey undaunted, 'Dr Joseph Kochs, resident alien, we might say, of little old Ireland. You know him, I believe?'

Chapter 28

It would have been an exaggeration to speak of the Colonel as the doctor's hero. Following the revolution in Iraq, the plastic surgeon had been left to his own devices and method of escape. Happily, (and no thanks to the Colonel) he had found himself a safe haven in Ireland and had never looked back. It was hardly surprising, therefore, that there had been other people in the world (now long dead) to whom the doctor would have looked up in awe, if circumstances had been different. But he had managed to keep his mouth shut over his racial feelings. Besides, for a time, he knew where his bread was buttered. Over the years in Iraq, he'd been given almost a free hand to work on faces of unfortunate and understandably reluctant subjects of his infamous master. Indeed, during the Colonel's reign of terror - the secrets of which had for too long been kept from the eyes of the world - many such faces were required to be altered and, in some cases, even obliterated. The wishes of Colonel Doomsday were hardly to be questioned, if one knew what was good for one. Yet, conveniently for Dr Kochs, the Colonel somehow appeared to sympathize with the darker side of this clever surgeon's character - his interest in the macabre, his sinister coolness when making the first cut into the flesh of a new victim. Murders, of course, were part of the normal menu of 'Government policy' during this reign of terror. But it was often expedient, and certainly more interesting, to trust in plastic surgery where a more subtle solution needed to be found for the nation's 'security'. And Dr Kochs was just the man for the job. Working for the Colonel in this way he'd had a field day.

It was, therefore, particularly fortuitous that Dr Kochs should be in residence in Ireland just at the time his former master should have need of his services. If ever there was clear indication of Allah's thinking, this was it. Most people had to wait for the next life before being endowed with a brand new countenance. If surgery was to be the means by which the Colonel would gain power in the old country once more, then who was he to question the will of Allah?

'Allah be praised.' exulted Dr Kochs rather too eagerly at the other end of the telephone on receiving the news from Mustafa, currently in residence in 'Little Caprice'. 'I shall be happy to help.'

The Colonel's bodyguard had long suspected the surgeon of working for as many sides as possible. Uncharacteristically, and inconveniently perhaps for some people's peace of mind, Mustafa had travelled and read extensively and had never forgotten the story which broke in all the newspapers at the time of that creepy little rat called Fuchs who, if it suited him, would work for anyone. And what a weapon *he* had tucked away! Judging from all the photographs and newspaper cuttings which Mustafa had collected over the years, Fuchs could well have been the grandfather of 'Dr Kochs'. They were the spitting image of one another.

As far as the Colonel was concerned, however, old Kochs' talents were sufficient for immediate purposes. Nuclear weapons, alas, would have to wait until he could smuggle back into the old country and worm his way into power for good.

The House of Baghdad

Worming one's way in - that was it. The more the Colonel contemplated the new situation in Iraq, the more he was finally convinced his old methods of violence and terror would no longer work. A leopard may not be able to change his spots but, unlike an old dog, there was no reason why he should not learn new tricks.

****

It was soon arranged. Mustafa, bless him, had volunteered to be the first to have his face experimented upon. After all, despite his personal mistrust of Dr Kochs, he had always been quick to acknowledge the talent and sheer genius of the little German surgeon. In fact, some of the new faces given to recalcitrant and stubborn dissidents back home were, to Mustafa's mind, too good for the bastards and Dr Kochs had, consequently, been ordered to 'mix things up a bit'.

So Mustafa had little hesitation in suggesting Kochs should begin working on him. It might give the Colonel some encouragement. But, to his surprise and delight, his master insisted he should be the first - Allah had willed it - and what Allah wills let no man.......

It was finally agreed that, considering the difference in the size and shape of head, the Colonel should not go for the Nasser look, despite his late father's hero-worship of the man. With the popular ratings on Iraqi TV currently swinging between Arid Aziz and his good-looking opposite number Faisal Hussein (with a discernible bias towards the younger man with the film-star looks), even Yudie conceded that if Dr Kochs could make him appear the image of Anthony Eden in his heyday, all memories of

British Imperialism would perversely be forgotten and its deeds forgiven. And dissatisfied Arab women would swoon in droves round him resulting in votes for the young Hussein being transferred in favour of the mature man. All he had to do would be to use his considerable guile and presence to have himself democratically elected. After all, if lesser mortals with a conspicuous absence of charisma could do it in England, how much more chance had he in his own deprived country?

Yes, damn it. He'd go for it. He'd always fancied himself as an actor. This could be his big chance. And if asked to play the part of Colonel Doomsday in a Hollywood blockbuster, what better man for the job than he, Yudie himself?

****

Dr Kochs, as was his wont, arrived bang on time. As the grandfather clock struck three in the lobby of 'Little Caprice', the surgeon put his finger to the bell and waited. Mary O'Reilly, who doubled as receptionist, answered the door.

'Oh, yes, Dr Kochs. We are expecting you. Do come in.'

Dr Kochs shook his umbrella and stepped inside.

'Thank you, Mrs O'Reilly. A nasty day again.'

'Indeed, indeed. Never mind. I'll soon have a nice cup of tea ready to warm you up.' Mary took the surgeon's top coat and hung it up on the rack beside the clock.

'Ah,...... Mrs O'Reilly. What would we all do without you?'

'Get away with you.' Mary O'Reilly waddled off to the kitchen while Dr Kochs entered the reception room to be greeted by Shaun O'Casey and then by his old master Colonel Doomsday and Mustafa, his trusty bodyguard.

'My word, Joseph. You look younger every day.'

'*You* are looking extremely healthy these days. Welcome back to... er..'

'Civilization, were you about to say?'

Mustafa smiled at Dr. Kochs, whose embarrassment and temporary loss for words, somehow imbued the atmosphere with a certain awkwardness, a touch of deference for the past, a kind of silent showdown, wherein the players could find their places and settle themselves before making the next move.

'Life has not been so bad for me and Mustafa,' insisted the Colonel, breaking what might have developed into unwanted tension, 'how about yourself?'

The Colonel was determined to start his new career of a smooth politician as he meant to carry on. What better opportunity than to make a good impression on a former subject? Admittedly, he'd always paid the surgeon well for his services. But the fact the revolution had, unlike many others in the world, actually changed the lives of the average Iraqi in terms of freedom of speech and freedom to travel might well have given the doctor food for thought, if nothing else. Besides, Colonel D-Day had done nothing in the way of helping the man to safety. The doctor seemed content enough at the moment, but his good health appeared to be due more to O'Casey's efforts than to those of the Colonel.

'I am very well, thank you, sir. I have found peace and contentment, here in Ireland - thanks to your friend and mine.' The doctor looked benignly upon Shaun O'Casey.

'Besides, you had your own considerable problems, I imagine.'

Yudie breathed a sigh of relief. 'Still do, Joseph. But with your help and skill I could, despite everything that has happened, find myself accepted back home as a new man. And for that, my dear friend, I shall be for ever in your debt.'

It was the first time the Colonel had called Dr. Kochs "my dear friend" and the first time he had ever contemplated being in his debt. But then, the man *was*, it appeared, in a tight spot. If he had a mind to ask, the surgeon could demand a hefty fee for his services, or perhaps he could even afford to refuse the job altogether, now that the revolution had taken hold. Yet if he denied his former master the chance to regain power with a new image, who could say what fate might befall him, here in Ireland? No, it would be unwise of him to do anything to jeopardize his new, calmer life-style. Moreover, with the encouragement of O'Casey himself, he had begun to develop another talent - painting in water-colours. Who could tell? Maybe it would not be long before Shaun would be able to slip one of Dr Koch's efforts into a collection of Impressionist paintings that he'd been acquiring over the years? They had become the envy of collectors within the Pale. Beyond the Pale, people chose not to notice, and he was happy to leave it at that.

There had, however, been several occasions since leaving Iraq for the doctor to 'keep his hand in' regarding his primary skill. If O'Casey saw no other reasonable method of persuading people to see things his way, (to his mind elimination had become passé and boring) then surgery, under anaesthetic, tended to shed a new light on matters.

Surgery, without anaesthetic, would have shed an even more startling light. But O'Casey was, at least, humane. And Dr Kochs always appeared willing to oblige. If the Colonel had paid him well in the old days (and he always had), then Shaun O'Casey could match that with no trouble at all. It was a gentlemen's agreement and Shaun took pride in upholding his countrymen's reputation for generosity.

****

In a little more than six hours the operation was over. But it was several weeks before the bandages were removed and the Colonel took his first look at the face in the mirror. The surgeon believed he'd done a great job. He liked to think of his creations as his babies - much as a writer regards his books - or at least as eggs which, with a little luck, hatch into enough success to provide him with a bit of money; a track record and 'something to leave for posterity'.

'What do you think, sir?' The doctor stood back, and held his breath for the reaction. The Colonel looked at himself and studied every angle, every crevice, every line. It seemed an eternity before he spoke and Dr Kochs began to wonder whether he should have let the knife slip and had done with it. The ears were different - they no longer stuck out. The forehead, somehow, was made to look more intelligent, less parochial. The moustache, an easy job - and nothing to do with surgery as such - nevertheless had been trimmed to match the new, better-looking features. The line of the chin matched perfectly the line of the forehead and the whole ensemble gave the viewer an impression of strength with grace, authority with wisdom, power with dignity. There was also a touch of humour and understanding which, unfortunately, went unnoticed by Yudie himself. Yet there was no doubt - here was a man for all seasons, a man who would touch the hearts and appeal to the imagination of the newly liberated Iraqi people. The women, and maybe some of the men, would go wild.

'It's fantastic! Praised be to Allah!'

The doctor sighed with relief - mixed with disappointment. 'Praised be to me,' he himself would prefer to have said. But he held his tongue and considered himself lucky. Perhaps, after this achievement, he would still be No.1 in the Colonel's book of plastic surgeons? Yes, he felt glad he'd resisted the temptation to do his worst with the knife. Or could it have been weakness and fear that had stayed his hand?

'Wonderful job, Joseph. Wonderful.' O'Casey shook the surgeon's hand and giggled. 'A ringer for Anthony Eden. Those politicians better watch out.'

'Congratulations, Joseph.' Mustafa had to admit the effect was magnificent. The Colonel would have no problem - on image alone - in persuading people to vote for him. And if he managed to avoid the sort of disastrous mistake which brought down his late British look-a-like, there was no reason why he shouldn't stay in power till……

'I shall be faithful to the end, sir. Count on me.' The old surgeon's words unnerved the Colonel. 'What do you mean, till the *end?* Sounds ominously near, the way you put it. Too near for comfort.'

'A natural death, of course, sir. *You* will outlive me, never fear.' And with that, the Colonel looked deep into the surgeon's eyes. Strangely, he could detect no trace of animosity. The little old doctor, who reminded Mustafa of Fuchs, could be trusted, decided the Colonel. After all, he was only a spitting image. It couldn't be one and the same man. Could it?

'What do you know about nuclear fission, Kochs?'

'Nothing, sir.'

'Right. Well, you can have a go at Mustafa's face, now.'

Mustafa laughed. His master had a sense of humour, after all. Once he was back in power, perhaps he would even be given some credit for it.

Chapter 29

In Brazil, the media were having a field-day rarely enjoyed in their chequered history. The disappearance of the Colonel and his bodyguard would, in Joshua Rainberg's opinion, remain a talking point forever if the fugitives were not caught and dealt with. The fact several newspaper editors were convinced both men had been murdered by MOSSAD, an accusation publicly endorsed by Franco Daconni, served only to leave the way open for an Israeli pursuit of them.

Other papers and magazines took a more sceptical view. **'DEAD or ALIVE?'** questioned Time, whose sales in Brazil suddenly picked up from a half-hearted trickle to a voracious raid on every newspaper stall in the country. An in-depth but lucid study awaited its readers of the history and nature of dictators and that of Colonel Doomsday in particular. Rarely seen photographs of the man filled the pages together with comparisons of well-known poses of his infamous father Sodom the Lesser. If only the papers had known what a dramatic change had come over Colonel Doomsday so very recently they would have fought like cats and dogs for yet another twist to the tale.

Maria, bless her, had shed all the tears of which she was capable - there had been few, despite having had such an interesting time during the Colonel's brief stay in her country. As expected, she was back with Manuel from whose face she would love to have wiped that infuriating smile. Her old friend and godfather, Pepe Fernandez, afforded himself a sigh of relief. Yet another burden had been lifted from his tired shoulders and at last he could manage a smile or two. He could even afford to go to his grave, safe in the knowledge he had kept faith with Maria's dead parents both of whom he'd loved as much as he loved their daughter.

In Iraq, the media geared itself to an endless discussion of the story. And professors, young and old, vied with foreign journalists in an analysis of the situation. Believers and non-believers were equally divided. And those who believed the Colonel was alive, tussled with an intriguing moral problem. Should Iraq stretch out a brotherly hand to the Colonel and welcome him back into the bosom of the family? Should the country play host to its prodigal son? Should Iraq join forces with Israel and track him down, put him on trial - and hang him? Or should the country grow up and renounce retribution for ever? The world would be watching. And once it had seen the real maturity of Iraq with its own eyes, it would do everything in its power to ensure the new democracy continued to flourish. The Colonel would see the error of his ways and fall down on his knees in the mosque praying for forgiveness. Better still, he might even enter the new Parliament as an MP and publicly declare his allegiance to the new constitution. The TV cameras would pick up another sensational scoop. He might even shake hands with Arid Aziz and Dan Levy and the world would be witness to the greatest public political climb-down in history. Egg would be dripping from the faces of the hard-liners who had managed to remain in the country. They had never ceased to revile Prime Minister Aziz over his handling of the country's affairs and warn him his Government could never achieve what only Colonel D-Day could achieve - a united nation under one flag. But the nation had seen what the Colonel could do and had turned its back on his bloody ways. But if he really had changed for the better, what a scoop for the new democracy. Who knows? If he played his cards right he might even succeed Arid Aziz as Prime Minister or take the place of President Bazrani, the Ambassador's elderly father? Allah would be praised indeed, if Colonel Doomsday really had changed his spots. 'There is more rejoicing in Heaven over one sinner that repenteth than ninety and nine souls that are pure'. And for that, perhaps the Koran might stretch a point?

In the camp of the non-believers, there were those who were saddened by his death and those who rejoiced.

'Good riddance.' shouted an Opposition MP on the reopening of Parliament after the summer recess. Mid-October was a good enough time to voice such abuses; and in the presence of TV cameras, it was just as effective as singing 'The Red Flag'. In any case, Faisal Hussein's party had modelled itself on the British Labour Party and had soon learned how easy it is to turn 180 degrees without the public noticing.

In Ireland, the story was discussed with no less vociferousness. Yet only a handful of VIPs knew that the man of the moment resided in their midst. But unlike many of their compatriots who would have blabbed to everyone if they had been privy to the information, they continued to keep their counsel. O'Casey had done a good job in picking his men. It was just another example of his many, considerable talents.

Commensurate with their fondness for a loveable villain, many people of all nations harboured a quiet admiration for the Colonel and his efforts to evade capture. If he was dead, he was dead. But if he was alive, they hoped he'd pop up again somewhere, not necessarily in order to do his worst but to pick up the pieces and start all over again. The spirit of Errol Flynn's swashbuckling adventures, seemed to have revived visions of better times in the memories of the older generation and a new toast had suddenly been invented in many of the watering-holes of the south. 'To Colonel D-Day', they shouted. 'Doomsday does it again.' Fears and doubts entered some hearts, while the hopes of the IRA, who the world thought had finally been laid to rest, were quietly raised once more.

In Clonakilty, people went about their business with their customary gentle pace. Darts were still thrown in the local pubs, Guinness consumed in steady quantities, guitars played by brave English ex-pats and 'to be sure, to be sure' echoed round the walls in response to each and every theory over the Colonel's likely whereabouts.

In the lounge of 'Little Caprice', the Colonel and Mustafa sat glued to the television set for the news bulletins and for those continual transmissions of Dan Levy's 'House of Baghdad'. Shaun O'Casey tapped Mustafa on the shoulder. Tipples of Jameson were quietly passed to his world-famous guests. And two pairs of square eyes looked up into his face. 'Thank you, Shaun. You treat us too well.'

'Not at all, not at all. I t'ink it'll soon be time for ye to leave these old shores for a new life, gentlemen.'

'I believe you are right, Shaun.' Mustafa raised his glass to the cause.

'To President D-Day.'

'President D-Day.'

'Steady, my friends. One thing at a time.'

Could the Colonel be learning? Could he already be a changed man - to match his new face? Could he, at last, be ready to listen to good advice, to go through the laborious process of working his way up to power through means fair - rather than foul? The Anthony Eden look was already growing on him. Perhaps it was just as well, since he had no intention of developing a penchant for plastic surgery - like some pop stars Mustafa kept talking about. He was either brave or foolhardy enough to go through it once - if this didn't work, well, at least he could join the queue of the rest of the world's doubles. He might even grab a part in a film as Eden playing opposite Colonel Nasser in "Eden's Bête Noire". And speaking of films, there was always the possibility of being asked to play Colonel D-Day in that Hollywood blockbuster. With a little bit of manipulation from a clever make-up artist, (rather than Dr Kochs with his ready knife) he was sure he would begin to look and certainly feel like his old self again. There would be no difficulty in learning about his real soul. For him, acting that part would be second nature.

'Look at them, sir. Look at 'em. Doesn't it make you sick?'

Mustafa's opinion of Arid Aziz and his opposite number Faisal Hussein was becoming increasingly jaundiced. 'They think they know it all.'

'But they love it, Mustafa. They love it. And so will I.......'

'You'll wipe the board, sir.'

'No doubt about it,' agreed Shaun, settling into his chair beside his two guests. The images displaying themselves on the screen may have been well known to audiences across the globe. But compared with what the Colonel could do, they were bloody hams.

Almost as if the collective thoughts of the three men had been transmitted telepathically to the producer, the TV presenter appeared on the screen and announced a 'New Faces' competition for prospective Members of Parliament. The competition would be the first of its kind anywhere in the world. It had been initiated by a joint committee which included the 'two crazy Englishmen', the Caliph, John Broadbridge, Jim Rosenberg, and Dan Levy himself. Whilst at first the idea had been opposed both by Arid Aziz and Faisal Hussein on grounds of unfair competition and unprofessionalism, (jealousy apparently didn't come into it) they had soon come round to the idea, believing it to be an ideal opportunity not only to show 'unlikely hopefuls' how damned difficult it really was - but also to show them the door. 'Everybody thinks it's easy,' sniffed Arid Aziz. 'OK. Let 'em try.' And Faisal Hussein soon agreed with the Prime Minister. After all, the Opposition was supposed to favour power to the people.

The competition was to take place during the Christmas recess and the entrance fee charged to each competitor would help further in the upkeep of the Chamber as well as going towards the fees of the TV crew. It may have been considered mad by many people but the idea would not only tickle the fancy of many a budding MP but would provide Dan Levy with yet another way of maintaining those high ratings whilst offering more absurd entertainment for the Christmas season. The man was already a multi-millionaire from this programme alone and he continued to be prepared to knock out anyone with his bare hands who seriously questioned either his nice little set-up or Iraq's new-found sense of humour.

'The competition is open to the world and any winner not an Iraqi citizen will be given a chance to take out Iraqi citizenship. Entries for this unique competition must reach us by November 5th.' A wry smile crossed the face of the announcer - an Iraqi who'd studied English History in the UK - and who no doubt hoped the ghost of Guy Fawkes would do his worst by wrecking the Chamber and putting an end to all the nonsense, once and for all.

'*This* is the break we've been looking for, Mustafa.'

'I agree, sir. You *must* go for it.'

'Can't lose,' echoed Shaun O'Casey. And the three men drank a toast - 'To the success of Colonel D-Day.'

'Sorry. *President* D-Day,' corrected Mustafa.

'One thing at a time, gentlemen.' Perhaps the Colonel really was a changed man.

'OK, OK,' began Shaun O'Casey excitedly, 'now we have to have new names for both of you.'

'What about O'Casey? *My* little thank you, Shaun?' The Colonel was beginning to enjoy himself.

Shaun laughed, while Mustafa simply grinned over the idea.

'I appreciate it, to be sure. But I t'ink a name a little less known to certain of our brethren might be wiser?'

'How about Donovan?' suggested Mustafa lightly.

'Oh no, Mustafa. Not another pop star?'

'I'm afraid he was, sir.'

'Was?'

'Well, the one I'm thinking of hasn't been seen or talked about in years.'

'Good. That's for me. Besides, I like the name.'

Shaun O'Casey sighed with relief. Of all his political and business connections, there were so many Donovans amongst them that one more, soon off to partake in a risky experiment in Iraq, could do no harm.

'Right then, gentlemen. Donovan it is. As the surname, though. Shame Anthony Eden was an Englishman. But at least he was damned handsome, like us Irish, eh?'

'Quite.' Mustafa decided to keep the discussion short and sweet.

'Now for the Christian name.'

'*Christian* name?'

'*Oh* yes. We have to 'play the white man', Colonel. Sorry about that. But it's all in a good cause, don't forget.'

'How about Jason?' teased Mustafa, pushing his master's good humour to the limit.

'No, Mustafa. No more pop stars, please. If it's got to be Donovan, which I admit to liking, make the first name strong and old-fashioned. Why not just plain John?'

'John Donovan. Yes, that's good,' agreed Mustafa and Shaun.

'Now, for *you*, Mustafa?' The Colonel, slumped in his chair, felt O'Casey was rushing things a little.

'Has it got to be Irish? Might look a bit suspicious for both of us to be Celts. No offence, Shaun.'

'None taken, Mustafa. OK. What d'ye suggest?'

'How about a Spanish name?'

'Why not?'

'Something like Bueno?'

'Ah, that's a good 'un.'

'Pun taken.'

'And the other names?'

'How about making it sound a little more classy? You know, with a nice-sounding middle name?'

'Like Perez, you mean?'

'That's it. Something - Perez Bueno.'

'Got it. Antonio Perez Bueno.'

The House of Baghdad

'Excellent. Yes. Antonio Perez Bueno.'

The Colonel began to feel a little jealous of Mustafa's new name. Somehow, John Donovan no longer felt quite right. A frown furrowed his beautiful new forehead and he had begun to take on the guise of Anthony Eden in the last throes of his dying Premiership. That would hardly be the image people would swoon over.

'Now, look, Shaun. Much as I love you Irish, the lilt of your tongue, the romanticism of......' (romanticism? What the hell did Colonel D-Day know about romanticism?) 'I really feel I should have a name that reflects the spirit of my eyes.' The spirit of his eyes? What could the Colonel mean? Death and destruction; murder, rape and pillage? Or 'get in my way and I'll kill you' maybe? He had always possessed those eyes. They were the eyes of his father. Yes, Sodom the Lesser had those eyes - cruel, greedy, manic. And the set of the face matched the intentions of those eyes. But Yudie, his son, had a new face - a face skilfully sculptured by the doctor, chiselled and moulded with care and imagination. The skin pigment didn't really matter - Eden looked wonderful after a holiday in the sun. But the eyes? No. The Colonel would have to take an Arab or Mediterranean name.

All right, all right, all right. Let's see, now. How about Gonzalez?'

'Oh, very droll. Now, come on, gentlemen.' The three men racked their brains. 'I'll take an Arab name,' insisted the Colonel. 'Something like Yussef,.. er..... Khomeini?'

'Pushing t'ings a little, don't ye t'ink?', questioned O'Casey.

'Oh, damn it. Yussef Khomeini it is. It will show my respect for Iran.' The Colonel appeared adamant. 'It will aid my triumphant homecoming. Allah will be at my side.' The Jameson, it seemed, was beginning to have a profound effect upon the famous fugitive. Perhaps all that surgery had been performed in the wrong department?

And Mustafa and O'Casey wondered what tomorrow would bring.

Chapter 30

Dave Fletcher switched off his word processor and leant back in his chair to stretch himself. He'd been working hard on his new book entitled 'The Lure of Power' and had finally succumbed to the lure of a break. Ensconced in his flat overlooking Lake Geneva, he'd scarcely had time to avail himself of the pleasures of the flesh or of the tittle-tattle currently enlivening even the most circumspect restaurants in town. And there were many such restaurants.

The antics of the Iraqi Parliament, it seemed, had permeated even the hardest of hearts and there was even the likelihood of one enterprising young TV producer raising the finance for a Swiss version of 'The House of Baghdad'. The proudest of all neutral states, it was feared by some, was in serious danger of corruption from the new sense of fun running amok in the Middle East. At least people knew where they were with Sodom the Lesser and Colonel Doomsday. A democratic Iraq could de-stabilize the world.

Dave swivelled round in his chair to switch on the TV set. He liked to keep abreast of world events despite his concentration on the book which, thank God, was finally approaching completion. Once he'd read and approved the proofs, he'd treat himself, he decided, to a little trip to somewhere warm in order to wind down and re-charge the proverbial batteries.

The TV burst into life. The presenter, face already contorted with barely-controlled mirth, was in the throes of giving details of the new competition for budding politicians: 'Entries for 'New Faces" he announced, calming himself with difficulty, 'must reach us by November

5th......' Dave Fletcher could no longer contain himself and his laughter, resounding through the ceiling of the flat below, brought anxious feet running to his door.

'Mr Fletcher, are you all right?' asked the caretaker lady, her eyes bristling with concern not so much for Dave's welfare as for the reputation of the building. Like Chestertons of England, the Swiss agents knew just what pressure to put upon their employees in order to maintain the status quo.

'I'm all right, Anna, thank you. It's just something I'm watching on television.'

'Oh, I thought you may have had someone with you?'

'It's not a crime to laugh, is it, Anna, or to have someone with me?'

Anna raised her eyebrows and turned on her heels. If it was not exactly a crime, to laugh on one's own remained decidedly suspect - and to have someone with one, well......

Dave returned to the television set in time to watch several unlikely candidates for the competition being interviewed in the streets of Baghdad by an Englishman whom he recognized. 'Good God. It's John Broadbridge!' Dave Fletcher had heard, via the BBC, how his colleague had taken rather badly the success of Dan Levy's 'House of Baghdad'. But John had to be respected for turning his natural jealousy into positive thought. And though his 'Baghdad Line' would never be able to match Levy's remarkable TV Programme, he had decided to make his services available to the American, perhaps in the hope of getting in on the act. One never knows. Success can sort of rub off on one, can't it? That was John Broadbridge's belief, anyway. Besides, his friendship with the Caliph had matured into a good business arrangement - instinctively the Caliph appeared to understand Englishmen and he'd made clear to his friend that he never need return home, particularly if the mere mention of Swindon remained the cause of his otherwise inexplicable migraines.

'Where do you think the Prime Minister has gone wrong?' he was seen asking an especially vociferous hopeful in a busy market street. 'Ha. You ask me that? You can see for yourself. The country's going to the dogs, its going to the dogs. The young people are on drugs, running around stealing from anyone so they can pay for those drugs. Shouting abuse. Shouting……..'

'Begging your pardon, sir. But that's what you're doing - shouting……'

The man, elderly, with grey hair and large bulbous eyes had seen it all and should have known better. He calmed down and attempted to conduct his argument more or less in sign language. It got the crowd interested and John Broadbridge decided to direct the microphone to someone else. 'All right,' the irate lady began. 'Why can't women be in Parliament? Why can't women have the vote? Why is it always the men who give the orders? We want our freedom, too.'

John Broadbridge wondered what he'd got himself into and, for a brief moment, a vision of life in his home town flashed through his mind. But he dismissed the picture from his brain and persevered with the interviews. Mad the people may be, but life in this place could never be dull. And anything was better than migraine.

The announcer came back on to the screen to reveal the details of the competition schedule. Out of the thousands of entries expected by November 5th, a number of winners would be selected by a draw to correspond with the exact number of MPs, the idea being (thought Dave Fletcher) that the people could see for themselves that democracy really did exist and that there was always an alternative to the House of MPs for whom they had voted in a rash moment of ignorance. Dave Fletcher could see the reasoning behind it all. It was obvious that both the Government and the Opposition - together with the President - hoped such a fiasco would prevail during the competition (rather like the first 'trial' for Dan Levy's programme) that the public would count their blessings, thank their lucky stars and look forward to the return of the real MPs after the Christmas break.

Dave had seen enough. He switched off the TV set and returned to his processor.......

> *'The world would appear to have gone completely mad,' he began, 'and with the speculation and excitement surrounding Colonel Doomsday's mysterious disappearance, Iraq, it might seem, has finally taken leave of her senses. If one can cope with a Country which has lurched from one extreme to another within a few months, then I would have no hesitation in suggesting Iraq is the place to be, right now. Brutal dictatorship, to loony Left antics in the space of a year, would have sent the average First World country spinning off its smug, well-plotted axis. But Iraq has never been like that. She has never been content. Ever since the ruthless bombing of the Kurds by the RAF in the early 1920s in an attempt to force their integration into the*

mainly Arab State, Iraq has never enjoyed peace as we Westerners know it. We may have suffered two terrible World Wars, in which millions died and lives were shattered, but, between those wars and more especially after the Second, there has been a peace which we in the West take too readily for granted.

Let us hope what is going on in Iraq today is not a serious aberration of democracy or merely a show for the amusement of cynical Westerners like myself and a way for a few greedy people to make money. Rather, let us hope there has been a fundamental and permanent shift from brutal dictatorship. If this is indeed the case, then we in the West should do everything in our power to encourage and foster the new State, rather than allow the return of a dictator whose only interest could be to exploit its teething troubles and snuff it out.'

Dave Fletcher printed out his leader and picked up the phone to book his flight to Baghdad. He had prided himself on being a man for all seasons. He had covered the revolution with brilliance and distinction - perhaps he'd be just in time to cover another.

****

The plane from Dublin touched down at Baghdad airport at exactly 4 p.m. local time with 'Jussef Khomeini' and 'Antonio Perez Bueno' on board. It was not exactly going to be like the homecoming of the great Ayatollah Khomeini.

But then - as Shaun O'Casey chose to put it (rather cruelly, in Mr Bueno's opinion)- 'beggars can't be choosers'. There were no crowds to greet the Colonel, to fall down on their knees before him, to kiss his hands and feet, to fawn on him or to sweep him off somewhere in a great limousine. With Antonio beside him, standing in for an otherwise engaged Allah, Yussef Khomeini could, at best, hope for a safe passage through Customs, a bumpy ride in a taxi and an undisturbed night in a seedy hotel-room somewhere down town. Yet, if the two of them could keep their heads down for a few days without arousing suspicion, it would not only be a miracle but it would surely be yet another sign of Allah's munificence in the face of all reason and justice.

'Did I say that?', the Colonel thought to himself. How could anyone doubt the Colonel's change of heart? He had a new name and a new face to go with it. And with his faithful bodyguard by his side, perhaps even a new heart? A leopard was one thing - a man, another. The people would have to trust him. In time, they might even get to like him. With a photo of 'Anthony Eden' on every household wall, every shop front, every street hoarding, how could he fail to win over the people and make them his to rule, manage and bend to his iron will? The people respected strong leaders. With this weak Government in power - allowing a ridiculous parody of Parliament to run riot - the so-called leaders were asking to be displaced, asking to be made a fool of - asking to be taken advantage of. And the Colonel was here to do just that.

They had both made it. They had passed their first test, back in the old country.

With scarcely a second glance paid to them as they politely handed their immaculate passports to the desk official, they were 'waived' on with as much interest as a morose employee at Malaga airport. They soon collected their baggage, which they had kept down to a minimum, and calmly walked through the 'Nothing to Declare' section of Customs. There was a brief moment of panic when a woman, laden with goodies, barred their way to the exit. But she caught the eye of the officials who pounced on her en masse. While the unfortunate woman was being 'turned over', they walked by and out into the lobby, unchallenged. Outside, taxis lined up to offer their services. Without hesitation, they took the first one and drove off to a modest hotel.

'My God, sir. I could have sworn I had Anthony Eden in the back, there.' The taxi-driver had done a speedy and efficient job and had arrived at the hotel, ready and willing to help his fare with their luggage.

'He does look a bit like him, now I come to think of it.' Señor Bueno remained the perfect diplomat as well as bodyguard. His old self, Mustafa, would have been justly proud. He gave the cabby his money. And they booked in as Yussef Khomeini and Señor Antonio Perez Bueno - businessmen.

The man behind the desk raised his eyebrows, for though he was too young to know anything about Anthony Eden, the gentleman did look distinguished (in a heavy sort of way) and his companion, massive by any standards, at least acted the gentleman. Their passports were in order and there seemed no reason why they should not stay. 'One, or two rooms, gentlemen?'

'Two, please,' said Señor Bueno, signing his name in the register. The Colonel did likewise... 'Yussef Khomeini, Esq'. The receptionist raised his eyebrows once more, handed the men the keys and instructed the boy to assist them with their luggage and show them to their rooms.

The evening passed off without mishap. After a quick shower (yes, even this downmarket joint had a shower - things were looking up for the old country), the two men came downstairs for a light meal and a drink at the bar. A number of people noticed them (who would ever be able to ignore them - apart from Spanish airport officials?) and one old lady kept smiling at the Colonel, who began to blush until he remembered who he really was. Señor Bueno, for his part, seemed to attract a couple of Iraqi hookers who, apparently, used the bar regularly as a pick-up point for new clients. Things were certainly looking up - as far as Señor Bueno was concerned. But, for the moment, he would have to behave himself.

It was decided an early night would be the wisest thing. They both slept like logs.

****

The afternoon 'House' was packed. All the short-listed candidates had, during the morning, rehearsed their speeches - long, short, good, bad and indifferent. And all the entrants were assured there was nothing to be nervous about. This would be only a dummy run. The occasion would enable them to get used to the idea - the Chamber, the procedure, the atmosphere and, last but not least, the cameras around them. Dan Levy, of course, had every intention of using the 'dummy run' as a separate programme - to be transmitted at *his* convenience. It would be hilarious, he decided.

But Mr Deputy Speaker, who had agreed to forgo his holiday in order to explain the procedure to the candidates (and, naturally, to collect the money promised him), believed there should have been more time allocated to help the candidates.

'Nonsense,' shouted Dan Levy. 'They only have to make a goddam speech.'

The Deputy Speaker looked at the American with wonderment that such an ignorant man should be allowed to have his way in Baghdad, as if the city were merely an outpost of the American Empire. Perhaps it was. In Colonel Doomsday's day, the man would have been hounded out of the country - if lucky. More likely, he'd have been tortured - then shot - if he hadn't already pegged out from his 'maltreatment'. Oh, if only the Colonel would return and save the country from ruin. Arid Aziz was not a bad man, in his odd way. But, well,... the man was a liberal (albeit under a Right-wing banner) and as for that cocky young Faisal Hussein, dishing out Left-wing morals like confetti……

'Forgive and forget', he was fond of quoting. What sort of creed was that? Call himself a proper Iraqi? Call himself an Arab? Even our enemy, the Jew, had learned a few facts about people in his time.

The Deputy Speaker's mind wandered on, whilst Dan Levy looked down the list of candidates and checked the names against the proposed speeches, 'Bills' and questions. Since it was really his show (and both Arid Aziz and Faisal Hussein, now on vacation, were glad, for once, that it was), he'd arrange the chaos *his* way. He'd amend, axe, omit, cut - do anything he saw fit in order to get what *he* wanted in the can. In that respect, he was no different from any other TV producer in the world. If the participants ended up with egg on their faces - too bad. Dan Levy, who could neither be seen nor heard, would come out clean. And whilst distancing himself from the innocent participants, he could make the thing fit into any shape or form he damned well chose.

Yussef Khomeini. Somehow, the name stuck out like a sore thumb. Dan checked the name again against the man's speech. But there was nothing except a question against Mr Abbas's speech on extradition. Abi Abbas, with designs on the premiership, had put down a strong motion for the extradition of the elusive Colonel. The fact the Colonel was either dead or in hiding, did not seem to bother him. He was adamant. The man had to be found and brought to justice, or Iraq would have no peace.

The question proposed by Jussef Khomeini, on the other hand, read: 'Why do we not invite him back? With the country's new liberal and forgiving stance in place, surely it could find room in its heart to forgive a man - even one........' (Dan Levy noticed the candidate did not say '*that* bad'. He simply said 'even one as strong as Colonel Doomsday?'). 'Who knows', the question went on, 'given another chance, he would more than likely serve his country well and go on to be a great Prime Minister? Rebels have been known to change their spots before. Besides, England didn't do so badly under a dictator.'

Heavens above. Maybe this candidate was sticking his neck out a bit too far. Nevertheless, even Dan Levy could recall a British Prime Minister of the '80s bludgeoning the country into shape with a rod of iron, before being kicked out of No.10 for winning three elections in a row.

The House of Baghdad

Dan looked at the list again, at the name Yussef Khomeini, at his question and at the original and bold way the candidate had put his case. UMM. Maybe this guy really knew a thing or two? Had he 'been here' before? Or was he a goddam plant of that creepy Ba'athist Party?

Chapter 31

7 p.m., London time. And millions of viewers crowd round their television sets to see some more Iraqi hopefuls make fools of themselves. They'd seen enough of the home grown breed.

In Iraq itself, people were glued to their sets to watch ordinary folk having a go at governing. Politics had suddenly become fun. And it beat the pictures, any day.

In America, Dan Levy's programme had not only survived as Top Soap from Coast to Coast but millions queued for as many shares as they could grab in the crazy show.

Since the start of the series more than six months before, Jack and Martha Johnson had never missed a transmission. To them it was as natural as breathing and eating. In fact, since they had both become staunch addicts of the programme even the steak sandwiches had begun to take a back seat. Moreover, there were no kids to worry about, shouting and screaming, demanding this and that and slamming doors. Jack and Martha could concentrate on their favourite sport, second only, of course, to those bedroom frolics which they themselves had improved - as a result, it seemed, of their avid interest in those spunky Iraqi affairs.

So Jack Johnson of Atlantic switched on his set and settled back on the sofa with his partner in crime. No more did Martha flit in and out of the kitchen, fussing over this and that, making mountainous sandwiches to keep her Jack at home. No, nowadays they watched 'House of Baghdad' together - without interruption. And then they'd go out to dinner at a proper restaurant where they would discuss the programme in great detail over a juicy steak and chips or a hot Mexican dish and a good bottle of wine. They had grown up, matured, reached out in life. And if 'The House of Baghdad' happened to be the cause of this miracle, so be it.

'Jesus, Martha. This is gonna be good. 'New Faces'. Get that. Maybe we should have the same thing in Washington?'

'Shoosh, Jack. Here it comes.' The enormous head of a peasant farmer loomed in front of the camera and immediately backed away. Being on television wasn't that good. The voice of the presenter softly droned in the background and the intimacy of his hushed, husky voice could have come straight out of the commentary box of the World Snooker Championship at Preston, England. The scene was set: the lights, the camera men, Jim Rosenberg, Dan Levy, the two English ex-pats sitting up in the gallery with great grins on their earthy faces. The coughing and chatter died down and a hush descended upon the entire Chamber. You could hear a pin drop. Jim Rosenberg signalled to the Speaker to start the proceedings. He was the only professional among the 'politicians'. But he seemed as nervous as a kitten. After all, he was an actor, too. He opened his mouth to speak but nothing would come out. It was as if Allah was punishing him for agreeing to participate in this farce in the first place. Allah should never be mocked. And those who did mock him must pay the penalty.

The man looked around at the faces staring back at him in the packed Chamber, faces which spelt panic, ignorance, foolhardiness, foolishness. And he had been the one who had tried to help them, who tried to get their speeches in some kind of order, who tried to show them how to stand, how to hold themselves, how to sit down again without a fuss, how to…….. Oh, God. What had he gone and done? No wonder that devious old Arid Aziz and equally devious young Faisal Hussein had both agreed to the idea. They damned well knew it would be a disaster and that, when they returned after the Christmas recess, the public would breathe a sigh of relief. For they would be able with a clear conscience to snipe at professionals. And the MPs in turn would be ready and able to fight back. Everyone would know where they were.

Jim Rosenberg waved frantically at the Speaker to begin. But nothing happened. And Dan Levy began to sweat. Jesus. Maybe this was going to be like the pilot programme that had dried up but out of which, admittedly, a working agreement had been reached that had finally led to a huge and undeniable success. But Dan had never shown the pilot (publicly, at any rate). This damned programme was going out live - to an audience of millions. To be amateur was one thing; to be incompetent, another. Rich as he had undoubtedly become, Dan Levy was darned if he would fail now; darned if he would disappoint millions of viewers across the globe and see his Number One slot slide into oblivion, or worse, be taken over by 'you know who'.

But just as he was about to ignore the Speaker's attack of stage fright and instruct one of the MPs to begin without him, the man suddenly found his voice.

'Er,…… Order, order,' he croaked. It was quite unnecessary.

The Chamber was already as silent as death. One of the contestants giggled and at least the programme had got off to some sort of start. 'The Bill to be debated this afternoon......' At last the Speaker had found his courage. Moreover, it was loud and clear........ 'is Mr Abbi Abbas's Bill on the extradition of Colonel Doomsday. All those in favour, say Ay.'

'Ay,' came from many mumbled voices.

'Those against, say No.'

Only one man said 'No'.

'The Ay's have it.' The Speaker had jumped the gun. But so had the Members of the House. For his part, the Speaker was so relieved to have found his voice, that he had difficulty controlling its flow. Maybe it was a Freudian slip on all sides, for he had witnessed and heard for himself a tremendous response to his charming faux pas. Everyone laughed except a lone MP who had managed to squeeze himself onto the Government Front Bench. If he had visions of turning this mob around to his way of thinking, he'd have a devil of a job on his hands. 'I am sorry,' apologized the Speaker with a smile, 'I suppose we ought to listen to the speech, first?' Everyone laughed again. And this time, even the handsome loner with the distinctive English countenance, managed a suggestion of a smile.

'Mr Abbi Abbas.' The Speaker benignly signalled with his finger for the debate to begin.

Abbi Abbas rose to his feet and glanced around the packed Chamber. A few would admit he possessed some kind of presence, albeit of a disturbing kind. With a turned-down mouth, deep lines hardening his face and a distinctly furrowed brow, he gave the impression of a less intelligent Enoch Powell - perhaps a half-brother or family idiot who had suddenly been let out of hospital for the day - with strict instructions given to his minder to return him by 6 o'clock. He was directed to the dispatch box, for not only was he known to have a burning ambition to become Prime Minister when Arid Aziz could be got rid of, but also, his desire to have the Colonel brought to justice and to take the credit for it, remained overwhelming. Dan Levy had gleaned these facts for himself. And it all appealed to his warped sense of humour. To see a man argue his case with manic conviction in front of a packed Chamber of complete amateurs and to an audience of millions at home in front of their sets, was something he couldn't resist.

MOSSAD had never been known to pussyfoot around. They were intelligent people, whose highly trained mercenaries knew what they were doing. In Dan Levy's mind there could only be one scenario as regards the Colonel - MOSSAD had shot the man and his bodyguard, set the bodies and villa ablaze and gone straight to the funeral of Felix Esbano as if nothing had happened. According to many reports, even the President believed the bodies to be those of Yudie and Mustafa. He may even have been involved in the plot. But which President were we talking about?

Dan was no politician. He was a TV and movie man. But then, anything which had an angle to it, he'd turn to his advantage.

'Mr Speaker, Honourable Members,' began Abbi Abbas confidently, 'I am not here today to try to undermine our new system of Government, so recently forged on the anvil of sacrifice - the blood, sweat and tears of our glorious revolution. The memories of that event are too vivid, too real, too painful for glib comment from any of us here today. Yet, my friends,' (Abbi Abbas attempted a Churchillian impersonation but the lisp didn't quite come off so he continued, as best he could), 'my friends,' he repeated, 'is it not reasonable to ask ourselves how best we can protect our new democracy from predators, whether they be foreign or native? The debate for the extradition of Colonel Doomsday has gone on now for many months......' (groans were voiced and heard throughout the Chamber. And a crack, it seemed, had appeared in the unnatural calm of the broadcast. But it was 'early days' and Dan Levy and Jim Rosenberg remained relaxed. Dan even found himself smiling up at the faces of the two Englishmen who gave little thumbs-up signs in mild response......). 'But I believe,' continued Abbi Abbas 'that it is a debate which *has* to be resolved once and for all.' (Coughs were now heard throughout the Chamber and one contestant tried to interrupt. But Abbi Abbas, in true parliamentary fashion, politely refused to give way.) 'I do not believe the Colonel is dead. What I do believe is that he is not only planning to return to this country in order to seize power but that he intends to wreak revenge on the United States of America for his father's ignoble defeat.'

Laughs of derision greeted this last phrase. But it was that word 'ignoble' that somehow perturbed a number of contestants. If they had been real MPs they would have picked up the point and exposed Abbi Abbas for the amateur he really was. But they allowed the man to continue.......

'It seems to me,' pressed Abbi Abbas, raising his index finger in the manner of an English Minister for the Environment with a sticky shopping-list or poisoned chalice, 'that we ignore this matter at our peril. If we do not have the resources to catch this monster ourselves, then we should, without delay, ask MOSSAD to do it for us. I'm sure they'd be delighted.' This brought the reaction Dan

Levy wanted. Uproar prevailed so that the Speaker, who had done a good job up to this point, had to revert to apoplectic shouting to bring the Chamber to its senses.

The cameras whirled once more and smiles appeared on the faces of their operators. The voice of the presenter, which at first had been so delightfully and respectfully subdued, coughed and spluttered into activity and pleaded with the audience back home not to switch off. It was highly unlikely anyone would.

'Ah, Martha. This is great. If we hang on a while we might catch 'em mixing things up a bit.'

'Don't be silly, Jack. Arabs don't fight fisticuffs. They throw stones, or get behind a gun.'

'Well maybe we'll see some maniac do that. Remember the guy with his gun at the back of the Prime Minister? Which episode was it, now?'

'Oh yes. I remember. And someone knocked the gun from his hand, and….'

'Yeah.' Jack and Martha were both glued to the set, wondering what the outcome of the day's show would be. Even 'Dallas', in its heyday, could hardly match this for drama. And this Iraqi stuff was for real.

Abbi Abbas at last sat down to a reception he neither expected nor desired. But the Speaker, with great difficulty, finally settled the MPs and called upon a Mr Yussef Khomeini to reply to the proposition. (Dan Levy had seen the question tabled by the man. He knew replies in the form of a question could, in the right hands, be devastating. Already the man had impressed him. If ever there was a PM or President in the making it was this man.)

Yussef Khomeini rose to his full height and calmly waited for the remaining hubbub to die down. But he didn't have long to wait. His very presence, his stature, those eyes, those vibes and that stillness - inherited from his father - all combined and came to his aid. No gun had gone off. And no shots would be fired while this man had the floor. The Chamber fell silent and all eyes turned to him - this imposing man with the English look.

'Mr Speaker,' he began slowly and assuredly, 'Honourable Members, I have listened with great interest to the Honourable Member opposite and to his simple, straightforward but, I believe, flawed proposal for dealing with Colonel Doomsday - a man who, as we all know, left this country to take up residence and a new life in Brazil.' (There were a few light guffaws at this remark and Yussef allowed himself a little smile, as intended.) 'I say flawed proposal, Mr Speaker, for not only does it presuppose the Colonel to be alive but it gives, in my opinion, the best opportunity Israel has had in years - and by that I mean an opportunity to do what it jolly well likes and to take a mile where we have authorized an inch.'

The Chamber was riveted. This man was special. Who was he? Where did he come from? He didn't look like 'one of us'. Yet he spoke our language. And we liked what he'd been saying. He had the floor to himself. No-one spoke but he. And no- one would speak until he had finished. He glanced round the Chamber and continued. 'Mr Speaker, I have an alternative proposal which, at first, may shock some of us. But if we think about it carefully, we may all come to the same conclusion. I propose we use simple psychology to flush the man out. In other words, if we just allow our new liberal democracy to literally invite him back, we can virtually make him serve us - rather than the other way round. *We* will be the masters. Not Colonel

Doomsday. And all the world will see our new State is truly democratic. In any case, why should the Devil have all the best tunes?'

Was Yussef Khomeini talking in riddles? What was he really saying?

'I'll tell you what I'm saying,' he challenged, catching their thoughts and fears, 'draw him out. Make him return on his own steam and at his own expense. Offer him an opportunity to make amends, to turn his considerable talents to good rather than evil. Who knows? He could even be the first dictator to become Prime Minister of our great new democratic State and the first to repent.' Tears flowed from the eyes of some of the older MPs and Yussef Khomeini sat down to considerable applause.

It wasn't what they had expected to hear. They had not come to hear another sermon on Christian virtues from Faisal Hussein. And it wasn't a particularly good speech. But, by golly, it had made them think. If the Colonel was dead, he was dead. But if he was alive, why should Israel poke its nose in to nab him? Yes, who else would Israel feel entitled to nab on Iraq's behalf? But it wouldn't be on Iraq's behalf, would it?

The more they thought on these things the more they judged this Yussef Khomeini to be right. A true democracy should be able to cope with a repentant dictator. This was Iraq's chance to test that democracy. And if the man publicly renounced his past before Parliament and the world, what an asset he might be in the defence of the 'realm'.

Chapter 32

Next morning, the world woke up to the news of a truly remarkable situation. The latest transmission of 'The House of Baghdad' in the form of 'New Faces' had caused a sensation in Iraq. The big man with the English look had stirred more than a few memories in the hearts and minds of millions everywhere. He had become the talking point of business lunches across the globe. Could this man be for real? Would he become a real MP on the convenient death of a member of Arid Aziz's party? Or would he force the pace of change, cause the downfall of his Government and declare himself dictator? Dictator? Who said anything about a dictator? Yet somehow, he looked like a dictator despite a certain similarity to the late Anthony Eden. Now, *there* was an interesting man - an intelligent, elegant, smooth and democratically elected MP who, as Prime Minister, nurtured more than a serious desire to kill Nasser. Maybe this 'new face' in Iraq intended to kill President Bazrani?

Arid Aziz was furious. So, too, for different reasons, was Faisal Hussein. Christmas recess notwithstanding, neither man could resist 'looking in' at the debate on his television set. Children were ordered to be quiet or be put to bed while Daddy watched the end being driven into the wedge of his possible displacement. Both men had agreed to the experiment, imagining it would never be taken seriously.

But it had been taken seriously. And if the present Government stood a chance of surviving, something had to be done - *and fast*. Arid Aziz picked up the phone and dialled Faisal Hussein's home number. Both men had long agreed that, in an emergency, each would be free to disturb the other - even during a recess. As far as Arid was concerned, this was an emergency.

'Why, Arid. Nice to hear from you. Did you see 'New Faces'?'

'Yes, I did.' Arid registered concern. 'We have to do something about it, Faisal.'

'Well, what's done is done. But I agree, we can't have this man disturb our cosy little set-up, can we?'

'Quite. With you I can deal. But this man would upset the delicate balance to which we've all contributed in achieving understanding with Israel.

Faisal grudgingly agreed that this, indeed, was the case.

'So, what do you propose to do?'

'I propose to telephone the President and suggest setting up a meeting with this upstart.'

'A meeting? Have you gone mad, Arid? You want to give him a chance?'

Arid listened with quiet satisfaction to his opposite number propounding a hard line on the current issue occupying the political scene. Oh, the ironies of life!

'It's not a case of giving him a chance to overthrow the democracy for which we have all fought, my dear Faisal. It's more a case of allowing democracy to work. It should, after all, be seen to work.'

'You sound as if you believe this man with the strange Western face may, in fact, be the Colonel himself?'

'Well?' Arid waited for Faisal's gasp.

'You're not serious?'

'Think about it, Faisal. We both remember his presence - the atmosphere he'd create around him. Take away that face - a face, by the way, which somehow wouldn't look quite right, even on an Englishman - you've indicated as much yourself - and you have the Colonel. It's uncanny. I don't like it, Faisal. I don't like it at all.'

Arid Aziz seemed genuinely upset and even the young, dashing Faisal Hussein, his official opponent, had begun to have his own doubts.

'Um. Well, maybe you're right, Arid. It's a macabre thought, I must say.'

'We have to be sure, my friend. Will you back me on a little investigation into the matter?'

'But I thought you intended to give him a chance?'

'Officially, yes. But unofficially, I feel we must investigate. After all, my dear Faisal, we have to guard our nests, don't we?' "Feather our nests" would have been more accurate but even Arid, who had been diligent in getting his English quotations up to scratch, (it had been an on-going competition with the Caliph for years) felt that "feather" smacked a little too much of English suburbia and meanness. Despite his acknowledged faults, Arid had always prided himself on being fair.

'Well, Arid. You must do what you think is right. Personally I have my doubts about the Colonel being here in our midst. The idea of a brutal dictator of Doomsday's calibre calmly delivering a speech on 'New Faces' as if he hadn't anything better to do doesn't quite wash.'

'But that's just the point, Faisal, don't you see? We both know how cunning the Colonel was. He would have done anything to stay in power. And I believe he'd do anything to regain it.'

'Just supposing he's alive, of course?'

'Of course.'

"Umm……. OK, Arid. You go ahead and contact the President. Unofficially, you have my support. Officially…….."

'Understood. Thank you, Faisal. And have a good vacation. Regards to your family.'

'And to yours, Arid. See you soon.'

"Bye.'

"Bye, Prime Minister.'

****

Yussef Khomeini had wasted no time in capitalizing upon his success in the Chamber. As soon as the broadcast was over he was inundated with congratulations, questions, good wishes, pats on the back and an approach from Dan Levy himself. 'Hell. You gave it to 'em, there, sir. Excellent performance.' 'Thank you,…. er….. Mr Levy.'

'I have a little proposition to put to you, sir, if, er….. when you've finished with your fans?' Dan Levy winked at the 'new star', in anticipation, perhaps, of a good, profitable relationship.

'Oh, of course.'

'They've given me an office, here, sir. Room No.9, on the first floor. If you care to join me?'

'I shall be there in a few minutes.'

'Great stuff. I'll be waiting.' Dan Levy thanked everyone with a sweep of his huge hand and walked out of the Chamber in the direction of his office.

Antonio Perez Bueno, who had been sitting in the public gallery during the broadcast, decided to hold back until the crowd had dispersed. He could sense no bad vibes about the place and felt it would be wiser to allow his boss the honour of congratulations, genuine or otherwise, to continue for a few moments. Only then would he casually approach him and accompany him to Dan Levy's office. He had overheard and understood the gist of Dan Levy's offer. And who knows? Maybe the producer would offer him the part of the Colonel's bodyguard - should he, of course, by chance be considering making a film about the great man. He and his boss had often discussed the possibility after watching yet another of Dan Levy's provocative programmes. It was obvious this Mr Levy never stopped looking for new ideas and angles in order to keep himself 'up there'. Well, a film on the Colonel would be just the ticket.

Yussef Khomeini offered his au revoirs to the remaining MPs as Señor Bueno approached, nursing his 'Order of the Day' brochure so thoughtfully distributed to people in the public gallery.

'Hello, Mr Bueno. Would you care to join me for a little meeting?'

'I should be delighted, Mr Khomeini. Thank you.' Señor Bueno's deferential bow did little to allay the nervousness of a few remaining MPs. Intelligent as he undoubtedly was, there seemed no way he could disguise the impression of heaviness even if he tried. 'Congratulations on an excellent speech.'

'Thank you.'

Señor Bueno smiled at the lingering MPs, who quickly collected their thoughts, if not their belongings, and departed.

'Well, Mus……. I mean Antonio…..' Perhaps the strain was beginning to tell. Señor Bueno smiled on his boss and they walked out of the Chamber with commendable poise and self-control.

Tony Sharp

****

'Ah, Mr Khomeini. Do come in.' Dan Levy beamed. As soon as he set eyes on the massive Antonio Bueno looming behind his 'new star', he knew he'd got his film. 'Mr Khomeini.' Dan stretched out his large hand and shook his star by the hand. Antonio stretched his own hand out to shake the hand of the wealthiest producer in the Middle East. And even Dan Levy was impressed. Señor Bueno dwarfed the producer, who knew he'd sign the man up for the part of bodyguard as soon as he'd popped Khomeini in the bag.

'Take a seat, gentlemen. I have a great proposition to put to you both.'

The two men sat down and listened with interest to what Dan Levy had to offer. If the producer seemed a little hasty in his enthusiasms, he'd certainly proved himself in Baghdad. And if he made an offer for them to play the Colonel and his bodyguard in a blockbuster film to be shown all over the world, who cared if they never got back into politics again? After all, everything was politics.

The kudos resulting from such an achievement would more than compensate for any failure to become master of Iraq once again. And even if he never made another film in his life, Yussef Khomeini would be able to write his memoirs, disclose his true identity and put his fingers up to the world. Such is the perversity of life that his country might even plead for him to take control, in spite of everything.

'Well, gentlemen. I think I can say with near certainty, and without offence, that you strike me as people with whom I can do business.' Jussef and Antonio made no comment and moved not a muscle. And Dan Levy continued undeterred. 'And I think you can already see, I am not a man to let grass grow under my feet. After what I have seen of your performance in the Chamber today, sir, I am prepared to offer you the star role in a new film I'm making on the life of Colonel Doomsday. Are you interested?' Dan Levy took his cigar from his mouth, and, looking Jussef directly in the eye, waited for an answer.

'Very much, Mr Levy. But my face......'

'Oh, that. Well, with a little bit of jiggery-pokery in the make-up department......'

Jiggery-pokery? Didn't he mean......?

'Don't worry, my friend. No need to go to the extent of plastic surgery. Not these days.'

A million thoughts swept through the minds of Yussef and Antonio. What they had been through as Colonel D-Day and Mustafa could fill a hundred novels. They had ended their careers with those names and, with plastic surgery, they had embarked upon new lives - with new names. If only they had known that one day they would be asked to play themselves in a major film, they might never have gone through with it. Oh, the twists of fate. What was it all about?

'Well, Mr Khomeini? Leave the make-up to us. I know you have it in you to do the part.'

'All right, Mr Levy. Thank you. I accept.'

'Great stuff. You'll be a smash over night. And you, Mr Bueno? Would you be interested in playing the Colonel's bodyguard?'

'I'd love to, Mr Levy.' There was little hesitation in Antonio's response. He damned well knew the Colonel would want him by his side in emergencies. What better opportunity than to be on the set with him?

'Splendid. Now, you may be wondering why I haven't asked either of you to do a test. Well, I'm in a hurry. An American disease, eh? Hope you will forgive me.'

'Of course, Mr Levy.' If only Jussef could afford to tell the producer that he, too, was in rather a hurry. But he held his tongue.

'As far as I am concerned, Mr Khomeini, you have passed your test with flying colours - in that Chamber.'

'Thank you.'

'And *you*, Mr Bueno, will……'

'Lick into shape?'

'You've both got the job. I've already drawn up contracts without the names. Have a look at them, now. Mary, my secretary will type in your names before you sign.' Dan Levy passed the papers to the two men who sat and studied them with due care and attention. Yes, there really seemed no reason why they should not sign. Everything appeared in order and the fees offered to them as artists were... well, considerable. At least - for artists.

The men looked up to Dan Levy whose smile said it all. 'Happy?'

'We are happy with this, Mr Levy. Very generous - for our first movie.' Yussef smiled a wicked smile at Dan Levy which the producer could have sworn he'd seen somewhere before. Who the hell did that smile really belong to?

'Good. Mary?' Dan's secretary took the contracts and, in her little room, quickly typed in the names of her boss's new stars. Back she walked into Dan's office.

The House of Baghdad

'Thanks, Mary. Now, if you'd both kindly sign *here*, and *here*, I will sign against your signatures at the bottom, Mary will be witness, and we're in business.'

The deed was done. They all shook hands and Dan Levy suggested a refresher from his drinks cabinet.

'Ah, Mr Levy. We shouldn't, but... oh, why not?'

'It's a special occasion, gentlemen.'

'It is, indeed. I'll have a gin and tonic, thank you.'

'And I'll have a whisky and soda.'

'Right.' Dan Levy poured out the drinks including a large whisky for himself and returned to his desk. 'Bottoms up, gentlemen.'

'Bottoms up,' they all smiled and drank up, while 'Mustafa' shot 'the Colonel' a look of wry contentment.

Chapter 33

President Bazrani listened carefully to what his Prime Minister had to say over the telephone. The suggestion that Yussef Khomeini might, in fact, be Colonel Doomsday in drag was dismissed out of hand. Arid Aziz had always loved his little jokes with the President. Since the revolution, the two men had hit it off in their respective capacities and agreed that a laugh a day was all that would be needed to keep the doctor away.

'But my dear Arid,' said the President, firming up, 'someone may well have done something nasty to the Colonel's face during his stay in Brazil but really...... I don't see him voluntarily having plastic surgery in order to make a fool of himself in the Chamber.'

'But he didn't make a fool of himself, sir.'

'The man you and I saw, I agree, did not make a fool of himself. Far from it. Apart from your good self, of course, and an occasional, well-constructed, if misguided speech from Faisal Hussein, this man Yussef Khomeini delivered the most powerful and articulate speech I've heard since I opened Parliament. As far as I can recall, Colonel D-Day never made a speech in his life. No, Arid, I'm afraid I cannot believe the man is the Colonel. It's not his style.'

'Well, I'm still suspicious, sir. I'd like to check it out.'

'Check him out, by all means. In fact, I have a suggestion.'

'Go on, sir.'

'Why don't I invite him here to dinner with his wife? I'll then be able to form a proper impression. I could phone you next day. What d'you think?'

'Brilliant, sir. Would you do it?'

'Why not? Better still - you come as well, with your wife.'

'Won't he feel we're ganging up on him, sir?'

'On the contrary, it'll spread the pressure a little, don't you see? The women will balance things up - in their inimitable way. And then the three of us will have a good chat in the study. What d'you say?'

'Fine by me, sir. Thank you. Hattie and I would love to come.'

'Good. You contact him and set it up. Wednesday or Thursday of next week - best for me.'

'All right sir. Leave it to me.'

"Bye, Arid.'

"Bye, Mr President.'

Arid Aziz put the phone down and took it up again to dial Dan Levy's office. Levy would surely have a contact number or address for the mystery man who, last night, had so galvanized the Chamber and perhaps the world. 'New Faces', indeed, thought Arid. Damned sure this egg is no new face.

'Yes?'

'Oh, is that Dan Levy?'

'Yep. Can I help ya?'

'It's Arid Aziz, here, Mr Levy. The Prime Minister.'

'Oh, yes, sir. What have I done now?'

'Relax, Mr Levy. The programme was splendid. So impressive, in fact, that I want to speak to you about this Yussef Khomeini.'

'Yeah. Good little performer, eh, sir?'

'Indeed, Mr Levy. So good that the President would like to invite him and his wife to dinner.'

'To dinner? Well, now, sir. I dare say I could allow my client to have dinner with the President?'

'Are you his manager, already, Mr Levy? You do work fast.'

Dan Levy laughed and sat back in his swivel chair to consider the matter. 'That's an idea you've given me, Prime Minister. In the meantime, I have signed him up for a major role in my new movie.'

'Have you, indeed? And what sort of movie is that, may I ask?' Arid Aziz's mind wandered through the gamut of celluloid horrors, from the grottiest of so-called hard porn to modern productions of Macbeth. He would like to have made a wild suggestion to Mr Dan Levy that perhaps Yussef Khomeini should play the part of Colonel D-Day in a film where the dictator actually gets his deserts - in the form of a nice slow death on a rack of red-hot spikes, with naked women running around him keeping him alive a little longer in agony. But he controlled his thoughts which, perhaps, were too good for a man like the Colonel.

'It's a movie in which Yussef Khomeini stars as Colonel Doomsday. How about that, Prime Minister?'

The Prime Minister would loved to have put the phone down on this cocky American. But not before giving him a piece of his tongue for stealing his ideas. 'I don't believe it.' he croaked.

'You betta believe it, sir. He jumped at the idea.'

'Jumped at it, did he?' The picture was becoming still clearer in Arid's bruised mind. He was suddenly given heart to carry on. 'All right, Mr Levy. I am not a jealous man. Good luck to Yussef Khomeini. I look forward to seeing the film. In the meantime, perhaps you'd be good enough to inform him the President has invited him to dinner next week?'

'Next week? Well, now, Prime Minister. I intend shooting next week. But what day had you in mind?'

'Wednesday or Thursday, Mr Levy. Will you get him to ring my secretary this evening?'

'I will do my best, sir. Count on me.'

'I do, Mr Levy.'

Blast the man. Blast both men. The bastards! The bloody ba……..

It took a good thirty minutes for Arid Aziz to calm down. It was a long time since he'd had such a strong attack of raging jealousy. This Dan Levy is only here five minutes before he's forming a corporation and broadcasting a No.1 soap opera across the globe. That nice Englishman, John Broadbridge, hadn't a look in…… Hadn't a chance in hell with a man like Levy around - five minutes the bugger had been in Iraq! And now this Yussef Khomeini comes along and, before one can bat an eyelid, the man takes Parliament by the scruff of the neck and lands himself a fat part in a major movie. It wasn't right. It just wasn't right. And to think the bloody bastard might well be Colonel Doomsday himself.

Arid prepared to pour himself a large Dalwhinnie whisky and sit down in his favourite armchair in the study to think. He even considered phoning the Caliph and joining him and John Broadbridge on one of their little sessions of Lagavulin 'sniffing'. But as yet, Arid Aziz was only a gentle novice in the whisky fraternity. He had never really appreciated fine whisky ever since a 'friend' poured half a bottle of Teachers down his throat as a schoolboy prank. After recovering from the most violent sting at the back of his tender throat, he had thrown up in the toilet and vowed never to touch the evil stuff again. A reassuring lecture from an elder convinced him his friend was very wicked to ply him with Teachers in the first place and when offered a wee drop of gentle Dalwhinnie, as a really friendly introduction to an exclusive club, his fears had duly been calmed. Moreover, Arid decided that, given time, his unfortunate childhood memory would sink for ever into obscurity.

The Dalwhinnie bottle sat there on the shelf, beckoning him. 'Come on', it said, 'I will do you no harm, but a lot of good. Drink me slowly and you will feel better'. He did as the bottle commanded, and within two minutes, he had become a new man. Evil thoughts of revenge receded into the past and a glorious light shone before his eyes. 'Phone the Caliph,' said the voice, 'and he will show you things of which you have never dreamed.'

And so it came to pass, the Three Wise Men sat down to drink Lagavulin. 'Oh wondrous light, oh star of Bethlehem, just say 'Lagavulin' and we will enter in.'

****

Yussef had had a long discussion with his man Antonio on the night following his 'debut' in Parliament and the signing of the film contract. It had been a momentous day for both of them. Not quite like the old days, of course. But different. Very different. And Yussef, for one, had already begun to get into the swing of it. Given time, the old days of mastering his country by force might seem like a childish game, an aberration of the mind and waste of talent, a period of stunted growth or a mere nightmare. This yapping in Parliament lark was quite enjoyable really - like acting in a play or field game - with the Speaker as arbiter.

And now this film contract. Who wouldn't have jumped at the chance? Even at the risk of exposing himself to the world, Yussef considered it would all be worth it. Besides, if he made a damned good job of it, Levy would be more inclined to protect him by also becoming his manager. And if Yussef himself, once the film was made, sank some money of his own into Levy's company, well... The possibilities seemed limitless and the hopes of the 'Colonel' and his man rose by the hour.

Yes, Yussef would certainly attend the President's dinner. He'd have to say his wife had died some years back and so......... Well, he'd be happy to go along alone.

'I don't think I should join you, sir. One of them might twig.'

'Unfortunately, I agree, Mus...... I mean, Antonio.' It was on these private occasions that Yussef would allow himself a forgivable slip of the tongue. Nevertheless, both men tried to keep to the new names at all times and act their parts well. After all, they were soon to be *paid* actors. It was part of an actor's stock in trade to 'be the part'. How times can change.

'I'm still somewhat concerned that the line we take should be consistent.'

'I agree with your thoughts, sir. Our visas as businessmen should suffice, I think, but the sudden change-over to actors may raise a few more eyebrows.'

'But it's a free country, Antonio. We should take advantage.'

'We have, already. Allah be praised.'

'Yes. And we'll go on doing just that. I shall play the democratic card for all its worth, with one exception.'

'Israel?'

'Exactly. It seems to have done the trick, so far, hasn't it? On our little walkabout this afternoon, the number of people congratulating me on that point, was most gratifying.'

'So, if the President asks you what your ambitions are, what will you tell him?'

'I will tell him the truth, Antonio.'

'The truth?'

'I will tell him I wish to become Prime Minister, or President.'

'Or both?'

'No, Antonio. That would be a mistake. Don't forget these people have memories of me in my capacity as Colonel D-Day. To covet both positions at the same time would smack of, er....'

'Dictatorship?'

"Umm. How I miss it, my friend.'

Chapter 34

Never had the world's media known so much fun. The Colonel's 'flight' to Brazil was one thing; his 'disappearance' in suspicious circumstances, another. But now, every day that passed, more theories as to his whereabouts were propounded by the most accommodating sources - ranging from hardened and hard-done-by prostitutes who supposedly knew the Colonel intimately or merely wished to 'get in on the act' to effete bishops - some of whose boyfriends insisted they had sucked off the Colonel at a wild party given by President Gonzalez in return for a handsome but never- to -be-repeated tip.

In the UK, *The Sunday Times*, which for years had taken the place of *The News of the World* in terms of popularity, with loud headlines and gross pictures, devoted a whole section to the Colonel - his history, background, methods, motives and likely ambitions.

The paper firmly believed the Colonel was alive and kicking, kicking the system, somewhere in the world - biding his time when he would gain power once more and satisfy his desire for revenge by letting loose his secret weapon on the free world.

The News of the World, by contrast, displayed its leader story in discreet type, reserving only one inside page to a healthy photo of Maria, the Brazilian President's wife, posing for a few grateful British photographers, hopeful for a spot of first hand knowledge. The leader story was short and succinct: *'The Colonel is DEAD. Let us forget him and go on to better things'*. If an example were ever needed of a world turned upside down, one only had to look at the British press.

Der Speigel took a more serious line and warned the world of a new catastrophe. *'Hitler was ours; Sodom the Lesser, theirs. But Colonel Doomsday - when he decides to surface - will truly threaten the world. Let there be no mistake: one bomb on New York will be the cause of the Third World War.'*

Le Monde decided to break all its vows of cultural purity and publish in three languages, so there would be no misunderstanding. **'FIND THIS MAN',** it insisted. No one quite knew, however, whether the President had actually joined the world community or was merely suffering an understandable attack of pique at being 'overlooked' by his former ally.

Time displayed a handsome photo of the Colonel on its front cover. It looked nothing like Anthony Eden but then, how could the magazine know the extent of Dr. Koch's creative talents? The article inside favoured the murder theory. Despite its own attempt to investigate what it had to investigate, the CIA, for reasons best known to itself, had decided to fall out with MOSSAD. Moreover, neither organisation would say whether or not it had access to any document supposedly code-named Project Jerusalem.

Joshua Rainberg and Dave Adams, for their part, had held a further meeting with President Gonzalez (much to the chagrin of Franco Daconni) and had returned to Israel. Daconni would like to have believed Joshua Rainberg was feeling the heat and had scarpered back to Israel with his mate, before he, Daconni, could close in on them and arrest them for the murder of Colonel D-Day and his trusty bodyguard. What a scoop that could have been for the detective. He'd have been honoured and decorated beyond his wildest dreams. But a small voice kept telling him not to be silly and to grow up...... 'The President is withholding vital information. Your friend is right. I am your friend.'

My God. Franco Daconni had never heard 'voices' before in his life. And if he had, he would hardly have listened to them. He'd always been a down-to-earth, practical man, hardly given to hallucinations or even the odd attack of amnesia. Raised from Italian stock, from a long line of peasant farmers, one of whose brave sons had escaped the escapades of the great Garibaldi in the 1840s and had found himself by a tortuous and devious route on the east coast of Brazil - a penniless refugee with a funny accent but damned determined - young Franco had fond memories of his grandfather who would relate tales of *his* father's little escapades and brushes with the law. 'Franco, my boy', he'd say, banging his pipe on the mudguard of his old open-top tourer and displaying a row of teeth that had seen better days, 'you can make it if you try. I have not done so bad. Keep out of trouble. But if you can't resist the underworld, then be a policeman. That way you will have regular meals and a pension. Can't lose, my boy.'

And so the years roll on and Franco Daconni finally makes it - as Chief Detective Superintendent: not quite Chief of Police but superior, he kids himself. To Daconni's mind, the latter post smacks of mere 'wide boy power' with no brains. To be Chief Detective Superintendent is something else. And at last he has landed himself a plum case - the murder of an ex-dictator, a man whose newsworthiness is second to none. He goes to the scene of the crime only to catch, red-handed, two members of the Israeli Secret Police. Yet these men appear to have had permission to be there in the first place. 'What the hell's going on?' he asks. 'But the President,... that's it, don't you see?,' says the voice insistently, 'MOSSAD have inside information. Demand to see the President.'

The small but nagging voice had finished and Franco Daconni sat down to think. Maybe the voice was right, after all? What had he got to lose? So, he phones the President.

'Yes, Franco. What have you come up with?'

'What have *you* come up with, sir?'

'But Franco, *you* are the detective.'

'May I come and see you, sir?'

'Why, of course. But you sound so dramatic. What's on your mind?'

'I'd rather talk about it when I see you, sir.'

'All right, three this afternoon.'

'I'll be there, sir.'

Damn. Damn the man. He was surely hiding something, the slippery bastard. The voice was right. Over the years he'd held his post, Franco had never really warmed to his President. And as those years went by, the distance between them had widened further. The more Daconni thought about the case of Colonel D-Day, the more he knew something fishy had been going on behind his back and that come rain, or come shine, Manuel Gonzalez would simply plead innocence and stick to his line. But what was his line? Whatever he told Franco, would doubtless be just another fabrication.

Daconni's frustration had reached boiling point. He even considered paying another visit to O'Death, if only to beat the shit out of the little creep. But the more he thought about that approach the more his own flesh began to creep. Oh, damn it. If he could gain no satisfaction from the

President, he'd call it a day and simply close the case. 'Unsolved Murder, Number.....?' There were so many in Brazil. What was another one, even one as tantalising and high-profile as this? Daconni would simply slump on to the next problem, bide his time, draw his pension and write his memoirs. Then, maybe, people would begin to listen to him.

But the personal and professional problems of Franco Daconni could not have been farther from the minds of news editors. As well as an avalanche of reports of 'sightings' coming in from the usual cranks, trouble-makers and inventive schoolchildren, mindful of a quick buck, the newspaper offices, TV centres and broadcasting corporations were inundated with requests from agents that their erudite clients should write articles and/or appear on easy-going chat shows and drop their individual bombs of inside information or pet theories. Such was the flow of information, misinformation and downright lies, that comedians across the globe vied with each other to see who could put the wind up their audience the most effectively.

Meanwhile, Dan Levy's office was overloaded with requests for a repeat of 'New Faces'. The experiment seemed to have tickled the fancy of the most unlikely viewers. And all Dan Levy could do was to oblige, adding a transmission of the pilot programme which he'd kept under his belt for a 'rainy day'. Anyway, he was now so busy with setting up the film about the Colonel, that the fewer distractions that came his way, the better. He was glad his 'Flying Circus', as John Broadbridge still chose to think of the whole caboodle, was virtually running itself. And even Iraqi newspapers were beginning to join in the fun, though to some Western minds, a fair degree of refinement was called for. *'If Iraq had known it could have so much fun'*, suggested one cynical but perhaps innocent editor, *'it would never have got rid of the Colonel.'*

Most national papers, however, were more than content with the idea that Iraq had opened up, relaxed and joined with other nations in the pursuit of happiness. And most had caught on to the idea that laughter may not, after all, constitute an affront to Allah.

'If anyone can understand what our country has suffered all these years, it must be Allah', said one bright editor. *'If he has chosen to guide us through devastation and wretchedness to a better world where we no longer have to look over our shoulders, or be watchful of our fellow citizens for fear of betrayal, then who are we to resist such change? Who are we to suspect anyone who chooses to laugh rather than cry?'*

For their part, people in the streets clamoured to get near their new idol with the English look. He was certainly built like an Arab and he sported those big, indigenous eyes. Yet the rest of his face cut the dash of a foreigner and one, moreover, who seemed thoroughly at ease with himself - confident, yet almost courteous, with a touch of elegance for good measure. Beside him, a pace behind, walked a big, powerful man with a more Spanish look about him. If not exactly a ringer for a young Julio Inglésias, the man, nevertheless, did exude a certain amount of Latin panache, for what it was worth.

'Congratulations, sir. We thought you came over much better than that other lot.'

'What other lot, my friend? The Government?'

'Of course,' laughed the crowd. 'Arid Aziz,' shouted one young man, 'plays to the gallery for all he's worth.'

'Which is not a lot, eh?' The crowd laughed again and pressed forward to catch more words of wisdom from the lips of the Messiah. Could they be looking at the man who would make their country proud again? No one could deny they were enjoying their first taste of freedom; their first taste of democracy and opportunity to oppose. But they didn't want to lose their identity altogether. They didn't want to march completely in step with every other Tom, Dick or Harry of the outside world, to sink without individual trace in the great sea of international pressure. His English look notwithstanding, this new man, who with one tiny speech had stirred the imagination of a nation, could be the man to lead them. He had those vibes, that bearing, that... 'something'.

And with local elections looming on the horizon, they would be more than willing to give the man a sporting chance for his first step into Government. Who knows? He may even be polite enough to wait for the death of an MP and stand for Parliamentary selection.

But the crowd grew; he would soon have them eating out of his hand. As long as he didn't overdo it but used this hour as a test of his own self-control and acting ability, as an immediate and natural training-ground for his future part in the film, he'd be all right. The crowd pressed forward once more and his bodyguard felt the first twinges of anxiety for his master's safety. Yet if he lunged in and swept aside his master's keenest supporters with the swift body action of the old days, he might upset the delicate balance they were both trying to achieve in these early days of readjustment.

'Hey. *You* look a bit like Colonel D-Day,' a young man called out, 'doesn't he, Mustafa?'

Mustafa? Who said Mustafa? For a brief moment Antonio Pérez Bueno went hot and cold. Mustafa was such a common name in the Middle East that he shouldn't have felt any qualms about being recognized. But Yussef had no such qualms. He was now beyond fear. In any case, he could pin the whole thing on this acting lark.

The young man's friend spoke up.

'Yes, Ali, he does a bit.'

'Ah, silly. Don't you idiots know anything? These guys are actors.' someone else shouted.

'Actors?'

'They've come to Baghdad to make a film.'

Oh, God. Whatever next? Was there no end to this democracy farce? Give people an inch and they take a mile. Yussef's thoughts ran on. Had someone rumbled him? Or had Dan Levy's scheduled film saved him? He would never lose sight of the ultimate goal of power, back in this old country of his; but in this 'village' of Baghdad, nothing seemed sacred any more. If there were a stronger case for stifling the 'Freedom of Information Act', due to be debated in the next session of Parliament, Yussef could not think of it. This was not the Baghdad he remembered. But all things must change, they say. If he got back into power, 'they'd' see some changes.

'Now, who told you we're actors?' Yussef looked the man in the eye and he took a respectful pace back.

'But, sir. This is Baghdad. We all know.'

'You *all* know?' Yussef glanced around him, at the eager and delighted faces looking up with awe into his craggy face - a sort of dark, handsome hybrid of opposing cultures, chiselled into submission by the talented hands of a flesh artist.

The House of Baghdad

'We *all* know, sir. And we think it's great. Can I have your autograph?'

'But I haven't made the film, yet.' The words were out of his mouth. It was hopeless to resist. The lure of stardom on the silver screen was too much to bear for an ex-dictator. He already had his audience at his feet. They were here - hands touching him, happy, happy faces laughing, hands stretching out with grubby pieces of paper for him to sign.

He looked back at Antonio. Oh, it was all getting out of hand. But….. oh, what the hell? Why shouldn't he go along with it? Yes, this would be his defence at the dinner with the President. Acting would be his salvation. Thank God for Dan Levy. And he never thought he'd bring himself to thank an American - and a Jew at that! His only hope was that Allah's understanding and capacity to forgive remained limitless.

'Go on, sir. Sign them. They're on your side.'

'You, too, Mr,. .er.. You'll make a great bodyguard. Can't wait to see the movie. Oh, thanks.' Antonio bent down and signed some more grubby bits of paper. And then more of them wanted Yussef's signature, followed by Antonio's. They were all happy. And two box-office draws in the making breathed a sigh of relief and began thanking those lucky stars.

Chapter 35

'My dear. Did you see that dishy man on the television the other night?'

'What dishy man?'

'You know, the one with the rather Anglican look about him?'

'Anglican? Don't you mean Anglo-Saxon? Why don't you just say English and have done with it, dear?'

'No, Ann. I mean Anglican. Bishop of Liverpool and all that.'

'He's nothing like him, dear. Now, if you had said Anthony Eden, I might have been interested.'

'You sly old thing, you. So you *did* see him?'

'Of course, dear. Wouldn't miss Dan Levy's little show for the world.'

'Well? What do you think?'

'Umm…. Has possibilities.'

Two Government Ministers' wives had begun their day with positive thoughts. Ann, wife of the Foreign Minister had, for too long, been saddled with a reliable but stolid spouse in whom she saw little spark or reason for her to get up in the mornings or even to fight. She had married him for 'security' reasons and the opportunity to get away from her former paranoic husband in Morocco. War and revolution notwithstanding, she instinctively felt Iraq was the country for her - not quite as colourful, perhaps, as Morocco but more edgy and with a sufficiently closed society to protect her from snooping, wayward, ex-husbands. She had made a big mistake. For, though her new husband who had served Colonel Doomsday as Foreign

Minister, had been kept on in Arid Aziz's Government simply by reason of his experience and contacts with the outside world, there seemed every chance that he would soon be replaced by a younger and more 'flexible' man who would do what Arid Aziz told him. But another man had ridden into town. And his name was Yussef Khomeini. Ann had spotted him on the tele.

But so had Raisa Breshnev. Raisa Breshnev, the combination of whose Christian name and surname smacked of a vain hope that some sort of chic or semblance of power (or both) would thereby rub off on her later in life, had married Faisal Hussein during one of his trips to Moscow before he became leader of his Party.

She had accompanied him back to Iraq where they set up home - she to become a lecturer in Russian at the Baghdad Institute for Foreign Studies and he to find himself in Opposition for God knows how long. Though the couple appeared reasonably content with each other, only a year had passed before she was looking around for other distractions. Young and dashing though he certainly looked in public, she had soon come to view him as a boring and selfish little peacock. He might say the right things in the Chamber in front of Dan Levy's cameras, but, by golly, living with him was a different matter altogether. Ah yes, she had spotted Yussef Khomeini, all right. Who hadn't? The very presence of the man, those features, that voice and the way he disturbed and then inspired his audience with a few chosen phrases; the way he took his time, the way he looked at you. Ah yes. Jim Rosenberg and his team knew what they were doing with those cameras - and the stranger knew how to look into them. A vague thought momentarily crossed Raisa's mind that she had seen the man somewhere before. Could it have been wishful thinking? Anyway, she couldn't place him. And Ann had more to say.

'So, are you invited to the President's dinner on Thursday, Raisa?'

'No, I'm afraid it's going to be a very select affair. Though, what counts for select these days......'

'But, my dear. Surely Faisal has been invited?'

'I think not. Arid likes to keep things close to his chest, as they say. You should know that.'

'And so does Ali, my dear. We have not been invited, either.'

'I might have guessed. Never mind, dear. Why don't we both do a little digging and find out what's going on?'

'What have you in mind?'

'Faisal has his spies, my dear. And I'm sure Ali *must* have a few from the old days, eh?'

'Umm....'

'My dear Ann, I didn't leave Russia without bringing some talents with me.' Raisa Hussein seemed to have so many talents that Ann, her friend, wondered why she should need any help from another Iraqi.

'I have no doubts about that. Let's talk again tomorrow, shall we? 'Bye for now.'

"Bye, my dear.'

Yussef and Antonio returned to their hotel as happy as sand boys. They had been fêted and made to feel good by a crowd of ordinary people. They had signed autographs galore which made them feel happy. They had even spoken to an old man and woman who remembered the days of Sodom the Lesser. 'Oh yes,' said the old man sadly, 'play your part well, sir, so that our young people will never forget.'

'But I am playing his son, Colonel Doomsday.'

'What's the difference?' snapped the old man bitterly and turned on his heel to leave the actors a less critical audience to play with. But the remark had hurt. And Yussef had exposed himself to it. He would have to learn to take the knocks. This was a democracy, a country he hardly recognized. He had been away from it only twelve months and it had changed. Lucky for him he had not been recognized. Dr. Kochs had done a wonderful job and Yussef reminded himself to pay the old surgeon a compliment, if only to say 'thank you', next time he phoned Ireland.

'What an interesting afternoon, Yussef.' They had returned to the hotel and sat down in a quiet corner of the bar, and Antonio was determined to use all his powers of persuasion and encouragement to lend support to Yussef in his first real moment of doubt. 'We have to go through with it. We cannot crumble now. We haven't come this far and had, er.... you know what done...' (a customer had walked into the bar, made a fleeting glance at the two of them and had walked out again) 'only to back out now.'

The barman busied himself cleaning glasses for what he hoped would be a busy night for a change. He may have been listening to the conversation, such as it was, but Antonio doubted anything of any significance could have been overheard. Besides, people in town had already become accustomed to seeing them around together anyway and had assumed 'New Faces' to be a publicity stunt or a film in the making. The country was a democracy and the honeymoon of free speech remained sweet.

Yussef and Antonio drained their glasses, thanked the barman and went up to their rooms.

'Let's talk in my room, Antonio.'

'OK, Yussef.'

They entered Yussef's room, shut the door and made themselves comfortable in easy chairs in front of the TV set. But there was no time to watch TV. This would be their last 'conference' before Yussef's dinner date with the President. Antonio dearly wished he could be there with his master - to give him support and to fill in any awkward gaps in the conversation, to......

'No, Yussef. No. You know I appreciate it but I must play this one alone. The President may be able to accept both of us playing in the film but to actually go along to a political dinner......'

'No need to say any more, Yussef. I understand. I know you're right. It's just that I don't want anything to go wrong.'

'It won't, Antonio. Hey, *you* were the one just now urging me not to weaken.' Antonio smiled. 'So I was.'

'Now. Let's go over the strategy once more. The line we both take... We are businessmen - directors of O'Casey's construction company, right?'

'Right.'

'But we have acted in amateur dramatics in Dublin, Cork,..... Interested in politics, the politics of the free market, *not* the IRA - heavy as we may, indeed, look.'

'Agreed. What happens if you, Allah forbid, unwittingly slip into your old mannerisms - the way you hold and smoke your cigar, lift your glass, turn your head...?'

'Antonio, my friend. I am an actor, am I not? I have studied the background, history, nature and ambitions of Colonel D-Day in preparation for shooting and if I find the character has taken me over, I shall remind the President of the great British actors the like of which we see only too rarely, these days. Well, what d'you think?'

'Very good, very good,' smiled Antonio. 'Better see Dan Levy tonight or tomorrow morning. Go over the script with him, do a few shots, you know…?' It was Yussef's turn to smile.

'Agreed. You have to do your stuff, too.'

'No problem.' They grinned at each other.

'Do you know, I think we're going to enjoy this acting lark. At least our first contract shouldn't be too difficult to fulfil.'

****

The candles flickered across the dining table of the President's Palace, casting a myriad of dancing shadows on the walls and illuminating the pictures of suspect rulers of Babylon through the ages. Over the fireplace loomed a huge portrait of Nebuchadnezzar, looking down on his people and on anyone brave enough to enter the room. Yussef glanced up to the portrait he knew so well and began to dream of yesterday, when his father held sway and when he, Colonel Doomsday, took over and transformed this wonderful ancient building into the Palace it was today, when he had 'pushed the boat out' and wined and dined his officers and their wives while events overtook him and forced him from power.

'My dear Yussef, you're miles away. What are you thinking about?'

'Oh, nothing in particular, Mr President. Just doing my homework for the film.'

'Ah, yes. Arid has told me about that. You must tell me more over dinner.' They sat down to their first course of turtle soup, brought in by smart waiters, one of whom could have sworn he knew the back of 'that head'. Dr Kochs had, indeed, done a good job on the face, but the back of the head……? Maybe if the Colonel had grown his hair…….?

The wine flowed, and conversation bubbled away about those funny sessions in Parliament and about 'New Faces'. Laura, the President's wife had been studying the Colonel ever since he arrived. She, too, had seen him on television. And now, he sat opposite her in his dinner suit and bow tie, his fine features punctuating the canvas before her, his strong presence and well-modulated voice intriguing her. She instinctively knew he 'had something' - and she wanted it. Whatever it was he had, President's wives, it seemed, wanted it.

Laura. What an evocative name. She was no Maria, no ravishing beauty, no sex bomb. But she was attractive, none the less, in a refined, almost intellectual way. And she was the President's wife. Yussef would bide his time. He would do nothing to disturb the tightrope he was now treading. If he stood the slightest chance of winning back power, his steps would have to be measured; his nerve - steady as a rock.

The rib of beef was served, with potatoes and carrots and a fine claret brought up from the cellar that Yussef imagined had been raided before he'd had time to change his underpants…….how long ago was it, now? Maybe the culprit was the President, sitting here beside him. Oh, how it hurt to know that had he been wise, had he been able to see and if only he'd……. if only. Colonel Doomsday, son of Sodom the Lesser, all-powerful ruler of Iraq had had it made - if only he'd known wisdom. But the taste of power was too good to let go, too seductive, too good to hand to someone else. Power corrupted him. And he had to go.

'More rib beef, Yussef?'

'No thank you, ma'am. That was quite sufficient. It was delicious.'

'Good. Call me Laura, by the way. We don't stand on ceremony in this place', she lied. She looked at him with a longing, hopeless pleading; a soft, almost servile hope. He hated that look. But he might have her, yet. Even he could be caught unawares......

The President decided to ignore his wife's little games - until she had come to her senses. She was not the type to flirt, in his view. And, in any case, he'd have to know a hell of a lot more about this newcomer before he'd decide whether he'd be worth making a fuss about. President Bazrani, for all his charm, remained a chauvinistic pig.

'We all thought you made an excellent speech, Yussef', said Arid Aziz, attempting to dispel any trace of patronage in his tone whilst congratulating the newcomer on an achievement few could dream of.

'Yes, so did the women', piped Hattie, his wife, determined to lend support to Laura in her 'hour of need'.

'Thank you', replied Yussef simply, putting down his knife and fork on the empty plate. It was a good meal and with the claret....... it was sufficient. He smiled at the assembled company, conscious he was being watched, studied, investigated. Iraq had come through bloody wars and revolution: he knew that as much as anyone, except he had escaped the worst of it. *He*, who had once exercised the power, remained untouched, unscathed. Only the plastic surgery had marred his equilibrium; and even that appeared to be paying off. Maybe Allah was an actor, after all. And for such an honour bestowed on him, *this* subject would not shirk his responsibility.

'So, what is your next move?' asked Hattie directly, taking another sip of her wine and smiling her devastating smile that unnerved the majority of men who came her way.

'Er, I think that is something we men will be discussing in a moment, my dear.' Arid Aziz shot his wife a sly look, hardly appreciated by her, but which, nevertheless, helped to save the day - as far as Yussef was concerned. Yes, he was on trial all right. But if a thorough grilling was about to take place in the drawing room, he would prefer it to come from the men alone. Much as he admired women - especially between the sheets - they seemed to have an unerring knack of asking the most awkward and loaded questions without the softening agent of humour.

'Well, Yussef, if you have had enough to eat.......?'

'Oh, yes, Mr President. No pudding for me, thank you.'

'In that case, we'll leave the ladies to their dessert and coffee while we... er, are you ready, Arid?....... drift into the drawing-room and take a brandy. What d'you say?'

'Fine by me, sir.'

The men took their leave of the women who looked up to the 'mystery guest' with varying degrees of interest. Arid's wife, Hattie, had seen photographs and old newsreels of Anthony Eden that her grandmother had shown her and she remembered the old lady treating herself to a quiet swoon whilst pretending no woman would feel safe with him. Maybe the old lady knew a thing or two, but, like a good trouper, was the last to admit. Yussef, on the other hand, exuded a certain brutality that stirred women's breasts and flung their menopause to the winds. And no lady would want to admit that. Or would she?

'We'll see you later, chaps', said Laura, keeping up an image of modernity and giving Yussef a last lingering look. She was even on the point of giving him a little wave of her tiny hand before Hattie stopped her.

Chapter 36

The three men settled into soft leather chairs by the fireside in the drawing room. Yussef had prepared himself to answer questions without obvious evasion. He had nothing to worry about, he told himself. His papers, passport - a wonderful job done by O'Casey (an expert on these, and other matters) - were in fine fettle, his money, as yet to be deposited in the bank of his choice, was as good as anyone's. His credentials as a businessman and director of O'Casey's construction company could all be verified - supposing the President and his men could even bother to look that far. His career in amateur dramatics could be vouched for in any Dublin pub they cared to name. There were enough O'Casey 'lookouts' and friends in high and low places to see the Colonel had a drama CV 'as long as yer little ol' arm'. And, in any case, the way things were being run in Baghdad right now meant almost anyone could enter the country - and had - and almost anyone could enter whatever damned competition took his or her fancy. No, if he didn't drink too much brandy but controlled his emotions, Yussef, actor extraordinaire, would remain untouchable. Besides, in Yussef Khomeini, Dan Levy had a new boy, a star in the making, and one which he seemed keen not to let slip. Yussef felt cautiously optimistic, if nothing else.

'Umm. Wonderful brandy, Mr President.'

'Thank you, Yussef. Cheers.'

'Cheers, sir.'

'Cheers, and congratulations, Yussef.' Arid Aziz raised his glass and prepared himself for the 'inquisition' of the 'newcomer' to Iraqi society. 'How do you see this thing developing?'

'Well, sir.....'

'Do call me Arid.'

'And my name, I'm afraid is Yussef', chuckled the President.

'Well then, I'll stick to Mr President, if you don't mind, sir?'

'Not in the least. Very chivalrous.'

'Well', sipped Yussef, looking Arid straight in the eye, thankful for a further relaxation in the atmosphere, 'I would be a liar if I said I have no ambition......'

'Now that you've had a little taste of power, eh?' pressed Arid dryly.

'I'd hardly call making one speech on 'New Faces' a taste of power, would you, Mr President?' President Bazrani appreciated Yussef's deference to him, whilst Arid already knew his man would be a tough nut to crack.

'But it was a powerful speech, was it not - if a little short?' Arid remained determined not to let his 'would-be rival' off the hook. But Yussef had prepared himself well. Besides, he knew what it was to exercise power; he'd been there - in the top job. In some people's eyes, he may have been a touch too brutal about it. But he'd been there.

'Well, that's very kind of you to say so, Arid. I can only do my best.'

Under his breath, Arid had already begun to seethe. And Yussef was beginning to enjoy himself. If he'd known it was going to be this easy, he would have insisted on bringing along his bodyguard, if only to see him joining in the fun. But all things considered, he knew he'd done the right thing. Yes, he'd continue to play safe, act the part and wait for tomorrow when he could be himself. Oh, if only Dan Levy knew what a prize he had signed up.

'You certainly impressed Mr Levy - enough, er.... to offer you a contract, I believe?'

'Yes, he did, Arid. Signed me up, there and then, as a matter of fact.'

'Well, congratulations, old man. You seem to have struck gold in Baghdad.' The President had caught the touch of bitter jealousy leaking out of Arid's now very dry mouth and the look he had just thrown the latest challenge to Iraqi politics. This was going to be fun, he thought.

'I am pleased for you, too', lied Arid. 'What is the film about exactly?'

'It's about Colonel Doomsday'. Yussef took another sip of his brandy and waited for the reaction.

'Oh? So soon?' The President presented Yussef with the beginnings of a grin and the latter wondered whether his host had rumbled him, after all. But he dismissed the thought and followed up the President's rhetorical enquiry before suspicions could grow. 'Dan Levy doesn't strike me as a man to let grass grow under his feet.'

"Grass grow..."? Dan Levy's words, weren't they? But Mustafa had also used them during the Colonel's days in 'the wilderness'. The phrase had finally come in handy, and he had timed its delivery to perfection.

'We all know what you mean, Yussef. We know exactly.' Arid had begun the conversation with his customary probing but, on this man, now firmly in his sights - relaxing and drinking brandy with the ease of a professional and answering each question with an ever-increasing jab at his pride and ego - nothing he'd tried, so far, had worked to his satisfaction. And the blasted man was shooting back answers with which he had no other option than to agree. 'So, where did you learn to speak like that, Yussef?' Ah, that should trip the bugger, thought Arid. The man had booked into an hotel with another man and they had registered as businessmen - a euphemism to hide a multitude of sins.

'I learned the language in Ireland. Amateur societies helped of course. So relaxing, after business.'

'Which is?' piped the President, determined to 'get one in'.

'Construction Company. Antonio Bueno and I are directors of the 'O'Neil Construction Company'. Great firm. High quality stuff. We thought we'd take a look here, you know, and try for some business.'

'Why not, Yussef? We still have much need of Western expertise. And Ireland has not been slow in providing much of it, eh?'

'Indeed not.' The President seemed pleased European companies still found Iraq an attractive place in which to do business. And to his mind, Yussef Khomeini had passed the test. Arid Aziz had, from the start, been the one to suspect the man. And so now he would allow his Prime Minister to wind up the case for the prosecution while he, the President, would busy himself topping up the drinks and passing round the cigars.

'Not for me, thank you, sir.' During his time in Brazil, the Colonel had caught on to the pleasure of cigars from his man. But considering the impact upon sensitive souls on watching the films of his own father coolly smoking a fat cigar while petrified men were taken to the back of the room and outside to be shot, he thought it better to refuse the offer. Associations can play havoc with people's minds and Yussef Khomeini had no intention of associating himself with Sodom the Lesser, his cruel father - just yet. After all, he was still on trial. And easy chairs, brandy and cigars could not fool him.

'Well, you seem to have cracked it with the ladies, Yudie?'

The President almost dropped the brandy decanter as he turned to catch the dramatic high point of this enquiry, so skilfully manipulated by his wily PM. The bombshell, accurately laid at the newcomer's feet, would surely shake him? But Yussef remained calm. Not a finger did he lift. He continued to swallow his second measure of brandy, already plied by his host. It was a very fine brandy. Gently, he put the glass down onto the side table provided for him, and took up the challenge.

'Cracking it with the ladies, as you put it, has always been a hobby of mine, I cannot deny. But there are only so many hours in the day, are there not?' Yussef smiled upon Arid Aziz and the President in turn. 'As for Yudie,' he continued, unruffled, turning his gaze back to Arid and continuing to smile quite naturally, 'I have already done my homework on the man. I'm sure even Dan Levy has not overlooked the Colonel's nickname? Though why he should pick on me so quickly as an ideal choice to play the part......'

'Surely, modesty is not one of your virtues, Colonel?'

God Almighty. This Arid was becoming a bore. Women were supposed to be the bitchy ones. Compared with Arid Aziz, they were sheer amateurs. Even the President froze with fear. His Prime Minister had always shown himself more than capable of extracting the truth from people and by providing two stings for the price of one in his interrogations, he had rarely failed. But Arid had already used up one sting and it hadn't worked. Would this one do the trick? Even the President, who by now had returned to his chair and had consumed more than half his 'refresher', sat up for the kill.

'I think you are going to love this film, Arid. Maybe, by the end of it - if I do my job properly - you may not wish to be reminded of that awful period in your recent history?'

The President relaxed. If Yussef Khomeini really was Colonel D-Day, as Arid seemed to suspect, he damned well had to take his hat off to the man. He might even consider resigning the Presidency in favour of him - if that were the truth. But if the man was merely a respectable businessman with a secret yen to be a star actor, having done a bit of amateur stuff in 'little ol' Ireland', well,..... all he could say would be 'Good luck to the man'. And to Arid: 'You should be ashamed of yourself'.

****

'I'm sorry, Arid. I cannot share your misgivings about this man. To tell the truth, I like him. I never liked Colonel Doomsday.'

Yussef Khomeini, the President's unusual guest, had just left. President Bazrani and his PM were alone together in the drawing room, still arguing. The President had believed his intriguing guest, Yussef Khomeini. It wasn't that the President was naïve - far from it. It was just that Prime Minister Aziz's analysis of the man didn't quite add up. Even if Yussef had told a few white lies about his age, his qualifications, amateur dramatics - all that sort of stuff - would he have gone to the trouble of having plastic surgery and returning to Iraq in the space of only twelve months

The House of Baghdad

after the revolution, only to run the grave risk of being rumbled not only in the Chamber but in this, the President's official home? No, it didn't make sense - unless the man was mad. And that, he most certainly was not. The man had to be genuine. And Arid Aziz had become a neurotic, defensive and jealous old fart.

'Have it your way, Mr President. I have said my piece. You'll soon see I was right, all along.' It was time to go. Yussef Khomeini's departure had disappointed the ladies. 'You old spoilsport, Arid. I bet you gave him one of your usual roastings and frightened the poor man away.'

'That poor man, as you call him, my dear, is no chicken. Nor is he innocent. He's been around - he's not afraid of anything or anyone. Moreover, I'm convinced he's Colonel Doomsday in person.'

'What? Colonel D-Day? Impossible.' The President's wife Laura, naturally, had joined Hattie, the PM's wife, in condemnation of Arid's hard and cruel theory about a man who had not only behaved impeccably over dinner earlier but had just rescued her favourite Ming vase which, in her understandable nervousness, she was about to drop on the floor of the lobby. He had handed her back the ornament with the most gallant kiss of her hand, had bade her and Hattie goodnight and left in his car. If Arid had found him to be the ghost of Anthony Eden who had decided to pay a visit to Iraq and atone for the past sins of the British Empire, she might have been inclined to believe him. But Colonel Doomsday? Never.

'Well, Arid, old man. I believe you're out-voted tonight? Makes a change for you, I suppose?' The President had retained his good humour throughout the evening. He was pleased his wife had agreed to the little soirée, after all, if only to put his own mind at rest over the issue of 'the talk of the town'. God knows, there had been enough speculation in the papers about Colonel D-Day to last a thousand years. It was so refreshing to meet a normal, healthy and intelligent businessman who had the energy and good humour not only to seek contracts here in Iraq which would benefit the economy of each other's country but to join with gusto in the 'New Faces' competition as if he hadn't a care in the world. He had shown himself to be a darned good sport. And despite his Iranian parentage he seemed to have been blessed with the good fortune of a little Irish blarney and cheerful disposition. A man whose character was farther from that of Colonel Doomsday he could not wish to meet.

'Mr President. It's always a pleasure for Hattie and me to attend your dinners - no matter who your special guests might turn out to be. Do……'

All right, all right, Arid. No need to embarrass the President.'

'I love him, really, Hattie. At least he keeps the old grey matter ticking over. There are too many well-meaning bores around, these days. Arid could never be accused of being……'

'Well-meaning?' Arid was determined to help out the President, forestall his own wife and leave the Palace on a good note.

'Off with you', smiled the President. 'Goodnight, Hattie.'
'Goodnight, sir, and thank you. Goodnight, Laura.'
'My dear.'

Chapter 37

'OK. Cut. Cut.' The voice of Dan Levy boomed out across the square in front of the President's Palace. Jim Rosenberg had been good - as director of those successful broadcasts of Parliamentary proceedings and even of the dramatic one-off 'New Faces', which had stunned the Government. But the requirements of a major movie - that was a different matter altogether. Dan Levy's determination to bask in the glory of success meant that he must, like the late Sir David Lean, take control of the whole caboodle. He would take command of his own damned ship, and if it went down into a fathomless pit he would go down with it.

But it wouldn't be like that. It would be as spectacular and successful as any of Lean's great epics. Everyone would go to see it and everyone would be talking about it for years to come. As for those Oscars - they were there for the taking. And Dan Levy would be there to take them.

'OK., Yussef. Lift ya arm a little higher.'

'Like this?'

'Perfect.' Yussef had done what the man had asked of him. After all, he had to grow into the part. If he were to give too much too soon he might give the game away. The President, bless him, had given Dan Levy permission to use the frontal and several rooms of the Palace for the filming of this important movie. The world should know the truth, he'd said, the stark truth about the Colonel. And then, perhaps, the people would be less inclined to demand too much too soon. Every revolution had been like this, whether bloody or peaceful. 'Look at Russia', he said on the phone to Dan Levy who had telephoned his secretary for the purpose of gaining all necessary access to buildings, streets, battlefields, airfields, army barracks, you name it - in order that the film should look authentic. 'I felt so sorry for Mr Gorbachev,' said the President, 'he had opened the gates of opportunity, and a flood of impatient rivers drowned him.'

'Is that how you feel about *your* country, Mr President?'

'My dear Mr Levy. Keep this under your hat but if I had known what a greedy, impatient lot my own people would turn out to be, I might have called for the restoration of Colonel Doomsday myself and gladly stepped down.'

'You're not serious, sir?'

'I might be.' The President remained wistful and extraordinarily honest. Dan Levy found himself wanting to open up to the man. 'Wait until the film is finished, Mr President. I believe you may then think twice about abdicating.'

The President laughed. 'Resigning, you mean?' He agreed to reserve judgement of his people until he had had time to see and react to the film. 'Now, in order to make things easier for you, Mr Levy and so that you can make the film as speedily as possible without, of course, sacrificing the high standards which I'm sure you've set yourself, I am prepared to give you carte blanche on the entire city.'

'That's mighty generous of you, sir. But what will the Government say about that?'

'The Government?' The president seemed a little hurt. 'If, by the Government, you mean the Prime Minister, Mr Aziz and I, Mr Levy, have a very good working relationship despite the fact he is convinced your star, Yussef Khomeini, is none other than Colonel Doomsday himself.'

'What? You crazy? Tell me another.'

'I agree with you, Mr Levy. I think Arid Aziz has become somewhat paranoid about things, lately. Your 'New Faces' competition didn't exactly help matters.'

'Ah, it's competition in its true sense, eh? Can't stand the heat?'

'I think you have it. Never mind, we will use the making of your film to put his fears to rest, eh, Mr Levy?'

'What happens if the people really clamour for the Colonel to take *your* job, sir?' The President chuckled. 'Let's cross that bridge if and when we come to it, shall we?'

'OK. by me, sir. I shall be using the street crowd as extras. All right by you?'

'Will you be paying them, Mr Levy?'

'Paying them?' The President let out a guffaw of delight at Dan Levy's credentials.

'Of course you won't. How silly of me.'

The early morning rehearsals had gone extremely well. In fact, Yussef Khomeini's acting ability, under pressure, had impressed Dan Levy so much that he wished he'd encouraged the people to get out of their beds and come to the set, so that he could shoot the balcony scene there and then. Despite the good account Yussef had given of himself in the Chamber in the full glare of the cameras, Dan Levy, in all honesty, had not expected the man to be *this* good when it came to playing Colonel Doomsday. As always, he'd been in a hurry and had signed him up, together with his colleague - the big husky brute with whom even Dan would think twice about 'mixing things up'. No, Dan Levy had simply followed his hunch. His instincts had always been good. What he could not know, perhaps, was that those instincts would hand him an instant star. If Yussef Khomeini never made another film in his life, Dan was certain that, once it was on general release, the 'new boy' would remain a star in the minds of countless men and women across the globe.

'Like this, Mr Levy?'

'Yes, like that. It's perfect, Yussef. Just do it. It's great. Frightening.' Dan Levy's words were music to Yussef's ears. Moreover, the more he succeeded in the eyes of this powerful American the more his man, Antonio Pérez Bueno, smiled. Casually sitting on a box behind the Director's chair, he had watched his boss open up and come into his own. It would be his turn soon. Eagerly he awaited Dan Levy's instructions to get on the set and work in tandem with his brave master.

'OK, Antonio. We're ready for you.'

Antonio got up from the box, and walked up on to the set. He smiled at Yussef and took up his position, marked out for him.

'OK, Antonio?'

'OK.'

'Good. Now Yussef, imagine the crowd are down there, cheering and waving and making a lot a noise. But the noise is for you - the great Colonel Doomsday who is about to deliver them from the bonds of America.' Dan Levy was chancing his arm. But it worked. Yussef, with Antonio one pace behind him, stepped out on to the balcony of the Palace, smiled and raised his arms to the 'crowd' below. The cameras whirled and Yussef made ready to speak. 'My people,' he boomed, 'I stand here before you today in celebration of our glorious State which has withstood the pressures of the outside world. You, my people, have stood steadfast in the face of.......'

'OK. Cut.' Dan Levy had seen and heard sufficient for the moment. But it was great, as far as he was concerned. Even Yussef's voice had changed - subtly changed into someone else's. By Christ, it sounded just like the Colonel's voice. Jim Rosenberg had managed to buy a couple of tapes from a disgruntled dissident by whom he had been approached in the market a few days ago. The tapes had been made during the Colonel's hey-day, when he'd often try to imitate Adolf Hitler in front of his closest and most loyal guards. The 'dissident' standing in front of Jim Rosenberg may well have been one of those guards. Who could tell? But those tapes sounded interesting. Rosenberg had played them on the vendor's machine there and then and liked what he heard. The deal was struck and Rosenberg rushed back like an excited schoolboy to play them over to Dan Levy.

'All right, all right Jim. One thing at a time. Don't let's confuse the guy. He's doing OK. His voice is so damned close, anyway. We'll play him the tapes only if absolutely necessary.'

But it hadn't been necessary. Yussef Khomeini had finally let go. He had got into his stride. It was the balcony that did it. And Dan Levy, via President Bazrani, had provided it for him. All that was needed now was the crowd.

'OK., everybody. Let's break for lunch.'

Dan Levy walked across to his new stars and held out his massive arms in a bear-hug gesture. Both Yussef and Antonio duly obliged, while Jim Rosenberg settled the crew and then walked inside the Palace to phone Dave Fletcher's hotel.

Dan Levy knew it would be good to engage the services of the man who, more than anyone before him, had written so poignantly, if a little cynically, about a nation whose ruler had been so effectively deposed but whose name and memory was about to be immortalised on the silver screen. Dave Fletcher of the BBC, now a man of letters, honours and standing in the world, had seen the best and the worst of Iraq's recent history. He had forsaken his hideaway in Switzerland to have the pleasure of witnessing a unique experiment - 'New Faces', Iraqi style. He had seen and reported on the revolution itself, the bloody part of the story. Surely now, after finishing yet another book which must have exhausted even his stamina, he would not be able to resist the fun of reporting in a cameo appearance in a major film, a play within a play, shot here in the heart of Baghdad for release across the world? Dave Fletcher's fame had reached the corners of the globe. To engage his services now would, indeed, be a scoop for Dan Levy and his corporation.

'Why, Mr Rosenberg. I'd be delighted. Right up my street, tell Mr Levy. I'll do it for real, and see what happens.'

'Great stuff, Mr Fletcher. That's just what we want. Give people the jitters.'

'Like the 'War of the Worlds', you mean?'

'Couldn't have put it better myself'.'

****

It had been a pleasant lunch, despite the meanness of Dan Levy in the hard liquor stakes. Nevertheless, there was enough wine left over to drown the crowd that by now had gathered in the square before the Presidential Palace. Some

The House of Baghdad

of Jim Rosenberg's scouts had gone round the town informing people and urging them to come along and enjoy themselves in the film. They would not be paid but there would be food and wine for them after the job was done.

In the event, it had been unnecessary for Jim's lads to expend their energy in this way for, by 2 p.m., word had got around that something exciting was taking place in the square and that it might be fun to go along and join in.

Dan Levy stood up on his rostrum and addressed the crowd. 'OK., folks. I want you to co-operate with us as best you can. If I am satisfied with the result you will be given food and wine to take home. Are you willing to help?'

'Yes, yes,' they shouted. Already, Yussef could spot many of the faces who had clamoured round him in his walkabouts after the broadcasting of 'New Faces'. And they recognized him, despite his make-up and uniform of Colonel Doomsday. They recognized him, preening himself for his master performance. And they liked what they saw. With a mighty roar of encouragement, they joined forces to give the film a kick-off which they felt it needed but for which Dan Levy had not yet asked. 'Colonel D-Day,' they shouted. 'We want Colonel D-Day.' How could they know? Even the makeup artist had not quite finished with her charge. But it hadn't mattered in the slightest. 'Colonel D-Day,' they shouted again. Then another chant began to take its place. 'Yudie, Yudie, Yudie! We want Yudie!' The younger members of the crowd had decided to forgo proper titles and plump for an easy sound. How could they know?

'Yudie, Yudie, Yudie!' they shouted again.

'OK, OK,' protested Dan Levy, swaying on his rostrum and looking, by the minute, ever more like the great Mike

Curtiz of 'The Charge of the Light Brigade'. All that was missing, it seemed, was the whip.

'*Quiet,*' he shouted. And suddenly, by golly, the crowd hushed. Somehow they knew this was more than the making of just another film. Somehow they knew this to be special. They couldn't quite work it out but they could sense they were in the midst of making history. They - the humble people of Baghdad - were about to take part in an extraordinary event. Could it be the homecoming of the man they had kicked out of town barely a year ago? They had touched the hand of a man who walked amongst them the other day, who had earned their admiration, who had signed their grubby pieces of paper, who had looked kindly upon them. Could he be this man in front of them, waiting for his cue to come alive and rouse them into adoration of him and submission to his will? Could he be the true one, who would make Iraq proud of itself once more and different from the rest of the world? Could he be the Messiah that Iraq deserved?

'OK, folks. Quiet - *please.*' The remaining hubbub subsided and all was quiet. 'Right, my friends. When I say 'Action', all you have to do is talk amongst yourselves as if you are expecting Colonel Doomsday to appear on the balcony. He had said it. 'Colonel Doomsday'. The man had said it. There was no mistake. All the crowd had to do would be to act naturally. But how could they act naturally - when it really came to it? How would they react to the 'actor' about to appear before them as the dictator incarnate, or as the make-up girl could, as near as damn it, make him? She had kept her fingers crossed. Dr. Kochs had done a pretty good job on the Colonel's face. But then, so had she.

The House of Baghdad

The clapper-board clapped. 'Colonel Doomsday. Balcony Scene. Take 1.'

'*Action,*' boomed Dan Levy before getting in close behind his camera.

The Colonel moved out on to the balcony at a leisurely pace, closely followed by his bodyguard and a couple of extra armed guards who took up positions behind them. This was no acting. A gasp issued from the crowd below and a helicopter buzzed low over the Palace, coming in from nowhere.

The Colonel stepped forward and made ready to speak. The crowd were already silent, not sure whether to laugh or cry.

Could this be for real? Was this why films were made? To frighten people, to......?'

'*Cut. No, no,*' shouted Dan Levy, - facing the crowd once more. 'Listen. When the Colonel walks on to the balcony you're supposed to *cheer*. Get it?'

But those guards looked ominous. They looked real. And so did those guns. 'Never mind them,' insisted Dan Levy. 'OK. Let's take it from the top.'

The Colonel and his entourage duly obliged and went back into the Palace to await instructions. Oh, how the Colonel yearned to let off a volley of bullets that would bring Dan Levy crashing down off his perch; how he yearned to fool the world and order that airliner to drop its nuclear load direct on New York. Oh, how he wished...... He pulled himself together. 'One day,' he said to himself. 'One day.'

'Colonel Doomsday. Balcony Scene. Take 2.'

'*Action.*' This time everything went to plan. Out stepped the Colonel, Mustafa, the two armed guards and the crowd roared with delight. They knew now that the whole thing had been arranged. It was all part of the show. They should have known this crazy American would come up with something to frighten them. They began to relax and imagine they were in the presence of Colonel D-Day himself - in one of his good moods.

'My people,' boomed the Colonel. 'I stand here before you today in celebration of our glorious State which has withstood the pressures of the outside world. You, my people, have stood steadfast in the face of American aggression. I pledge to you that one day those wrongs perpetrated against our beloved nation will be avenged.'

Dave Fletcher, who had been quietly sitting 'in the wings' for the last twenty minutes, was suddenly gripped with a violent stomach-ache. He never suffered stomach-aches as a rule. But when he did, he would read them as unmistakable symptoms of psychic revelation. He'd had this 'gift' since boyhood and through the years he'd grown to appreciate and take advantage of it. There was no doubt in his mind - the actor up there was no actor. He was Colonel Doomsday. Besides, Dave had seen too much of the dictator to be fooled by this man basking in Levy's attention. And it was Dan Levy himself who'd given him, Dave Fletcher, journalist extraordinaire, Nobel Prize winner, a brief to do his worst - to say what he liked. He'd say it in his inimitable way - it would lend a touch of authenticity to the whole thing. Like mustard on beef. And the underpinning of that authenticity was to be provided by the link-up with the BBC - via John Broadbridge here in Baghdad and Peter Watson in London. If Mr Watson's sense of humour had ever been in doubt, what was about to be broadcast to millions across the world would dispel any such notion for years to come.

The House of Baghdad

Moreover, Dan Levy had struck a deal with Columbia News to video the making of his film and transmit it live on prime news time across an America still hungry for more of Mr Levy's delicacies. If only the people knew that what they were shortly to see on their television sets was no publicity stunt, no intentional joke. But who cared? Anything Dan Levy put out had to be fun.

The link-ups were complete and John Broadbridge's 'Baghdad Line', which for months had taken a somewhat resentful and lethargic back seat, was about to be given an unforgettable boost. The airwaves bristled as the cameras rolled for the final take of 'Colonel Doomsday'. This time, there would be no interruptions, no hiccups. The whole thing would be live. For real. And the world would be witness to an extraordinary one-off.

With a camera trained on his whimsical face, the crowd roaring in the background, Dave Fletcher prepared to deliver his comment on the drama going on behind....... 'Here comes the Colonel,' he began ominously, 'stepping out onto the balcony he knows so well. And, with what appears to be a genuine roar of approval from the crowd, he raises his arms in ironic appreciation...... And now, as he turns to go back inside, he gives a final wave to the people, while drawing to his side a prize infinitely more desirable than mere power. And by that I mean the President's own attractive wife. I wonder what he will do next? About this man, nothing would surprise me. Now,..... when I was a small boy, my mother would tell me stories. But if she had told me pigs could fly, I would never have believed her. After all I have witnessed in Iraq over the past twelve months, I know they truly can.'

Maybe this time, Dave Fletcher's free and wicked throat would finally be cut by one of Allah's children, if not by Allah himself. Dan Levy would soon be busy cutting to perfection his unexpected and unwitting thriller. For, minutes later, a helicopter rose up into the cloudless sky to head for the airport. It was not meant to make it. An almighty explosion ripped the machine and its occupants to pieces - **and the pig was no more.**

About the Author

TONY SHARP, an Oxford graduate in Music, embarked upon a teaching career before turning to the pop/jazz scene. After two years back at Oxford as University Organist, he gave harpsichord 'recitals' on CBC, BBC TV and The South Bank, London and worked with named artists as a writer and session musician.

Writing books, he maintains, now provides him a measure of sanity.

His first fantasy novel, 'THE GUV'NOR', was published by Regency Press, London.

Printed in the United Kingdom
by Lightning Source UK Ltd.
99092UKS00001B/98